"*Oklahoma Odyssey* has original, non-stereotyped characters and a wealth of details from everyday life. The characterization conveys . . . a commendable ethical view of human nature. At the same time, it does not indulge it what seems to be the prevailing practice of dishing up violence and sensationalism."
—JOHN NESBITT, author of *West of Dancing Rock*

"*Oklahoma Odyssey* perfectly captures the era of the Oklahoma land rush in a story that is rich in historical detail. . . . Mort surrounds Euly with a compelling cast of characters and a story that both surprises and feels inevitable. It's a terrific book that illuminates a lesser-known part of American history with a plot that will keep you reading through its crisp turns."
—STEVE WIEGENSTEIN, author of *Scattered Lights* and the Daybreak Series

"As mythology is a hybrid of history and lore, so too is *Oklahoma Odyssey*, with a slurry of characters with crosses to bear as they inhabit the borderland of Kansas and Oklahoma Territory. . . . Mort's keen attention to detail and refusal to oversimplify and homogenize keep the tension elevated in this commanding portrait of Americana."
—SIDNEY THOMPSON, author of the Bass Reeves Trilogy

FRONTISPIECE. Photograph by William S. Prettyman, 1893.

OKLAHOMA ODYSSEY

JOHN MORT   *A Novel*

UNIVERSITY OF NEBRASKA PRESS | LINCOLN

The University of Nebraska Press is part of a land-grant
institution with campuses and programs on the past, present,
and future homelands of the Pawnee, Ponca, Otoe-Missouria,
Omaha, Dakota, Lakota, Kaw, Cheyenne, and Arapaho Peoples,
as well as those of the relocated Ho-Chunk,
Sac and Fox,and Iowa Peoples.

Library of Congress Cataloging-in-Publication Data
Names: Mort, John, 1947–, author.
Title: Oklahoma odyssey: a novel / John Mort.
Description: Lincoln: University of Nebraska Press, [2022] |
Includes bibliographical references.
Identifiers: LCCN 2021037423
ISBN 9781496229731 (trade paperback)
ISBN 9781496231987 (epub)
ISBN 9781496231994 (pdf)
Subjects: BISAC: FICTION / Historical / General |
FICTION / Westerns | LCGFT: Novels.
Classification: LCC PS3563.O88163 O38 2022 |
DDC 813/.54—dc23
LC record available at https://lccn.loc.gov/2021037423

Set in Garamond Premier Pro by Mikala R. Kolander.

Pretty soon they would all begin to live like kings.

—LAURA INGALLS WILDER, *Little House on the Prairie*

Thanks

Thanks to Dr. Daniel Swan for his valuable time—and knowledge of Osage weddings. Thanks to the language department of the Osage Nation; any errors, of course, are my own. Thanks to the Oxford Public Library of Oxford, Kansas, for informing me how you crossed the Arkansas River in the 1890s. Thanks to Kara Evans, Missouri Valley Special Collections librarian in Kansas City, for information on Mr. Spalding's college; and to Rebecca Hamlett, librarian at William Jewell College, for information on women's options in the 1890s. Thanks most of all to the Springfield Writers Workshop, with me all the way.

OKLAHOMA
ODYSSEY

I

I

His Father's Son

uly Kreider left Jericho Springs, Kansas, an hour before sunset, wagon loaded with ten-pound sacks of cane sugar, twelve silver dollars in a Mason jar beside him. A good sum, but Euly simmered. He hadn't received enough for his apples, hardly twenty cents a bushel after crating charges.

"I'll go to Newton!" he called out to his horses. He'd learned that in Newton, twenty miles west, buyers paid up to thirty-five cents a bushel. The only buyer in Jericho Springs was Giles Cabot, stationmaster, postmaster, telegraph operator, undertaker, usurer—anything and everything for which he needn't break a sweat. Euly was just an ignorant Mennonite kid in the estimation of that Englische scoundrel.

Cabot knew that Euly's father, Barney, had gone to Missouri again. Never send a boy to do a man's job, that's what Cabot thought, but when would Euly be regarded as a man? He'd turn twenty-one in February. He read and ciphered as well as his father—probably better than Cabot.

Euly tried to convince himself that it didn't matter how young he was. Everyone had a bumper crop this year. In November, apples dropped with the barest gust of wind. And what did his father always say? "The only way to make a profit in this world, Ulysses, is to offer a man something he can't do without."

A man could do without apples.

Ulysses was Euly's true name. His father loved Greek literature and had christened his son after Homer's great adventurer.

Brave Ulysses was two miles outside of town, a mile and a half yet from home, before he calmed. He realized he'd been cold for a while. Rain drops splashed off the bill of his straw hat, and if he were a wagering Mennonite he'd have bet the rain would turn to ice by midnight.

Gerty tugged more insistently at the light load, knowing she was nearing her warm stall and cracked corn. Maude picked up her pace slightly but she was an old gal and nothing excited her. "Hey, ladies," Euly clucked, and pulled back on Gerty. He considered his final chores for the day: unhitching the big Belgians and throwing them some hay, first of all. Always take care of your horses. You'd die without them.

He ought to sort apples for tomorrow, but dear Lord, he was tired. And what was the point? At Cabot's prices, he might as well press them all into cider.

He'd banked the fire in the morning, so he'd have coals, still, to bring up the flames. He'd thrown an inch of navy beans and some salt pork into a pot of water, and they should be perfect. He doubted he had energy left to make cornbread but the beans would be delicious. He'd crawl under his blankets and read from *The March Upcountry*—another of his father's adventure stories.

The Belgians turned into the Zimmerman Woods and the steel tires slipped and thumped as they cut through little towers of half-frozen mud. The woods were pleasant in the summer and courting couples drove out from Jericho Springs for picnics and to walk along the creek, stealing kisses. Now it was nearly dark and the woods grew shadowy, with only the bare sycamores distinct, shining dully in the half-light. The narrow road seemed to tunnel into endless blackness, and Euly's cheeks stung from the sparse, icy rain. He pulled his scarf to his ears and murmured, "Easy, easy," to his horses, who moaned ritually. They loved him. They knew he'd guide them out of the dark.

He heard a rider behind him. Not a draft horse, because of

the quickness and lightness of the striking hooves. Euly had spent many nights alone, scaring himself with Edgar Allan Poe and Washington Irving as the wind howled, the house creaked, and the fire danced. He imagined Giles Cabot on his trail, hell-bent on knocking off his head with a pumpkin.

Such foolishness aside, highwaymen still haunted these parts—last month, down in Coffeyville, they'd finally cornered the Dalton Gang. Euly took a deep breath and aimed his team into a thicket of wild plums. Gerty whinnied and lifted her head high in annoyance. "Hush, girl," Euly told her, as he reached behind the front gate and grabbed his shovel. He sprang from the seat, found a shadow, and lifted the shovel like a club.

A black horse came at a gallop. Even in the poor light, Euly could see the lather on the poor beast's neck. He calculated where he'd step out and swing his shovel—but stopped. He recognized the sleek shoulders, the proud steps of King Arthur, the Cherokee stallion Euly's Uncle Helmut had given to his adopted daughter, Katherine.

Orphaned Kate and motherless Euly had been raised together, before Euly grew old enough that Barney, his father, could use him on the farm. Euly was almost two years older than Kate. He thought of her as his sister.

Euly stepped from the shadows. "Kate?"

She slid from the saddle, threw her arms around his neck, and buried her head in his chest. She sobbed, and Euly patted her back and waited for her to compose herself. Kate was not given to hysteria; thus, something terrible must have happened. "All right, Kate," he said. "It's all right."

Barney had brought back the infant Kate from his travels and handed her off to Elise, his sister-in-law. Elise and Helmut were childless. No one could predict the disposition of an adopted child, and some said, because of her dark skin, Kate must be an Indian. Or of mixed blood, because her hair was almost blonde. But the Mennonite tribe were famous for their good deeds and many families adopted waifs. Kate had been around the church and school so long that the blonde-haired, blue-eyed German-Ukrainians had forgotten she was a foundling.

Kate was popular enough and not bad-looking. Over summer, she'd turned down two proposals.

Euly grasped Kate's arms and gently pushed her back. "What is it, Kate?"

"Uncle Barney! He's been shot!"

Panic settled on his blood like a fast poison, but Euly had always feared this. His father ranged too far, carrying freight that men not only needed, but would kill for. "What happened?"

It rained harder now. "I rode in to Cabot's for the mail. I saw your father on that boardwalk where the old men sit. I started to cross the street to say hello—looking where to put my shoes in all that mud. Uncle Barney was talking to Monte Truman—"

Owner of the principal saloon in Jericho Springs, the Santa Fe. The same boardwalk from which that one-legged Union veteran, Sy Wentzler, reached out with his cane to trip little boys. "Where were the mules?"

"The mules! In the alley where they unload. Ulysses, Uncle Barney is—"

"What time was it?"

"About four, I guess."

He'd missed it all by fifteen minutes. "Tell the rest," he said.

"A rider came galloping down the street, like somebody with bad news. Then he veered toward the saloon, drew his pistol, and shot Uncle Barney down!"

"Ahhh," Euly murmured.

"I don't think Uncle Barney even saw the man. Monte Truman fell, too. He cried out to the Lord, and begged for mercy, and crawled along the boardwalk. The rider dismounted and grabbed your father's bag. Then he jumped on his horse and galloped off south before anybody had time to scream. Oh, Euly, I just stood there in the mud. Paralyzed."

Apples, he thought. I was worried about apples. From a distance, Euly heard his voice: "I'm so sorry you had to see that, Kate."

"Me! I—"

"And it was noble of you to ride so hard."

"Your father lies dead, Euly. How can you be so calm?"

"I am not calm, Kate." He swallowed. His father, his Uncle Helmut, had both taught Euly to restrain his emotions. In business, in every line of work, reason was your greatest ally, if only because the people you dealt with were invariably emotional. "I am not calm. But it will serve no purpose if I . . . break down."

"I understand." Kate stroked his arm in the darkness and placed reins in his hands. "Take King Arthur."

The stallion didn't like anyone but Kate, but the wagon was slow. "You can handle the team?"

"Of course! Do what you need to. *Go.*"

Euly swung up to the saddle and pulled back on the reins. King Arthur bobbed his head and rolled his eyes toward Kate but Euly turned him without trouble. "Give our friends some oats," he called out to Kate. "And an apple each. I'll be there when I can."

"I'm so sorry, Euly!"

"Make some cornbread, if you're up to it," he said. "I left beans on the stove."

2

Jericho Springs

Barney Kreider was the youngest of four sons, barely a man when, with Helmut and Ananias and Ronald, his brothers, he emigrated from the Ukraine. They were pacifists fleeing from Czar Alexander's imposition of universal military service after the Crimean War. They arrived in Kansas in 1874, purchasing great blocks of grassland from the railroads.

Barney's brothers were hard-working, God-fearing, tradition-bound Mennonites who founded a little Germany in Harvey County. The Kansas plains were not dissimilar to the Ukrainian steppes and the brothers were clever farmers. Each brother gathered to himself a section of fertile land, and though they struggled at first, the turkey red wheat they planted eventually made them rich.

Barney was more adventurous. Rising at four for devotionals, backbreaking work until noon and another round of devotionals, he found enervating—and boring. He took for his own a forty-acre heel of land under a bluff where he planted apple trees and raised a few acres of corn and oats for his stock. He had water: Zimmerman's Creek began on his land, a trickle out of the strewn rock.

When his young wife, Evangeline, died in childbirth, Barney placed his infant son, Ulysses, in the care of his brother, Helmut, and Euly's Aunt Elise. And then Barney was off to see the world, or at least the world of Kansas. He became a freighter who ran whiskey at night, traveling back roads and open country as far away as Carl Junction, Missouri. His business took a profitable turn when Kansas went dry—in 1879, thirteen years before his murder. Kansas was dry but a man could buy whiskey right on Main Street. That is, if somebody hauled it in.

Barney hauled myriad other things to places the trains didn't go, so he was useful to the community, but the church, not to mention those annoying Temperance women, didn't approve of him. Had his sins been less nocturnal, or more local—if he weren't brother to such prominent wealth—he might have been shunned.

The not-quite-apostate Barney never complained that his brothers occupied the most fertile land. They made money, to be sure, but never stopped working. Barney enjoyed his rather mysterious trips, his Cuban cigars, his Missouri whiskey. Euly suspected he'd had a woman somewhere, or more than one.

EULY TIED KING ARTHUR to the big Conestoga wagon and gave Prince and Pauper, Barney's mules, some oats in feed bags. The rain fell steadily now and he disliked leaving the mules in harness, but it couldn't be helped.

Except for an apple crate full of traveling supplies, the wagon stood empty. He couldn't locate the lever-action Marlin, which Barney kept in a scabbard attached to the headboard. Euly had ordered the rifle from Montgomery Ward and given it to his father a year ago last Christmas.

He entered the back door to the Santa Fe, passing the racks of beer and sarsaparilla bottles and a dozen oak barrels stacked two high. He stood in the dim storeroom, allowing his eyes to adjust, and looking across the tables and chairs, which kerosene lanterns lit only a little more brightly. Half a dozen customers, indefatigable regulars, huddled near the great stove in the center of the room. In the best-lit corner, four glum-faced men sat playing poker.

Behind the bar, one arm in a sling, a bandage around his forehead, Monte Truman waved his free arm and declaimed on his heroism. But Truman, though something of a braggart, was a fair man, at least for an Englische. Euly had read somewhere that before their lives were finished people came to resemble their names. Perhaps Truman rang true. Anyhow, his father liked Monte, and he'd become vital to the man's business because of the fine whiskey he carried from Carl Junction.

Euly brushed the rain from his sweater, tucked in his shirt, and lifted his suspenders so that his pants pulled higher from his boots. He straightened his wide-brimmed hat and stiffened his back.

He came up behind the two men who listened as Truman told his tale. He'd tell it many times in coming years, but now he stumbled at points, and flushed, and paused to spit tobacco juice into a tin cup. Ordinarily, Euly would have waited politely until he was recognized, but he was cold and short of patience. Perhaps more loudly than necessary, he said, "Where did they take my father?"

The listeners turned on their barstools. Truman stepped back and stared. "Euly! Oh, what a tragedy it is! I cain't say how—"

"Mr. Truman, where is my father?"

"At Cabot's, young man, where else? Listen, I—I couldn't do a damn thing. It happened so quick!"

Euly nodded. He refused to cry. The poker game broke up and the players gathered around the bar with the dedicated drinkers. Several men reached out to pat Euly's back. Brave Ulysses held up his chin, and said, "Father had a Marlin .32."

Truman stared at him in wonder even as he reached under the bar and produced the rifle. "Nice little gun," he said. "Kinda light. You ain't chasin' after that man!"

"No, sir," Euly said. "But I ordered that Marlin from Montgomery Ward so my father could defend himself in his travels."

"Aw," said Truman. "Barney was a fine man. Proud a *you*, always was. 'Euly's a hard worker,' that's what he said."

"Shot him down like a hog," said one of the poker players—

Gibbs, that was his name. Horse trader, if you could call his half-starved stock horses. He bought them, or maybe stole them, from the Osage down in the Territory.

"Eddie Mole! Murderer!" said another of the poker players, Malachi Bauman. Euly recognized him by his mutilated ear. Bauman was a hulking fellow whose face had been rearranged from prize-fighting.

"Don't get no notions, son," Truman said. "The Mennonites know best in these matters. Let the law take care of it."

"I will," Euly said. He felt dizzy, like at his Aunt Elise's school when he had to make a speech. The layers of tobacco smoke in this gloomy place didn't help. "I will not seek revenge, but who is this man Mole?"

"Was a buffalo hunter, then a bone picker, until they wasn't no more buffaloes—and no more bones," Truman said. "He throwed in with an ornery bunch, they robbed a bank way over to Emporia. That's what we know. Cabot says Mole kilt two men—there's paper on him. Son, he's halfway to the Territory by now."

Cabot again. Jericho Springs was so small it didn't have a peace officer. One-legged Sy Wentzler held the job for a time, but he was always drunk. Cabot was justice of the peace, but for matters more violent than a wedding you had to telegraph Newton.

"You better believe I'd go after him," said the fighter. "I could find him down there, too. Killed my old man? Shit."

"You never knowed your father, Malachi," Gibbs said. "Anyhow, you couldn't find him. *I* could."

"I'd lay up and wait for him. I'd ambush the bastard."

The profanity hurt Euly's ears. "There's the barrels," he said. Truman nodded but with a blank face. "The barrels?"

"The empties. My father would bring in new stock, and—"

"Shore, son, we'll load 'em up for you. Listen, you don't have to be so—so—so *solishus*. Nobody here gonna cheat you. What kinda men would we be, iffen, if we—"

Euly picked up the rifle. "Thank you, Mr. Truman."

"Your father was a good man, son. Tell you this: gonna put a crimp in *my* business. That Missouri whiskey was special. I gotta deal with bootleggers now."

Euly stood at the front door, looking into the rain. Now he cried, but he'd pull back every tear before he reached Cabot's.

Truman followed him for several steps. "You awright, son? Aw, you ain't. You cain't be."

And there were calls from the little crowd: "Anything you need," and "We'll ride with you, boy," and "U.S. Marshal ul get him! They'll hang that guttersnipe!"

Euly smiled. Negotiating the Santa Fe hadn't proved so hard. His father had been popular with drunks.

HAT PULLED LOW, Euly ran across windy, sopping Main Street to the opposite boardwalk, and stared back toward the Santa Fe. The town had gone dark except for the saloon, an unsteady light at Ammon Krughoff's bank, and Cabot's gaslit enterprise near the depot. Conquer your dread, he told himself. This was the worst of days and he faced a hard winter, but best get on with it.

Though not a witness to the murder, Euly couldn't shake the image of his father grasping his chest and falling, and then the gush of blood as his heart pumped its last. He stood at Cabot's long window, staring at the blurred image of something wrapped in oilcloth on a long, steel table. As he gathered his resolve to enter, Giles Cabot stuck his nose into the rain. "You poor boy," he said. "Come in out of the wet!"

Euly allowed himself to be guided into the "funeral parlor," which ordinarily was a packaging room for rail shipments and a post office, but Cabot had swept the floor, dragged in the table, and placed chairs against the walls. Euly shook off the rain and stood awkwardly, staring at the covered body, while Cabot maintained his sympathetic smile.

Fortunately, Uncle Helmut and Aunt Elise had been waiting, and Elise called out to him in a weak effort at cheer. "Annelise," he murmured, slurring together "Aunt" and "Elise" as he and Kate always had, and as most of the congregation also had come to do. Euly dropped into a chair beside her, holding the Marlin rifle between his legs. Surprising him, his usually unexpressive Uncle Helmut reached across and squeezed his knee.

"Young man," Cabot said, stepping from behind his desk into the light. "There are times in every life when the darkest sorrow descends. We navigate such trials by our faith in our fellows, and in God. We may feel—"

The speech didn't quite fit the moment, and Helmut stared glassily. Annelise turned to Euly, her pale face shrouded in a black bonnet, her blue eyes glistening. "He's right about one thing," she whispered. "This is the time for family. Lean on us, Ulysses."

"Oh, Annelise." He fought the temptation to lay his head in her lap, as he would have a few years before. He put an arm around her shoulder and said, "We'll get through it."

"What are you doing with that rifle?"

He nodded toward Cabot, and said in German, "I am going to shoot Mr. Cabot."

"Euly!"

He returned to English. "He gave me a bad price for my Ben Davis apples."

She smiled. "Worth shooting him for?"

"No, ma'am." Euly laughed. "The rifle was Father's, that's all."

Cabot wanted to sell them a cast iron coffin, but among the Mennonites anything more than a well-fitted wooden box constituted vanity. Cabot went on about transporting the body, and rent for the space in which it lay, until at last Helmut rose. He was over six feet tall, though gaunt, as if suffering from consumption. He wore his broad black hat—always wore it. With his full black beard, he made Euly think of the fierce abolitionist, John Brown.

Helmut jabbed a finger. Though he understood English, he usually spoke in German, particularly to the Englische. He said it gave him an advantage in business dealings. "Money! Money! *Wie viel geld?*"

"Oh," Cabot said. "Who can consider money at such a time? I believe ten dollars might be fair."

Helmut dropped two silver dollars on the counter. "Goot?"

"Very good, Herr Kreider."

Now Euly began peeling back the oilcloth. At this Annelise hurried forward and grasped his shoulders. "Euly, he hasn't been dressed."

Cabot placed a hand on Euly's wrist but Euly batted the man aside and stared at his father's face. He could not have borne the dead eyes but they were closed, and otherwise the thin hair, the gray face didn't resemble Barney Kreider. His soul had fled . . . somewhere.

He stared at his father's incongruous deerskin boots. Barney Kreider was fond of those boots. Some Indian woman made them.

Euly's fingers traveled over the heart, still sticky with blood, stopping at last at the waist and parting the oilcloth again. "Mr. Cabot, where is his belt?"

"Of course." Cabot paused, as if he'd made an answer. Anger clouded his eyes. "I assumed the preparations would be here, and so I removed . . . the effects."

"He kept two twenty-dollar gold pieces in that belt."

Cabot slipped into his small office and returned with a japanned metal box. Euly lifted the lid and felt two round shapes under the leather. He plucked out a pocketknife as well, and his father's railroad watch.

"Thank you, Mr. Cabot."

"You should be more trusting of your fellows, young man. At such a time as this—"

"My name is Ulysses. Or you could call me Mr. Kreider."

"In the future, I certainly will." Cabot folded his arms over his vest. "I'm sorry for your loss, Ulysses. I liked your father."

"Ulysses," growled Helmut, pointing to Barney Kreider's covered feet. *"Nehmen sie seine füße."*

Take his feet. Euly's German was only fair, and sometimes

he had to pause to work out a translation. He clasped his hands under the deerskin boots, while Helmut lifted under the shoulders. They carried the body out to the alley and pulled it onto the bed of the black buckboard.

Annelise followed, holding the Marlin by the trigger guard like a dirty diaper. "Thank you for everything, Mr. Cabot," she called back, and Cabot said, "So, so sorry," and then the three Kreiders stood in the rain, negotiating.

"He should be buried with my mother," said Euly. "Up above the orchard."

"Certainly," Annelise said. "Come stay with us, Euly."

"You know I can't, with stock to feed. And apples. I still have apples."

"We'll send Johnny Heart down to help."

Euly nodded. Johnny was his best friend. "The service . . . it won't be at the church—?"

"Of course, at the church, Ulysses," Annelise said. "Where else?"

"I only meant—"

Uncle Helmut hulked above, clapping his big hands on Euly's shoulders. He was crying—a stunning and marvelous thing to see. *"Mein bruder. Mein kleider bruder."*

"Our little brother," Annelise murmured.

ACCORDING TO HIS FATHER'S railroad watch, Euly reached home at midnight. The rain had turned to ice and his clothing had soaked through. The darkness around the barn seemed absolute and might have frightened him, but he'd been awake for twenty hours, dragged through the bloody day until his every sense dulled. Teeth chattering, sneezing, he held his hand steady enough to light a lantern, then back King Arthur and the mules into stalls and throw them some hay. Maude slept on, her lips fluttering with snores. King Arthur kicked at his unfamiliar stall and screamed out that he was in charge, but the mules were exhausted and made indifferent vassals. Euly gave each animal half an apple, setting King Arthur's atop the stall gate because the stallion might bite his fingers.

He staggered toward the house with his hat pulled low, his saturated boots like machines his body was attached to, dropping into puddles, slipping on ice. Inside, he reached for the lantern, but confusingly it was already lit, burning so low it issued no more light than a birthday candle. He opened the stove door and found the fire free of ashes, burning with steady yellow flames. Shivering, he dropped his coat and pulled off his wet clothing, until he stood naked, rotating before the stove like meat on a spit.

His second pair of Levi's sailed across the room. "I'm not your wife, Euly! Put those on!"

He jumped behind the stove. "Sorry, Kate. I forgot—"

"Not that you couldn't use a wife. This place is a mess."

"I'm alone so much, I forget the niceties. And Father is—was no guide."

Kate came near and handed him a shirt. "How was it?"

He couldn't answer.

"Do they know who . . . ?" At the far end of the table, she moved a stack of books to the floor and sat. "Who the killer was?"

"Someone called Eddie Mole. A bank robber. He's killed before."

"Are you going after him?"

He sat at his table, pushing back dishes and books to make a place for his plate of beans. He broke off a chunk of cornbread and held it up in a salute. "Thank you, Kate."

"Are you?"

"I wouldn't know how, Kate." Euly's face twisted in agony. "The Church preaches against revenge, you know that. We're supposed to leave it in God's hands. To the law."

"What are you going to do?"

Euly threw up his hands. "Get through the funeral. Bury him with my mother."

Kate laughed. "I mean, in life."

"I don't know. I have all these apples to sell, Kate, and I need to find someone besides Giles Cabot to buy them. I'll take up Father's freight runs, I should imagine. You?"

"I was never close to him. Every Christmas, he gave me twenty dollars. Never spoke to me. I want to draw, Euly."

Kate was an artist, or fancied so. At Annelise's urging, she'd hung her portraits and landscapes all around the schoolhouse, begging public approbation, but no one came, much less commented. The Mennonites were too busy for Great Art, too insular to appreciate it, or they thought it decadent. Kate painted glorious sunsets and collapsing soddies but also Johnny Heart of Oak—in strange, almost comical poses, as a great chief or sullen warrior.

"You're talented, Kate. I wish I had such talent."

"It's a curse. I can't bake cookies or join in quilting—"

Euly finished his beans. "Fine cornbread, though. What about Johnny?"

Kate averted her eyes in the soft light. "What about him, Euly?"

People said she was bold to go about in men's trousers and to spend so much time with Helmut's hired hand, an Osage Indian. "Well," Euly said. "The two of you sneaking off to the creek."

"You're insulting!"

"I'm Euly, Kate. The fellow who always tells you the truth."

"I don't know, Euly. I don't *know* what Johnny wants. Are people talking?" Kate opened the stove door and shoved the poker into the coals.

"Not really," Euly said. "Frieda Hausen asked me about you two."

"That old maid! Out to sabotage happiness anywhere she sees it. Listen, where are we gonna sleep? You wouldn't send me outside on such a cruel night?"

His belly was full. Sitting before the warm fire, Euly found the sound of ice bouncing off the tin roof almost comforting.

"Once upon a time," he said. "On cruel nights, we curled up together."

"Get that out of your head, you lecher!"

He laughed. "I could sleep with Maude. She snores and licks my face right at dawn."

Kate laughed, too, and pointed to the space before the stove. "There's plenty of blankets."

He sank toward the floor as more blankets fluttered above him. He heard chunks of wood shifting in the fire box, and out in the barn, one long, indignant wail from King Arthur.

His first image was always of the two of them as children, sitting on a pew with their legs straight out as Annelise fussed with his collar, and Kate's unruly blonde hair. Almost asleep, he murmured, "My father is dead."

She didn't answer. Perhaps she slept. In a low voice that was almost a prayer, he said, "Thank you, Kate, for helping me through this."

"Oh, Euly," she whispered. "Who else?"

3

Johnny Heart of Oak

They hit hardpan two feet down and threw off their coats, sweating despite the cold air. They chiseled their way with picks and a pike, prying out chunks of limestone and chert, before at last leveling the bottom. They sat for a time on the mountain of dirt, Johnny smoking his pipe, Euly looking across at the grave of his mother, Evangeline, whom he never knew.

The sun showed itself, the wind calmed, and they picked apples for three hours more, sorting them into the wagons, throwing the culls into baskets for cider.

Two blessings: first, they'd so far been spared a deep freeze. Apples were usable after freezing but lost their crispness and couldn't be sold for much, not at all to the railroad. And second: with one day remaining before the funeral, and two wagons, they could haul seventy bushels to Newton.

There was a third blessing: working so hard kept Euly's grief at bay. Right now, he didn't understand how a man such as Eddie Mole could exist, though there were plenty like him. Oklahoma Territory would be a better place when such men were exterminated, but why did the Lord allow these monsters in the first place?

The answer the Church gave was that good and evil raged on, neither victorious until the Day of Judgment. Or even, more cynically, that behind every bad man another one stood, and hence, almost as a practical matter, it was best to leave it all to God. Euly had heard this since he was a toddler and it was cold comfort.

Life was work. Keep working! They pulled the wagons into the barn, unhitched and fed the animals, and the next task was to fix supper for two weary men. Some of Helmut Kreider's fine smoked ham, scrambled eggs, fried potatoes, and canned corn. Men who looked after themselves seldom ate so well but Euly was grateful for Johnny Heart's help. For his friendship.

He tried to say so. "Johnny, I appreciate—"

Johnny waved a hand. "We are friends. And you are a good cook, Little Hero."

At the boarding school in Pawhuska, Johnny read both the Bible and Homer. He shared with Euly a love for the *Odyssey*, which was akin to certain Osage stories with its fantastic adventures. Learning that the boy who followed him around had been christened Ulysses, Johnny Heart took to calling Euly "Little Hero."

And for another reason. Twelve years before, when the first steam threshers reached Kreider wheat fields, little Euly crawled up high to a seat by the boiler, fascinated by the deafening plunge of the pistons, the clanking and hissing and feverish heat. He shouldn't even have been there, but the men didn't completely understand their new machinery and were engrossed in feeding the thresher, a spinning, maniacal god that sought your fingers for an offering.

A long flat belt wound from the thresher back to the boiler, and only Euly saw when a hanging strap from Johnny's suspenders caught on a protruding wire from the belt's seam, jerking him awkwardly, almost comically toward the engine's pulleys and massive flywheel. Johnny had time to reach for his pocket-knife and cut his suspenders, but the great machine was unfamiliar, the moment irrational. As if released from a spell, the men yelled out, but only eight-year-old Euly was calm enough to push forward the clutch, bringing the belt and the flywheel to a thunderous stop. Euly spared Johnny from a crippling injury, maybe even saved his life, and became the Little Hero not only because of his name.

Johnny had a nickname, too, at least with Euly and Kate: Noble Savage. One Christmas, Euly gave Kate a set of watercolors—his first order ever from Montgomery Ward. When she was fourteen, and had graduated from water colors to oils, Kate painted Johnny in buckskin, then wielding a tomahawk, then up on King Arthur with his raised lance. Two summers ago she'd painted Johnny in profile, wearing war paint and a somewhat tattered headdress. "You're my noble savage," she said.

"The Osage do not wear the headdress," Johnny explained. "If that is a requirement for noble savagery."

"What do they wear?"

"A bandeau made of beaver skin. Or a Stetson hat."

"Well, I don't suppose kings go around wearing their crowns all the time, either. Not when they're taking a bath or out fox hunting."

"Alas, I am only an ordinary savage," Johnny said—ironically, Euly supposed, though Johnny's face remained stoical and it was hard to know.

Of course, Euly hadn't been there to overhear their conversation, but Kate always relayed what went on between them. Kate and Johnny were his two favorite people and they should marry, though the matter was delicate. It could be said that Johnny was a Mennonite, even though born and raised an Osage. And Kate was white, even though if you had dressed her up in Indian clothes, you'd have thought her Cherokee or Ponca or Quapaw or Osage—any of those tribes that had been dumped into Oklahoma Territory to make room for white settlers. How would the tribe react if Johnny and Kate announced their marriage? That is, the blue-eyed, German-speaking Mennonite tribe from the Ukraine?

"Do you want a baked apple?" Euly asked. "With brown sugar?"

"If some of your father's stock lies about."

"That's all right? An Indian drinking?"

Johnny shrugged. "I am part French."

Euly struck into the cold across the dogtrot to enter the other room. This had been his father's office, where he figured his profits and read at a rolltop desk made from bird's eye maple, ostentatiously trimmed with black walnut. A more abstemious Mennonite wouldn't have owned it.

Five shelves of books: Mark Twain, Nathaniel Hawthorne, several of the Waverly novels—Barney used to read to Euly from *Ivanhoe*—Dickens, Shakespeare, Cervantes, Dante, Plutarch, and Aesop. Homer, of course, and the plays of Aeschylus. A lifetime of reading, and perhaps his father's finest legacy, more so than the dogtrot house, two wagons, two freight teams, one three-hundred-pound sow, an apple orchard, and possibly five hundred dollars in the bank. He'd find out when he talked to Banker Krughoff.

He had to make room in here for apples, at the moment his only source of income. Even after the journey to Newton, one hundred bushels would remain. He'd keep a low fire until he could process them.

He caught up two five-gallon oak casks and returned to the warm side. "Missouri whiskey. Kansas cider," he said.

Johnny sat under the only window, a hardware purchase with a sash that he had raised halfway. A thoughtful gesture, as he had fired up a pipeful of his foul tobacco. But Johnny could do anything he wanted and have a drink besides. Euly mixed whiskey with last year's hard cider and handed the cup over. Stout stuff.

He took a long slug himself and lay on his bed. It occurred to him that Johnny also needed a place to sleep but weariness washed over him. He dozed, and woke, and thought Johnny went outside for a time. Convinced he'd heard a rifle firing, he sat up. He slept again, and when he woke Johnny lay on the pallet of blankets Kate had made up when Barney Kreider was killed.

"Noble Savage, what do you do on the reservation?"

Johnny took the winters off and soon would leave. He didn't answer. I shouldn't tease him, Euly thought. Johnny *was* noble. "I am like you, Ulysses," the Indian said. "I make a great plan."

EULY READ BARNEY KREIDER'S fancy railroad watch: 4:30. He stumbled to the stove in his wool socks, donned gloves, and scooped ashes from the live coals. He fanned the coals with the bellows until the fire roared. He began coffee and threw pieces of salt pork into a skillet. He dipped hot water from the reservoir into a saucepan and dropped in potatoes.

Lord, his head ached.

Johnny stomped in, announcing he'd hitched the teams. They stood near the stove, gulping coffee and eating potatoes along with the pork and chunks of cold bread.

Johnny lit his pipe. "A bad night for you, Ulysses?"

"Yes." He'd dreamed of his father shot down, rising to resist, being dragged through the mud by the outlaw, Eddie Mole. Euly laced his boots, pulled on his wool sweater, coat, and floppy-eared Ukrainian hat, then stepped onto the dogtrot.

The house was two large separate rooms with a wooden platform, the dogtrot, between them, and one long roof over it all. Barney and Helmut Kreider threw it up in a week, using the mental blueprint of a house Barney had seen down in Arkansas. Euly had just arrived to live with his father. Hardly ten, he sawed the green oak sheeting and handed it up to the men.

Below freezing, Euly judged, and the air spat snow. He retrieved the stinking buffalo robe from the other room and offered it to Johnny, along with another floppy hat.

Johnny also wore suspenders and a gray woolen shirt buttoned to the neck, because the uniform reduced the number of insults hurled at him. Neither Johnny nor Euly boasted a beard, their fur hats stood out, and each man's hair hung to his shoulders. But their coats were black and square-cut, their boots heavy and durable. They looked Mennonite enough—or Brethren, or Amish, or Quaker, all of whom had founded colonies in these parts. Because bishops and elders kept making changes, sometimes Euly himself couldn't tell the tribes apart, and certainly the Englische couldn't.

The Englische admired Mennonite industry, and the turkey red wheat, or winter wheat, that they'd brought from the Ukraine made Kansas prosperous. Still, they were a strange folk. They weren't Russians, but Germans. They'd fled to the Ukraine because of a quarrel with Catholics over baptism. Then they fled to Kansas when the czar wanted their young men to carry rifles.

Their pacifism made them stranger than Baptists or even Catholics. The Mennonites were strange enough that it followed they'd welcome Indians among them, maybe even Negroes.

THE ROAD RAN DUE west, five miles of it through flat Kreider land. In fact, the hills ended east of Jericho Springs, and from what Euly had read the land lay rolling, almost flat, all the way to the Rocky Mountains. In the tall grass, travelers on the Santa Fe Trail had imagined themselves on a great ocean. Not an adventuresome route, not muddy, not menaced by outlaws, and the teams plodded along, making six miles an hour in the crisp air. Even under an army blanket Euly grew cold, but the sun rose at his back, and the golden land awakened with the screams of prairie chickens and the pure melodies of meadow larks. A coyote skulked ahead of them, then disappeared into the grass, chasing a rabbit or groundhog.

He reached the railyard at Newton and turned Gerty and Maude onto a fast, black road made of cinders. Newton wasn't a big city but it boasted an active railyard and a buyer who seemed not to care whether Euly was Mennonite or Moroccan. Johnny pulled up with the mules as Euly unloaded, and the buyer, an Irishman, retained his glum expression.

Euly thought they should celebrate. He offered Johnny five dollars for his work, which the Indian refused, and then suggested they eat in a restaurant. They found a place frequented by rail travelers, but the sign on the window read:

No niggers
No Chinamen
No Injuns.

"Go, Euly. Bring me some bread."

"No." Two doors down stood a German butcher's shop, where Euly bought cheese and bread, liverwurst, and sarsaparilla. They drove their empty wagons two miles toward Jericho Springs, stopping at a grassy creek so the stock could water and forage. The mules pulled their empty wagon near a midsized cotton-wood and stripped bark with their teeth.

Euly had sold his apples at forty-one cents, less only a penny for crating. Thus he returned home with $28.40—two weeks wages for a farmhand, better than Cabot's price by ten dollars.

Still, he was miserable. His father was dead. His friend couldn't eat with him because his skin was brown. "How do you stand it?" he asked, by which he meant not only mindless hatred, but life itself.

Johnny shrugged. "Soon I go home."

4

Vengeance Is Mine

Barney Kreider, whom Annelise and several other women had cleaned and dressed in a black suit, rested with his gray face studying the church rafters. Euly much admired the well-fitted coffin, made of red elm on short notice. He'd be sure to thank his Uncle Ronald and pay him for the handsome wood.

He wasn't so sure what to do about Pastor McAfee. He knew it was customary to pay preachers for the marriage ceremony but what was the etiquette for funeral orations? Two silver dollars, as his Uncle Helmut gave Cabot? If anything in life came free, a funeral should, and Euly didn't want to waste his apple money. He disliked McAfee.

Pastor Peter McAfee wasn't born a Mennonite. In the '80s and into the '90s, convinced that hard work and devotion to God would triumph over poverty and sin, families from several parishes adopted street kids, mostly teenaged boys from Chicago. But what the Mennonites thought of as an offer of freedom the boys regarded as slavery. Bearded patriarchs, speaking half in German, tried to extract a day's hard work from young thugs who, before they could begin, needed "work" defined. The only reward was food—lots of food—and Bible lessons.

The boys refused to, or couldn't, adapt to field chores. They smoked, they drank, they picked fights. They came together in gangs to harass picnics and wedding parties. Most never learned to read and terrorized their teachers and fellow students. In time they were moved into a home for incorrigibles, from which most escaped and found their way back to Chicago, there to finish their angry, short lives.

The exception was Peter McAfee, who climbed from illiteracy to the seminary in eight years. He even learned German. Everyone loved to tell the story, and yet Peter McAfee's admirable struggle hadn't made him admirable. Humility sat on the pastor's face like an insult but he read something in Euly's eyes, too, and suppressed his contempt. Euly didn't accept the man's moral authority. Maybe that was it.

Euly sat with Annelise and Helmut, on the right with the men—in plain white shirts buttoned to the neck, eschewing the audacity of ties—behind them. The women—in black or gray wool, the craven glory of their hair covered with black bonnets—sat on the left, but mysteriously the unmarried among them, ranging from a giddy fourteen to a hopeless twenty-eight, had clumped together. Like nuns in their plain dresses, like unadorned angels, they looked up with grave eyes at the unmarried pastor, ordained not a year before by the little Mennonite college in Halstead. McAfee offered no encouragement, but the young ladies were encouraged nonetheless. Perhaps the young pastor's cloak of indifference seemed like holiness.

McAfee had to be endured but only for a day. Euly glanced over the congregation. Where was Kate?

"An unholy sin has been committed against you, Ulysses Kreider," said Pastor McAfee, dropping his head, almost meeting Euly's eyes. "But know that the grievance you have is everyone's and we must find strength in one another. To seek vengeance, to allow violence to beget violence—"

Why did everyone assume he sought vengeance? If Euly undertook revenge himself—never mind that Eddie Mole was a mad dog killer—he usurped God. *Vengeance is Mine, I will repay, says the Lord.* Euly had heard that verse since he was five. Even his father quoted it.

The pastor's voice grew quiet so that you had to learn forward to hear: "Sisters and brethren, here is the hardest part—and again we draw from Romans:

If your enemy is hungry, feed him;
If he is thirsty, give him a drink;
For in so doing you will heap coals of fire on his head."

Biblical paradoxes fascinated Euly. It was almost as though God couldn't make up His omniscient mind. Repaying evil with kindness remained revenge, if the result was heaps of fire on the offender's head.

Unless you could work yourself into such a selfless state that you fed Eddie Mole out of divine love, out of the love that Jesus showed on the cross. Was any human capable of such love?

"Now, when we have been wounded, when we are outraged, when the world might look upon us and say, 'You are justified in your revenge'—" The young pastor paused and his eyes bore down on Euly. "We must resist. Friends, ye faithful, we must submit to the will of God. We cannot know His ways but we do know that they work toward justice. We know that on the Great Day He will reward those who have remained true to His holy word, and turn away sinners. Sisters, brethren, young and old, and oh! those wronged and those grieving, submit. Fold yourself in His compassion. Submit."

He'd heard this all his life, too, though never from his father, not the late renegade, Barney Kreider. Do not simmer. Do not plot. Make your spirit submissive before the Lord. Euly lifted his face so that everyone could see the tears in his eyes, while moans and sobs rose from the good Mennonites of Jericho Springs. They might have concluded that what they saw in Euly's agonized face was an expression of grief and submission, when in fact what they looked upon was rage.

But toward Peter McAfee, not Eddie Mole, whom Euly fully intended to leave to the discretion of the law. The dour pastor hadn't a single kind word for his father! For imperfect Barney

Kreider! Maybe they should have laid Barney out, and drunk to his life, at the Santa Fe.

Euly's legs trembled. Almost, he screamed at the pastor, "My father was a man! A good man!"

But Euly forced himself calm, mimicking his friend Johnny's stoicism. Reason, he lectured himself. Logic. No point in hating Peter McAfee; hatred was manna for the dour pastor's husk of a soul. The man was a waste of time.

THE ELDERS HAD DECREED every Mennonite house and barn should be painted a dull red-brown. Annelise fought the good fight for a white church and you'd have thought she'd grown horns. Everything must be plain, plain, plain! Snow sparkled on the slate roof of the white church like a divine blessing, and Euly cried at the purity of it. Then he suppressed his tears because the day was half-finished and he had work to do.

He slipped McAfee two dollars and stood with Helmut and Annelise Kreider, smiling stoically. Excepting Kate, the unmarried women filed quickly by, trying mightily not to giggle because today was merely church to them, their weekly social outing with a somber twist. Most offered the obligatory hug, holding their bodies apart.

But sixteen-year-old Jenny Muenster, who'd grown two inches since last Euly saw her, pressed herself against him, then looked at him with tearful blue eyes. She held out a paper bag with a straight arm. Euly smelled oatmeal and realized that Jenny had baked him cookies. He mumbled, "Thank you, Jenny," before averting his eyes.

"So kind, Jennifer," Annelise said, almost too warmly, and the old woman embraced the young one. "Come with me, Euly," she said, in her sternest tone, and Euly, holding the cookies under one arm, trudged after her, grateful to escape small talk.

Men and women dispersed, speaking of weather and winter wheat, temperance and imminent marriages, quilting and baking and threshing machines. Buggies parted the infinite white fields, some turning toward the gravesite, others toward Sunday dinner. Horses whinnied, wheels squawked, and the churchyard became a spongy, sopping mass of mud and dirty snow.

I have to bury him, Euly thought, and then all of it will be done.

Annelise led him into the dull brown schoolhouse, and they sat opposite each other on student desks, Euly on his own desk from six years before. Annelise was tough enough to keep order among lanky farmboys who sometimes brought knives to school. She loved learning, lamenting she could take her students only through the eighth grade. She encouraged Euly to read every book in the schoolhouse, even those superfluous to the elders' view that knowing the Bible, Anabaptist history, and long division was all a Mennonite farmer would ever need.

"I have something difficult to say, Euly. Your father, Barney—" Annelise paused and looked up at him painfully. Euly loved his aunt and wished he could make things easier for her. He reached into the paper sack and passed her one of Jenny Muenster's cookies.

Annelise smiled. "Jenny's a kind-hearted girl."

Euly stared over her shoulder at the piano and shuddered with a minor guilt. Three years before, at a Sunday afternoon picnic, a game of Old Crow rose—little different from tag, but using a knotted gunnysack, which you threw at the next candidate to be "it." Few girls played but Jenny threw the sack with surprising force, striking Euly below the eye, then running into the empty schoolhouse. Euly ran after and cornered Jenny behind the piano.

Then something bewildering happened. As he raised the gunnysack, Jenny looked up him in fear—not fear, but terror. Like a fox in a steel trap, aware it soon would die. Did Jenny read something in his eyes?

His aunt said, "Euly, you're alone now. You have a farm. It's not too soon to be thinking about . . ."

On the frontier, you didn't wait around forever.

"Jenny's a practical young lady. Mature for her age."

"Yes, ma'am," Euly said, but wondered what this talk was really about. Not blue-eyed Jenny. "Annelise, where's Kate?"

"She's leaving us, Euly." Annelise looked toward the piano, too, and nodded. "You know she has been unhappy with the Mennonite way."

Euly shook his head. "With farming. With the clothing. With no outlet for her painting. But—"

Annelise grabbed his hand. "Ulysses, Katherine is your sister."

Some part of him had always known. They thought alike; sometimes, they blurted out the same sentences. "My father, he found the little girl—"

"In Missouri, yes. We told everyone that Kate was an orphan, that her poor, abandoned mother died in childbirth—"

"Like *my* mother."

"Like God-fearing Evangeline. But this woman—she was your father's . . . I don't want to say the word. Barney couldn't raise the child alone, so Helmut and I, we took her in—you know. You know. I couldn't bear children, Euly."

The schoolhouse seemed tiny, the world immense. "Why didn't you tell us? We could be—"

Annelise dabbed at her eyes with a handkerchief. "Your father took you back when you were ten . . . I didn't think how close you and Kate were. Like Kate's brother, Ulysses! Oh, I know it's confusing. Maybe we were wrong. Barney didn't want—it seemed wiser—we didn't want the shame upon her."

"What shame? That she was half-Indian? Or that Barney Kreider was her father?"

Annelise turned her head. Her old, white cheeks reddened. "I've read so many books, Euly."

He stared at his gentle aunt, baffled. "Yes."

"And still I don't understand the human heart. I don't . . . know a *thing*, Euly. Barney named her—he was generous—in his will. If you can, Ulysses, imagine your father's torment."

My father's cowardice, he thought. Kate's life, his, belonged in some old English novel. "Annelise, where *is* Kate?"

"Waiting for you. Just . . . go on home."

HE RODE GERTY HARD the half mile to Jericho Springs, and thought, what is the sense of this? We don't bury him until three; why should I punish my poor horse? He slowed her to a walk as he reached the Zimmerman Woods, then dismounted, a mile now from his farm. He came upon Kate almost at the point where she'd stopped him four nights before.

She wore a black, collarless wool coat cut below her waist, a Mennonite coat out of which mushroomed a dark blue skirt with a pattern of small red stars. The splash of red was an Englische touch and seemed defiant, as did her snarled, blonde hair. He reached out and touched an ear. "You'll freeze, Kate. Take my hat?"

She laughed. "Your silly, floppy hat?"

They embraced, then stood apart again, both of them crying. "I can't stand it, Euly."

"Stay. No one will blame you."

"They will, Euly. I'm a—I don't know *what* I am."

"An Indian, that's what I think. Why didn't Annelise—?"

"She's our *mother*, Euly. Like a mother—"

Behind them, King Arthur and Gerty drew together, the sleek male, the ponderous female. They snorted and their breath hung in the cold air.

"Our father—" Euly began.

"Was never a father to me. Hardly to you."

"He never struck me. He taught me about books. And tools and mules and apples."

"He worked you night and day."

Euly smiled. "*Das Leben ist Arbeit.*"

"Yes, yes, life is work," Kate said. "If I had a penny for every time Uncle Helmut says that!"

"Mostly, Father was absent. And I would say . . . remote. He wasn't an evil man, Kate."

She frowned. "Shall we talk all day, while they lower him into the grave, on the question of evil? He hauled whiskey, but no, he wasn't evil like Eddie Mole. Barney was lonely. I pitied him. No woman in the church would have him, no decent women among the Englische."

"Half the farm is yours."

She laughed and reached for King Arthur's trailing reins. "It's a poor farm, more a curse than a blessing. I have heard Uncle Helmut say so."

Euly reached deep into his trousers, and handed her the two gold pieces. "These were his."

She turned them over in her hands and returned them. "Something Uncle Barney, our father did, Euly: set aside money for me. You'll see the will. The farm for you, money for me. And, best friend there ever was, you are my brother."

Euly looked away in embarrassment. "Sometimes, I thought we'd be together."

Kate swung up to the saddle. "You'll do as a brother. Might do as a husband, too. Will you take care of King Arthur for me?"

"You're going on the train."

"Isn't it ironic? Uncle Barney—*Father*—made it possible. I'm going to Kansas City to study art."

Euly stepped near and took her hand. "What about Johnny, Kate?"

"We spoke. We—Euly—I don't know." Kate's eyes glistened. "He's older. He's . . . Osage, and I have no idea what I am. Everything needs to calm down, don't you think?"

"Will you write?"

"Soon." She pulled on the reins, goading the stallion with her knees and turning him; he whinnied, as if he enjoyed her harshness. Euly swung up to the saddle as Kate trotted away on her black horse.

He drew near the dogtrot house. He tied Gerty to the pasture gate and then twisted among the dozen or so buggies before plunging into the camouflage of his orchard, Limbs hung heavy with fruit, still, bending to the ground.

According to his railroad watch, he was precisely on time for his father's burial. Bearded men held shovels, while women stood in their long black coats, and black shawls, and black bonnets. Four big men lowered the box. Johnny Heart of Oak handed him a spade and Euly threw the first dirt. Then the women and children sang and he fell to his knees, but Johnny drew him up again. It was an Englische hymn, and everyone's:

> Yes, we'll gather at the river,
> The beautiful, the beautiful river;
> Gather with the saints at the river
> That flows by the throne of God.

Five men shoveled dirt, and five more after them, as Euly stood back. He didn't hear what Pastor McAfee said, he didn't care, but knew it was over when Johnny drew him down the bluff and through the orchard. "I will come tomorrow, Little Hero. We will kill your pig before I go."

The men and women filed down from the bluff, with several Englische among them, including Monte Truman and Giles Cabot, both of whom shook Euly's hand. They were his friends, each said, like they'd been friends to Barney. Helmut and Annelise hung back as if to speak, but left without a further word. Jenny Muenster stared at him but also remained silent.

Men promised help and offered smoked sausages. Women gave pies and roasts and candied sweet potatoes. Don't be a stranger, people said. The bad times pass, and remember, you have friends. Come see us for Christmas.

Buggies turned east and west, and south toward Jericho Springs. Ulysses Kreider fed his stock. He started for the orchard with two baskets but felt chilled to his soul, and gave it up.

Yes, everything needed to calm down. What could be more calming than death?

He built up the fire and ate a piece of apple pie. Then he poured a brace of his father's illegal whiskey and sat near the stove, listening to the horses in the barn and the wind in the trees, as if another voice might speak.

5

To Kill a Pig

Every spring Barney Kreider brought home five or six piglets, which he—or, rather, Euly—fed through the summer on pasture and produce, as well as the golden corn or barley mash that remained after distillation. Up in the fall, when the pigs turned into hogs approaching three hundred pounds, Barney hauled them to auction in Wichita or even Coffeyville, depending where his freight runs aimed his wagon. But he always saved one pig for slaughter and now his son faced the chore.

Euly sharpened every knife he owned. He rolled out a steel barrel, half filled it with water, and built a fire underneath. Above, he rigged the chain-hoist to a stout loop of rope he could slide along a horizontal oak limb. He manhandled the cast-iron cauldron nearby, for rendering lard, and built another fire. He brought out two tables, the lard press, the sausage grinder, a dozen dishpans, and several wide, galvanized tubs.

Johnny Heart drew up at seven. He carried a bed roll, food, and a rifle.

They went to the house to warm up. They drank coffee and didn't speak. At last Johnny caught up Euly's Marlin and walked to the hog pen, where the sow lay in a patch of sun, head tucked between its hooves like a dog might lie, remnants of snow glistening around it. Johnny held the rifle up to the blue sky, threw it from hand to hand, and sighted it toward the Zimmerman Woods.

"I gave it to my father," Euly said. "Good for varmints."

"I will buy one for myself someday." He handed the rifle to Euly. "It is your pig. You should kill it, Little Hero."

Euly dropped the rifle onto a post and chambered a round, as Johnny Heart climbed over the fence and kicked the hog. It refused to stand, so Johnny reached low and pulled the animal's springy tail. The hog rose irritably, squealing, and pranced sideways. It saw Euly and stared, appearing to squint.

"Between the eyes, and an inch above," his father always said. Barney Kreider was an indifferent marksman, however, and even from thirty feet had once missed that sweet spot, hitting the snout, grazing off the thick skull. The hog shrieked in outrage, then staggered about in confusion, head rolling, so that another shot proved difficult. A bad memory, but Euly remained calm and his aim was true. The hog fell and in seconds Johnny Heart slit its throat, catching some of the blood for sausage.

A chorus of protests rose in the barn, horses whinnying, mules croaking, one set of hooves, King Arthur's, pounding against a stall.

They dragged the throbbing carcass toward the hoist and ratcheted it over a tub. Johnny slit the belly, pulling back a little from the stench, then sliced out the heart and liver, dropping them into the sausage pan. He trimmed more fat and cut through muscles, until the intestines oozed into the tub.

While he scalded and scraped the hide, Euly knifed away the filmy membranes, and more fat, from around the intestines. By then Johnny had split the hog with a saw and brought the halves to the other table. Now the bloody business of cutting meat into hams, ribs, and bacon began.

They worked together to uncoil the small intestine and cut it into six-foot lengths. Euly held each length low while Johnny stood high on the step ladder, pouring cup after cup of clean well water through the narrow openings. At last Euly peeled the low end back like a French cuff, and the weight of the falling water slowly forced the entire gut to turn inside out. Johnny returned to render lard while Euly lay out the slick lengths of intestine like white snakes on the table, and rubbed each with salt, until the hog's most practical organ could be stuffed with its own dead flesh. Life was work, task upon task, but sometimes Euly stepped back in awe. Intestines came from another world. He held his hands over his own belly, and marveled at the mind of the Creator, fashioning such machinery.

In seven hours, not stopping to eat, they hung bacon, hams and shoulders, and links of sausage on wires in the smokehouse, and closed the damper on the applewood fire. Three hours of daylight remained, and though he didn't want Johnny Heart to leave, Euly filled a flour sack with pork chops, biscuits, and apples, and held it out.

"At daylight, Little Hero."

"We'll have a fine supper."

Johnny fed the stock and checked on the smokehouse while Euly made cornbread with cracklings, and fried some potatoes, but plenty of food remained from the funeral. They ate apple pie warmed in the Dutch oven, then sat in the kerosene light, exhausted at four in the afternoon. Johnny held out a wrinkled paper:

WANTED

$1500 Reward for the Delivery to Justice of

EDDIE MOLE

Also known as Irish Charlie, Sid DeBoer, and Nat Sobel. Height, 5' 8; fair complected; black eyes; bushy moustash, sloping fourhead, partly bald in front; wears hat low down; rounded showlders with slight hump back; mangled right foot which he throws sideways when in a hury; 2 long scars above the club foot.

WANTED

for the murder of Barney Krider, an honest merchant,
late of Jericho Springs, Kansas.

Wanted for bank robery and murder of innocent
persons in Emporia, Kansas.

Wanted for horse thievery near Pawhuska, Oklahoma
Territory, and the murder of Suzy Niabi,
an Osage Indian woman.

Contact United States Marshall's Office Wichita, Kansas

WANTED DEAD OR ALIVE

Euly stared at the grainy image, unsure if he'd be able to recognize Eddie Mole, at least without his bowler hat, or unless he persuaded the man to take off his shoes. He said, "Did you know Suzy Niabi?"

Johnny looked away. "At the boarding school—when I was a child. She was kind to me. A bad woman, they said, but full blood."

"And there are not so many full bloods, is that what you mean?"

Johnny grunted. "We should kill Eddie Mole, Little Hero. One thousand, five hundred is very much money."

"He is skilled with firearms. Even if I could do it, I'd be profiting from revenge."

Johnny nodded as if in agreement. "Your white preacher would take revenge, as you call it."

Euly laughed. "The Mennonite tribe is all white, except for you."

"The preacher is whiter than white. But does he not say feed your enemy, give him drink? To kill him with kindness?"

"That's Paul, the apostle. It means—" Euly stopped. He wasn't sure what it meant.

"The method is interesting."

"Is there an Osage method?"

"I would not know. I have never killed anyone. They made us go to the boarding school and maybe I am more white than Osage. But my grandfather, he might say, you trail him. You camp somewhere; you wait. When he is not being a bad man, when he is drinking or with a woman, you shoot him."

"You could kill a man like that?"

"Is he a man?" Johnny shrugged. "We could throw a rope around him and drag him to Wichita. The thing to avoid—"

"Yes?"

"Is being killed yourself."

Euly smiled. "I am a Mennonite, Johnny. At least I'm enough of a Mennonite to know killing is wrong. Even of an animal like Eddie Mole."

"You killed the pig, an animal."

"A pig is born to be eaten! A pig has no soul!"

"The Osage would say, even a pig has a spirit. A mean spirit, maybe. Not so mean as Eddie Mole."

Euly couldn't answer.

"Are Mennonites a tribe of fear?"

"You *are* a Mennonite, Johnny. You know we are not."

"What if Eddie Mole wanted to kill your sister Kate?"

"I would defend her. As I would defend you." Euly paused. "How long have you known Kate is my sister?"

"I always thought so. She is so brown. And tall, like the Osage. But she told me last night, Ulysses, when she came to say goodbye." Johnny looked away. "As she wept."

"You two belong together."

"This is not a settled matter. I am . . . older." For an instant, Johnny's dark eyes flickered with pain, and it struck Euly that his friend's usual stoicism was somewhat cultivated. A face for the white man.

"Kate needs to be alone for a time," Johnny went on. "So do I. So do you, but this is not what we were discussing."

Euly frowned.

"Think on this, Ulysses." Johnny frowned, too. "With a name such as your father gave you, the name of a great hero, how can you not kill the pig with two legs? From a high ridge, without noise, like a raven descending. Or we haul him to jail and they hang him while reading from the white man's book of law. It is not a matter of honor with such vermin. Would you not kill a wolf or a panther if it attacked your sheep? Avenge your father, Little Hero, and take the money."

Euly threw up his hands.

"Maybe I will find him for you, Little Hero."

6

Hard Winter

Ammon Krughoff, the Mennonite banker, called Euly in from the street to inform him that a mortgage payment was due on his farm. Also, Barney Kreider owed small amounts to the blacksmith, the harness maker, and of course to that omnipresent Englische, Giles Cabot. Strictly speaking, Euly might not owe his father's debts, but he'd build up some good will if he paid them, and he did need to take care of the mortgage. The good news was that his father's account would wipe out every debt, including the mortgage, if Euly wished to proceed that way.

Euly looked down the street, where a phalanx of temperance women, like a Roman battle formation, stood before the Santa Fe's swinging doors. "Lips that taste liquor will never taste mine," one sign read. The women only grouped in fine weather or Monte Truman would be out of business. He might be in any case if he couldn't find a new source for whiskey.

If Euly paid off every debt, he'd be solvent, he'd be a land-owner with two fine teams, but his operating capital would be reduced to sixty dollars. Enough to pull him through the winter, but little more. He tried to think like a businessman. "If my farm were free and clear, and I had a notion for investment, could I borrow money?"

"Yes," Krughoff allowed, stroking his white beard. He'd been a banker in the Old Country, too. "If you presented us with a worthy proposition, your credit would pass muster."

"Have you some notions, Brother Krughoff?"

"Your farm isn't worth a great deal, Euly. However, Zimmerman Road comes to a T almost in front of your house, and that road takes you to Newton going west, and to Emporia headed east. It's an excellent location if they grade the road and lay down gravel, which Harvey County is discussing."

"Location for what?"

Krughoff shrugged. "Something more than apples, I should think."

HE SPENT A WEEK in his father's office, pressing apples until he had two hundred fifty gallons of syrupy, brown cider. A saleable commodity through February or so, before the cider turned hard, and he had sold twenty gallons when ten inches of snow fell. He figured Monte would buy the hard cider at perhaps a quarter a gallon. Better than if Euly let it turn to vinegar, worth no more than a nickel a jug.

He set several gallons behind the stove, sipped on it through the day, and dropped off to sleep mildly drunk. Another foot of snow fell, and once more he shoveled out his paths.

"I am Barney Kreider's son," he announced to no one but the cosmos. He added sugar and yeast to the cider, and in six weeks raised the alcohol content to—he guessed—around 14 percent. Not a subtle wine, but on the prairie subtlety was little in demand.

He tapped fifty gallons of raw wine into wooden pails and set them outside during a bitter cold snap. Every morning for a week he scraped ice from the tops, until he'd lost half his volume, but he raised the alcohol content to somewhere between—he guessed—25 and 30 percent. Applejack.

Now what? He pumped up his lantern and sat with his stockinged feet propped on a metal bucket by the stove. More snow fell and he tried Emerson: "To be yourself in a world that is constantly trying to make you something else is the greatest accomplishment." A puzzle. Did people try to make him into something else?

He tried Thoreau: "I find it wholesome to be alone the greater part of the time. To be in company, even with the best, is soon wearisome and dissipating. I love to be alone. I never found the companion that was so companionable as solitude."

Maybe so, if you had lived a life to retreat from. If you were a famous writer. To Euly, being alone just seemed like loneliness.

He picked up the *Odyssey*, his father's beautiful, leatherbound edition with its lush color plates. When his father was gone, Euly always turned first to Book Six, where the beautiful Princess Nausicaa came to King Odysseus's aid after he'd lost everything at sea, giving him food and clothing and falling in love with him. A painting by someone named Lord Leighton featured beautiful Nausicaa standing in a doorway, her long legs outlined beneath a translucent white robe.

Staring now, he imagined Jenny in Nausicaa's clothes, or shedding her robe for a bath in the Whitewater River. Golden-haired Jenny was not far away, at the end of a lengthy, cruel journey; she lived ten miles down the road toward Newton.

The snowbound road. The snowbound road that stretched out like a vast ocean.

"Ahhh!" he shouted, and ran to the barn, where he pushed the stock out into the snow, and cleaned three stalls, and climbed into the mow to throw down hay, and stood looking over the infinite whiteness. Not a wagon, not even a horseman, had passed for a week.

The animals couldn't find forage in the deep snow, and moaned and whined and whinnied to be returned to their snug stalls. As he led them in big flakes filled the sky again, and he hustled into the barn buckets of black walnuts he'd stolen from the squirrels in the Zimmerman Woods way back in October. First, he hulled them, then crushed them in a vise, and then sat near his bed, by the hardware window, to pick out kernels. He had to pick walnuts by day because his lanterns didn't yield enough light.

Such tedious work drove him mad. He found himself on the dogtrot, squeezing off rounds at starlings with his father's Marlin .32. He dug a path around the house and then ran in circles, shadowboxing. He went down to the barn again for a long talk with Maude. "You're a good horse," he told her. "You've pulled freight for almost as long as I've been alive. I've got to make some money, but do one more year for me, Maude. Then it's nothing but apples and spring water for you!"

Maude took an apple from his hand.

The snow melted a little but he couldn't do field work, and the Zimmerman Road was too muddy to get through.

He returned to the walnuts. A bucket yielded about a quart, or Mason jar full, and he had twenty-five buckets, but on his best day Euly filled only three jars. He could sell them to the Widow Kearney, who ran a bakery out of her little house, at fifteen cents a jar. He gave up, picking out the big pieces only, and throwing the rest in the stove. Ten days of granny work, maybe three dollars.

In one day, he read *The Scarlet Letter*, which in his last year of school, the eighth grade, he'd found boring, but now he understood the agonizing subtleties that Hawthorne intended. Hester Prynne reminded him of Kate, not Jenny. Kate wasn't exiled or fallen but she'd gone away to sort things out, and she'd never again quite fit among the Mennonites.

I wonder if I do.

"HULLO, THE HOUSE!"

In the third week of February Euly was out in the barn, saddling King Arthur for a trot down the Zimmerman Road, to see how difficult it would be to get through. He hadn't heard a voice, other than his own mad ramblings, since New Year's Day.

His visitor was Monte Truman, who could be here for one reason: he hadn't found a new source of whiskey.

"How are you, sir?" Euly tried to make his voice sound like his father's.

"Couldn't be better, young Mr. Kreider. Excellent. Hard winter for you?"

Euly looked away. "Being snowed in is tedious."

"Evrybody sorry for you. They ain't found that sonuvabitch, have they?"

"Don't know if anybody's looking."

"They'll run him down, reward like that." Monte sighed. "Reason I come out today, Ulysses, them damn temprance women."

Euly knew a deal was coming. "Sir?"

"Kansas is dry, evrybody knows, but a man needs a drink a whiskey now and then, don't he? All right, I run an illegal business, but that law's *wrong*. These women, they come by evry warm spell—and I don't operate on Sundays, out of respect. I know men can be loud, shore they can. And looks like, man's gonna drink up all his wages—when he's got little children, hungry, to home—I send him on his way. Ain't that right?"

"Yes, Monte."

"Well, these women stand out there singing their damn hymns, and I ain't got nothin' against religion, but you might as well close your doors. This time, Saturday night, one of 'em snuck around back, and taken an axe to your poor ole daddy's barrels. To come right to the point, Euly, I ain't got nothin' but beer to sell. And sarsaparilla. Got lots of sarsaparilla. Wondrin' if you mighten have left a little a your daddy's stock."

"Not a drop," Euly said, though he still had five gallons. "I'll show you what I do have."

They went into the house and Euly poured Truman half a cup of applejack. Truman sipped as if drinking the finest wine, frowned, then drank it all. His eyes widened, he coughed, and a look of mindless contentment spread over his face. "Tastes like California brandy. Dollar a gallon, all you got."

He had no other buyer, but Euly said, "I'm holding out for two dollars on the applejack."

Truman nodded. "Shore, Euly."

He did argue over the wine. Euly asked for a dollar a gallon, but it was harsh wine, and a last resort for Truman's customers even if it were sweet as plums. Truman was almost angry, and Euly could tell it was true anger, rather than a bargaining ploy. They settled for fifty cents, and Euly could scarcely contain his joy.

They walked toward the road, two businessmen pleased with a deal. "Harvey and Butler Counties gettin' together," Truman said. "They gonna lay down gravel on the Newton Road."

"You could make eight, maybe ten miles an hour with a good rig."

"You cain't stop progress. 'Fore you know it, be steam cars runnin' up and down. Fifteen miles an hour!"

"They'll never replace horses."

"Naw. That would go against nature. Anyways, businessmen in Jericho, the bank, Giles Cabot, talkin' about fixing that hog waller through the Zimmerman Woods. Gonna have to, we want Jericho to survive. Railroad ain't gonna be enough. Point bein', you got one helluva location here, Mr. Euly Kreider."

"What would you do with it, Monte?"

"I'd find me a pianer player, and a good cook, and put in a roadhouse. And a purty girl, too, in a long, white dress."

"What's the girl for?"

Monte laughed. "Sing songs to break a fella's heart."

EULY STOOD AT THE school door, watching Annelise. It was Saturday evening but he'd find nothing to do in Jericho Springs. He was bored with his own cooking. Maybe she'd feed him.

Annelise had lifted all the chairs atop the desks and mopped herself in his direction. She did everything. Taught school, brought in a big garden, fermented sauerkraut, counseled the troubled, visited the sick. He'd never been angry with her. She was almost his mother.

She sat opposite him, not startled in the least, and he didn't have to ask. "Kate's in a boarding house, a fine establishment, and she's already in school, Ulysses. Barney's money made it possible, though we'd have helped."

"You're proud of her, Annelise."

"Euly, I am! And I'm not worried, truly I am not, except—"

"She's alone in the big city?"

Annelise laughed. "I'm not worried about her safety. Or falling into wickedness. A woman with an education, Euly, that will be her burden. She sets her sights high, but what can she do in this world? Go around in bloomers, complaining about the terrible lot of women? Is that enough for a life? What will content her, Euly?"

"Maybe a schoolteacher, like you."

She seemed not to hear. "For that matter, Ulysses, what are *you* going to do?"

"Start a business."

"Really." She seemed pleased. "Doing what?"

"I haven't decided. Haul freight where the railroad doesn't go. But the farm is free and clear, and I've made a little money."

"From pursuing Barney's trade, I hear." She smiled but her voice was not reproachful.

He said, "I came to apologize, Ma'am."

"We were in shock, Euly." She waved a hand. "I might equally apologize to you. Keeping it all a secret—"

"Everything needs to calm down. That's what my sister said."

"An adage for life." Annelise rose and shoved her mop toward a clump of dirt. She whirled about and stared at him mischievously. "Euly, it's almost spring. Everything will start over in God's universe. Why don't you ride over to the Muenster farm?"

He glanced away. "I worry that you are too much Jenny's champion in this."

"Not at all!" Annelise laughed so hard that Euly was embarrassed. Her laughter at last resolved into something akin to a giggle. "No, Ulysses. You're a hard worker, you're good with livestock, and you know fruit. You're intelligent. You have ambitions. You're no Apollo but if you take a bath now and then, and put on clean clothes—they don't have to be new, but clean—most any young woman would be interested."

He laughed. "I believe that's an endorsement."

"It is. The world will close in on you soon enough. You're a young man with possibilities. Behave like it."

7

The Courtship of Jenny Muenster

On a bright morning in early March, Euly rode King Arthur to the Muenster farm, a poor, sandy piece of ground bordering a swamp twenty miles west of Jericho Springs, along the Whitewater River. Cecilia Muenster, Henry's wife, walked behind a mule with its ribs showing, nearly finished with harrowing a garden patch of over an acre. Jenny spaded holes for potatoes, while the four barefooted littluns wielded hoes and rakes bigger than they were, cutting rows and covering vegetable seeds. Jenny wore a faded smock, baggy trousers, and stiff-looking chore boots too large for her feet. Sweat glistened on her cheeks and her blonde hair whipped in the wind.

Cecilia and Henry had two teenaged boys, Milton and William, who might have helped, but perhaps they were preparing the fields for corn. Euly's instinct was to tie King Arthur in grass and grab Jenny's shovel, but Cecilia threw him a hard look and Jenny seemed panicked. Maybe he wasn't as welcome as Annelise implied he'd be, but then Henry Muenster, from his chair in the sun, waved a hand and called out, "If it ain't Euly Kreider! Come to see us?"

Henry was barefooted, too. Euly tried not to look at his crooked, blackened toes.

Henry had caught a minie ball in his lower back at Fredericksburg, and according to Euly's Uncle Helmut, *"hatte nicht arbeitete seit."* Hadn't worked since. Hadn't raised a hand in the spirit of enterprise that made America a great country, unless you counted fathering six children.

Rather than fight, many Southern Mennonites rotted in Confederate jails. Pacifism was a reason why they'd left the Old Country. But Henry never liked farming. He joined the boys in blue because he figured they'd win and that he'd be able to talk himself into a sinecure. So he did, cooking for a general and driving a mess wagon behind the lines. He should never have been in peril but that minie ball floated in out of nowhere, knocking Henry down as he flipped bacon and stirred grits.

What he did after the war wasn't altogether clear—he claimed he'd been a conductor for the Union Pacific, a seed salesman, and a janitor for a great Mennonite church in Toronto. In the late '70s he limped into Butler County and found work in Mennonite country—always the man on the wagon, because of that chunk of lead that crowded his spine.

Plain, stoical Cecilia Hostetler clung to her little farm after her strong young husband, Erik, died from smoke inhalation when he tried to save their burning house. One of the founding Ukrainians, Erik was widely mourned, and men in the congregation planted Cecilia's corn, put up hay for her cows, and castrated her barrows until a new husband could be recruited. Henry was lame but available. And since he'd fought for the Union, he drew a small pension.

The problem facing Euly—the first problem—was firewood. Henry and his husky boys, the twins Milton and Will, couldn't keep up with the cookstove. They dragged fallen branches up from the swamp with the mule and stacked them on a rickety scaffold outside the kitchen window, through which Henry could angle branches into the open fire box. The kitchen was always smoky, therefore, but it didn't matter so much when Cecilia forgot to push in half-burnt branches, and they fell to the floor. The floor was dirt.

"That system could be improved upon," Henry allowed. "But hit's jest about the best I can do. I tell you there's days,

Euly, I cain't stay on my feet. You know, I was wounded at Fredricksburg."

Euly caught another glimpse of Jenny, this time with a fleeting smile, but it seemed he needed to talk to Henry for a while. "Yes, sir. That must be a burden for you."

"Oh, I don't complain. But violence is a terrible thing and that's all war is, organized violence. Had to do it all over, I don't know. It brought on terrible suffrin.'"

"You freed the slaves."

"I reckon we did, Euly!" Henry looked off toward the swamp, and the great West beyond, and his eyes moistened. "We was so sorry to hear about Barney. What a terrible tragedy for you!"

"Thank you, sir. I'm doing all right."

"Cecelia and me, we been prayin' for you."

"Prayer is a powerful force."

"More powerful than a cannon! Now, what I mean to say, Euly, them twins, they're good boys. Yes, they like to have their fun, and I'm not the kind of daddy who would deny them that, because I know that when you get down to brass tacks, when push comes to shove—"

"Yes, sir," Euly put in.

"They're hard-workin' boys. All they need is a lively example and if an enterprisin' young fella like yourself—and I've heard nothin' but good about you, Euly, and for shore and certain they's a purty young woman there in the potata patch, she praises you to the skies!"

"Yes, sir." The crux of the matter was that Henry wanted Euly to saw up a rick of wood, and in the process organize the work in a manner that inspired his industrious sons, who needed only inspiration to do the work themselves. The task seemed so straightforward and simple that it puzzled Euly, but when he went down to Henry's sagging barn he discovered that the man's crosscut was rusty and dull, and his bucksaw blade broken.

"Always borrow, never return," Helmut said, when Euly rode

over for a saw set tool, a wire brush, and several files on Henry's behalf. Helmut meant Henry, not Euly.

"When I was a little boy, you said to me, 'Keep your tools sharp.'"

"*Möge Gott uns helfen*," Helmut said. God help us.

Back at the Muensters', Euly discovered that Henry didn't own a vise, so he pushed King Arthur on to Newton, where he spent three dollars on a four-inch bench model. He considered that the sweetheart whose hand he had yet to hold was becoming rather an expensive proposition. Nonetheless, he intended to solve the firewood problem, because helping your neighbor was almost a commandment.

And the trip to Newton proved fortuitous because in the town's massive hardware he realized what his business would be. He loved the gleaming saws, the barrels of nails, the horseshoes and harness, the ballpeen hammers, the rolls of barbed wire, rifles and shotguns, even electric lights! He might have been Archimedes in his bath, shouting, "Hardware!"

As he rode back he planned how to erect his store. He'd pour a cement floor with a real foundation—a time-consuming process, but he could do it in sections. Rain wouldn't affect it.

Newton was the best place to buy studs. He'd heard of a big sawmill down by Wichita that sold siding. He'd raise the building before May was out.

Sawmill? Just as Jericho Springs was too small for a real hardware, neither was there a nearby sawmill. Ronald Kreider ran one but only for congregational needs. Maybe he'd sell his machinery. Euly would stock hardware *and* lumber. He'd pull in farmers for miles around. He'd put all those amateurs—the liveryman, the blacksmith, even Giles Cabot—out of business. Who owned the Zimmerman Woods? He'd buy it! He rode home and fed his restive stock.

By dusk the following day—waiting for Milt and Will to appear, so he might pass on his wisdom—Euly had sanded, oiled, and sharpened the crosscut and replaced one handle. He installed one of the new bucksaw blades, each of which had cost him twenty-three cents, and sat for a moment as if awaiting congratulations, but no one came forth.

He did not like being exploited. Except for Jenny, he did not like this family.

Maybe he was wrong about her, too. He recalled one of his father's pronouncements: "Look at the mother." Cecilia's only expression was a scowl.

Subduing his anger, he built two sawhorses using Henry's scrap lumber, then dragged everything in place by the woodpile. He sawed one log as noisily as he could but still the twins failed to appear, and now the sunlight waned. He caught up King Arthur and headed for home again.

He'd almost forgotten about Jenny but now he saw her in the garden, sowing radish and lettuce seeds, and setting out kohlrabi plants. Euly sat astride King Arthur, studying her. She'd thrown off her bonnet and her blonde hair glowed in the dying sunlight. He stared at her bare feet and thought of naked Nausicaa.

She turned. "Did you come to see me, Ulysses?"

"I meant to. Then I did some work for Mr. Muenster. And I began daydreaming—"

"Castles in the sky. I build them every day."

"You and your mother work so hard. If I were—" He stopped, considering his words. "Doing men's work. Then you go into the house and work half the night."

She dropped her eyes. "Father is unwell."

Not truly your father, he thought. You're like Kate and me. He meant to say something harsh, but she seemed sad, and then, from out of the swamp, he heard a mourning dove: *Ooo. OooWAHooo.* You heard them in the mornings and evenings when the air was cool. No matter how hard he worked, how foul his mood, he stopped to listen. Maybe mourning doves were part of what Thoreau talked about—if you were already reflective, their call was musical accompaniment to living alone.

"I do have my own tasks, Jenny, but perhaps I can help a little more."

"And perhaps we can find some time together, Euly. Would you enjoy walking in the woods?"

He shivered in the saddle. He wanted to buy her some shoes. "Yes."

"We could pick flowers."

Indeed, the air smelled of lilacs, and he almost dismounted, to be near her and . . . well, he had no plan. No matter, because then Cecilia stepped into the yard and yelled, "Girl! You get in here!"

Jenny tossed her hair and looked up at him in the failing light. Down in the swamp the mourning dove called again, or he imagined so.

HENRY OFFERED OTHER PROJECTS, such as fixing the roof of his chickenhouse, which he'd built around an oak tree years before. The oak had grown, pushing up the cedar shakes, causing water to run in and rot several rafters. "Might put a tin roof on there," Henry said. "Last a lot longer. Way things is now, them chickens don't like it how wet it is, and they wanna roost in the barn. Cain't never find no eggs."

By now, Euly saw through the old schemer. "I cannot buy your tin, sir. Perhaps I could haul it for you when I am working on my own projects. I drive to Newton now and then."

"That's a good idea, Euly. I'll send them boys over to your place. We could trade labor for some tin."

Euly refused to show his anger. The barefooted twins had appeared once. They went amiably to work and Milt quickly broke the bucksaw blade. When Euly returned from the barn with another, he made out two stick figures, loping over the ridge.

The boys were feral. Fifty years earlier they'd have been mountain men. They disappeared for days, hunting deer and prairie chickens, and trapping beaver along the Whitewater River. Later, Jenny spoke of her brothers with a rueful affection. "They was smokin' their awful old corncob pipes right in the house," she said. "Mama made 'em sleep in the barn with the cats and the mice."

Euly kept his tone amiable. "It may be a good idea, Mr. Muenster, but I don't believe Will and Milton to be reliable enough to pursue the work I have in mind."

For a moment, Henry seemed confused. He recovered himself and laughed. "Well, Euly," he said. "I understand your point of view."

EULY HAD THOUGHT JENNY was a fine young woman who would share his dreams, and that together they'd build an empire. He wanted to appear wise before her and perform heroic deeds worthy of his name. But Henry's antics and Cecilia's sullenness cleared his head and he didn't return to the Muenster farm.

Kate and Annelise were kind, easy to be with, but they were kin. The other women he knew lived in novels. They were city women who never left their drawing rooms. Servants attended them and they did no work, or nothing Euly understood as work. The two Beckys were instructive: the schemer Becky Sharp, in the long-winded *Vanity Fair*, and the dependent Becky Thatcher, in *Tom Sawyer*. If the two were at the ends of a spectrum, where did Jenny Muenster fall?

She worked. The girl wasn't allowed to do much else.

He hadn't been, either, but he worked no harder than Annelise and Helmut. Their house was filled with love, their food was good, and they knew how to laugh. Living with them, perhaps he'd formed a false model of how men and women got along, how families pulled together.

His father and he made another sort of family. Barney Kreider worked him hard, too, but also gave him responsibilities, and provided books.

Not to mention shoes.

Most every young woman in Jericho Springs was spoken for but when he rode into Newton any number of girls smiled at him, not at all discouraged by his plain garb—Mennonite girls with merry eyes, blue as Jenny's; *Englische* girls with brown eyes, in bright hoop skirts and puffed-up derrieres. He veered into the ether and pondered the significance of a lingering glance.

Stewing over flirtatious glances was foolish. Staring into space was time consuming. Yet when the night stretched out and he writhed in misery, he understood what that old bachelor Paul meant when he wrote that it was better to marry than burn.

When he lusted for a Newton girl, he felt disloyal. He thought of Jenny in her drab linsey smock and bare feet. He wanted to rescue her.

But damn, that family!

Jenny singled him out. That was in her favor, wasn't it? That of the twenty or so Mennonite boys she'd gone through school with, she favored him? Again he recalled that odd day when he'd trapped her behind the piano. She was twelve—much closer to Becky Thatcher than Becky Sharp. She liked him but something frightened her. Had old Henry beat her? Worse?

Hoping he'd see her, he hitched Gerty to the buckboard and drove to church. Three weeks, an eternity, had passed. Jenny stared from across the broad aisle, her eyes full of lightning, and he felt guilty because he'd abandoned her. *Still*. Could he, at fifty, be happy with the woman she became? Once you chose, among Mennonites, the only escape was death.

They strolled by the creek, where he attempted to kiss her even though she was angry. No. Out of pride, she *pretended* to be angry. And with parents such as hers, she couldn't afford much pride. He'd thought he came from a low place, but compared to Jenny he stood on a mountain. He said, "I'm sorry, Jenny."

"So am I, Euly."

He put his arms around her waist and she bent back fiercely. "Mother and Father were so mean!"

"Yes."

"I said to Mama, 'Euly likes me. And I like *him*.' And I said, 'How does a young lady get on in the world?'"

"Maybe she doesn't want you to get on, Jenny. You're her hired girl."

She shook her long hair. "You saw her in a bad light. Mother can be—"

"She drove your sister away." The eldest Muenster girl had run off with a tinker.

"Anna was wild! I could never . . . abandon my *mother*." Her eyes had filled with tears.

"Not abandon her, Jenny," he said. "But a young lady has to find her own place, just as a man does."

She dried her eyes with a sleeve. She bent to pick three blue flowers that grew out of the gravel. "Not like a man, Euly," she whispered.

"What are those?"

"Sweet Williams, sweetheart. Don't you know *anything*?"

He kissed her. The back of his neck felt warm and he didn't know what to say. He looked up the hill toward the church. "They must be looking for you."

"They assumed you'd bring me home, Euly."

Indeed, he'd driven the wagon. "They set a trap for me," he murmured.

She fell silent.

"I will not be their hired man! Not when your brothers, both of them stronger than me—"

"They're good men, Euly."

"They're lazy and conniving, like Henry."

"No, Euly," she said. "They know the farm is hopeless. They know they have nothing. They want . . . they *need* . . . an opportunity."

He never noticed what women wore but now he took in Jenny's gray woolen dress, so like every other woman's dress except for a thin white trim around her neck. He realized that Jenny had worn the dress for years. It was the only dress she had.

The old dress made her breasts seem prominent and he fought the urge to touch them.

They sat close together on the bumpy road to Jericho Springs, and maybe it was a trial run as man and wife. Farmers and farmers' wives called out and waved. Marriage was crucial but hard, and once a couple was seen together the Mennonites allowed for long engagements, and relatively unconstrained joy. Joy, not frivolity, but if lighter moments failed to emerge, perhaps the match was not made in Heaven.

As they forded the creek, she lurched against him and they kissed. The kiss was long, insistent, and Euly drew back in shock at his own lust. Jenny gave off more of a jolt than applejack. She was good at kissing, and Euly wondered if she'd practiced with someone.

He talked about songbirds and crops and the novels he'd read, postponing the day's true subject until they'd reached his farm.

He stopped at the post office to check his father's box and found a curious lot of mail: letters and cards, fliers from implement companies in Kansas City, temperance screeds, and a new Montgomery Ward catalog. He drew out a pregnant envelope from Johnny Heart and almost opened it, but he had a pretty young woman to entertain. He stuffed everything in a leather bag to read later.

"They're going to fix this road," he said, as Maude trotted through the Zimmerman Woods. She was peppy today, like she was ten years younger.

"It's real muddy," Jenny agreed, her speech more restrained now. She seemed vexed.

They walked about his little farm. The apple trees bloomed, but apples bore heavily one year, lightly the next, and he'd have a small crop. "The bright side is that I won't need to thin," he told Jenny.

"Apple blossoms are so beautiful," she said, her blue eyes fixed upon him. "Nothing is prettier except plums."

He nodded. Apples blossoms *were* beautiful. Plums, subtly more so.

"There are no flowers around your house, Euly."

"Oh?"

"A home needs flowers. When you're feeling sad, at least there are flowers."

"My father and I—"

"It's possible to be *too* practical, don't you believe that, Euly?"

"Maybe it is, Jenny." He laughed. "I don't stop being practical long enough to find out."

"Have you ever seen a play?"

"I have not. They put them on in Newton now, at the college."

"Could we go?"

They walked about on the cement floor of what would be his hardware. Puddles had formed where he'd failed to keep the wet cement level. "It's hard to do everything by yourself," he explained.

"I could help," she said. "Maybe not with cement work but I can drive a nail." She walked to the center. "You will be here, holding the rafters together, while I nail to the plate."

He shook his head. "You couldn't."

"I could. But I worry, Euly."

Not planning to, he drew her close. "About what?"

"The inventory."

How did she know a word such as inventory? "I don't—"

"It will take a great deal of money to stock your hardware, won't it? Perhaps Brother Krughoff will loan you some—"

"But not all." He nodded. "I haul freight, Jenny. I am never idle."

"Still, it could take a long time to earn enough. And you won't have customers overnight."

He sighed. "Castles in the sky."

"No, Euly." She drew a finger down his nose. "I could find work in Jericho Springs."

"You'd make so little, all your money would be taken for room and board. Unless you—"

She fell apart from him. They walked arm and arm to the house, not speaking, stopping by the cistern and kissing, their hands everywhere. He picked her up in her gray Sunday dress and carried her a little way. She kicked herself free and he caught her. He fumbled with the top buttons of her dress. She batted at his hand and fled inside.

He sat at the rolltop desk while she built a fire for tea, sliced some of his bread, and brought strawberry preserves out of her bag. She made those preserves, he thought. Grew the strawberries, put up the jam. For three Sundays, she'd carried that pint jar to church, watching for him.

The mail contained two checks for his jobs hauling freight, and an invitation—from, of all people, Giles Cabot—to bid on a weekly run to Newton, carrying hardware. Was Euly supposed to undercut the railroad?

But he forgot everything, even Jenny as she danced by the stove, when he read Johnny's news clipping.

CONGRESS VOIDS TREATY

Lands Opened; Cherokees Lose Long-Standing Claim

Guthrie (O.T.), Mar. 3. With its appropriation of $8.3 million, the U.S. Congress has met treaty obligations from 1891, entered into with the Cherokee Nation. For such considerations the Cherokee Nation forfeits all claims on lands bordering central Kansas, the "Cherokee Outlet," known more popularly as the "Cherokee Strip."

In question has been the Cherokee Nation's legal standing in the matter. Payments to the Nation for use of grasslands by cattlemen's associations ceased in 1890, when President Harrison ordered the army to begin removal of cattle and capital improvements from what the Department of the Interior has estimated to be 6.5 million acres. The spurious claims of certain Cherokee homesteaders, many among them white men, have also been voided.

Speculations arose today from Wichita to New York City of a poor people's land run, reviving popular memory of the extraordinary Arkansas City spectacle of 1889. On April 22, an estimated 50,000 entered the O.T. in their rush for claims, establishing the proud cities of Guthrie and Oklahoma City in a single day.

And Johnny had scribbled across the bottom:

Land Run from Caldwell Sept. probly

Without a word, Euly crossed the room and handed Jenny the clipping. As she ate her bread and jam, she frowned. "I don't even know where Caldwell is. What does it mean?"

He tasted the strawberry jam on her lips. She pulled back, irritated. Then she pecked at his cheek.

He said, "Caldwell is one hundred miles south. On the Oklahoma line. It's our inventory."

"I don't understand."

"People will rush in, Jenny. They'll be crazy. They'll come in their wagons, they'll drop off the train, with nothing. They'll need shovels, axes, harness, pots and pans, soap, rifles, hats, shirts, shotguns, gloves, sledge hammers, corn meal! Everything! And Brother Krughoff will loan money on it, I *know* he will. Do you see, Jenny? We'll build up a *monstrous* inventory. A biblical inventory! We'll find a place down there to store it—there's time! And we have two wagons. Do you see? Do you see?"

"I do, Euly," Jenny said. She threw him a curious look. "And this great thing, this wondrous, reckless adventure, will you undertake it all by yourself?"

"No, Jenny," he said, pulling her close. "You're my, you're my—"

But in his free hand, holding it up behind her shoulder, he read the other news from Johnny. His Mennonite soul twisted in grief and apprehension and he wondered if he had deluded himself with his barefooted girl, his hardware in the sky. Johnny's postcard, mailed two weeks before, contained five words:

"I know where he is."

II

8

Not Like the Old Days

His first three days out of Jericho Springs, Johnny Heart of Oak made ninety miles. He rode an uncomplaining mare, a blue-eyed paint with Choctaw lineage that his grandfather, Buffalo Dancer, named Soquili.

Johnny would see his grandfather soon. He would see him about horses to make up a bride-price. Johnny knew Kate's uncle, the patriarch Helmut Kreider, didn't require the horses. It was an Osage custom. But Buffalo Dancer raised fine horses that would put the shrewd old white man off his guard. He'd lust for them and give up his niece.

First, Johnny had to find the bad man. Eddie Mole ought to be killed by Johnny's young friend, Ulysses Kreider. Johnny should only count coup. And yet if Johnny killed the bad man, he could claim fifteen hundred dollars and have enough money to marry.

This was not his plan. He wanted to shame the young hero into action and the two of them could divide the reward. Still, if you hunted a man and carried a rifle, who could predict what might happen?

JOHNNY GUIDED SOQUILI AROUND the little towns and the homesteads, burying horse and rider in the tall grass. He enjoyed the illusion that he and Soquili were alone under the boundless sunshine, that he was a hunter in long-ago times, that these remained Osage lands. They hadn't been since '72, the year he was born.

When he was a little boy, his mother, Mira, told him he was of the Sky People, the *Tsi-Zhu*, who descended out of heavenly chaos to land on a great red oak, the tree where all life began. Probably his mother no longer believed the story. She had become a follower of the Great Jehovah, rather than Wa-Kon-Da. She had become a Baptist because of her husband, a white preacher named Emmet Baxter.

To Johnny, educated in the boarding school at Pawhuska, the Osage story seemed no more fanciful than the white man's tale of Adam and Eve. He named himself "Heart of Oak" to honor the Osage myth, but he had no true Indian name. He was Emmet's adopted son, John Baxter. Whites called him by his Indian name while the Osage used his white name.

John Baxter urged Soquili up to a high, rocky copse with a thin stand of blackjacks and sumac, intending to meditate on marriage, murder, and the mysterious universe. Up here two inches of snow covered the sparse forage, and he measured out oats for Soquili. Raking aside the snow, he built a fire, brewed coffee, and set pork from Euly's pig to fry.

He was coming home late. In previous years he took leave of the Mennonites after their feast of thanksgiving.

John Baxter ate his hot pork, splashed coffee into a tin cup, and then dragged over two rotting logs and threw them onto the coals. The coals flared, sizzled, and gave off great billows of smoke in the waning light. He cut a dead cedar with his hand ax and the flames leapt high again and the logs burned steadily. He added another cedar and another until the flames rose half-way to Heaven.

Then Johnny danced around the fire and brandished his rifle—his father's rifle, a 15-round Winchester .44, the 1873 model. His father's name was Misai, or White Sun. Misai died in a fight with the Kiowa in 1875, somewhere far west in the

Cherokee Outlet. Johnny was only three. He held no memories of his father.

As he danced, he made up a song:

I am John Baxter, John Baxter,
Fatherless John Baxter.

I am John Baxter, John Baxter,
Only a hired man.

I am John Baxter, John Baxter,
I work for the white man,

I have no tribe.
I have no horses,
I have no land.

I am John Baxter, John Baxter.
I seek a wife.

Wah-Kon-Da, Wah-Kon-da,
I am John Baxter,
My spirit soars,
One with all things.

From points around the copse, slipping in the snow, Johnny cocked the Winchester and sighted slabs of limestone at what he judged to be one hundred yards, and two, and four. Chinks flew away from his first two rounds but not from his third. He aimed higher and thought he hit the far rock on his second try, but in the failing light he couldn't be sure. His father's old rifle was fine for hunting in brush, but he might need something better for a man galloping at a distance.

Grandfather Sun tugged his light over the horizon. Through his binoculars, Johnny made out the lights of several towns along the territorial border; Caldwell was three miles ahead. He'd had the notion to spread out his bedroll by the fire but thought how cold the night would be. He envisioned waking half-frozen beside dead coals.

Johnny had lived with the Mennonites too long. He liked a roof over his head and to keep his feet warm. He saddled Soquili, who skittered about, not understanding why she had to work again even though she'd found no bed in the snow. Man and horse journeyed down the hill toward the lights.

IN THE EARLY 1880s Texas longhorns lumbered up the Chisholm Trail to the railhead at Caldwell, driven by teen-aged cowboys craving faro, liquor, and painted women at the Red Light Saloon. Gunfights were almost predictable and the Indian who ventured into such places, even if he belonged to a trail herd, was either fatalistic or a fool. But by '85, trains stretched deep into Texas and the herds stopped coming north. Troublesome men still passed through Caldwell and they could find whores if they needed to, but the city began to slip into its destiny as a sleepy farm town. With the Cherokee Outlet two miles south, Osage and Ponca were welcome, or their annuities were.

At the livery Johnny rubbed Soquili down and gave her one of Euly's apples. For another quarter, he stored his gear in an adjacent feed room, which boasted a board floor and a cot, and he saw no signs of rats. Perhaps he could have taken a hotel room but so simple a thing was a chore among the whites, even in this enlightened year of 1892. One manager might take your money; another might curse your "red" skin. Maybe the sheriff would visit, wondering why you were in town after dark.

Johnny preferred the stable. The brown Jesus was born in such a place.

At the general store he bought a wool scarf and heavy shirt, anticipating at least two more days of cold riding before he reached the Osage town of Hominy, where his band, the Upland Forest People, had settled. Buffalo Dancer's ranch lay five miles to the north.

He bought a box of .44 ammunition and a pouch of fancy Virginia tobacco.

Then he sat in a dim corner at the Hereford Café, where he warmed up with coffee, fried chicken, carrots from a can, and rye bread a little past its prime. He listened to a white man with a carpenter's pencil lodged above his ear and an old Negro who wore a soiled slouch hat—tradesmen. Farmers had gone home by now; most merchants had closed their doors.

A new bank was going up, the carpenter said, which meant work for masons. It seemed the Negro was a skilled bricklayer.

The winter so far had been mild, but with little moisture following a year of drought. Farmers might switch to dry land crops—more wheat and sorghum, less corn.

Rumor had it that the federal government was about to release the Outlet for settlement and that the army would supervise one final land run, probably in September. Soldiers already mounted patrols to oust squatters, called "Sooners." Both Caldwell and Arkansas City would be prime starting points for the run and a great deal of business would come to Caldwell, from blacksmithing to lawyering, from serving meals out of tents to whoring.

This was extraordinary news and Johnny rose to gather up copies of the Caldwell *Post* from around the room, giving his two fellow diners a nod.

If you rode due south from the Kansas border, the Cherokee Outlet was about seventy miles wide. It butted against the Arkansas River, and thus the Osage Reservation, on the east, and stretched westward almost four hundred miles if you counted the panhandle, or "no-man's-land," that brushed up against Colorado and New Mexico. The government called the land an outlet because that's where the transplanted tribes, most all of them clustered along the Arkansas, had traveled through on their way to hunt buffalo.

When the buffalo disappeared, the Cherokees amassed a fortune renting the land to big ranches and trail herds from Texas, because the tall grass, the blue stem, made fine pasture. Now, under pressure from speculators and citizens' groups, the federal government had bought the land. They'd deployed their blue coats to chase out ranchers and squatters, even pulling down their buildings.

Johnny wasn't an American citizen and couldn't file a claim himself, but he knew where the best land lay. His half-brother, Billy, could make a claim, and so could his white friend, Ulysses.

Now the carpenter and the mason talked of a murder from two nights before, of a deputy named Horst. He'd confronted a bad man at a saloon, "The Barn Dance," south of town.

"Should never gone after him," the Negro said, waving his old hat at a fly.

"Foolish youth," agreed the carpenter.

Johnny lifted his voice: "How was this man called?"

The two men were startled but civil enough. "Robert Lee Horst," said the carpenter.

"No, sir. I refer to the murderer."

The carpenter shrugged. "Don't rightly know."

"They's so many," said the Negro.

JOHNNY WRAPPED HIS FEET in several gunnysacks, because if you kept your feet warm, the rest was easy. He lay under three wool blankets that were too short for him, so one arm stuck into the cold, but that was a tenet of life. One part of you *should* be cold, so the rest of you might revel in warmth, as you denied yourself blackberry cobbler in order to savor your roast beef, or selected boards for a table not for their perfect grain, but their knots and whorls.

Kate was beautiful. But her wiry hair could be considered an imperfection, at least as Johnny understood the standard of beauty among the Mennonites. And she had big feet. At six-foot-five, Johnny stood six inches taller than she, and yet his own feet were two inches shorter. They'd slapped them together during one of his posing sessions, on a languorous Sunday along Zimmerman's Creek.

As he slipped into a pleasant dream of Kate, Johnny heard gunfire. You dared not sleep deeply among the whites.

Yelling, cursing, running feet. He reached across for his Winchester and waited for footsteps to go on by. They failed to, and the big barn door that faced Main Street creaked open. A shape the size of a man stumbled into the half-light, with the moon casting a long shadow before him. The dark man fell, rose, and ran toward Johnny, while another man-shape appeared in the doorway, something gleaming on his chest. "Calhoun, they's no sense in this. You cain't get away."

The man named Calhoun, who smelled of whiskey, stopped about three feet away, then steadied himself on the half-door to the feed room. Johnny held his breath. He knew Calhoun couldn't see him.

The drunk brought his handgun up to the half-door, cocked the hammer, and aimed. Though Johnny was already reacting, he wondered almost whimsically what a Mennonite would do, because wasn't he partly a Mennonite? Could a faith be so nonviolent, so fatalistic, as to allow a man to die?

Johnny lifted his rifle by the barrel and brought the stock down hard on Calhoun's forearm. Calhoun groaned and sank to his knees, while his handgun skipped over the board floor and then into loose hay. Johnny held the rifle on the fallen man and called out, "I have him! Do not fire!"

They dragged the man, who complained that he'd been ambushed, over to the jail. The sheriff, a short, stout fellow with thick, oily hair that glistened in the coal oil light, pushed the drunk into a dank cell and kicked him.

Calhoun howled. "That Injun broke my arm."

"I'll send for the doctor," the sheriff said, but motioned to a chair for Johnny, poured coffee for them both, and pushed several oak logs into the stove, before taking his own seat behind the desk.

"You said you'd send for the doctor!"

"Didn't say when," the sheriff answered. "Hadn't been for this good man here, you'd a kilt me."

"I wouldn't. I'd a aimed for the floor. I need a doctor!" Calhoun shrank to his dark corner, sobbing.

The sheriff turned to Johnny. "You was sleeping in the stable?"

"In the hotel, you can never be sure—"

The sheriff puffed on a stubby cigar. Johnny didn't mind the stink of it. "Oh, we're a welcoming town, Caldwell is. Redskins, black skins, greasers, we got 'em all. You're so tall, you must be Osage. Only your hair ain't right."

"Summers, I work for the Mennonites."

"Where's this?"

"Jericho Springs."

"Ah huh. North a Wichita." The sheriff nodded and seemed to lose interest in Johnny's origins. He stared toward the office's one dusty window. "Every time I gotta shoot some sonuvabitch, Council tells me the bad ole days, them whore-mongin', shoot-up-the-town days, is a thing a the past. Stopped when the longhorns stopped." He faced Johnny again. "What's your name?"

Johnny paused. "John Baxter."

"I'll take your word for it." The sheriff laughed. "I'm Frank Turnstall. I'm in a position to offer you employment, Mr. Baxter."

"An Indian deputy?" Johnny laughed, too. "On which side of me will you pin the target?"

The sheriff leaned back in his chair, exhaling cigar smoke. "Hunert a month."

"That is very much money, but—"

"Shut your piehole!" the sheriff called out. Calhoun had begun moaning again. "Sorry, Mr. Baxter. I won't lie to you. We lost a man two nights ago, my fool brother-in-law."

Johnny reached deep inside his layers of clothing for the wanted poster. "This man? Did he kill your deputy?"

The Sheriff studied the poster, nodding. "Yeah, I seen this. The trollop said he wouldn't take that bowler off, even in the act."

"Which way you think he went?"

"Not back north. You know this Osage woman, Suzy Niabi?"

"A long time ago." Johnny sighed. "She was killed near the town of Ralston."

"That's right. Somebody—some whore—said he has a ranch down there. More like a shack, I reckon. You going after him?"

Johnny nodded.

"Well, you can bring Eddie Mole right here, Mr. Baxter. To this jail." Sheriff Turnstall pointed to his cells.

"You'd hang him?"

"I told you, it ain't like the old days. He'll get a trial."

"There's a United States judge in Fort Smith."

"One in Wichita, too." The sheriff shrugged. "Assuming Mole's holed up for the winter around Ralston somewheres, and lessen I got my geography wrong, Fort Smith would add a hunert miles to your travels, and through some pretty ornery country. We'd love to process Mr. Mole right here, John Baxter. We'll get your money for you.

"Tell you something else: Council put up five hunert dollars their own selves; that would net you two thousand dollars. Lot a money down on the reservation or anywheres else I heard of. Robert Lee wasn't worth a damn, he was runnin' around on Brenda, but he died in the line a duty."

9

Comes with the Snow

As he crossed into the Cherokee Outlet, Johnny saw many tracks, cut up with wagon tires, but shortly the horse prints separated, most heading south down the Chisholm Trail, only a few pointing southeast. Of these, most were unshod Indian ponies. He figured Eddie Mole rode a shod horse, and in several miles two sets of horseshoes remained. By midmorning one of these, carrying a heavy load because the hooves pressed more deeply into soft ground, veered south, following a trail to some forlorn ranch.

The remaining prints had to belong to Eddie Mole, and indeed he seemed headed toward Ralston, as Sheriff Turnstall had suggested. Ralston sat across the river from the Osage Reservation's most southwestern corner, and Osage and whites mingled there.

Long ago, when he was a boy, Johnny visited Suzy Niabi in Ralston.

Mole's trail followed the Chikaskia, a meandering, salt-and-gypsum-filled creek that flowed southeasterly into the Salt Fork. Johnny cut across loops in the Chikaskia along the hunting trails he'd known as a boy. He struck the Salt Fork perhaps ten miles from the Arkansas, where he discovered Mole's inevitable campsite, up a ravine from the water. Mole had built a fire and left behind an empty can of beans, coffee grounds, and smears of tobacco juice. No coals burned from the fire but the ground remained warm. Mole was a day ahead.

Johnny could ride another two hours and make a cold camp; with an early start, he might catch up with Mole late tomorrow. But did he want to confront the man? Let him reach his destination and settle in. Edge up slowly and plan how the man could be captured. Then telegraph Ulysses.

Meanwhile, both he and Soquili needed rest, and maybe he could flush something to eat, a rabbit or chicken, that would go well with pinto beans.

The drought had rendered the Salt Fork into a muddy stream that seeped along in a series of shallow, frozen-over ponds. Johnny stepped out onto one and the ice broke in the middle, while shadows flickered beneath. He had no fishing gear but looped his rope around an ice-encased sycamore branch, tied it to the saddlehorn, and urged Soquili to pull. She slipped, caught her footing, then turned over a sheet of ice perhaps ten feet across. "Good girl!" he shouted, as three great catfish flopped onto the sandbar.

Johnny beat their flat heads with a rock, but still, they lay gasping. It was difficult to know when a catfish died.

He repeated the process until he had six big catfish, one the size of a small dog. For the last two, he waded the frigid water to herd the sluggish fish into even shallower places, and heave them onto the sandbar with his hands. He enjoyed this sort of fishing, which he thought he might have invented.

Working with ice, and with the cold, cold fish, chilled him more that he should have allowed, with no fire made and darkness near. His feet grew wet, his fingers stiffened—a reckless thing in winter. He'd behaved like a silly boy, heedless of the rising wind, the falling temperature.

Clouds fell to the earth and the blizzard began.

But this land was not the flat prairie, where sometimes you could get lost even under blue skies. Though intent on his catfish game, part of him had remained conscious of the bluffs back from the northern shore, two hundred feet behind him. He turned into the snow and led Soquili to an overhang of wafered limestone, out of the direct wind, and tied her to a stunted cedar. Others had camped here and he salvaged bits of dry wood from old fires. He kindled a flame with sulfur matches and brittle cedar twigs. He flung off Soquili's saddle and tore again into the whiteness, following his own footprints so as not to become lost. He captured branches and small logs from drifts along the Salt Fork, every stick he could find. He trimmed the straightest poles with his hand axe, leaned them against the cliff, and thatched them with cedar branches to repel the snow. He heard his frantic heart, thumping inside his frozen body.

Given more time, he could have constructed a better shelter, but he couldn't see, and finding the overhang, building a shelter in minutes, constituted a miracle. He murmured his gratitude to the white god and Wah-Kon-Da, though he held no certain belief in either. Wah-Kon-Da was in all things, even the blinding snow, but you couldn't speak to him. He, in fact, was more akin to an "it." Only the whites made a "him" out of Wah-Kon-Da. Thank you, every god, everywhere. I behaved stupidly and do not deserve grace.

He had a destiny. He would not die by this dried-up river.

Johnny built the fire high and smoke drew up a cleft in the rock, a sort of chimney. He took off his boots and wet socks and held his feet to the flames. After a while, when his fingers began to work again, he beheaded and gutted the largest catfish, speared it with a sharp stick, and leaned it into the fire. He placed his coffee pot on live coals, settled back, and lit his pipe. The Virginia tobacco was strong and he wished he could add sumac leaves, but still, with his coffee, his warming feet, he felt a moment's contentment. He missed summer. He missed his true love, Kate.

No sumac leaves, but in the process of cleaning out his saddle bags a cotton tobacco sack fell free. He recalled its origin: his impish brother, Billy, handed him the sack in March, when Johnny swung up on Soquili for the long ride to Jericho Springs.

In the dim light, he shook out half a dozen greenish peyote buttons, dried and shrunken since last spring.

Johnny had never smoked, never chewed peyote. Peyote visions were for religious purposes, though that wasn't what Billy's white friends in Bartlesville wanted it for. Johnny laid out the buttons on his blankets, not knowing what to do with them. He stared through his fire into the swirling wall of snow that when the wind shifted north, sifted through his brush arbor. The storm had intensified. It might not blow itself out for another day. Johnny bit off a small piece of a button: it tasted so bitter his jaw clenched. He nearly threw the sack onto his fire.

Instead, he placed the sack on a flat rock and hammered at it with the butt of his knife until the cloth tore. When he pulled away the ruined sack, he had flakes and shreds and some coarse powder. He pinched several portions of powder into his tin cup, poured coffee over it, and drank the potion down, grimacing as he used to from Buffalo Dancer's medicines.

He felt nothing. Bobbing about on Soquili's flanks through sun and wind and rain, the buttons had lost their potency.

He drew on dry socks, spread out his bed roll, and crawled under a blanket next to Soquili. Her lips moved as she snored, and he wondered what she dreamed of. He listened to her deep, peaceful breaths and slept for a time himself. He sat up, warm on one side, cold as the rock on the other, and tidied his fire, pulling to the center logs that had burned in half. He needed more wood.

The snow had drifted a foot deep in places but his path down to the river remained clear; in twenty feet he lost sight of his shelter, but at that point he made out the river. The snow whisked about his ears. Johnny didn't know what time it was, he'd never carried a watch, but high above, out of the east, a diffuse, quaking, almost ethereal light sent rays into the snow, and he concluded that this must be morning. How could he have slept so long?

He raised a pile of branches at the river's edge, using it as a marker as he ranged upstream. The wind blew and the snow stung his face, but he laughed at the adversity. He was surprised, under all his layers of clothing, that he sweated.

Returning to his pile of wood, he saw a man standing and looking at him from a long sweep of gravel down the stream. No, a woman, and she turned and ran as if afraid of him. "Sister!" he called, but the woman plunged through the snow and leaped onto an ice floe that . . . something was wrong here. The little river stretched out endlessly, while the ethereal light pierced the snow, enfolding the woman as she leaped from iceberg to iceberg, trying to reach . . . Ohio?

There were no ice floes. The Salt Fork became a series of shallow pools again, covered with snow, and he realized he'd imagined the woman, Eliza, a character in a novel Kate gave him. A trick of the faint light, and he thought, *foolish John Baxter*.

He dragged his driftwood up the path and erected a new pile before his shelter. He went to work with his hand axe and then ducked inside with an armload of fuel. Soquili sat on her haunches, quite unusual for a horse, and stared with her intelligent blue eyes. It seemed she was about to speak. "What! Horse!" Johnny said.

He found that he could stand his full height. His shelter was much larger than he'd realized, a sort of cavern that dove into the bluff in a dozen dark pockets and cul-de-sacs. He pulled a small log from the fire and held it out for a torch. Light jumped ahead of him down the cavern walls, round a corner, to a wide place where the sun shone down on six inches of pristine snow.

He turned about: he'd left the rock face. He turned again and spied a house on a hill. As he watched, houses appeared along a street that ran down to a dock beside the great river. Not the Salt Fork. The Arkansas.

He'd been here before.

He turned again: nothing but snow behind him. How would he find his way back?

The house on the hill was the only one to show smoke. Though it stood half a mile from the river, Johnny reached it in a few steps. A lone figure paced before it, stabbing at a doe that had been hung from a crooked sycamore limb. The woman turned, holding high her bloody knife, but Johnny saw only her large green eyes.

The woman motioned to the deer. "The man you seek killed it."

"Sister! How do you know this?"

She stabbed savagely at the doe. Entrails spilled, splashing against her high boots, slinking across the bloody snow. Her green eyes almost closed in the cold wind and her long hair blew stiffly backward, as if frozen. She held out the knife, hilt first, while motioning toward the house made of rough oak sheeting. "I will prepare a meal."

The knife was alarmingly sharp. The doe had stiffened but was pliable enough to be skinned, which meant that Eddie Mole—or someone—must have killed it almost at dawn. If so, was he in the cabin even now?

Where were the half-wild dogs? They should be screaming for their portions, and fighting over guts, but no dogs prowled this village.

It was not a village but the memory of one. Ralston.

He sat within. She sliced the carcass into smaller and smaller offerings, placing them on plates. The meat kept bleeding.

"He brought you this meat," Johnny said. "A gift."

"A payment," the woman said. It was warm inside the house, smoky, stifling, and he had difficulty seeing. He smelled something disagreeable, something rotting, but couldn't place the source. Wraith-like, the woman appeared out of the dimness to offer him a hot porridge of honey and hickory nuts. The porridge filled him with magnificent energy.

"You gave him this," Johnny said.

The woman knelt in one corner before a shrine to Jesus, singing tenderly, mournfully as an ethereal light shone down. Her face was so pure Johnny began to cry. He thought of brown Madonnas in little Catholic churches from Wichita to Hominy. "They said I was a devil. They said I stole their men."

Johnny squinted and pulled his head erect. "How are you called, Sister?"

"It snowed the day I was born," she whispered. "I am Comes with the Snow."

The woman's angelic face broke apart like smoke and floated away, her long body trailing behind. She sat at her school desk, a thin, frightened girl. Her nose and mouth were sharp, delicate.

"I knew you at the school."

"Much later, John Baxter." The little girl looked up at him, her eyes full of love. She said, "The whites called me, 'Suzy Niabi.'"

The whites thought everything about you was wrong. They issued names like writing tablets and white chalk. Names without the spirit of Wa-Kon-Da, without meaning.

"We didn't know where we were, John Baxter. We didn't understand the stairs and crawled up them, and slid down on our bottoms."

He himself had seen the bewildered girls, who never spoke, even when the gray school mistress shook them and screamed into their vacated faces.

They stood on the hillside, looked down over the village of Ralston, and eastward over the winding river. Johnny wanted to right her wrongs. "Have so many died here?"

Only one from a knife.

Suzy Niabi wore a deerskin skirt with red stitching, and a cotton shirt from the trading post embroidered with red horses. As she turned on the barstool, drink in hand, her long hair fell forward and her pretty ankles gleamed. Clumsy, oafish men stumbled across the dance floor, growling and snorting, wanting Suzy Niabi. Eddie Mole caught up her hand and the two staggered up the hill toward the house with its rough oak siding.

"Where is he, Comes with the Snow?" Johnny screamed, as the walls of the cabin disintegrated and darkness stretched in all directions.

"You will find him."

The monster, kneeling between her naked legs, brought the knife down into her belly again and again.

"Oh! I will—"

"You have a part to play, John Baxter," said Comes with the Snow. "But you will not kill him."

GRANDFATHER SUN LIGHTED ALL the world, shining from the unfathomable blue, feathered to the east with a velvety cobalt. Hours had passed, perhaps a day and more, but Johnny could not recall saddling Soquili again or finding his way down to the Arkansas. He climbed the hills to the west in a cold trance, following an instinctive trail, perhaps guided still by Comes with the Snow. He stopped to harvest sumac leaves for his pipe and as a small gift for Buffalo Dancer, then climbed through a grove of walnut trees where the snow lay thin. He could have shot a dozen squirrels, bounding over the leaves after nuts.

He crossed a sort of plateau, picking his way around weathered limestone formations, until, on the southern edge, low cliffs pushed out in a ragged line. Grassland stretched below the bluffs as far as he could see, some of it green, still, with patches of snow under rises and along dry creeks.

Johnny preferred the high ground, the woods. He crossed a draw with standing water and followed it upwards to a spring. By the pool stretched an outcropping of grass that would have been lush in the summer, and even now showed green at its roots. A man could make a home here if he wished to hide from life. A lonely man, a man without a wife, without even a tribe, might come to this place to make his peace with Wah-Kon-Da.

He gave Soquili a handful of oats and then tied her to a post oak in the little pasture. He strode up to the plateau again and walked over ground strewn with boulders, where little grew but red cedars and prickly pear. He dropped to another outcropping of ragged cedars, densely-packed, where he suspected deer slept. The trees fell away and he crawled forward until he reached the cliffs again. A hundred yards eastward, his eye followed a creek idling through the tall grass—the creek from the spring where he'd staked Soquili.

On the northern side of the creek, by the low cliffs, lay forty acres ideal for cattle or sheep; it wouldn't even be necessary to fence it. Perhaps five acres of cultivated land, a fallow cornfield, lay to the south, streaked with snow, but bare ground showed through. The soil was black, not red—land rich enough for a Mennonite. This easternmost piece of the Cherokee Outlet looked to be its most fertile and it had water!

Here was the place to make your claim and someone had. Where any sensible homesteader would have placed a cabin, Johnny saw one.

He drew out his binoculars. The cabin door jerked open and Eddie Mole sauntered into view, wearing only the top of his longjohns and his bowler hat. He threw a bottle and it crashed against a rock. Cradling his genitals in one hand, he waddled toward an unsullied snow drift to urinate, and turned his broad chest toward Johnny.

The distance stretched six hundred yards. He'd need to compensate both for higher elevation and the Winchester's drop. He couldn't miss and hope for a second chance against a man like Mole.

The deed *might* be done. Not from the cliff, but at dawn he'd steal down to the creek and wait behind that split cottonwood. Two hundred yards.

Or he could relieve Emmet Baxter of the Sharps .45-.90 the man had kept from his buffalo hunting days, and still used for deer hunting. With such a weapon, with enough impact to smash through a buffalo skull even at a thousand yards, he could make the shot from the cliff. But to secure the Sharps, and return, would take at least four days. And—

You are not a killer, John Baxter.

He retreated to the spring, built a fire, made biscuits, and cooked a catfish. He smoked his pipe, mixing sumac leaves with tobacco. His stomach felt uneasy, perhaps still an effect of the peyote, but he slept curled up near the coals until he heard crows gathered above. He opened his eyes and Grandfather Sun had set another day on fire.

He returned to the cliff with no sure plan, but he believed that he'd slept late for a purpose. Oversleeping, he could not hide by the split cottonwood and wait for Eddie Mole to stagger into his rifle sights. Wah-Kon-Dah did not speak in words but perhaps, nonetheless, he had spoken.

In an hour, no more than two, blue-black men astride brown horses rode out of the west—fourteen buffalo soldiers. Oh, what a delight to see the blue-black men confront Eddie Mole, who shook his head, disbelieving his shift in fortune! Perhaps matters seemed worse for him because his eviction came at the hands of black men who once were slaves. Mole brandished a rifle—which he quickly lowered when fourteen revolvers and carbines issued from holsters and scabbards and pointed toward him. Mole fell to his knees in the snow and clasped his hands. Through the binoculars, Johnny read his lips, "I got rights!"

Mole must have thought they meant to hang him, because one black man walked out with a rope. Mole rose, his face calm. The soldier walked past him, tied the rope to a post, and nodded to a man with bold yellow stripes on his coat. That man urged his horse backward and the rope stretched tight, but the post was too strong.

The black man with the yellow stripes shrugged and motioned toward the troop's supply wagon. The man on the ground retrieved a red can and poured from it along the south wall of the little house. Mole motioned violently and ran inside, returning quickly with two canteens, a parfleche with food, and a bulky gunnysack that could have held anything. In moments the house was on fire, but Mole didn't even look backward, instead walking directly toward Johnny, spreadeagled in the snow atop the short cliff. Mole disappeared below, where Johnny heard the outlaw's restive horse and Mole's gravelly voice: "Eat it. It's all you're gonna get." Mole coughed. Tobacco smoke drifted up. Then the bad man was silent and Johnny didn't stir, until the house had turned to charred wood and the soldiers rode off east.

The soldiers didn't know Mole was a wanted man. They didn't care. Their mission was to oust squatters from the Outlet before the great land run, nothing more.

Mole emerged on a mud-colored mustang, heading southwest toward the land of outlaws and maybe the Canadian River. Johnny took aim on his back. He shivered from lying so long in the snow. His fingers had numbed but still he couldn't miss.

You are not a killer, John Baxter.

"Comes with the Snow," he whispered. "I feel no more for this man than I would for a rat in Helmut Kreider's barn. My motive is the money the whites will give me. Money for a wife! Why should I not kill him, as I would smash a scorpion?"

Comes with the Snow didn't answer. Wah-Kon-Dah spoke only with a gust of wind that howled along the cliff, and yet Johnny knew the truth: killing Eddie Mole was not his destiny. His destiny lay before him, rolling out toward Grandfather Sun, rising splendid and orange from the east. Mole's stolen land: the beautiful, black dirt, the spring-fed creek, the long, natural corral. Free for the taking.

10

Buffalo Dancer

I n Pawhuska a plunking, tinny piano rose with boys' voices
for "Sur le pont d'Avignon," which was at once charming
and unreal. Indian children, singing in French! Of course,
in the time of Johnny's grandfather, Auguste Choteau had come
among the Osage to trade for furs. Many Frenchmen took Osage
women for wives—Johnny himself was one-eighth French.

The French were long gone, defeated in faraway wars, replaced
by the Americans who slaughtered the buffalo, starved the Indians, and took dominion. The catchy little tune was American
as much as French; even the Mennonite children, one generation removed from speaking German, sang it.

L'on y danse, l'on y danse.

A woman in gray stood at the door, clanging a small brass bell
which Johnny remembered from his childhood. Several boys
pushed and shoved into the schoolyard for recess. One tried to
climb a tree but this was mere bravado in the bitter air, under
a sky that spat snow. The boys hurried inside again except for
the tree climber, who stood at the wire fence, staring at snow-
covered Johnny. Johnny waved, but the boy turned away without expression and the schoolyard was again deserted.

Still a prison.

His eyes fell on a cedar log building that had fallen into dis-
repair. He remembered stealing out from the second floor—he

spied the very window—onto an elm and slithering down the trunk. The cedar building was the bakery then. He and George Snapping Turtle found corn muffins, honey, and cinnamon rolls. Every boy loved the cinnamon rolls, as sweet as they were alien, and they tasted all the better when the old watchman shuffled by, the light from his lantern throwing grotesque shadows on the walls.

Johnny had never been in the army, but he'd listened to the crippled veterans on the boardwalks of Jericho Springs, talking of privation and carnage. Every death was halfway an accident. Any day could turn cruel. You lost weight from the physical strain and the bad rations; you lost fingers from the rough work and firearms. But never again would anything you did have such consequence. Never again would you make such friends, with whom you shared things you could never tell, such as that time you gunned down your evil lieutenant. The army was pure misery but you loved it, too, because once in a while you happened upon cinnamon rolls.

Boarding school was Johnny's hitch in the army. The whites belittled his culture, suppressed his religion, tried to replace his language, but also they taught him English, mathematics, and literature.

He'd clung to that fence like the boy did, on a bright spring day when it was almost time to go home for the summer. From two hundred feet away he saw the green-eyed maiden, Suzy Niabi, so forbidding, so cold she seemed to belong to another species than the drab girls surrounding her. Was it only her beauty? No, she was restless as a panther, and she had plans.

He was nine, she twenty-five or more, but her eyes fastened on him, too, as if they, only they, knew a secret that would set them free. A magical valley, a kingdom of peace. It was as if she were enslaved and he the only man with the power to free her— that is, if he were a man. They'd go about robbing white men's banks and burning the churches of their righteous women.

She was from Hominy and belonged to his band. Possibly,

she was his cousin, but she had no family to return to and anyhow she'd grown too used to the white man's ways. She'd worked
at a big hotel in Fort Smith, Arkansas. People seemed suspicious of this. Maybe her work at the hotel had little to do with
housekeeping.

But the Quaker agent appreciated her talents and hired her
to coach the frightened little girls in reading and even in deport-
ment. Otherwise, the girls learned cooking and sewing; the
Quakers thought, as women, the girls would serve as domestics.

Maybe Johnny's puppy love bemused Suzy Niabi but she was
never cruel. She was somewhere between a mother and a lover.
As the sister he didn't have, she asked how he felt today, and
reached through the fence to touch his brow. When she took
his hand, he trembled, because every princess was part witch.
Indeed, when she withdrew her hand, he held a silver dollar.

"I love you," he said.

"I know," she said. "I love *you*, Little Man."

"Run away with me."

Like a drink of cold spring water, her laugh, her smile invigorated him. "Where would we go?"

John Baxter hadn't thought so far. "Somewhere . . . there's
good water. Where the fishing is good."

"What about cinnamon rolls? Will we find cinnamon rolls
there?"

Johnny hung his head. But Suzy Niabi took his hand again
and whispered, "I know it's hard here, and lonely. But the Quakers won't beat you and there's food enough. Learn all you can,
John Baxter. Someday, you will rise, and I'll help you."

He stared up miserably. "Are you leaving?"

She shrugged. This time, Suzy Niabi left a Barlow knife in his
hand. It was a gift for a boy, a cheap knife that wouldn't hold
an edge, but he kept it many years.

Three summers later, Johnny dreamed of Suzy Niabi. She was
dressed all in deerskin like a maiden of old, moccasined feet dan-
gling off a rock that overlooked a clear, deep spring. Then she

stood with him—not the little boy, but an older man—above
a vast, grassy plain.

It was a vision, a sign from Wah-Kon-Da. One morning before
dawn, he drew a gentle mare—Soquili's grandmother—from
Buffalo Dancer's corral and rode her bareback to Hominy. He
visited the general store, the feed dealer's, the lodges of his uncles,
and all were happy to see him. They offered venison jerky or
porridge or hard candy but no one had much to report con-
cerning Suzy Niabi. "So beautiful," an aunt said.

A toothless old woman in the wheelwright's shop said Suzy
Niabi had gone to Fort Smith to work in a hotel, but Johnny
knew this much already.

The wheelwright, a white man, called out from his shop,
"What you want with her?"

"She is my sister. I have a message from home."

The white man offered a thin smile. "She's got a house in
Ralston, son. Up on the hill."

By the time Johnny reached Ralston, the sun had tumbled
halfway down the western sky. Nor had he reckoned on crossing the Arkansas River. But even amid the cattails on the eastern shore, he could see the house—a gray, clapboard cabin, the
only house on the only hill. He led the mare through a stand
of cane, through willows and cottonwoods, detouring pools
of water filled with turtles and minnows, until he reached the
river itself. Little rain had fallen and the river was low but still
he was afraid to swim his grandfather's horse, and he hid her
in a glade where she had water and grass. Then he stuffed his
moccasins under his rope belt and swam the river.

He was a good swimmer, the current wasn't strong, and in
not too long he reached the other shore, perhaps three hundred
feet downstream from Ralston. He crept along a grassy alley
lined with outhouses, horse barns, and vegetable patches, and
had only glimpses of the horses and wagons on Main Street.
He heard snatches of conversation, a hammer striking an anvil.

He followed a grassy path up the hill and knocked on Suzy

Niabi's door. He was a man calling on a woman. But when she opened her door, he was unprepared for how old she was and couldn't find his voice.

She clutched a green robe to her neck with one hand, toweled her hair with the other: he'd surprised her in her bath. Her eyes seized him with anger but her anger melted into puzzlement, then the warmth of recognition. "John Baxter," she said. "So tall!"

Indeed, almost as tall as she. And he was man enough to imagine her without her thin robe, but he felt he should not have such thoughts and looked away.

"Come closer," she said, her green eyes full of kindness. "Am I so mysterious?"

"I dreamed of you."

"A nightmare!"

"You showed me the future."

She nodded. She glanced toward the door as she dried his hair. "You swam the river, John Baxter? To see *me?*" She brought her towel to his wet hair and rubbed vigorously. "Sweet boy!"

Johnny didn't like being called a boy. Something seemed to collapse in her green eyes, to pull him in but then halt him, and he despaired. He understood he couldn't know her truly, that he'd never come to the end of her. She *was* mysterious; she partook of magic. He kissed her and she pushed him away. He sat on her soft chair, bewildered.

She floated away and returned with a warm porridge of hickory nuts and honey. "I must change," she said, closing her bedroom door.

The porridge assuaged the weariness from his long ride and swimming the river, and when Suzy Niabi returned, wearing a long red dress and beaded, ankle-high moccasins, he said, "We belong together."

She nodded. "We *are* together, John Baxter."

She sat at her bureau, combing her hair black as a crow's feathers, and he stepped behind her and kissed her bare shoulder.

She turned, her eyes patient—and sad. She pulled him into the space between her bare knees, bent his head to her breasts, and kissed his cheek. "I am not your sister; I am not your mother. I am the one you leave behind."

"We are—"

"We are unique, John Baxter." She smiled. "We are impossible."

"I will be a man!"

"A man is like a tree. It takes many years to grow a strong one, with deep roots, who can survive wind and drought. Perhaps I will find you then, John Baxter." She pushed him away, laughing. "If only in a dream."

When next she spoke to him, almost twenty years later, her name had changed to Comes with the Snow, and she was dead.

HE RODE TO George Snapping Turtle's house but his old friend had gone hunting. His new wife stood in the doorway, ignoring Johnny's shivering, the ice in his hair, as behind her a teapot simmered. She would not give him food. He could not even warm his hands, but he understood. She was young and pretty, and he frightened her with his trail-worn appearance. Perhaps he frightened her more when he asked, "Do you remember Suzy Niabi? From Hominy?"

Irritation lit the young woman's eyes, as if to say, you come to my door, you whom I do not know, and speak of a prostitute?

Maybe that's not what her eyes said. Maybe they said, *She was not so beautiful as me. Not so beautiful as I was before I married.*

The young woman had wiry hair like Kate's and he felt a pang of loneliness. He turned away.

"Wait." She stepped out of sight and returned with two biscuits.

"Thank you, Sister."

She lowered her eyes. "Suzy was an evil one. She did not know Jesus."

He recalled Comes with the Snow's shrine. "I believe she did."

"She went with white men and robbed them. Sometimes, they were found dead."

"A white man killed her."

A baby cried and George Snapping Turtle's young wife sighed. "We should think of happier things."

She closed the door and Johnny felt lonelier still. Nothing remained for him in this town. Every time when he returned he hoped things would be different but he was always a visitor. He had more friends in Mennonite country.

He crawled into an abandoned lodge east of town and built a fire in the crumbling rock chimney. He found hay for Soquili and pulled her inside, too, and rocked back and forth on his frozen feet as the fire drew strength. He sang for Comes with the Snow and for Kate whom he loved, though she had gone away to the white man's big city and perhaps his love was unrequited. Maybe only his horse loved him.

L'on y danse, l'on y danse.

THEY SAT ON BUFFALO DANCER's little porch, a long lean-to he'd added onto the south side of his lodge. Johnny shook out sumac leaves, crumbled them into the powerful Virginia tobacco, and each man filled his pipe. Smoke hung in the still air and the westering sun split the afternoon.

Stallions screamed in their separate pasture, fenced out from the barn, through Buffalo Dancer's woods and down to the Arkansas. They were pliant, their rutting time dormant, but you could never quite trust them short of turning them into geldings.

Buffalo Dancer maintained no certain breeds, no papers, though he knew every horse's lineage for several generations. He matched fine stallions with likely mares, and sold sturdy, healthy foals. All of his horses were sought after, if not on the reservation then with dealers in Arkansas City or with the Cherokees. And enough of the white man's ways had rubbed off that he kept his profits in a bank, so as not to tempt whites bold enough to invade the reservation. Or degraded Indians who drank up their annuities and showed no respect even for an elder.

There was a famous incident, in fact, when Johnny's several uncles, old men themselves now, trailed a horse thief off the reservation and hanged him. Afterwards, the whites puffed and threatened, but no Osage talked.

"I need horses, Grandfather."

The old man pushed up his shapeless hat and nodded. "A good horse is your friend."

"I have saved two hundred dollars."

"This tribe that will not fight should pay you more."

"Yes, they should. But they have taught me much."

"To farm?"

Like many Osage—like Johnny's uncles—Buffalo Dancer was ambivalent about farming, though he raised oats and put up hay for his horses. Johnny tapped out his pipe and pushed more tobacco into the hot bowl. This old man had partly raised him. Why was he so nervous? "Grandfather, I find satisfaction in growing things, as you do in breeding horses. The Mennonites have taught me how to farm, yes. And also, maybe, how to succeed in the new world."

"If success in this new world requires horses, is it new?"

Johnny laughed.

For a long moment, Buffalo Dancer squinted into the sun, causing Johnny to wonder if his grandfather were going blind, but then his eyes met Johnny's. They were clear, brown eyes that shone brightly out of his leathery face, as ancient and warty as the Osage Hills. "I will give you horses because you sit without making noise, and smoke good tobacco with an old man. I would give you horses even if you ate my food and slept all day, because you are my favorite grandson. Like many of the young ones, you have not found your way. Yet you do not drink the white man's whiskey or seek out bad women in Ralston. If you need something I can give, I will give it. However, I must sleep now. While I sleep, you can shuck my corn."

Buttoning his coat and pulling down Euly's Russian hat, Johnny walked to the corn patch, shooed the crows away, and peeled back the canvas on his grandfather's wagon. He drew on gloves and began throwing up the corn he shucked. The task should have been finished six weeks before, because some of the stalks had frozen to the ground and mice had founded little cities around the ears.

After a while, Johnny built a fire from the dead stalks and warmed his hands. He returned to his saddle bags for a coffee pot and lit his pipe while the coffee came to a boil. The patch was about three acres and would take him most of the week. Johnny didn't mind. The work was important but you couldn't do it wrong. Thus your mind sailed over a thousand landscapes as you considered the nature of revenge and love and how spirits sometimes pointed the way.

In the evenings, sitting by the wood stove in the dim lodge, Johnny told Buffalo Dancer the story of his tentative young friend, Euly Kreider. He described Eddie Mole, who shot Barney Kreider dead in Jericho Springs. He told his grandfather of Comes with the Snow, how he'd tracked the murderer into the Outlet and held him in an uncertain aim.

"The world is full of these white devils."

"Some whites are good. The Quaker agent."

"He is a stiff man who speaks truly. Your spirit woman also speaks truly. Let the white man kill the white man."

"The outlaw is worth two thousand dollars, Grandfather." Johnny sighed. "I lusted for it."

"Have you become a white man, then?"

"White men run their world with money. They respect the man who has it."

"Until they steal it. There are Osage valleys, plenty of flat land, where you can plant your corn."

"The good ground is taken, Grandfather. And every drop of water."

"You have become ambitious. Have you found a woman?" The old man laughed. "My bashful grandson! Is she with child?"

"No!"

"I hope she is not white. White women never stop talking."

"She is mixed blood, very tall. Osage, I believe, though she was taken as an infant and no one knows."

"Strong?"

"Very strong. She rides a bold stallion."

"This is good," Buffalo Dancer said. "You need money for a farm and horses for a wife?"

Johnny bent his head. "Yes, Grandfather."

Buffalo Dancer squinted at the sun again. "Worthy. Worthy, Grandson, but I must sleep. I will pray on this matter while you clean out the barn."

So Johnny crept around the stallions and cleaned the barn. In cold weather, when no insects tormented him, it was not such a bad job. He enjoyed its simplicity, even its humility. He'd dump a wheelbarrow load of steaming manure in the cornfield, look up at the cold sky, and think of his long journey from the school to Mennonite country to Buffalo Dancer's fallow fields. What did Helmut Kreider say? Life is work, every sunlit, precious moment.

He stepped into the dark lodge, and encountered waves of heat and smoke with the camphoraceous smell of cedar. Buffalo Dancer chanted but Johnny couldn't see him, and he almost expected fearsome green eyes to bear down and seize his soul.

He began splitting the gnarled logs behind the lodge. His uncles had dragged up driftwood from the Arkansas, everything from near-worthless cottonwoods to red oak, which burned hot all night long. Buffalo Dancer had cut the logs into stove lengths but the knot-filled Osage Orange chunks required wedges and a maul, not to mention a specialist in humble work.

As he fought the last log into submission, Buffalo Dancer called for him. "I have the answer."

"Thank you, Grandfather." Johnny leaned on his maul, and wiped his sweat with a rag. "What is the answer?"

"Long ago, in a time of drought, the buffalo had gone away to their secret country. The hungry people sent a messenger, a beautiful young maiden, to Elk Head, your great-grandfather. The girl said, 'Our people are dying; they have no squash or beans or corn. They can find no animals to kill.' So Elk Head prayed. He prayed for a week. He held the rite of vigil—and by and by, he was able to enter the land of buffalo spirits. 'My people and yours have lived together many years,' he told the buffalo chief. 'But now you have gone away, and my people are starving.' The buffalo chief nodded his great head. 'It is true what you say. Our tribes have lived together for many years. I say to you, I will send a few of us to a special place for you to kill. This is so your babies will not starve.'"

"What does this mean, Grandfather?"

Buffalo Dancer squinted. "It means I must talk on the singing wires."

Pawhuska, Johnny thought. You rode to Hominy for supplies and to visit friends. Pawhuska was tribal headquarters, where you conducted business—faraway business, if it required a telegraph.

"What shall we do after that, Grandfather?"

"Hunt the buffalo."

Johnny nodded, trying not to seem skeptical. His uncles— and that great buffalo slayer, Emmet Baxter—claimed that the old man had a spiritual connection to buffalo.

When he was ten years old, the nameless boy wandered from the camp where women cured hides and dried meat. He found himself being chased by a massive old bull, bellowing its rage. Men understood the peril, but the bull was too far away for their lances or arrows. Then a strange thing happened. When the bull charged so near that the boy could feel its harsh breath, he danced to the right. The buffalo turned, and turned again, as the boy led him in circles. The old fellow had one eye and couldn't see Buffalo Dancer unless he kept turning. The men rushed forward and shot arrows into the bull's neck and lungs.

Johnny didn't voice the obvious: "There are no buffalo." He didn't want to imply that Buffalo Dancer was crazy or senile, because the old man was as wily in his tribe as Helmut Kreider was in his. Johnny had to wait for Buffalo Dancer to reveal his magic. He had to have faith. He said, "Do you have more tasks for me, Grandfather?"

"No. It would be a good time to visit your mother."

11

Down by the Riverside

When she opened the door Mira had no greeting, but wrinkled her nose in an exaggerated fashion and turned away. She poured hot water from the cook stove's reservoir into a galvanized tub and thrust out her hands impatiently. Johnny laughed but his mother didn't, so he pulled the tub a little into the bedroom for privacy's sake and began throwing out his clothes. He wondered if she'd have cared if he stripped before her. He towered over her, but to her mind, he was still her little boy.

He sank into the hot water, folding up his long legs, feeling foolish, then warm. He hadn't felt warm for a week.

"You come home so late. And so filthy."

"Forgive me, Mother. My friend—"

"The white boy?"

"Yes. He entered a time of troubles—"

She raised a hand to silence him and disappeared with his soiled clothing. As the water cooled, she returned with a fine deerskin shirt, a gray Stetson such as his stepfather wore, and moccasin boots. With these she placed heavy denim jeans and a wide belt with a brass cavalry buckle, featuring crossed sabers and a superimposed 7. Hard to say where that came from. Some dead trooper, perhaps, from Kansas days. But it was his belt, not his brother's: Mira made it for him.

She sat by the window, lifted the sash, and lit her clay pipe.

Now and then she parted the curtain, as if Emmet would return. He didn't approve of smoking. "We are having a feast today," she said. "For our prodigal son."

Today was Sunday, so something was going on at the church. But the Baptists were always breaking bread, and Johnny, arriving without notice, couldn't be the reason.

"I am no prodigal, Mother. I have not wallowed with pigs nor envied their food. And I have no inheritance to squander." He did not mean to sound reproachful. The farm would go to Billy, who had worked it along with his natural father, Emmet Baxter. The farm was profitable, Emmet ran it well, but Johnny had never wanted it. He could tolerate Emmet, and the Baptist bulwark of Emmet and Mira, only in small doses.

Mira handed him a soft cotton blanket to dry himself. As he dressed, she knelt to mop up the water under his feet. "No, you are not a prodigal. But you work in a faraway place, live with white people, and you have no wife. A man without a wife, without children, is a dangerous thing in the human world. Without a wife, you are lost, my son."

He pulled on the deerskin shirt. "I believe I have found someone, Mother. Where is my brother, Billy? Where is Emmet?"

Mira offered a ritual frown. "You must call him Mr. Baxter, or Reverend Baxter. Is your woman Osage?"

"Mixed blood."

Mira's frown became a smile. "Such good news! We will have the wedding right here. Reverend Baxter—"

"Kate has yet to consent. Where is Reverend Baxter?"

"At the river. Now that you are clean, we shall have our great feast. Why would she not consent?"

"I need to gather up horses, to find land. I need to prove myself worthy."

"Of course, you're worthy. Are you not my son?"

He helped her pack Emmet's Studebaker wagon with sweet potato pie, hominy salad, bread, apple butter from Mira's trees, and a pot of strip meat—venison—soup, with peas and wild onions, that he remembered her making when he was little. Mira had learned to cook white people's food and her English was good. She wore a long dress like Annelise, high black shoes, and a sober black hat with a half-veil. She was tall, slender, striking. She was one-quarter French. But she would never be white, which mattered not at all to Reverend Baxter, her hard-working, loyal, grateful husband.

That she wasn't white mattered to the whites in Bartlesville, and to Mira. The Quakers, and the Jesuits before them, came among the Osage with compassion and honesty, but you couldn't enter their wider world without encountering heavy condescension. Emmet and Mira could eat at either of Bartlesville's restaurants but were always ushered to a back room by the stores of canned vegetables. In the mercantile Mira was attended to last, spoken to in pidgin English, and charged more. She could not even sit on the cold wagon while Emmet conducted his business, because then a gang of teenage boys materialized, making their pig noises mixed with "Squaw. Squaw." In the end, Emmet couldn't drag Mira east—she'd accompany him only to Pawhuska.

Even as a child, Johnny knew the marriage was troubled. Mira accused Emmet of wanting her for access to Osage land. This was true, Emmet could never convincingly deny it, and by and by Mira deluded herself that her husband meant to poison her so he could marry a white woman. She took Johnny and the infant Billy to live with her parents, Buffalo Dancer and Turkey Feather.

The reverend wasn't a subtle man. He didn't understand how you could hate your own skin, any more than he might hate his bulbous nose or missing right hand thumb. He built his God-fearing Osage wife a fine house with an indoor pump from the cistern and an upstairs bedroom for the children they both hoped for. Mira would give him two sons to work his farm, and all he required otherwise was that she cook and sew, tend her vegetable garden, and curl next to him in the winter. He wasn't a reverend then, but an aging, illiterate buffalo hunter lucky to find any woman, white or brown, who'd welcome him into her bed.

They worked it out. Johnny, the part-time son who preferred living with his grandparents, and who spent the long winters in boarding school, never understood, except that marriage must be difficult and families were strange.

As Johnny tied the horse to an oak above the picnic site, Mira unwrapped her brilliantly colored sashes: one of chevrons, dyed red, orange, and a faded blue; and one of the traditional lightning-and-arrow design, black and orange. Fringes dripped from both, with white trading-post beads woven in. Johnny pointed to his deerskin shirt, also featuring lightning and arrows, and two trails of white beads, marching around his chest. "Beautiful, Mother."

"It is something to do in the winter. While my eyes can still see."

"Do you sell them?"

"Yes, they sell in Pawhuska." She frowned. "Even better at the store in Bartlesville, to rich people. We women meet once a month, and weave, and gossip, and eat things that make you fat."

"Keeping the old ways."

"Young women come, too." Her eyes lit up. "Beautiful young women, my son, who need husbands should the woman from up north refuse you."

"You train them?"

"Someone must," Mira said, smiling. "They can't blow their own noses."

BELOW THE WOODED HILL, the Reverend Emmet Baxter, in his long coat, Sunday Stetson, and black rubber boots, stepped onto the ice of the Caney River. The Caney was a small stream, diminished by drought, and the congregation did not seem alarmed. At least the adults didn't. The six children clung to their mothers, except for one full-blooded girl, who ran to the shore and stared at the reverend; maybe she was near-sighted. All the children wore summer clothes and shivered accordingly.

"Hallelujah!" Reverend Baxter cried, bringing down his axe. The ice cracked to the other side of the river and sent off a high-pitched moan, as if some big animal had died in the cold and lonely woods. The reverend stepped nearer the shore; two men joined him, and soon they'd chopped away a section of open water.

The reverend lifted high his Bible but did not refer to it, giving a short-but-fiery sermon on sin and redemption that for Johnny struck familiar resonances. He didn't listen attentively, even when Mira plucked at his sleeve and motioned. He smiled and studied the reverend, who, busy as he was, nodded.

He caught sight of his half-brother, Billy, sitting with a pretty girl at the far side of the little park, on a slab of limestone between two great oaks. A white girl, but Billy had attended a one-room school for whites near Bartlesville, and he was a whim of nature, half-Osage but with blond hair and freckles. He waved and Johnny weaved through the congregation, nodding to those he knew, stopping for brief conversations.

An old woman who said she'd known Turkey Feather grabbed his arm, grinned toothlessly, and offered him pemmican flavored with wild plums. Johnny thanked her and chewed thoughtfully as he watched the proceedings. He couldn't remember the old woman's name.

Six mothers pushed their children forward, releasing them near the shore into the care of the gentle reverend, who called each child by name and opened wide his arms. They entered the icy water crying, or crying out, or marching to their doom, as their mothers' faces filled with joy. One by one the children went under and failed to drown. But the water shocked them and afterwards they splashed about like dogs, thrashing their way onto dry land.

Johnny joined the singing:

What can wash away my sin?
Nothing but the blood of Jesus;
What can make me whole again?
Nothing but the blood of Jesus.
Oh! precious is the flow
That makes me white as snow;
No other fount I know,
Nothing but the blood of Jesus.

Laughter rose from the crowd when the reverend came out of the water, threw off his boots and socks, and nearly fell backward into the Caney. Though not much given to smiling, he smiled, and Mira rushed up with clean trousers and a gray wool sweater. The children were handed mugs of hot cider, while their sisters and brothers held up blankets, and their mothers peeled off their wet clothing. The nearsighted Osage girl couldn't stop crying but the others began to calm, and pretty soon all stood by the fire in warm clothes, held hands, and sang:

Jesus loves me! This I know,
For the Bible tells me so;
Little ones to Him belong;
They are weak, but He is strong.
Yes, Jesus loves me!
Yes, Jesus loves me!
Yes, Jesus loves me!
The Bible tells me so.

The congregation had grown and included not only Osage and mixed bloods, but also whites. The deeper Johnny pressed among them the more unfamiliar they seemed. Men stared menacingly—but no, it wasn't menace, not hostility. The men stared competitively, as if he were about to issue a challenge. And not all of them: several donned foolish grins, and a man he didn't recognize called out, "Johnny. Come visit."

Their wives looked at him longingly—or with an affected disdain.

He would ponder this. He was only a farmhand and yet he held bold plans for the future. He had work to do but believed Kate would consent in the end. Maybe this explained his confidence, and his confidence explained the admiring glances.

As he neared Billy, a surprising thing happened. A mixed blood girl, with brown skin but with the blue eyes of a European, crossed his path. She didn't look at him, seemingly intent on a stir in the woods. Johnny turned his head but saw nothing out of the ordinary. The girl stumbled and he reached to help her. He found himself facing her, holding both her arms, while she looked up as if helpless. Johnny released her arms and mumbled an apology, and a woman called out:

"Blossum, you leave that man alone."

Laughter erupted behind his back and Johnny hurried to his brother's side as if to a life raft. Yellow-haired Billy laughed. His girl, awaiting her introduction, looked up with bright, admiring eyes.

Johnny turned. The children, washed clean of their small sins, had lined up to be fed. Their mothers stood proudly behind their dishes. Men stepped into the serving line, Reverend Baxter leading. He slapped backs, shook hands, and told a funny story. As he blessed the food, his eyes filled with tears.

Johnny remembered that about him. Emmet Baxter broke into tears at appropriate but also inappropriate times, and his eyes fled to a painful place. No one ever said anything. People pretended nothing had changed and in moments Emmet recovered.

Even with so much going on, so much fellowship, eyes rolled Johnny's way. The girl named Blossum stared openly at him. So did other young women.

Always, he'd stood near the back and left early, but now a powerful spirit had descended on him, as if Comes with the

Snow were still at his side. He felt as though he were destined for a run of good luck and great deeds, after so many years of stubborn fortune and small deeds. The spirit said, *see how the people respect you? This is your time.*

"That's some shirt Mother made you," Billy said.

JOHN BAXTER WOKE TO a screeching he remembered but couldn't place. He dropped his feet to the floor and plumbed for his bearings. Moonlight through the upstairs window lay in long rectangles on the board floor.

He heard his brother's soft snores. In the golden light, they'd talked until late of a murderer named Eddie Mole, Johnny's adventures in the Outlet, and then Billy's succession of girl-friends. There were saloons and roadhouses in Bartlesville and the girls there liked to dance. Billy took the girlfriends for granted, a source of wonderment for Johnny. Billy seemed prouder of prizes he'd won at a Cherokee rodeo.

"I try not to compete with a horse," Johnny said. "I connect with her spirit, what she is willing to give. Then we are friends."

"Yes!" Billy said. "But Soquili is a gentle mare. What about a horse that's mean? Then it's your will against his and you must tame him."

"Not with an iron bar, I hope."

"With an iron *will*."

They fell asleep with talk of buffalo hunting, something that only old men had done, killing massive, mythic beasts as fero-cious as mountain lions. Every man was diminished without the buffalo. Lions padded over the plains and every year or so a man killed a bear in the Osage Hills, but the buffalo had defined the tribe. "What does our grandfather mean to do?" Billy asked. "Will he conjure buffalo from thin air?"

Perhaps. Johnny stepped softly to the window in his wool socks and long underwear, and looked toward the machine shed. Frost gleamed on machinery. Puffs of moisture rose from the barn. A blurry Emmet Baxter hunched over his workbench, lit brightly by the gas lantern, like some ghoulish creature in an old tale, playing his discordant song as he pushed a file over saw teeth.

Mira's grandfather clock struck five and a three-hour ride awaited him. Johnny pulled on his shirt and trousers and crept downstairs, carrying his boots so not to wake Billy. The house was cold. He shoveled ashes into the coal scuttle, added two small logs and some carpenter's scraps, and squeezed the bellows until flames burst from the coals. He started coffee.

Then he pulled on his boots and buttoned his coat, carried the ashes to the garden, and stopped by the corral gate. He whistled, shivered in the wind from the west, and whistled again. Soquili came up noiselessly, her breath steaming in the moonlight, and nuzzled his shoulder. He pulled at her mane and offered her a cube of sugar from his coat. He scooped up oats and attached her feedbag. Soquili was a gentle mare, as Billy said, and Johnny treated her gently. No trick riding, no bravado, and that women admired such things mystified him.

Kate was not that way.

When he opened the shed door Emmet didn't hear. He rocked forward with his file—and cried. His eyes were puffy and red and he pulled in little sighs and gasps.

Over there in the corner, almost thirty years before, Emmet Baxter beat Johnny for drowning kittens. Johnny found the kittens and held them down in a horse trough, amazed how they writhed under water, until they stopped writhing. By the third kitten, he understood that he was killing them, and exactly then Emmet hovered over him with his belt.

When his stepfather set down the file to adjust the saw, Johnny said softly, "Emmet."

Emmet Baxter turned on his stool. His red eyes filled with terror.

"I'm sorry to disturb you, sir. I need to ask a favor."

"Shore," the reverend got out, his eyes rolling left and right in confusion. Johnny looked away, giving Emmet a moment to find himself. He pointed to a curious set of objects mounted above the workbench: an empty whiskey bottle, a Continental Cubes tobacco tin, and the long Sharps rifle. "I need to borrow your needle gun."

The Reverend's face was weathered, stern, but not as hard as the child in Johnny remembered. The old man said, "It ain't to be used, John."

"Yes, sir."

"I keep that bottle, that tobaccy, that big gun to remind me of the old days."

"Yes, sir."

"Looking north, looking south, you couldn't see the end of 'em. Seemed like it couldn't be. I shot fifty-four one day, three dollars a hide, left the meat for the wolves. All they done with them hides, they made flat belts, run from the flywheel on your steam engine, and they come back later, they taken the bones, they ground 'em up and made dishes. I have dreams about it. Woke me up tonight. Knowed I couldn't sleep so I come out to the shop."

Johnny toed the dust of the shed floor. "I understand."

"I'm sitting up high, kinda floatin' in the air. I shoot, and I load, and I shoot. I got to kill 'em fast because somebody's gonna stop me. Maybe the Lord God. I got to get them all kilt before He tells me I'm crazy."

"Never saw a buffalo," Johnny whispered.

"Then I'd get me a bath and whore it all away. I was an evil man, John."

Johnny wanted to comfort his stepfather but he'd never known how. "Reverend, you have atoned with your good works. And if there is no atoning, what can we do but live?"

"Praise Jesus," the reverend said, his eyes glistening. "Shoot a deer, that gun blows they heads off. What you want it for?"

"Buffalo Dancer says we are hunting buffalo."

Emmet Baxter looked dumbfounded, but turned and brought

down the gun. They went out into the cold morning and Johnny lifted the heavy rifle toward the sky.

"You cain't hit the moon with it," Emmet said. "Only, it'll shoot out a mile for certain. You know how to use that tang sight?"

Johnny flipped it up. "You look through the peephole, and—"

"Adjust your yardage there on the side."

"Good as a telescope?"

"I reckon not. Some of them telescope sights, they got the distance built in, but that tang sight's awful fine. Past five hundred yards, this gun bears a little right. I love your grandfather, John, but there ain't no buffalo. I kilt every one."

A sliver of orange emerged to the east. They turned and Billy led Soquili and his own horse, both saddled. Johnny smiled. He couldn't fool blood kin.

"Goin' with you, brother. He's my grandfather, too."

"You—"

"You cain't say I'm too young. No more you cain't."

Johnny nodded.

They went inside and drank coffee while Mira fried bacon and eggs, and pulled her plump biscuits from the Dutch oven. Johnny looked up a little in awe of Emmet, whom he had never truly known. The old man's eyes glistened with a light some might have called holy.

"Tell me of your true love," Mira said. "Is she strong? Does she love children?"

Billy slumped in his chair, grinning. Johnny hadn't wanted this scene. He would have left, astride Soquili, like a thief in the night. Yes, Mother, Kate is strong, and of course she loves children. Johnny laughed. He supposed, after all, that he had a family.

12

The Last Hunt

They left the hills and the tall, brown grass stretched before them with gentle rises and slopes. The wagons rolled easily now and as the hours dragged by, and cold air settled, boys threw stones at squirrels in the haggard blackjacks, and then bullied the girls. Their mothers slapped them and the boys ran off a distance, then ran back, crawled into the wagons again, and slept.

The little caravan stopped at the snowy cliffs. Below lay swamp, frozen-over lagoons and icy ground, but no one could see the Arkansas through the deep fog. The children stood up, chattering, a little afraid, as their mothers braked the wagons. A boy leaped to the ground and ran to the edge, where he leaned forward even as his mother screamed.

In his lifetime Johnny had journeyed a score of times to Arkansas City, but it seemed to him he'd followed river banks all the way north. Never this broad, low ground, never this fog.

The uncles turned toward Buffalo Dancer, who slumped on his wagon seat, his wrinkled head poking out of his blankets like a turtle's head. His favorite granddaughter, Lavinia, tugged back the reins. Red Deer, a big man sitting heavily on his little sorrel mare, made a guttural cry. Buffalo Dancer stepped down but did not look at Red Deer. He shuffled to the rear of the wagon, where the Jersey cow was tied.

The cow, weaned from her calf a day before and carrying a

heavy bag of milk, had struggled to keep up since daybreak. Buffalo Dancer loosened her rope and allowed her to lie down. As she moaned, he sat in the thin snow, took her big head in his hands, and stared into her woeful, brown eyes. As if bestowing a blessing, he began to chant.

The uncles twisted about with their horses and muttered among themselves. Wives stood in exasperation, and soft-hearted Little River said, "Why do you torture her?" Only the children were quiet, because Buffalo Dancer carved clever toys for them, flutes and bears and hickory bows. They loved the old man, and this was their great adventure together.

Buffalo Dancer kept chanting, an old song which some of them knew:

I rise, I rise,
I, whose tread makes the earth to rumble.

I rise, I rise,
I, in whose thighs there is strength.

I rise, I rise,
I, who whips his back with his tail when in rage.

I rise, I rise,
I, in whose humped shoulder there is power.

Buffalo Dancer swept out a hand to the south. Grunting, Red Deer wheeled the sorrel, and the others joined him. A tall boy brought up the string of horses, and the wives hissed at their mules and horses and turned their wagons southward. As the procession melted into the cold fog, Buffalo Dancer nodded toward Billy and Johnny and pointed the opposite way.

Johnny heard a woman's voice: *Yes, to the north.*

He glanced at Billy, wondering if he'd also heard the voice, but his brother frowned and aimed his strong black gelding toward the expanse of fog. As they rode north, the cliffs grew taller for several miles, before breaking up into bluffs and hill-

PART 2

ocks that ran out eastward into the lowlands again. They dismounted and led their horses down a ravine that held a foot of snow, and at the bottom picked their way along the rockstrewn banks of a gushing stream. As the stream flattened into the swamp, they entered the fog. Now and then they paused to listen for the rest of the party, which had had a shorter path and by now must be deep in the depression. Billy thought he heard the ring of an axe, then shook his head. The cliffs were somewhere to the east, the river to the west, and while their trail might zigzag, they shouldn't become lost.

They entered a broad, soggy area without trees, with man-tall brush to either side of them where they held up their arms to ward off bending branches. The horses stumbled over the watery ground and grew confused. Their feet crunched through ice and they leapt from the little holes, whinnying in alarm. Fearing one would break a leg, the men dismounted, and dragged their own sodden feet forward. Still, they made progress. In warmer weather they'd have worried about quicksand, and water moccasins draped over branches, but their greatest obstacle remained the fog.

"Grandfather is crazy," Billy said. "Why did he send us this way?"

Johnny felt they'd entered a place of the spirits, that lost souls wandered in the awful whiteness. He did not believe Buffalo Dancer was crazy.

Both men fell silent when they heard a piercing wail to their left, and after that a guttural, piggish sound, like something fluttering in the wind, mixed with a quick panting. They blundered onward until sight of the buffalo cow emerged from the whiteness, a giant, mud-covered, gasping, red-eyed creature pinned under a great fallen oak, turning her head in her dying agony, but not crying out, not screaming like a horse. Beside her, a bull calf grunted and moaned and pawed at the mud. When he saw the men, he grunted like a boar and feinted charges toward them, giving up as grief overcame him and he returned to his mother's side. He nuzzled her face.

I see, thought Johnny. It is a sign.

Long ago, there was an evil white man, said Buffalo Dancer. His name was Charles Jesse Jones. He hated all Indians, yet he admired them, too, as you would admire a dog for its tracking ability, its sense of smell, its fierceness. Such men he called friends, and they were his scouts. Buffalo Dancer was one of them.

Jones killed buffalo and grew rich from their hides, in the country of the Kiowa and Arapaho, in western Kansas where the herds were so large a man could walk outside his camp and begin to shoot. In those first days, not even Charles Jones realized that if the whites killed the buffalo, they killed the Indian. Because there were as many buffalo as people. Seventy million, some said, and hunters could never kill them all.

After hunters had *almost* killed them all, smart white people came from the East and shook their heads at the slaughter, and wrote books. Jones became "Buffalo" Jones and expressed sadness about the splendid buffalo. He saw that something must be done to keep the species alive. South of Garden City, Kansas, Jones started a great ranch to preserve them.

He mounted expeditions to capture the last of the herd but soon discovered that subduing two-thousand-pound animals was almost impossible. So he hit upon the scheme of killing the mothers and bringing home the calves. Even this was difficult, because the calves were unruly to begin with, grieved for their mothers, and would not eat.

Here was Buffalo Dancer's great scheme, to earn money so that Johnny could woo his wife and buy a farm: buffalo calves. The evil white man, with his guilty conscience, would pay three hundred dollars for healthy calves.

Johnny was a farmer, not a cowboy, but he could form a noose. He motioned for Billy to do the same, then dismounted and tied the loose end of the rope to the pommel. "Easy," he told Soquili, whose eyes remained calm, but full of wonder. The two men came at the calf from opposite sides. Billy rushed, the little bull half-charged, and Johnny dropped the noose over its head. He pulled it tight and Billy dropped his noose as well— then reached out with his Colt revolver and shot the mother through an eye, twice.

The bull was a baby, but still he weighed four hundred pounds. He bawled out his rage and misery and attempted to charge, then wheeled toward his mother, but whichever way he strained, a rope pulled him back. The two men mounted their horses and the bull tried to run forward, then back between the horses, but Johnny yanked him westward. Several times the bull tangled in the brush, and when Johnny or Billy dismounted to free him, he tried to bite and kicked Billy in the leg. Johnny laughed. Billy cursed him and limped back to the gelding. Then the fog broke because they'd reached the river.

The little bull had worn himself out and tried to lie down. Johnny dismounted to push him along, and then the bull revived, snapped at Johnny's hand, and ran a few steps. They clumped through the ice and mud and at last heard the clamor of the hunters. As they entered the camp both men dismounted, left the reins of their horses trailing, and struggled forward with the little bull, whose neck bled from his struggles against the ropes, whose mouth frothed and issued guttural, growling sounds. Red Deer—with the other uncles behind him—stared, disbelief crossing his painted face.

Buffalo Dancer stood erect, his arms folded, wisps of fog twirling around him. He nodded and pointed toward a long rope stretched between tall cedars.

Johnny understood. They pulled the bull forward, and Johnny shortened his own rope and tied it securely. Billy tried to retrieve his rope but the bull almost bit him, and kicked up its hind legs, and Billy fell in the mud. All the children laughed. The uncles gathered with great authority and many sage pronouncements, but they didn't know what came next. At last one of the wives brought a pan filled with canned milk but the bull overturned

it, and snarled, and hissed, and made a long, stuttering, metallic growl, almost like a woodpecker banging its head at an elm.
Now Buffalo Dancer and Lavinia brought up the poor cow.
Her bag was so full she could hardly walk and she fell in the
mud. The children cried and urged her on. Johnny and Billy
hurried near and brought her to her feet again, until she stood
by the little bull. He snarled at her but she didn't do anything.
She mooed, and sniffed, and licked the bull on the nose. She
moaned in anguish and pain. The little bull nuzzled against
her and began to nurse.

THEY WERE FIVE DAYS in the foggy place. No one could
see beyond twenty feet, and the band began to rely on sounds.
To the north coyotes feasted on the dead mother. Johnny
heard them at night, one brute calling out, the others screaming at different volumes, until he fancied he could distinguish
individuals. He counted eight, but a day later, after the uncles
killed two more cows, another set of cries arose to the south.
Maybe five of them this time, feasting on forelegs and guts as
the camp processed meat until midnight and afterwards tried
to sleep. The dogs strained at their ropes and barked ceaselessly,
until Johnny wanted to shoot them too.

Next day, near the place where the uncles had killed the two
cows, they found an energetic female calf hiding in a cedar grove.
The uncles chased and roped her.

On the third day Johnny heard heavy feet, a mewling, and
pumped four rounds from his Winchester into a cow as her
monstrous head emerged from the white, curved horns tilted
toward him. Her female calf was a few months old, more man-
ageable than the little bull. He tugged it toward the river without calling for help, pushing sticks into the mud along his trail,
counting his steps, so that the uncles could find the dead cow
with their travois.

The uncles sought meat and hides but captured another calf.

To the south they came upon a herd of twelve in a cedar grove and the great bull charged them. He stopped, pawing the ground.

Red Deer explained it all to his children that night as they sat by the fire, huddled in agency blankets. The boy and girl were twins and Red Deer was fond of them. "The bull was very fierce," he said. "But we were not afraid."

"Did you kill him?" his son asked.

"We don't want to kill the bulls, when there are so few. Tall Man and Sleeps in the Woods ran left and right, beating on pans—"

"I don't understand about the bulls," the boy said.

"The bulls make more cows," Red Deer said.

"Oh."

"They shot off their rifles and the herd ran away while I lassoed the calf. I am very skilled with ropes."

"Why do you want the calves?" asked Red Deer's daughter.

"So your cousin, John Baxter, can find a wife."

"I don't understand."

"Nor do I. The mother came, even though the herd had left her. She was very brave, and very angry—"

"That was her calf!" the girl said.

"We shot her for the meat. We have very much meat; we may even sell some. We are a prosperous family!"

"But you killed her," the girl said.

"It is our way," Red Deer explained.

"It is our way!" the boy said.

So now they had four calves, but the female Johnny had captured was disconsolate. She wouldn't lap at canned milk or nurse from the Jersey cow. Children talked to her and petted her, but she hardly lifted her head, and ants crawled around her eyes. Even if they hauled her by wagon to Arkansas City, it seemed doubtful she could survive a train ride all the way to western Kansas.

The uncles killed another cow, and dragged back another calf, a feisty female that stood a strong chance to survive. This was no way for men to hunt, Red Deer said, loudly enough that all could hear.

Buffalo Dancer appeared to listen.

"There is a long ridge before you reach the cliffs," said Red Deer. "We should stretch out, women and children, too, and scream our war cries, and beat on pans, and the buffalo will run over the ridge, some breaking their legs. The rest will back against the cliffs and be easy to shoot."

This was the old way, refined many years before when buffalo were easily found, but Buffalo Dancer shrugged. "It does not matter how you hunt, Red Deer. You have killed five. I do not count the beast under the oak tree. You may kill one more."

"For the number of families?"

"Yes. One thousand pounds each."

"We could sell to the Cherokees."

"Others would say, 'Where did you find this meat?' The buffalo spirits have stated their will. Six and no more."

"Ah," Red Deer said. "My father speaks to Wah-Kon-Da now?"

Buffalo Dancer was seldom contradicted. Johnny would never again question him, because he had four calves to sell. Buffalo Dancer had been proved right, or prescient, or in touch with the spirits that lived in all things. But, perhaps because Red Deer was his oldest son, Buffalo Dancer said, "In my dreams."

That night Johnny dreamt of Kate. She wandered in the menacing fog. He wanted to warn her of the coyotes but never saw her face, only an ankle turning away from him, and once her frizzy hair, disintegrating in the mist. He called out, and in his last seconds of sleep had a vision of Comes With the Snow, her eyes wide as Kate's, her hair sleek and black but blowing up in the wind like Kate's, and the two women seemed the same.

He woke to bodies stirring in the fog and the camp breaking up around him. "What is it?"

Billy ran a rod down his rifle barrel. "Red Deer wants to hunt in the old way."

Johnny walked through the camp but could not find Buffalo Dancer. He decided to confront Red Deer. "Grandfather said—"

"He did not say how to hunt, John Baxter."

"But are there even fifty here? If you kill them all—"

"We are quicker this way and can go home to warm fires. We will kill only one, as my father says. How could we carry more meat?"

This seemed true enough. As Johnny rolled up his bedding, he didn't know whether he had a hunch or if Comes with the Snow spoke again: *Take the Sharps.*

Carrying the needle gun, joining the line of beaters and war-whoopers, he envisioned how things might have been for Misai, his father, thirty years before. Johnny doubted whether he'd have been a great warrior like Misai. He wasn't a killer. Farming came to him too naturally.

All the camp stretched out, except for a few fierce children and old people, left to guard the meat. You could not tell the women's soul-chilling cries from the men's, and the older children made a terrible racket with their pans and rattles. Many bodies passed through their tightening ring. They were all but invisible in the fog but Johnny felt the slithering of coyotes, the gliding leaps of antelope, brushing him like feathers. He heard the irritable chortling of raccoons and the hisses of opossums. Squirrels and mice ran, and every bird took wing, until the swamp fell silent.

When they reached Red Deer's ridge, the fog lifted all around, revealing a valley where water dripped from the cliffs above. A jackrabbit looked out at them from atop a limestone slab, but they saw no buffalo.

Except one. Halfway up the cliff, along an ancient pathway, a great bull bore down on Buffalo Dancer, who knelt and rocked back and forth. How did the old man get so far ahead of them? How did he climb so high? Was he there at all?

Eight hundred yards.

An impossible distance, but the number dropped into Johnny's head like a command, and he knew he had thought it, that Comes with the Snow hadn't put it there. He lifted the heavy rifle, and in the same motion flipped up the tang sight. He hadn't time to take his stepfather's advice and seek out a limb on which to prop the rifle. He steadied the barrel, aimed a little right, guessed at the elevation, and fired at the bull's head. The recoil knocked him backward two steps but he held his feet.

Nothing seemed to happen at first. The massive bull charged. Buffalo Dancer prayed. Then the bull stumbled and rolled to its knees. It struggled up but lost its footing, tumbling down the loose rock, tangling on a cedar improbably growing from the limestone. The cedar broke and the bull slid to the valley floor. Buffalo Dancer stood looking down. That's six, he might have said.

Screams and cheers rose down the line of muddy hunters. The uncles dragged the bull to a travois and all returned to the camp. Families loaded their wagons even as the butchering went on.

Red Deer came to see Johnny and punched him above the heart. "You are very ugly, John Baxter."

"Not as ugly as you, Red Deer."

"You are so ugly we must capture these buffalo babies to make your bride happy. She is hard to please!"

"She doesn't even—"

"True, I have not met her. Maybe she is even uglier than you." Johnny shrugged.

"But even though you are very ugly, and your bride is ugly, she has one thing to be proud of."

"And what is that, Red Deer?"

"Not even I could have made such a shot."

ARKANSAS CITY WAS ONLY twenty miles to the north, and beyond the swamp a frozen road paralleled the river, but Johnny and Red Deer, worried about the calves, made three days of the journey. The calves rode in the wagon but the men pulled them out midafternoon, staked and fed them, and covered them with blankets.

The sad little female died the first night. The other three females had begun to browse, but still their appetites were huge and they came near to exhausting the store of canned milk. The little bull had grown so attached to the Jersey cow that they planned to ship her as well.

At noon on the third day, they reached the rail yard, and staked Soquili, the buffalo, and the two mules in separate patches of ice-covered grass. The Jersey cow didn't need to be tied because she never strayed from her bull.

Red Deer refused to venture into the town. Johnny returned with two cases of canned milk, and soup and bread from the Harvey House. Red Deer said, "I cannot do that."

"What do you mean?"

"Go so easily among the whites."

"I speak English."

"Not as well as you, but so do I. I cannot humble myself."

Johnny nodded. "Some are not so superior."

"The ones who will not fight?"

"Yes. But I do not talk much."

Red Deer slapped his shoulder. "That is good, because you have nothing to say!"

They had reached the part of their plan, the rendezvous with Buffalo Jones, that seemed most likely to go wrong. Red Deer didn't believe you could trust any white man, while Johnny thought them trustworthy if every detail was clear in advance, and if the white man wanted the deal enough. Still, now that they had arrived, it seemed absurd that a mean old white man would venture three hundred miles to buy four animals. And at a dear price!

"Their word means nothing," said Red Deer.

In the morning Johnny ventured to the telegraph office, where he stood in line among suspicious white people. But two messages awaited him and he laughed; he almost danced. He caught himself and tried to look grief-stricken, because in every prairie town thieves watched the telegraph office. He walked down the street with his head low, and then laughed again as he turned toward their camp. What did it mean when you conceived an elaborate plan and it worked?

Billy had left Pawhuska with the bride-price horses.

Ten the next day, Jones strode out of the depot as Johnny walked toward it. The white man wore a white goatee and moustache, neatly trimmed, and a heavy, rawhide jacket with fringe down the sleeves but no beading. Johnny thought he might buy a broad-brimmed Stetson such as the white man wore, but that red scarf seemed pure vanity.

"Mr. Jones?"

Jones nodded but did not offer his hand. He looked up at Johnny with a trace of irritation, as if offended that Johnny was a foot taller, and Johnny sensed the man's contempt as they walked toward the animals. Red Deer was like this, too, among the Osage. You had to gain his respect with a bludgeon.

Red Deer glanced at the white man and stepped away. He made a fuss of gathering up the bull calf, almost tractable now.

The Jersey cow bawled.

"They'll do," Jones said, leaning over to spit tobacco. He gave Red Deer a cursory glance and handed Johnny the money. "Obliged."

"Thank you, sir," Johnny said. He opened the envelope and counted twelve hundred dollars in currency. "Do you need a bill of sale?"

Jones looked at him quizzically, then pointed toward a rail car. "Not necessary. It's real clear they ain't jackasses. And if they die, they die. But you fellows can help me load."

They led the milk cow first, and the bull, almost as tall as she, followed peaceably as a Hereford. The three females fought and required all three men to get them up the ramp: Johnny and Jones pulling ropes, Red Deer pushing the hind quarters. They tied the females to rings inside the car, twenty feet apart, and left water. They heard kicking and thumping as they walked down the ramp.

"I'm giving some thought to making the land run," Jones said, wiping manure from his hands with the red scarf, and tossing the scarf onto a pile of broken lumber. He drew another red scarf from his trousers pocket. "You know about that, Chief?"

Jones was a rich man with no need of land. He must be planning to speculate. "I have heard of it."

"Way I figger, man wanted a good claim, you'd have to place somebody down there in advance. Somebody knowed the country. What you think?"

"I am not the right one to ask, sir."

"You speak English better 'an me, John Baxter." Jones laughed. "That your Indian name? Not the Right One?"

Johnny smiled.

"I like Buffalo Dancer," Jones said. He stuck out his hand. "He's full a tricks. Tell him Charley Jones said hello."

JOHNNY GAVE RED DEER twenty dollars and bid goodbye. He wanted a bath but one of the two hotels appeared to be reserved for white people, the other full of riffraff such as himself. Afraid for his twelve hundred dollars, he washed up at a horse trough and slept at the livery next to Soquili, his Winchester on his belly. It snowed that night, the wind howled, and nothing stirred, not even rats.

But in the morning the temperature shot up with the sun and water ran in the streets. In a bank window he saw that today was March 24. You could have such a freak day in January, but everyone on the street knew this was different. White people smiled even at Indians.

Spring had come.

The girls at the Harvey House gave him haughty looks but served him, and then Billy arrived, and the girls, looking at Johnny as if for permission, couldn't stop flirting. Johnny almost wanted to stay another day to observe his brother in action, but chores awaited among those who would not fight, and adventures in the Outlet with Euly Kreider if his friend was agreeable.

He gave Billy thirty dollars.

"You're rich, Brother," Billy said.

"I may need your help for the run. It seems to me you cannot get to the good land without spotting someone along the way."

"I wouldn't miss it, Old Man."

Johnny rode a fine gray stallion out of Arkansas City, which made Soquili unhappy, but he had to control the stallion. Soquili followed the three beautiful mares, and he called to her from time to time, and she kept the mares tranquil. "Thank you, Buffalo Dancer," he said, and "Thank you, Comes with the Snow." He chanted, "I am John Baxter, John Baxter. I am a rich man." He fed his horses oats and they made their way toward the land where magic came only from money, and no spirit guide could help.

13

The Girl I Left Behind Me

Small!" insisted Phillippe Taureau, the large—the tall, the muscular, the unshaven—professor who claimed he'd studied at the Louvre with Louis Béroud, whoever that was, and Paul Cézanne. Taureau talked of masterpieces that covered entire walls, while demanding his class work on canvases not one foot square. Kate tried to understand. The small canvas taught you discipline and how to master detail with slight, precise strokes. If you excelled at small, one day you'd graduate to the large canvas and be set free. When?

Perhaps not for years, Taureau said, ambling through the class, studying Kate's tiny landscapes and sketches of Indians, frowning, moving on. How she longed for a word of praise!

Twelve of Taureau's eighteen female students hailed from Kansas City's best families. But they were a giddy lot, all older than Kate, all failures at their fancy Eastern schools, trying out art as a last resort before they retreated into spinsterhood. They were plump, or dense, or sickly. They were pathologically timid or shallow as the Great Salt Lake.

The remaining comely five slithered around the Master in their splendid dresses, sometimes daring to touch the hem of his garment. Only once had Taureau trained his hard eyes upon Kate, studying her springy hair, her bust, and her unwaspish waist—she disliked wearing corsets. Kate didn't believe she'd ever been scrutinized in so matter-of-fact, sexual a fashion, not by Johnny or any of the Mennonite swains. She supposed she was fortunate to avoid the complications if Taureau found her appealing, but still she was offended. By the man's rudeness, but also by his rejection. Why not me? she wondered. Do I have a crooked nose? Are my breasts too small?

One bright day in March, Professor Taureau deployed his retinue, each carrying a vase, a small canvas, and perhaps a sandwich, to cross the Hannibal Bridge through the sullen little town of Harlem, then into the wilds of the north. They made quite a procession, bright young women in silly shoes, piecing their way through the mud and horse manure, trying not to brush against the coal dust that coated everything, enduring catcalls from filthy men in half a dozen languages. They cowered midriver when a locomotive passed, with its clanking of rods and wheels, its gasps of steam, its plumes of soot.

Perspective, Taureau explained. Everything in life was perspective, and so it must be with art! From this northern perspective you could turn and see the city in its anguish and ambition: the ghastly Armour plant, spewing offal into the Missouri, but also the bright trolleys, climbing out of the stinking Bottoms as if toward Heaven. And the river itself, teeming with flat boats and barges, and Negroes from Mississippi Town, wielding their patched rowboats, pulling out catfish big as whales.

To the north nature resumed, in swamps and hillocks as pristine as Euly Kreider's Zimmerman Woods. Following his mysterious agenda, the great professor directed them to pick wildflowers, ferns, cedar boughs, and tall grasses, and to assemble bouquets. He offered no guidance, and these city girls put flowers with flowers, perhaps adding a fern for contrast. The professor asked the class to categorize each bouquet, and the verdict was always "romantic" except for one "baroque," a term decided upon after the rejection of "mess" and "brushpile."

Kate gathered an unfurled milkweed from the season before, an elderberry shoot with its tiny, green fruit, and several blackberry briars. To either side she placed delicate May apple blooms, sheltered by their umbrella-like tops. The class agreed: "Classical."

"Ladies, this is your style," the professor said. "Everything you do in life, how you see the world, will in some way express this style."

Kate said, "But what if you know that, Professor? What if you understand your style and don't want it to limit you? What if you deliberately change it?"

"Yes! So true!" Taureau said, with a magnanimous smile. "Dear ladies, Katherine has explained it to you. When you overcome your natural style, your humdrum self, that is art!"

Kate was pleased with the lesson. And perhaps Professor Phillippe Taureau was a fine teacher, although he hadn't studied at the Louvre, and his real name was Max Keaton, accused of embezzlement in Cleveland. When the young ladies next assembled, they learned from the embarrassed administrator that Max had left town following the confessions of a precocious fifteen-year-old from Quality Hill. The professor's private lessons had yielded a pregnancy.

Not that it mattered, but the comely five did not turn out to be society girls, depending how you looked upon society. The ladies worked the night shift for Annie Chambers, the famous madam down on Wyandotte. Given their vocations, who could blame them for seeking out culture?

THE MONEY FROM UNCLE Barney—Kate still found it difficult to think of him as "Father"—provided for her education. But because of Barney Kreider she was illegitimate, and Euly, whom gossipy churchwomen had determined she'd marry, had transformed himself into her brother. Her awkward brother, as familiar as her paint-stained fingers, as romantic as a frying pan.

Blameless, though.

Her most worrisome feelings, her anger, her confusion, centered on her father. What if he hadn't been ashamed of her?

What if "Uncle" Barney had come to her, confessed his sins, begged her forgiveness?

Maybe he would have. Maybe, as she fell sprawling and ignorant into adulthood, he'd have been forced to. Instead, before her eyes, Eddie Mole shot him dead.

She could not scold her father; she could not even weep. She could not be Barney Kreider's daughter, or her unknown mother's. Unlike Euly, she was an orphan.

In her dreams she saw her father across the street, looking up in surprise, falling dead before he could cry out. She struck out across the street, where mud and horse manure slowed her pace, pulling her down to the tops of her boots. She stood helplessly as the evil outlaw galloped away, and that drunkard, Monte Truman, himself wounded, screamed for help.

In other dreams she was naked, reaching in the darkness for something—someone—she could not quite see. She woke aroused, sweaty, and filled with shame. Was this the heritage of her wanton mother? One half of who she was could not be known; the other half sprang from a Mennonite outcast. Even if she willed unflinchable virtue, her birthright forbade it. Maybe her very soul was venal.

One frozen morning she woke and yearned with all her might to go riding on splendid King Arthur, out to the fields where Johnny Heart of Oak worked. She'd coax her man down to the creek, where they'd swim and almost-kiss, almost-touch. Always, he was a gentleman. Always, she was the aggressor, but in the end she was as shy as he. With relief she'd pose him on the bank, the little waterfall behind, and attempt yet another masterpiece.

But Johnny was an Indian. Marrying one in Missouri was *illegal*. Even in Kansas, how would they live?

She didn't need anyone. She felt homesick but a person got over that. Like the measles, the boardinghouse girls said.

Thus spake a bevy of flirts. Every one of them, encountering brutes, awaited Prince Charming.

She lived in the Big City now. You could drop in a little place like Jericho Springs five thousand times. She was a free woman with her small fortune, and she'd make something of herself. Before she was done, her paintings would hang by those of that French fellow's in the Louvre!

ANNELISE HAD KEPT UP a stream of letters since Christmas. She said Euly might marry that Muenster girl. The jezebel who ran off with the tinker? No, she meant Jenny, the blonde. Dear God. Brother, Euly, look around!

Maybe Kate shouldn't fault her, hailing from such a family, but Jenny Muenster was a humorless, avaricious little thing.

Kate caught herself. Jealousy? No, she felt a *sisterly* concern, and Jenny Muenster would make for a boring sister-in-law. Hardworking, to be sure.

Like Euly?

All right: a match. An ordinary, sensible match, and who was she to judge? She'd drop Euly an encouraging note, like a good sister should. No need to keep herself apart anymore.

She grew depressed, thinking, *I can never go back.* No one needed her, already she was forgotten, and like her father, she made a poor Mennonite. Too many rules about what color you painted your stock gate, or whether one horse or two should pull your Sunday buggy. They said it was a miracle when the tornado passed over and that God moved in mysterious ways when the barn blew away with all your cows. How could they believe such nonsense?

And she was, not to be delicate because the matter was hardly delicate, a bastard. Even less kindly, a bitch. She'd always be a bastard in Jericho Springs, among the submissive Mennonites. Even they couldn't hold the child accountable to the sinful womb. No one would shun her, not exactly, but she'd grow old wearing the scarlet "B."

Outside of Jericho Springs, in all the great world, no one knew. She could be—

What? What, in the spring of 1893, could a woman be?

Teacher. An honorable calling, but she'd wait a while.

Missionary. She didn't know how she felt about taking God's word to the benighted. She felt benighted herself.

Nun. She didn't wish to withdraw from the world. And those nuns she'd observed, with their veils like blinders on carriage horses, all seemed so sorrowful.

Author. Jane Austen? Harriet Beecher Stowe? How did they do it?

Secretary. Boardinghouse girls, Pauline and the duplicitous Greta, thought they could parlay secretarial work into marriage, but Kate wasn't a ravishing blonde. Her hair sprang out like wire. You needed to dress well and she knew so little about clothes! Perhaps you could simply be loyal, competent, good with numbers, and a fast typist. But you had to say "Yes, sir," and "Thank you, sir," and you made so little!

Nurse. Hard, depressing work. Those heavy bedpans. And long hours.

Laundress. Too hard. Dead at forty.

Factory worker. Too hard. Dead at forty.

Bargirl. You'd never starve, but not much better.

Dressmaker. Or milliner, though she didn't know anything about making hats. At least you could sit down.

Clerk. Better than secretary if you weren't chained to a desk, and handled interesting goods.

Prostitute. She laughed. Annie Chambers's whores dressed nicely, but their glory was brief, indeed. Dead at thirty-five.

Wife. Well, that would require a husband.

Mother. She could not imagine it.

And little else—except a painter. No one could forbid her from putting brush to canvas, even if she signed with a man's name.

Annelise wrote:

We are enjoying fine weather here, but Helmut worries over the dearth of moisture. He says the wheat is fine because we had so much snow, but the corn will do poorly. Instead, he will plant sorghum because it tolerates drought. He sends his love.

I asked if he had any pearls of wisdom for you, and he said, *"Das Leben ist Arbeit."* Life really is work, Katherine, but I worry sometimes that my dear Helmut will drop dead from it. I believe he would ascend straight to Heaven.

Speaking of work, I wonder if you would consider broadening your education. Many years may pass before your paintings sell. Because I could take you only through the eighth grade, you would have a difficult time even entering a woman's college, and I don't believe those foolish girls' schools, where they teach girls how to walk and hold a fork, would help you any.

The Church has Bethel College now in Newton and the Brethren have their McPherson College, and either might be more sympathetic if you wanted that college diploma. We would love for you to come home!

However, I have learned that there is a fine business school in Kansas City, founded by Mr. Spalding. I believe women are allowed to attend.

Perhaps you could augment your studies in art with some bookkeeping and stenography classes. What about learning to operate a typewriter? Several businesses in Jericho have them now, and they are everywhere in Newton. I suggest this because of how difficult it can be for an unmarried woman. Someone who can handle numbers is always in demand. Even if you are a farmer's wife, Kate.

It won't be long before some handsome young man comes courting. Do follow your heart, but be careful. You are an extraordinary girl! Your beau needs to be extraordinary!

At this an image of Johnny came to mind. Other than Euly and Helmut, he was the only man she knew. He was a hard worker, though not talkative. I never gave him a chance to talk, she thought.

Euly and Jenny bask in glory, they are so happy. But he's busy as Helmut and Jenny is equally as bad. When they are not working, they work. They need to take a day off and get married!

Euly hauls freight all day and builds his hardware by moonlight. God only knows how he'll manage when he has crops to tend to!

Well, we worked that hard when we came from the Old Country.

All anyone talks about is the land run. Some in the congregation will try. Lo, the poor Indian! We steal their lands then tell them to obey the law.

We have heard nothing about the outlaw.

I must go. I have three pies to bake and essays to grade. The topic was, "How My Mennonite Faith Will Help Me in My Life's Work." I don't believe you think it has, Kate, but be patient, and steady, and submissive to the Lord's will. Everything will work out fine.

Your loving Aunt Elise

Kate took her aunt's advice, enrolling at Spalding's Commercial College. She enrolled late, but catching up proved simple, compared to how she might fit in. She was one of three women in bookkeeping, while only one man wanted to type. Thinking of Professor Taureau's antics in painting class, she dressed severely for the business school, in black dresses and practical hats—almost Mennonite garb. No man flirted with her, which was both a relief and puzzling. Was she so homely?

She purchased three sports dresses at Bernheimer's, in green and red with modest floral designs, two of which went with bloomers. She walked everywhere and walking was easy in bloomers, but the young businessmen still did not notice her. Maybe the bloomers were why. They thought she *was* one.

City ways were city ways, but she refused to wear a rigid corset. She pulled on her comfortable Montgomery Ward bust supporter, which lifted her breasts and made them seem larger but still allowed her to breathe. She donned the third dress, a maroon affair with modest white lace and sensible sleeves that dropped respectably to the floor. Her hair was so wild it defied gravity, but she let it spring free, setting it off with a cheerful white bonnet. Several men eyed her. One—she could not understand!—with bemusement. Two others offered knowing leers. Had she achieved the appearance of an Annie Chambers girl?

She couldn't solve the mystery but all was not lost. Next day, when again she donned a sports dress and bloomers, a young man sat beside her. "Abner Pierpont," he announced with a determined sort of dignity, as if you might deny him his name. "I am from Philadelphia."

She introduced herself, smiling at his seriousness. "Are there no business schools in Philadelphia, Abner?"

"My father felt I needed a new start. Why are you here, Katherine?"

"My father felt that *I* needed a new start." She laughed. "I'm really an artist but I am advised to be practical."

He nodded. "Artists have such a difficult time."

Soon they were eating their lunches in a park across from the school. They studied together after classes. Her accounts of Mennonite life seemed as incomprehensible to him as did his of what sounded like a privileged life in the East. He'd attended Princeton, then a business school back home in Philadelphia, but somehow he'd always had to move on.

They ate in restaurants and the city brimmed full with opera houses. They saw *A Doll's House*, starring the popular actress Modjeska, about a woman, Nora, with an oppressive husband. Nora struck out on her own, and in a vague way Kate thought she should cheer. Yet the only marriage she knew intimately, Helmut and Annelise's, was so unlike Nora and Torvald's that they didn't compare.

Annelise had few options in life but she made the most of them, and Helmut was no tyrant, like Torvald. Annelise and Helmut's purpose in life was to serve God. They had known the czar's tyranny and were grateful for what America offered. Through endless hard work, they prospered.

Above all Ibsen's characters seemed foreign, and not because they were Norwegian. The idea of characters striding across a stage, reciting important words, itself seemed foreign. The nearest thing to a play Kate had ever known was when Annelise forced the eighth-graders to memorize scenes from *Julius Caesar* and self-consciously recite them.

And yet Kate did feel . . . *different*. She had that much in common with Nora. Why was she always an outsider? No one knew she was illegitimate. Was it because she was a woman who took business classes?

She wondered what Johnny would make of *The Girl I Left Behind Me*, a melodrama about a frontier fort besieged by Indians. Savages! Painted white men, bare-chested, some shooting arrows, some rifles, screaming like coyotes as they charged the noble soldiers. The heroine, pursued by a villain with a black moustache but also by a stalwart hero, seemed more a pretty prop than a character.

A silly entertainment, but the title brought to mind a painting by Eastman Johnson, which Kate remembered from a reproduction hanging at Annelise's school. A young, innocent-seeming girl looked across the boundless prairie, while her hair blew in the winds of a rising storm. The girl clutched her school books, hopeful but alone, bewildered by the vast, ominous horizon.

Abner walked her back to her boardinghouse and she never worried because they stayed on Main, lit by the amazing electric lights. Sometimes, Abner halted and stared down the unlit alleys. Kate jerked him forward.

Once or twice he took her hand. She didn't enjoy holding hands, at least not with Abner, because she was a foot taller and it threw off her long stride. Still, she'd never had a beau except for Johnny, the painted savage. Rather, the savage she'd painted.

Could Abner be thought of as a beau? Men were forbidden in her boardinghouse, so she stepped onto the street, dropping her head to a level below Abner's, and looked up with what she imagined to be great admiration, if not exactly love, in what she believed was correct posture for receiving a kiss. Abner pecked her cheek.

"Is there something wrong with me, Abner?"

Abner should fling himself at her with wild abandon. Afterward, with infinite kindness, she'd explain how she cared for him but that they could never be anything but friends. A man waited for her, a fine, patient man, back in her home town.

"Something is wrong with us both, Kate. That's why we are together."

IN THE MORNINGS THEY rode the streetcar east to Troost, comparing worksheets and preparing for tests all the way. Years later, when Kate reflected on her adventures in the big city, she realized that people had stared at them, that in the bubble of youth she hadn't understood. Perhaps these ladies in fancy hats and men in their department store suits envied their brightness and idealism, but also they disapproved. The rouge favored by white women never quite masked their outrage. Why outrage? And joining them, ever so briefly, the sidelong glances of the businessmen flashed with something like animal hunger, as if Kate and Abner were morsels of meat.

In the park across from the school, they practiced short orations on the future of American industry: the typewriter, the horseless carriage, labor unrest. Kate had chosen the topic of steam threshers, because she knew how much brutal work they saved, but also because agricultural issues were neglected at the school. She understood farming better than the stock crisis, which had made all her teachers gloomy.

As they crossed to the school, she said, "What did you mean, Abner?"

"Dear Kate." He struggled for words. "I don't wish to offend."

"Out with it."

"Kate, how can you not know?"

Abner's decorum angered her. "Say it!"

Abner looked away. "You're a . . . Negress."

She slapped him. He reached to readjust his glasses and his face flushed. "You can pass, Kate! You're passing here. In Philadelphia, among the Quakers—everywhere!—they *pass*. You're lovely, Kate. I love you. I—I *would*. If I—"

She looked up in agony. "I'm dark."

"Not so dark . . . brown. It's unfair to judge people that way. How could you not know? Maybe only me, Kate, because I—" Abner dropped his head. "It makes no difference."

She fled to the women's water closet, the only one on four floors, and stared into the mirror. Her curly hair! And what might she conclude about those dark eyes? When almost every Mennonite's, every German-Ukrainian's, were blue?

Damn Barney Kreider, she thought, even as she stepped to the front of the class. She had to concentrate; she had to exude confidence even if she felt despoiled. She stared at the disapproving, righteous young men, every one of them wearing a bowtie. They were a pack of wolf pups. Did it even matter how good her speech was?

Then she spied woebegone Abner, sitting at the back of the room, alone as always, looking miserable as always. He'd given an intelligent speech about the Brotherhood of Locomotive Firemen and Enginemen, a sort of union, and how badly American industry treated its workers. Workers were treated worse than horses but that would change in the new century, and change had to come if America was to prosper and remain true to its founding ideals. Abner's speech was received in silence, except for several throat clearings. Professor Bigelow said, "Thank you, Mr. Pierpot,"—not even getting the Philadelphian's name right.

"I want to talk to you about the Mennonites," Kate said. "And the great gift they brought from the Ukraine to America."

She held up her sketch of a cloaked peasant, wielding a scythe, and another of a horde of peasants gathered by a great steamship. "This is who we were," she said. Two men kept talking and Professor Bigelow moved near them, as Annelise used to with her rowdy eighth-graders. Perhaps the two young men would become pilots of industry but rudeness was rudeness. Anger infused Kate's blood like a tonic.

"Gentlemen," she said, with only a little irony. "Consider the steam thresher."

She rolled out her lithograph of a McCormick thresher, and then her sketches—ten times larger than Professor Taureau's dimensions—of men in long sleeves and slouch hats, wielding pitchforks, throwing bales of straw onto wagons, chaffing the kernels of wheat the thresher spewed out. The two miscreants laughed, and one said, *"Farmers?"* Professor Bigelow brought down his pointer across an empty desk and nodded to Kate.

Such scrawny specimens didn't matter, not when men like Helmut Kreider and Johnny Heart of Oak walked the earth. She lifted her voice high above their bowties, speaking not even to Abner but to an abstraction—Congress, perhaps. Or the bustling Mennonite nation. "Like the Israelites of old, they were a persecuted people. They were the best farmers in the Ukraine but when the czar wanted their young men to go to war, they refused. The commandment, 'Thou Shalt Not Kill,' was first among their beliefs. Thus they emigrated to the frontier of Kansas, of which they knew very little, except that in vast America you were promised freedom of religion. And opportunity. With hard work your family could prosper, and your children become doctors and teachers."

She placed another drawing, two feet by three, in the chalk tray of the blackboard. Here she had imagined the confused men in their Russian hats, the stoical women in their dark cloaks, the frightened children, as they exited from the railyards at Newton.

"They introduced a miracle crop: turkey red wheat. Conventional wisdom had it that you couldn't grow wheat in Kansas because in July the rains stop, the winds blow out of the desert, and the grasshoppers destroy what little grain you have left. Some of you gentleman come from farms. You know what I mean."

She had them now, anyhow half of them. Not all were pampered sons. Some had milked cows before daylight and mended harness by the flickering light of coal oil.

"The Mennonites brought *winter* wheat. You planted it in the fall, it germinated beneath the snow, and by April you could estimate your harvest. In June you took it to market."

She dropped her eyes and met Professor Bigelow's reassuring smile.

"These Mennonites made Kansas but they hadn't enough hands to chaff so much wheat. Thus the steam boiler, which powers the thresher, and the thresher itself, so that Kansas can bring its bread to all the world. Even more than cattle, turkey red wheat has built Kansas City, and made possible our gathering here today, gentlemen, in Dr. Spalding's fine school. Soon, still more ingenious machines will plow the ground, plant the wheat, and transport it to the granaries.

"Gentlemen, this is the genius of America: the starving, rejected peoples of Europe, overcoming every obstacle. We, the immigrants, love God and believe in the perfectibility of man. In America we undertake a great experiment not only for the privileged, but everyone. The humble, the displaced, the low-born will also rise! Everyone who works, with brains or brawn, will find his place! With farm implements, great locomotives, and electricity we will invent our way into the new century, the greatest century in history! *You*, gentlemen! You will bring business—industry—to the last frontiers of America. And the harvests will be beyond imagining!"

The applause erupted. Even the two rabblerousers rose and

whistled and Kate smiled. A tip to the orator: Turn your audience into heroes even if you despise them.

Professor Bigelow charged to the front of the room, clapping. "Wonderful! Class, did you note Miss Kreider's extremely effective use of illustrations? Are those yours, Miss Kreider?"

She was grateful for her teacher's admiration, for what was her first success in Kansas City, but doubt nagged at her. Her fine words had seemed true in the moment, but hadn't she simply regurgitated the sort of thing you read in the *Times?* True in a way, ideal, but the stuff of boosterism. As she smiled, and the young men milled about her drawings, saying polite things and even flirting with her, she thought of Johnny Heart of Oak, so tall and strong and noble, and so *brown*. She thought of the Negroes in Mississippi Town, lucky even to feed themselves. And what manner of creation was she? What? What? The humble, the displaced, the low-born will also rise? Maybe the white ones.

LIKE THE COUNTRY WOMAN she was, Kate donned the boots and trousers she'd worn for chores, and for good measure, a crumpled Stetson a workman had left at the boarding house. She liked dressing up for plays and when she went out to dinner, but she had work to do, and her dresses had cost too much to drag through the mud. In the early morning conventional folk had yet to show themselves, but she tied an old skirt over the trousers while descending Main Street to the Bottoms. As a laborer might his shirt, she tied the skirt around her waist when she struck off west toward Kansas.

She passed Hell's Half-Acre, a gathering of saloons and whorehouses, almost a town, hugging the brown Missouri.

A hotel stood at a right angle to the river. Clustered nearby she made out a livery, a general store, and then several saloons with second stories, where she could only imagine what went on. All the buildings were of rough-sawn oak clapboard, unpainted and weathered, and looked as though a strong wind might push them over. A hand-painted sign on the fascia of a restaurant, reading, "Oysters," had come loose on one side, and squawked in the sulfurous wind. Lanterns hung along the narrow porches of several buildings and might seem alluring, lurid, when the sun went down.

By the river a flatboat docked. Men unloaded barrels of whiskey, and one fellow in a black suit, carrying a samples case, got off and entered the general store. She sketched the men nervously, the long, trash-filled Main Street before them, the foggy river behind.

The sinners still slept. But no decent woman would linger here, and she eyed the little borough warily, as if a demon would reach out with his horny paw and drag her to the black depths. If I were a man bent on revenge, Kate thought, I'd look for Eddie Mole in such places.

She eyed an upstairs window. Maybe my mother was a crib girl, she thought.

SHE CROSSED THE KAW River on the Belt railroad bridge, and from up high saw the smokestacks of the Armour plant, pumping thick, black smoke over the little city behind. To the northeast, almost at the confluence of the Kaw and the Missouri, she saw shanties. She dropped down to a muddy river road, and then a trail, and then a brushy hillside.

She topped a grade and looked down upon Mississippi Town—not a town at all, but a cockeyed, rickety assemblage of logs and rough lumber that had floated down the Missouri and been patched over with Armour lard cans. She drew up a broken crate and sat within a grove of sumac where she could observe but not be seen. The air was stifling and a rancid odor rose from the Negro town. She sweated. She swatted at mosquitoes and pinched off ticks. Still, she leaned forward intently, clutching her sketchbook.

Men issued from the shacks, heads down, their strides forceful, as they climbed into her view, then veered toward the meat plant. Their clothing was ill-fitting, multicolored—castoffs. She was well dressed by comparison. A whistle blew and another of her notions floated away: that rancid odor came from Armour's stockyards and rendering vats, not the Negroes. She'd wondered whether *she* gave off that mysterious smell.

She caught herself. Full of prejudice, she was ill-suited for this adventure. She only knew what she read in the newspapers, the books, all written by white people. Even the children at Annelise's school, none of whom had seen a Negro, said they smelled peculiar. Maybe she should drop down to the path and sniff each man as he passed!

She placed a hand over her heart as if she could stop its racing. She sketched faces, drawing an outline she'd fill in later. The men laughed and talked as white men might, except they spoke in strange dialects that Kate had difficulty translating.

They were butchers. They did the meanest, most dangerous work. They killed big animals until they themselves were too injured or bent to lift their knives. Armour hired them because of how little they'd work for and because they couldn't complain no matter how they were used.

"I complain all the time," Kate murmured.

When the men had gone, she slid down from the sumac grove onto the twisting little street. She heard a baby cry, the clank of spoons hitting plates, but no one entered the sunshine until she had almost reached the Kaw. A young woman emerged from a dugout in the river bank, ducking under a burlap curtain, and stirred a cauldron full of work clothes. The boiling water had turned dark brown from slaughterhouse blood.

The girl had drawn her long, frizzy hair to either side in loose pigtails tied with small blue ribbons. She stared at Kate with blue eyes and Kate stared in return. She was so astonished by those blue eyes peering out of the black skin that she had no words. The girl spat and ducked behind the rough curtain.

"Sister!" Kate cried.

What had come into her mind was that the girl was a mongrel, a sideshow freak. What person, white or black, would feel otherwise? Then she thought, *I* am the freak, and stood over-heated and chagrined on the alien street. The blue eyes in the black skin were meaningless, like a blue-eyed goat in a herd of fifty with brown eyes. The girl was pretty and Kate felt a kinship.

"Forgive me, please," she called out. No answer, and Kate stumbled toward the shore, thinking, *Judge not, lest ye be judged.* She had been, hadn't she? If a friend called her a Negro, what did those proper women on the trolley think?

She came up behind an old woman who baited lines and threw them out. The woman was almost bald. Her body brought to mind a strip of bacon, brown and thin, with black splotches from some sort of skin disease. Kate might not have guessed she was female but for her patchwork dress, made from other dresses and strips of burlap. This time, Kate remembered what Professor Taureau taught: rise above yourself. The self that thinks, *mongrel.*

The old woman was friendly. Seeing Kate, she sat back on a bucket and motioned toward the fishing poles.

"Med'diss," she said. "I'm jes' po'ly; I ain't had no res' all night, them crazy niggahs drinkin en frolickin. You big an' strong, Med'diss, push dem poles down in da mud fer me? Them cat-fishes gonna pull 'em inter the river."

Kate cast the bait and shoved the poles deep into the moist clay. "Nothing but catfish, Mother?"

"They's suckahs, they's putch. You hep me wid da trap now."

Kate stood for a moment, processing the woman's strange speech. *Med'diss?* As she waded a distance into the water, she remembered a story in the newspaper about the African Meth-odist Church, bringing aid to the Southern refugees who washed up in Wyandotte and Mississippi Town. The old woman thought she was a relief worker.

The trap had drawn in half a dozen perch, a foot-long catfish, and two orange-and-green striped turtles such as Kate remem-bered from Zimmerman's Creek. Meanwhile, one of the fish-ing poles bent toward the water, and Kate hurried to pull in the largest catfish she'd ever seen. The fish nearly caused her to capsize, but with both hands on the pole she muscled it toward the shore, where the old woman unhooked it so quickly Kate couldn't see how she did it.

Kate laughed. "Mother, this is fun!"

The old woman clapped. "We got us a mess er fishes fer dinner, Med'diss!"

"My name is Kate. I am not Methodist."

"You a w'ite woman, I knows dat. You kin call me Nancy, Kate, an' I tanky fo' da hep."

"It's a pleasure, Nancy. You're a fine fisherman."

"You bring food, Kate? You bring money?"

"No."

"Why you heah fo'?"

She was here, Kate supposed, to see if she felt an affinity with the people of Mississippi Town, and perhaps she did, but not because her skin was brown. What did evil men say? One drop of black blood made you a Negro? But already she understood that only one in twenty was black as coal. Most were like saddle leather, or mud, or wheat. Others were brown and white like cowbirds.

Nor were white people anything like ivory, Kate thought. They had peeling, sunburned noses, and their babies came pink from their baths. But if she looked upon them with the eye of an artist, they were redder than the red man, who was never red. They were sallow from sickness, gray with age. They were dark as she was.

"I came to draw you," she said.

SHE GAVE THEM FLOUR, sugar, corn meal, sides of bacon. She supplied peroxide and bandages, liniments, ointments. She brought garden seeds, a shovel, a hoe. She brought a wide cardboard crate with round holes in its top, the first home for fifty Rhode Island Red chicks. She talked to an AME minister on the Missouri side and he turned over his stock of donated shoes.

Suppressing her disapproval, she brought chewing tobacco

and snuff. She fulfilled forty-two requests for Dr. Bersuch's Medicinal Bitters, more potent than Nancy's elderberry wine.

Guilt nagged at her for bribing the affections of these poor people, but she soon understood they'd never like her. In a narrow way they trusted her, but to them she was a woman of privilege, and "white." Though they had nothing, they regarded her with bemusement or mild contempt, because only a naive person would give away valuable goods.

Nancy, a sort of mayor, drafted Kate's models and routed them to a kitchen chair down by the Kaw. Sometimes, Kate moved the chair from shade to sunlight, or positioned her subjects with the river unfurling behind them. Everyone said "Yes'm," and "No, Ma'am," to the strange young woman who wore trousers. Kate gave each woman and child a quarter and offered hoarhound candy to the children. Working men propped up their sore feet, sipped warm beer or Dr. Bersuch's Medicinal Bitters, and fell asleep.

An ex-slave, George Washington, stared at his image and said, "Wi'te man's trick."

He was drunk. The bitters turned most men mellow but some howled until midnight, and even discharged shotguns. In the mornings, you might find them up or down the river, passed out in the weeds from bitters and the whiskey they bought at Hell's Half-Acre.

"Mr. Washington, I'm an artist," she said. "I won't trick you."

She dropped a quarter into his gnarled hand. His eyes filled with a mixture of hatred, wickedness, and—she thought she read him correctly—superiority. She drew back. In some towns, even in 1893, even at his age, George Washington would be beaten for that look.

He shook a Bible in her face, and his lips, no teeth behind them, quivered as though to admonish her. Then, as if a chemical reaction had concluded in his brain, he bent his head and his shoulders drooped. He seemed ancient, like a scarred, old tree deep in the woods. "You steal my so'," he said.

Maybe she did. She'd never drawn with such freedom. She modeled heads from different angles, pulling back, coming intimately close. She was literal one time and summoned the impressionists the next. She tried pencils, charcoal, ink, even watercolors. Demons emerged, and unexpected angels. When you froze their faces in drawings, when you synthesized squirmings, sneezes, and implacable stares, their essence remained on paper. Their essence, even when they laughed, was sorrow.

She took several drawings, signed K. Kreider, to the little gallery the art school ran. She had no sales pitch and was almost apologetic, but the director, Mr. Denby, couldn't stop staring. He was a short, unkempt fellow in a paint-smeared apron, with an upper body shaped like a pear. His bald head suggested a pear, too, and when he talked his wide jowls quivered. "My goodness," he said, his magnified eyes almost scary behind his glasses. "My goodness."

Mr. Denby hung three of her sketches in his Main Street window, by student still-lifes of apples and roses, and Denby's own portraits of Quality Hill ladies in their wedding gowns. Kate sat by the window at the less-than-fancy restaurant across the street, did her accounting exercises, wrote to Annelise, and ate the cheapest lunch. With her charity work her inheritance had dwindled, but she felt like the detective in a mystery novel who has stumbled onto a vital clue. Or like a gambler taken over by a demon.

On the morning and afternoon of the first day, perhaps two hundred people hurried by the gallery window, and not one paused to look at her work. Classes occupied her on the morning of the second day, but as she ate her sausages and sauerkraut, and lingered over coffee, an old man with a cane stopped to study her drawings. She stood at her table. "Go in," she murmured. "Go *in*."

He didn't, and two schoolboys came next. They pointed, brought their hands to their mouths in mock outrage, and then leaped about like monkeys. She could hear them screeching from across the street and clutched the table until her fingers went white. Despair rolled over her. Not ridicule!

Then she seemed to hear Professor Taureau's scornful laugh. You have to be tough, he'd say. You can't stand on the corner crying out about public stupidity. The task would never be done. The public wants noble birds, dewy-eyed kittens, and fluttering angels. They want burlesque. *That* public will never be interested in you, Kate, so why waste thought on them?

Still, walking back to her boardinghouse, her heart filled with doubt. What if her sincerest efforts were amateurish, and vulgar as those boys?

Next day, her practical upbringing asserted itself. Annelise and Helmut Kreider would have thought it unforgivable to waste so much time over a matter of pure vanity. You've learned to type, Kate told herself, and you're good with figures. Don't be a silly female, agonizing over something as frivolous as art. She'd had her adventure in the big city. Maybe she showed a small talent but she'd never go to Paris. The time had come to put girlish dreams behind her.

Done with art forever, she decided upon a last extravagance. She ordered oysters—packed in ice, shipped all the way from Cape Cod—but then sat looking at them, because they were *raw*. She worked up her nerve, piercing the slippery things with a strange little fork, dipping them in sauce, and bravely swallowing. Each was more tolerable than the last and she didn't vomit. She lifted her coffee and began a list of brand-new goals. She doodled some caricatures of Johnny. She missed him.

And at that moment, in the early afternoon of the third day, a well-dressed couple—easterners, she thought, though she couldn't have said why—stopped at the window, studied her drawings, and entered the gallery.

They emerged minutes later with a small, flat package wrapped in butcher paper. She knew the package held a drawing—perhaps two. She reached again for the coffee cup, and spilled it across the tablecloth and onto her skirt. She recalled the monkey-boys and began to cry.

At last she composed herself and crossed the street, determined to seem casual. Director Denby was all smiles. "My goodness gracious!" he said.

"Yes, Mr. Denby?"

He walked around the long counter and dropped a stack of silver dollars into her hands. "One dollar each," he said. "We never sell *anything* here, K. Kreider! In three days, you sold seven! Two only a moment ago. My *goodness!*"

She restrained her tears. "Your commission, Mr. Denby?"

He waved a plump hand. "Not today, Miss Kreider. Next time: ten percent. But first—"

"Yes?"

"I want you to frame them. Do you know how to do that?"

She nodded.

"Then I believe we can price them at five dollars each. It's marvelous work. And 'K. Kreider' is *so* mysterious. One lady said, 'This great artist, he must be a Negro!' Humorous, don't you think?"

"My goodness," Kate said.

KATE LAY ALMOST NAKED, trying to study for her finals. The material, on making a sales presentation, was uninteresting but simple. All she had to do was parrot what Professor Bigelow had said, but sweat crawled into her eyes. Kansas City boiled. What did she hate about her boardinghouse?

1. The bathroom at the end of the hall, which seemed always to be occupied.

2. Her cramped sleeping room, with a bed not long enough, so that her big feet poked into space.

3. Corn meal mush for breakfast, and chicken soup for dinner—but that chicken was only a rumor. And—

4. It was *hot*. Maybe it was the Missouri River and something the *Times* called "humidity," but Jericho Springs, two hundred miles distant, was never so warm. She moved her one chair near the window and propped her long legs on the sill in a most unladylike posture. She felt the suggestion of a breeze and read on. She dozed.

A hand squeezed her shoulder and she nearly fell off her chair. Yes, another thing—

5. She despised her landlady, whom you had to call Mrs. Jewison even though her husband seemed as absent as chicken from her soup. Mrs. Jewison was a voyeur. She barged into your room without knocking, hoping to discover you with a man or, only a little less evil, cooking your own food.

"There is a young man to see you," Mrs. Jewison said.

It had to be Abner. They hadn't spoken in three weeks, not since Abner had opined that she was a Negro and she set out to prove him right or wrong. She avoided him thereafter. Busy as she was, she hadn't thought of him. But something unresolved remained between them and now she felt guilt for her neglect.

She began combing her snarled hair and casting about for something unsoiled to wear. Mrs. Jewison still stood there, as if willing to supervise her conversation with lascivious Abner, and Kate frowned and advanced on the old woman, hovered above her, pushed her back with a frown.

"Miss Kreider, you know the rules of Carriage House. I have been liberal with you, but—"

Kate slammed the door behind her landlady and in moments hurried down the stairs, past her fellow boarders, Greta and Pauline and Myrtle in the tacky sitting room, talking about clothes and men and their own flawless virtues. They resented her attending school. They accused her of being rich. They were offended she wore pants.

Kate threw them a hard look and their heads snapped back

like snakes' heads. Oh, Jill and Sarah weren't such sourpusses and she smiled at them, but she felt in her soul that her life was changing. She didn't know what she'd do, but she couldn't remain here much longer.

Then she stood on the boardwalk, her petty resentments evaporating like the sweltering puddles on Main. Abner wore his best suit but a sling supported one arm, his nose was bandaged, and one side of his face, below a black eye, was cut and red and swollen. He looked toward the west: the prosperous heights of Quality Hill, the sprawl, the endless commerce of the Bottoms. She neared him with reverence, her heart overwhelmed with compassion, but her head filled with puzzlement. She placed a hand on his shoulder.

"We pretended, Kate," Abner said, not yet facing her. "We walked along in a cloud. But this place—" He swept his free arm over the city. "Is Hell."

She also stared west. The city had slowed at mid-day. You couldn't take a step without breaking into a sweat. "What happened, Abner?"

"Some would say, I got my just deserts." He turned to her now. In his eyes a war raged between defiance and shame. "I was . . . discovered somewhere I shouldn't go."

"They beat you awfully. Did you inform the police?"

"No! Not them!"

"But Abner, if you were attacked—"

"I *can't*." He looked up at her in agony. He wiped his face and droplets of sweat popped back immediately.

"Were you robbed? The police are there to help, Abner."

He dropped his eyes and mumbled. "Homosexual," she made out.

Homosexual, she guessed, referred to something shameful, but what concerned her was that Abner was hurt. She wanted to fix things. She felt as though she were picking at a scab but plunged forward. "I don't understand."

"Sodomite!" His face wrenched with anger. "Do you know *that* word, Country Girl?"

She stood stunned. Yes, she knew the word from the Bible.

"I'm going home, Kate."

"This moment? Let's . . . get out of the heat. Talk."

"I came because you were my friend."

Now she saw his luggage: one expensive-looking leather bag. "What about school?"

"Professor Bigelow—Dr. Spalding—they were quite decent about it." He patted his coat pocket. "I have my certificate. Third time's the charm."

"Philadelphia sounds grand. Maybe I'll visit you someday."

"I would like that."

"You were my rescuer," she said, realizing now that she'd rescued him as well. "I am sorry . . . for what happened." His beating was so severe, so vengeful, it must not have been for money. She couldn't imagine Abner doing anything to offend, unless his existence offended. *Something wrong with us both*, he'd said. Men knew what instinctively but she didn't. "All people are not—"

He shook his head. "I saw your drawings, Kate. You are talented. Weren't you afraid to go among the Negroes?"

"Should I have been?"

"I would be." He wiped his face again. She remembered his skin as reddish-white but now it was ashen. "I'm afraid of everything."

"It took courage for you to come all the way from Philadelphia to Mr. Spalding's school. To try again, Abner. Abner, you succeeded."

He picked up his leather bag and stared off vacantly. Kate tried to embrace him but he pulled away and she understood that to touch him, to mother him, violated whatever dignity he clung to. She stood not knowing where to put her hands.

Now she remembered her encounter with that fearsome word, "sodomite," in the Old Testament book of Kings. She asked what it meant in Sunday School class, led by her cousin, Frieda Hausen. Frieda, who also taught German at the school, blushed and murmured, *Sodomie*. But Frieda didn't know, other than it was some kind of wicked act that men performed on each other. Afterwards, they turned into abominations.

Looking at her damaged friend, Kate fought back revulsion. She was confused. She couldn't keep her voice from sounding artificial: "What will you do?"

"Father will place me in some little office down by the Schuylkill, and I will tally figures forever." Abner struggled with a smile. "But I will make a living from gainful employment. I will have my own private rooms."

They should have had dinner together, gone to a last play, but even coming to see her must have taxed him. He walked slowly down the boardwalk, his torso tilted forward from the hips like an arthritic person. Evil men hurt him, she thought, and wanted to carry his bag to the Union Depot, and look out for him on the train, and hold his hand until he found his place in Philadelphia.

So many in the world had no defense against it.

She fought off grief and hatred welled. She felt forlorn. She wanted to bury her head in Johnny's chest. But in her confusion, she felt a spike of clarity. Abner's plight filled her with sorrow, she'd be his friend forever if he'd let her, but something about him had always made her long for Johnny. She let her tears flow, even though the boarding house girls would see them as evidence of a jilting and want to know every sordid detail.

"KANSAS," JOHNNY HEART SAID, the day before she left Jericho Springs. "It means, 'a good place to grow potatoes.' But I think this city you go to has nothing to do with potatoes. I think it is a dangerous place for a woman from the Mennonite tribe."

"A *big* city, Johnny." Kate smiled. "Everything is there!"

"I went to the office of Mr. Giles Cabot, and studied his maps, and read his newspapers. This city is not for you, Kate. I wish that I could accompany you and protect you." He paused. The crowfeet around his eyes danced and his voice lifted an octave. "All the winter I will long for you."

Three days after her father's murder was the wrong time for Johnny, twelve years older, an Osage, to declare himself. She envisioned herself flying over the little town, a free spirit who never had to make decisions. A long moment passed and Johnny said no more, but she knew she hadn't imagined his words.

"One day, Johnny," she whispered. "Spring will come."

Without expression, Johnny handed her a "muff pistol," a two-barreled Remington derringer that she could hide in a bag or even a waist pocket. He insisted she learn to fire it, and they practiced shooting at whiskey bottles until, after a dozen rounds, from fifteen feet, Kate shattered one.

She'd been a perfect fool, wandering in the lowest realms of this violent city with only high ideals to protect her. Evil rose up and nearly killed poor Abner. Maybe *he* should have carried a pistol, but anyhow Kate had absorbed Johnny's lesson. She took the derringer everywhere. She clutched it inside her shirt whenever she passed Hell's Half Acre.

"Thank you, Johnny, dearest friend," she murmured, but thought, It is a terrible thing to arm yourself.

She had her work. That was the Mennonite way, wasn't it? When you doubted, when you stumbled and fell, then you rose, thanked God for the breath of life, and went to work. *Das Leben ist Arbeit.*

She bought Josephine, the mute, blue-eyed young woman in pigtails, a pretty dress and shoes. She set up a large canvas on an easel and posed her model by the river, but she couldn't summon the breezy confidence that had infused her sketches. Kate couldn't frame the painting convincingly. Was it the big space? Maybe, as Professor Taureau said, she wasn't ready.

She didn't know the girl. There lay the problem. "Where are you from, Jo?"

The girl answered with difficulty. "Sawanny."

"'Way down upon the Sewanee River?' Georgia? Florida?"
Jo didn't seem to comprehend and Kate consulted Nancy.
Nancy shrugged. "She jest on der boat, New 'Leans, St. Looey.
Slow."

"The boat was slow?"

Nancy pointed to her head.

"Oh." Now it seemed as though putting the girl in the pretty
dress, with the great river behind her, was wrong. What next?
Give her a pink parasol? Kate told her to change into her everyday clothes—an oversized gray shirt, a floppy hat, and a faded
skirt. The work clothes, discarded by white people, weren't right,
either.

It was those evocative blue eyes. Intelligence seemed about to
leap from them but never did. A white man had crossed into Jo's
ancestry somewhere; that's all those eyes meant. Kate's unknown
mother defined her but she didn't know how to explain this
to Jo, that they held something in common. The girl seemed
empty all the way down.

She put Jo in the dress again and pointed to a bluff that hung
above the confluence of the rivers. "We'll go up there."

Jo took a step toward her boiling cauldron and the piles of
bloody clothing from the Armour plant.

"I'll give you five dollars," Kate said.

Jo's blue eyes glinted. She was not so slow she didn't understand the power of five silver dollars. Possibly, the money was
sweeter because she did so little to earn it, or because the foolish white woman gave it, and Kate's heart sank because she
couldn't reach the girl any other way. Kate grabbed the easel
and Jo the box of paints and they climbed a steep, slippery path,
zigzagging below the crumbling bluffs stained black from wet-
weather springs.

They threaded through scrub oaks and found a grassy promontory. As far north as you could see, the brown river cut through
green parcels of farmland, all seeming to tilt upward into a gray
wall of clouds that shrouded the horizon. A storm brewed. She

posed Jo and sketched quickly, making mistakes she knew she could correct later. Painting was all about revision.

"We could go to a play, Jo," she said, but the girl simply stared. Some theaters would let them in but they'd have to sit in separate sections—unless Kate declared herself a Negro!

"I could teach you to read," she said, as much to herself as to Jo. All those charitable things Mennonites were enjoined to do: give to the poor, feed the hungry, tend the sick. She felt more and more sad. She couldn't help Abner. She couldn't help Jo. All she had, her only gift, was to draw.

Once again, the pose was wrong. The simple white dress contrasted with the black skin but seemed too billowy, even without undergarments. The shoes were too stylish. Kate had given Jo black gloves to hide her big, rough hands, but now Kate took the gloves away, the white woman's shoes, and pinned the skirt halfway up Jo's shins. The direct angle, highlighting the girl's pretty, imponderable face, didn't satisfy Kate, either. She turned the face at an angle, so that Jo looked off over the great valley, and the inchoate horizon, trembling with faraway storms. Then nature came to their aid.

Wind tore out of the north so that even Jo's stiff hair, freed of the ribbons the girl seemed so proud of, flew back. So did the white dress, bringing into relief the girl's figure and those daring ankles. The sky grew dark and Kate streaked black across dark blue to capture it, with the sun behind burning through a crack of cadmium red and yellow; her dark colors migrated to veridian for the bending tall trees, then brown and black and yellow for the swirling, white-capped river. She'd fill it all in later but she had to know her colors!

Kate gave Jo the gloves again, and the girl stood twisting them, holding her pose but then glancing toward Kate, her eyes not fearful, but mocking. Jabbing at the canvas, Kate caught one almost cobalt eye reflecting the black storm, and Jo's slight, playful, insouciant smile. The one thing Kate would never have thought possible in Mississippi Town: joy.

The rain overwhelmed them and they slid down the muddy path, with Kate holding her oilcloth cover gingerly so that it didn't brush against paint. Jo slipped ahead, lodging her bare feet against saplings, extending a hand to keep Kate from falling. They were sisters now. They ran across the rutted river trail to a clearing and what seemed to be a picnic shelter—two tables with a tin roof. The rain fell heavily as Kate read the hand-painted sign that commemorated the clearing as a Lewis and Clark campsite. She wanted to tell Jo about the great explorers but didn't know how.

SHE RETURNED TO MISSISSIPPI Town for several days, looking for Jo. She'd never encounter the same light again, but still she climbed the promontory for the perspectives of land and water and air. Her room drew plenty of sunlight, so much that she lowered the blinds to approximate a stormy day; she resented nightfall, when her one electric lamp, bright as it was, did not suffice. She worked six days and couldn't conjure another stroke. She knew she should put the painting aside, then resume work in a month or six months, but when the colors were fast she took the painting to Mr. Denby.

He seemed puzzled. He shook his head and thumbed through a stack of lithographs. He extracted one, mumbled something as he studied it, and Kate wanted to slap him. Finally, Denby turned the image toward her and caught her eyes.

"Oh," she said. "I didn't—"

The lithograph was of Eastman Johnson's *The Girl I Left Behind Me*. "You didn't know of this painting?"

"Oh, yes," she said. She stared at the woebegone girl, her hair like a flag in the wind. "I knew of it. I *love* Johnson's work. But I wasn't trying to—"

"It happens. These great images, they percolate in an artist's soul."

"I thought I was being so original. All I did was an imitation!"

"Nonsense," Denby said. "You made a sort of commentary, K. Kreider, and a reverent one. I think we can try for two hundred."

"But I—I just wanted you to see it, sir. It's not ready."

"Not at all the sort of thing you keep working on, Miss. You are not Eastman Johnson but you don't want to be! Never, never! Your painting is real. It's *raw*." Denby reached under the counter for his cigar box. "I can give you one hundred on account."

SHE VISITED MISSISSIPPI TOWN once more. No one could deny her successes: selling her sketches of ravaged faces, and then the painting. Especially the painting, and she wanted to tell Jo about it. Annelise would understand, and Johnny, but they were far away. With Abner gone, Jo was the closest she had to a friend. Success was hardly success if you were the only one who knew.

Kate planned to give her twenty dollars. She purchased a small, leather purse with turquoise Navajo beading to hold the treasure. "You've earned it, Jo," she'd say.

Jo wouldn't know what to do with such a fortune, but Kate would advise her. Clothes: she might even bring the girl to Bernheimer's. She imagined the girl's sparkling blue eyes, surrounded by the store's frilly dresses and hats. And practical things, of course. Food. Kitchen knives, plates, some cups.

A gun! Living where she did, how did the girl protect herself even from sober men?

No fire burned under Jo's wash pot. None had in several days, now that Kate thought about it. She found no cooking utensils, no furniture, not so much as a candle inside the shallow dugout the girl called home. The space was stale and disagreeable, like a cellar where a mouse died.

As always, Nancy sat in her kitchen chair by the Kaw, fishing. She seemed aware of Kate's presence even when Kate approached from behind. A hot wind blew down the water, and Kate stood, detached, wondering how she and Nancy could have intersected. "Nancy," she whispered. "Where is Jo?"

The old woman didn't turn her head. "She drownded."

"*Drownded?*"

"Jo one a dem gals in Hell Town."

"Drowned!" Kate knew nothing. True understanding was always down in the valley and over the hill. When at last you reached it, only regret remained. "A prostitute. That's what you mean. Someone . . . killed her?"

"S'all right, Kate." Nancy faced her at last, her black eyes glistening. "You good to 'er."

Kate clutched the leather purse, imagining the girl pointed into the wind, defiant as a mountain lion, and so innocent. "When?"

Nancy turned her head toward the water as if a catfish had struck. "Been a week o' mo'."

No one told her. That's how little she mattered here—but Jo hadn't mattered, either. What day she died held no importance when bodies washed up downriver every morning and were never named. Her silly plans! She resisted the temptation to throw her twenty pieces of silver into the mud, but what use was anger? Was she angry with Nancy? She placed the purse gently in the old woman's hand and kissed her bald head. "Buy food," she said. "Buy anything."

In the woods, she ran a distance, tripped, and tore open her trouser leg. A thorn raked down her thigh, but she welcomed the pain. It punished her for all she hadn't done for Jo and for Abner. Like a good Mennonite, she'd visited with suffering, but never thought, there but for the grace of God go I. Not overconfident me, she thought. I want to *paint* suffering. I'm a voyeur like Mrs. Jewison.

No. I didn't beat Abner. I wasn't so depraved as men who would lie with simple Jo. God help me, perhaps I'm shallow, but I meant well.

Kate sat with her back against an oak and grew conscious of a troop of finches, flying from limb to limb through the brush, their leader calling out to the others with each new perch. A squirrel dropped to the earth for some small prize, then scurried for the safety of the next tree. She heard a whoosh as a chicken hawk dove, barely missing the squirrel. She thought of her beautiful stallion, King Arthur, and wished she were astride him. Together, they could outrun evil.

She pressed a handkerchief to the cut until the bleeding stopped. I'll live, she thought. I'll be a great painter. I'll stop thinking so much of myself and I'll be a better woman.

Calm now, she walked past Hell's Half-Acre. Behind the saloons, pigs and dogs guarded their territories in the garbage. The pigs looked fat but she could see the ribs of the dogs. A big brown mongrel chased after a piglet until two sows mounted a defense. The mongrel bared its teeth and growled, then ran away, tail dragging.

She couldn't help but think of Jo, lying there in the garbage until some guttersnipe threw her into the Missouri. Or maybe she staggered out into the night, drunk, and fell off the dock. A nigger girl who couldn't talk. No sheriff's investigation, no preacher's sermon, no obituary. No grieving relatives to put her in a proper dress, bury her, and erect a stone.

She aimed Johnny's derringer toward the saloon, cocked the hammer, but of course she didn't fire. A rifle was a tool, but what good did a pistol ever do? Then she remembered the day Eddie Mole shot Barney Kreider down and a cruel answer came to her. She cried for Jo but also for her father, the whiskey drummer. His murder sent her to the city and gave her a career. Who could make sense of it?

THE ART WORLD WAS filled with abominations. Kate drew her conclusion because of how Mr. Denby behaved around patrons: fussy, lecturing, with well-to-do women, and fawning toward men. Certain men. Almost hostile toward others—who, she observed, were hostile toward Denby. Hostile enough to beat him and leave him for dead in an alley.

Denby would do anything for her. She wanted his recommen-

dation to the *Times*, where on June 15 a position would open
for a commercial artist. She thought she could make a living
drawing furniture and steam threshers for the classifieds. Professor Bigelow, who sometimes wrote for the business pages,
would also recommend her. She'd scored high with her finals
and certainly he liked her—maybe too much. A fiction about
her betrothed, due any day in the city, slipped into her dis-
tracted mind. She'd need to work until they could begin their
married life—

She laughed. She'd never been burdened with a surplus of
suitors. Maybe she should encourage Bigelow.

Should she leave Kansas City? She didn't feel safe anymore.
She could move to Newton, keep books for a department store,
and nibble at classes at the tiny Mennonite college. She'd be near
enough to her family to take the train home on Saturdays but
still could claim her independence. She'd be near Johnny, pre-
suming he wanted to be near *her*. She'd written him twice, filling
up pages with colorful accounts of her life in the big city, and he
hadn't answered. Yes, he spent winters on the reservation and
wasn't much of a writer, but his silence had grown unbearable.

She gathered painting materials and walked into the Northeast, where new streets and rows of fine houses stretched out
along Independence Avenue. Magnificent oaks and walnuts
were felled at alarming rates, according to the *Times*, displac-
ing Irish and Italian squatters. Following the trails, she passed
quarters to beggars: Greeks, Serbs, and one leering Italian who
took her quarter and trailed her for a distance, calling *"bella
donna"* and *"bella donna di colore."* Venturesome territory for a
woman, but she needed to work and she carried her derringer.

She followed Cliff Drive until the woods closed overhead,
and the way grew so narrow a wagon would have difficulty getting through. The only sound came from two eagles, startled
from their carrion deer. They tumbled out high in the air, then
hung on thermals above the Missouri River, lighting in the tall
cottonwoods on the northern shore. Kate climbed the steep

hillside and erected her easel on a limestone shelf with a clear view. She sat on a carpet of juniper-colored moss, laid out her brushes, and raised a pencil. She waited for her imagination to summon the river from the days when the Osage and Sioux traveled it. Subtract, subtract, she thought, but couldn't concentrate. Again she reasoned through a future in Kansas City, and an alternative in Newton. Neither excited her. She wondered where her mother was buried. Nowhere, the same as poor Jo.

Time drifted, clouds gathered, and the light quivered enticingly, but through her reverie she began to study the far shore, staring until details emerged, details most never saw. Kate saw not merely a blur of green, but sap green, forest green, seagreen. She saw willows with twisted trunks near the water, and blue herons and black-and-white kingfishers peering down through the opposed, symmetrical leaves. She saw young cottonwoods all at the same height, meaning that whatever grew before had died in a flood; brown-and-tan sycamores towered over them. Far below, a red fox poked her nose out of the grass, her kits tumbling after, no bigger than rabbits. "Watch out for those eagles," she murmured.

She heard a thrashing in the brush and her easy thoughts turned hard. It must be that rude Italian. She slipped away from the easel and cocked the derringer. She would *not* be a victim like Abner or Jo. She was *not* defenseless and had no fear even of taking a life. "I hear you, sir! Identify yourself!"

The thrashing continued, punctuated by sighs. Aiming downhill, meaning only to frighten her assailant, she fired. Now she lowered the pistol and waited. She made out a dark patch, a pattern of sleek black crisscrossed by green. She aimed left for the heart, and low because the intruder stood downhill. She fired.

"Katherine! That popgun is not for me!"

She fell back on the thick, cool moss, and looked up in wonder. He'd cut his hair white-man short, big city short, and held his Stetson in one hand. She'd forgotten how tall he was. He wore a black suit with a string tie and mother-of-pearl clasp. She felt something disintegrating inside. She felt warm.

Absurdly, he knelt. He didn't speak. She'd always carried their conversations, chattering enough for both of them—and a church committee, too. Now she had no words.

"I brought five horses to Helmut Kreider," Johnny said at last. "From Arkansas City, a long journey. I have money, Kate. Many tasks await us."

She laughed. "What did Uncle Helmut say?"

"He said, 'Those are fine horses.'"

"And Annelise?"

"She shed many tears. She said, 'Bring her home, Johnny.'"

He placed a small, home-made, black walnut box on the moss. Yes, yes, but she felt rushed. What had all their years of friendship meant, except that they belonged together? But there were problems, barriers. "Johnny—"

"This is what white men do when they seek a wife. I am Osage, I do not care about white men, but I want you to be my wife and we will live partly in the white world."

Kate heard herself saying the words: "Are we legal?"

"I went to the office of Mr. Giles Cabot and read from his books. We are not legal in this city. We are legal in Kansas. In Oklahoma, they have no law."

She opened the little box and stared at the ring. She had expected gold or silver but the ring was wooden. Not a random wood but Osage Orange, a deep red with brown striations, polished and smooth. She knew he'd made it. "Such a hard wood. How could you work with it?"

Johnny smiled. "Many hours by the fire. Many attempts that *became* fire."

"It's perfect," she said, looking up into his calm eyes. "But it is not so simple, my love."

She reached out to touch him, but he drew back, staring, his eyes stormy. She blundered ahead: "Some people think, they look at me, Johnny, they say one drop of blood is everything. They say I am a . . . Negress. Would you—do you . . . ?"

Johnny laughed. He laughed as she'd never heard him, almost bitterly. His laughter cascaded over the great river and the fox lifted her head. "I don't care, Kate," he said. "But listen to me. You are not a Negress."

"Ah," she said, and threw her arms around his neck.

"You are Osage."

IV

14

The Company

In the merry, merry month of May, Ammon Krughoff, the Mennonite banker, said no.

Euly was astounded. His concrete hopes, his future with Jenny, depended on a loan. His scheme to sell hardware to settlers making the land run seemed flawless. All it required was money and endless hard work, and Brother Krughoff knew that Euly was capable of the latter.

"You told me—Sir, I've been relying on this—that my farm could serve as security."

"I believe I said, 'for a worthy proposition.' Machinery. A new well, or seed corn. Even your new building, which I gather you've financed yourself. But five thousand dollars, young man, is ten years of work for your average fellow. Your farm isn't worth even a thousand."

"How much could you loan?"

"Nothing, Ulysses. It's too risky. Your proposition would not improve the economy and well-being of Jericho Springs. You would go among the Englische, where swindlers and bad men stand around every corner." Krughoff stroked his snow-white beard. "Your father—"

"My father!"

The banker raised a hand. "I say nothing against Barney Kreider. I never did. But he was involved in questionable endeavors, and tragic as it was, his death—"

"Like father, like son?" Euly jumped to his feet—but checked himself. He heard the banker calling after him, but if he lingered he'd have nothing to offer but anger. Like the prudent businessman he aspired to be, he calmed himself by the time he reached the street. Maybe one day a tornado would pass and he'd require the old banker's help to rebuild his barn.

"GO TO YOUR UNCLE," Jenny said.

She ran their fledgling hardware in the afternoons, doing a steady business in fencing materials, hats and gloves, and canned goods. She ordered staples and nails from the manufacturer in Boston and they undercut prices in town. Euly hauled oak lumber from the sawmill in Wichita, marking up his costs 20 percent while still coming in under Giles Cabot. He priced tobacco high, because men didn't want to drive another ten miles to find it cheaper. Tobacco, like whiskey, was something they couldn't do without.

Some evenings, if a flurry of customers arrived late, Jenny didn't go home. Euly slept in the barn and joined her for breakfast before leaving on his freight runs. One morning he came in early and surprised her at the sink, naked to the waist. She drew a towel over her breasts but slowly, sleepily, and they fell onto the bed. At last he pulled back, Jenny grasping at him angrily. He left the farm dazed and it was fortunate Gerty and Maude knew the way to Newton, because he didn't.

"He never loans money," Euly said.

"You been plantin' his crops. You're blood kin, Euly, almost like a son. Everyone knows how stingy he is, but they say he's got money stuffed everywhere. Get your aunt to work on him."

Euly nodded. "Even Uncle Helmut doesn't have five thousand dollars. Not in ready cash."

"You might be surprised what he has." Jenny kissed him. "Or the influence he can wield on Banker Krughoff."

On Saturday Jenny left for her parents' farm twelve miles away. He didn't want her to go but she had to deliver the small wage Euly paid her to keep up pretenses. Well, the kids were about to be married. Even if they weren't, Henry and Cecilia wanted the money.

"You could be a fancy lady for all they care," he said. He meant to make a joke and flirt with Jenny, too. Then again, he disliked his future in-laws and worried how he'd deal with them.

"I almost *am* a fancy lady," Jenny said, leaning down from the saddle, caressing his cheek. "The way you treat me."

"We have to get ahead," he said, not quite understanding. They'd discussed this. Didn't she want a church wedding? "We are going to be respectable. And *rich*, Jenny."

"Rich will do," she said. "Why don't we set the day?"

Why don't we, he thought, as he drove the wagon through Jericho Springs and up the long hill to his uncle's farm, carrying six lengths of galvanized stovepipe that Annelise had ordered for the school. Cabot didn't deliver, much less install, but Euly knew she'd thrown business his way more than once. He was so much in her debt already, and Uncle Helmut's, and now he needed five thousand dollars.

I want us to marry in triumph, Jenny, in the church as respected young Mennonites.

His proposition was sound and would set them up for a prosperous life. Nonetheless, five thousand was a fantastic sum, when he could raise not quite five hundred, and Jenny nothing at all. He had to make someone see the world through his eyes, and it wasn't as though he was a celebrated citizen with proven business acumen. Maybe in Newton he could take out a mortgage, say, for another five hundred. That made a thousand, but it took a long time to save money out of his freight runs and he had no apple crop this year. Even running whiskey wouldn't raise money fast enough.

Annelise stood in the driveway as if expecting him. She wore her Sunday clothes except for her new, brown, almost flamboyant bonnet. She untied it, ran her fingers through her hair, and pulled it on again. Something was wrong.

"I was about to throw a saddle on old Jerry," she said. "It's those infernal sheep!"

Strong language coming from Annelise and Euly smiled in sympathy. The sheep were a scandal. Henry Muenster had begged a load of hay from Helmut but Helmut wasn't much for charity. Henry promised quick payment and he did pay, leaving off two barren ewes while Helmut was down by the creek, planting potatoes. Helmut kept pigs and pastured cattle but he despised sheep, if only for their helplessness. It was spring and he was too busy to take the sheep to auction, not that the two together would fetch five dollars. "Another trick from Henry Muenster," he said. "*Ich schieße ihn!*"

He'd shoot him. No, but Helmut grew more irritable every year. He'd discharged his twelve-gauge over the head of more than one tinker and salesman.

Bandanna over his nose, Helmut sheared the ewes, then took them to an old sod-roofed cowshed on a rocky piece of ground he'd never tried to farm. A little spring provided water; he staked the sheep in new grass every several days. They munched their way through their halcyon days and knew enough to return to the shed at night. Toward fall, when he took a pig or two to auction, Helmut would load up those ewes as well.

"Ulysses, he's very late," Annelise said, and she didn't need to add that Helmut was ordinarily as punctual as a German clock. "We're going to town for dinner. It's our anniversary."

Their fortieth, which explained the new bonnet. Euly was ashamed he'd forgotten to buy them anything. "I'm sure he's fine," Euly said, and turned the horses without quite stopping. "I'll find him, Annelise."

The light had begun to fail and he cracked the reins to urge some speed from Gerty and Maude. They would never make racehorses but seemed to sense he meant business. They broke into a heavy trot down the grassy lane between wheat that grew lush and green despite the dry spring, and the milo Euly had planted, already beginning to head. "Whoa, girls," he called after something short of a mile, and turned off the lane onto the low, rocky hill where Helmut seemed most likely to be. The horses plodded up the grade, surefooted despite the loose rocks, as the sun dropped to the west, its long, fiery fingers gripping the dark woods.

He set the brake and crept up on the shed. He didn't hear whippoorwills or owls and his skin prickled with apprehension. "Onkel Helmut! Helmut Kreider!"

No answer. From the ridge above, with its outcropping of cedars and oaks, a crow in silhouette answered his call, and then, awakened from their sleep, an irritable chorus rose and fell. Euly glanced over the shed in the waning light. A half-roof, covered over with morning glories and sunflowers shooting up, sheltered loose hay, a block of salt, and grain in a lidded barrel. To the right stood the split-rail fence and the open gate to the pen. He made out a hand in the dirt by the gate and leaped forward.

Helmut lay face down, his hand outstretched. His face seemed wrong, as if an imposter lay in his clothes, but then Euly understood that the face was swollen, or perhaps covered with mud. He knelt. "Onkel," he whispered, and shook Helmut. He lifted his uncle's muddy hand and thought he felt a pulse.

The breeze carried a metallic, acrid smell; Euly recalled butchering day and lifted his head. He made out dark spots on white, the blood-streaked carcasses of the two dead sheep, and yellow-green eyes hovering above them. Those eyes caught the sun's dying rays and glowed red. Euly shivered, as if in the presence of a demon.

He half-stood, trying to identify the dark shape behind the eyes. He wanted to fit the image into that of a wolf but it wasn't a wolf. He licked his lips. Blood thumped at his temples. It was a mountain lion.

Most days, he carried the Marlin, but he'd killed a groundhog yesterday as it feasted on peas, and the rifle lay on his kitchen table to be cleaned and oiled. He remembered a pitchfork in the feed bin but feared that if he moved, the beast would spring.

Near Helmut's hand he made out a shovel, which apparently Helmut had tried to use. He reached for it without taking his eyes from the cat, and with the other hand turned Helmut on his back, gasping when his fingers dragged over the sticky blood. Again, he thought he felt a pulse. Holding the shovel so that he could quickly turn with it, he reached for his uncle's collar, and pulled him several inches through the gate. Then the mountain lion coughed and bent its long body low like a horse stretches. Down the grade, Maude and Gerty snorted in alarm, and then the lion sprang.

Euly swung the shovel at the animal's head, deflecting it, but the lion's thick paw hit his head like a nine-pound hammer and its claws pierced his heavy shirt as they raked downward. The cat twisted in the dim air, a massive, gray thing, yowling like a barn tom. Euly staggered back, braced, and lifted the shovel again. His head didn't feel right. Let out all the air, he thought, trying to make a joke to himself. The cat screamed so shrilly it was like a blow to his ears. Euly licked his lips and swallowed. Blood ran from under his hair but he couldn't attend to it. This time when the cat leapt, Euly stepped back simultaneously, swinging the shovel like a baseball bat, aiming for the animal's head with the blade edge. He heard teeth crunch, but still the cat reached Euly with its claws, raking down his thighs, stabbing his knee. He cried out. He knew he was hurt.

He braced for another leap but the cat streaked for the fence, screeching in what seemed like betrayal. With its long body poised on the top rail, it hissed and looked back, but through only one red eye slitted with a dark pupil.

"You had enough?" Euly screamed. "You had enough?"

His bravado lasted only an instant. He fought for breath, a heavy, desperate sound on the quieted hill. He drew out his bandanna and wrapped it around his head. He sweated in the cold air and shook with chill. He was fading and knew he must hurry.

He dragged Helmut through the gate with strength he didn't know he had and loaded the limp body onto the wagon, crying now because he couldn't tell, with all the dragging and pushing and bumping, how much damage he did to Helmut. "Onkel," he whispered. "Onkel."

He pulled himself up to the wagon seat, almost losing his balance. One leg couldn't take his weight, he felt a bone give, and he nearly blacked out. He discovered he'd turned the wagon around and found the crop lane again. He snapped the reins and Maude and Gerty stepped out in their awkward trot.

"I love you," he murmured, and he might have meant his horses, Helmut, Jenny, or the starry night. He thought wolves ran alongside the wagon, dark, fluid shapes that made no sound, but every wolf had been killed. He slumped backward on the seat and lost the reins.

HE SAID STARTLING THINGS about sheep and what Henry Muenster did with them. He raved about Jenny's beautiful breasts and how one time he'd come upon Johnny and Kate, swimming naked in Zimmerman's Creek. Confusingly, Johnny and Kate were *there*. Two brown people, his friend, his wonderful sister, and he tried to speak to them, but they blurred. Maybe that was all right, because indeed they were one. "I'm Osage," Kate said. "Did you know? Did everyone know?"

He blacked out.

"We need to form a company," Kate went on, or maybe she was Jenny. "Pool our resources. That's what they did for the run in '89. I have eight hundred, Father's money. Euly! Can you hear me?"

"I have a thousand dollars," Johnny said, bending near, holding a pouch. He'd cut his hair. "I dug comfrey root, Little Hero. I will make tea for your scrambled brain."

"I just have me," Jenny said, leaning down from the misty heavens, kissing his forehead.

"*She* thought of it," Kate said, jerking a thumb. "Brother, you're the president." She left with Johnny through the door, melting into the shimmering sunlight. Jenny held a cold compress to his addled head and washed his face. She turned him on his side, the one that didn't hurt so much, and rubbed him with something that smelled like horse radish and stung his skin. She threw away the stinking bandage and bound his head again, then slipped under the hot blankets and held him close. "Poor Euly," she said. "Poor, brave Euly."

"I am not brave," he said, though indeed he had dreamed he was a hero of old, sailing the raging seas with his fearful men at the oars, while he fought off one-eyed monsters and faithful Penelope rejected a kingdom full of suitors.

The funeral drew buggies from all the county. The Englische came, including Giles Cabot, and that could only mean someone important had died, and then he realized that it was his Uncle Helmut. I should be there, Euly thought, and willed his body to rise, but fell asleep.

Cabot stood in the doorway with his aunt. Euly heard her promise a thousand dollars to "The Company," whatever that was. Did the Englische hold a lien on the farm? He had to protect Annelise and dropped his good leg to the floor. Cabot turned away with a crooked smile, laughing. Then Annelise drew near, her face long and lined and ancient.

"Sleep," his aunt said. "It's over and you're going to Oklahoma on your great adventure."

"Uncle Helmut—"

"Is with Jesus. We didn't think we should move you to the church."

"He was hurt so bad and I couldn't—"

"You were very brave, Ulysses. I'm proud of you."

Then there were heavy boots on the porch and voices arguing over twenty-five dollars. "Make a nice rug," one voice said, and Euly almost knew who it was. "Please. Go away!" Annelise said, and Euly could hear the tears in her voice, the door slamming. In moments, Jenny's brothers, Will and Milton, stood outside the long window where Euly lay studying the brown schoolhouse, the white church, like a painting. The brothers held high a yellowish rag. No, it was the mountain lion. Euly tried to turn his head but felt too weak.

"You in there, Euly? Thought you'd wanna see what we done for you."

The brothers pushed the lion's head into the frame of the window, and Euly groaned, but the lion was a dead thing.

"Will shot him," Milton said. "Shore done *you* a service."

"He weren't nothing to track," said Will. "Bad hurt like he was. He wanted to fight some, once we cornered him. Reckon we done the whole county a favor."

"Ain't that worth a little something, Euly? Hell, ten dollars, what's that to a rich fella like yourself? We used up most of a day when we shoulda been plantin' corn."

Euly fell asleep even as the brothers boasted. He slept for hours, a day perhaps, and woke to the moon in his face. He didn't move for a long time, staring at the open space where the lion's head had appeared, wondering if he'd dreamed the episode like everything else.

He pulled his arm free. Reddish scars streaked up his wrist where the cat clawed him, but his arm was whole. He opened and clenched his fist.

He tore the bandage from his head. His neck had scabbed where the cat tried to find his jugular but he was all right. He could think without drifting off. He could plan. Could he walk?

He hopped to the crutches leaning against the window and swung out for several steps, but then fell across the bed and slept again. He dreamed that Jenny lay beside him, that his strong hand clutched her to him under her thin nightgown. He pulled his hand away. He wasn't dreaming.

"Sweetheart," she murmured. "Go ahead. What does it matter?"

"I'm not . . . well," he said, though he seemed to be.

"Pastor McAfee could marry us tomorrow. That's almost a church wedding, don't you think? Wouldn't that be 'respectable?'"

"You don't understand. We go to Caldwell, we come back in triumph, all the congregation turns out for the wedding—"

"I think you are very stubborn, sweetheart. Where would we sleep in Caldwell?"

"I'll find a place. I'll go down next week on the train."

"Don't you see, Euly? I can't . . . *be* with you, an unmarried woman—"

"You'll stay with Kate."

"I don't want to stay with your sister. I don't *like* your sister."

He sighed. Kate didn't like Jenny, either. "Anyhow, you'll be safe. Your honor, Jenny. Not a question! You must know that I would never—"

Jenny slipped from the bed. "I know," she said.

EULY ROSE BEFORE DAWN and wheeled into the kitchen to shake out the ashes and rekindle the fire. He made coffee and toasted bread, then sat on the porch as the sky brightened, his broken leg resting on a coal scuttle. He remembered swallowing spoonfuls of laudanum, Annelise and Kate holding him down, and old Doc Hortz miles away, cupping Euly's bare foot in his big hands. The doctor grinned, told some story about the war, and yanked hard.

Swirls of fog curved off to the south, following the creek, and now the chickenhouse came to life with the rooster crowing, the hens moaning and squawking. Down in the pasture, he made out Johnny, working with the horses he'd brought to Helmut for a bride-price. He wondered if those pretty horses were headed back to the reservation, along with Kate and her soon-to-be husband.

This is such a beautiful farm, he thought. Helmut kept it neat, and tolerated no inefficiency. He remembered his father, the last son, squeezed out of any inheritance except for the butt of rocky land that would only grow fruit trees. Now his only son would inherit the best farm in the county. Only twenty-one and he'd be rich. People would look up to him, the whiskey peddler's boy.

A buggy rolled up the road from Jericho Springs, raising dust. It had rained the day of Helmut's death but turned dry again. The wheat is almost ripe, Euly thought. The milo will hold through drought.

The last person Euly expected to see stepped down from the buggy, but Euly had fought off a mountain lion and was full of confidence now. So he smiled at Giles Cabot, and said. "A little early for breakfast, sir. But there's coffee on the stove."

"I apologize for the hour. I'm taking the train to Kansas City at 7:20 and wanted to talk to you before I left."

Euly added two sticks of oak to the fire, put bacon on to fry, cracked six eggs, and then the two men sat at the kitchen table. Kate breezed past, squeezing his shoulder, smiling, and Euly watched through the window as Johnny brought up King Arthur and Soquili, and the lovers trotted off toward the creek.

"I look at those two," Cabot said. "And wonder why I never married."

Euly cleared his throat. He tried to think of how a man of the world should reply to such a remark. "You never found the right girl."

"Perhaps." Cabot shook off his pensiveness. "Ulysses, I know a number of suppliers in Kansas City. I can vouch for you, explain the situation, ensure that they expedite your orders coming in from Caldwell."

Euly was not surprised. Annelise, perhaps Kate, had been at work. "That's kind of you, Mr. Cabot."

"Giles, if you like. Your aunt tells me you have raised around twenty-five hundred."

Euly shoveled the bacon and scrambled eggs onto two plates. "*They* have. I've been sleeping for three weeks."

Cabot seemed taken aback by so hearty a breakfast, but buttered a piece of bread and began eating. "We all know what you did, Ulysses. Trying to save poor Helmut. Very brave."

Euly shrugged. "You do what you have to do."

"Precisely. I want to join your company. I will put up the other twenty-five hundred."

Euly looked out the window again. The sun had risen over the treeline and lit up the dew on the church's roof. "I don't know what to say, Giles."

"Are you still thinking of your apples? That was long ago and I gave you a fair price."

"In Newton—"

"Enterprisingly, you took the remainder of your crop to Newton, where you received a better price. I gave you a fair price for Jericho Springs, where I am the only buyer." Cabot smiled. "Ulysses, you are the hardest-working young man I've ever seen. You're clever. But there is a phrase you need to learn."

"And what is that, sir?"

"'It's just business.'"

Euly laughed. "Yes, sir."

Cabot thrust a hand across the table. "Do we have a deal?"

"We do, Giles."

"I'll put it in writing. Five thousand dollars is a trainload of inventory. You'll need somewhere safe to store it."

"Yes, sir. I'm headed down there tomorrow."

"And find yourself an accountant. Someone to keep track of the merchandise, the expenditures, the profits."

Jenny was good with figures. "Yes, sir. About those profits."

"I don't expect half, with you doing most of the work. My contribution is a loan. Five percent, due by the end of the year."

Per annum, Giles would make ten percent. "Twenty-six hundred twenty-five dollars."

"If you agree." Cabot rose. "It's not an excessive profit, given the risk involved. I'm not being kind, you understand. I'm not being magnanimous."

"That's clear enough," Euly said, standing, gingerly putting weight on the cast, shaking hands again. "It's just business."

15

Caldwell

He couldn't sit a horse. So Euly rented a buckboard and drove a quarter mile north of Caldwell, where he found the sprawling barn he'd spied coming in on the train. It might once have been a symmetrical building, given that small, neat cupola, but lean-to after lean-to had been added, and sided with lard cans and scrap Santa Fe signage, so that it was hard to tell tool sheds from stables. Inside, maybe everything connected.

At last, Euly located a stovepipe and stepped down to knock on the door. He heard a quick scurrying. He reached to knock again but his hand dropped through air as the door opened, and he stared into a shotgun. Behind the shotgun stood an old woman not five feet tall.

"Ma'am," he said, stepping back a little.

The woman stared at his bare toes, pointing out of his cast. "What kinda religion is you?"

"Mennonite," Euly said, tipping his straw hat. He sensed she'd never heard the word and added, "We're like the Quakers."

"Peacebul?" She lowered the shotgun. "We'se gettin' along fine, good Baptists livin' heah doin' the Lawd's work, livin' overcomin' lives, only them Advents—"

"Adventists?"

"The preacher, Reverend Mister Daniel Walls, he claimed the Rapture was come and the fateful had all to go to Colorada."

Euly smiled. "That's what they said back in the Forties. They sold their worldly goods and gathered on a mountaintop, but Jesus never came."

"I git up one mornin', they left me with nary a word. Didn't pay their rent nor fer all the meals I cooked. I don't need no Bible lessons, Mister."

Euly nodded. Dressed in black, he supposed he looked like a preacher. Might be a useful sales technique.

"Now, I got a liddle bit a coffee left, mixed it with pig nuts."

She meant those bitter little hickory nuts. Back in the seventies the Mennonites had stretched their coffee, too, with chicory or even sumac. "Coffee would be fine. Who can say about the Rapture, Ma'am? There's no way to prepare for it except to live a virtuous and humble life."

"Humble," the woman said. "Amen."

"Where you from, Ma'am?"

"Cabool."

"Where might that be?"

"Down in the holler, fer certain. They call it the Ozarks."

"Name's Ulysses Kreider."

"Evangeline Mott."

"My mother was an Evangeline. In Latin, it means good news." He stared at the old woman. "Like what our dear Savior brought."

Euly took a chair by a table made of planks.

Evangeline stepped back. "Y'all hurt your foot, Ulysses."

"It's nothing much." Euly shrugged. "Evangeline, there's a big land run coming, down into the Territory, this September. Maybe ten thousand people will arrive."

"Rapture right heah!"

"I'm a hardware man. I want to sell these people my goods. I'd like to rent your barn for storage."

"What y'all pay, Mistah?"

Evangeline slid a cup of coffee before him and Euly took a sip. "Fifty dollars."

"For the summer?" Fifty was fair, and acting for the company, he couldn't throw money around, but how did the old woman even feed herself? "Oh, no," he said. "For a fine, commercial property like this? Fifty a month."

She'd made a good deal but Evangeline didn't gloat. She smiled. "You look around, Ulysses. Make yourself a plan. I got chicken broth and taters!"

"Mighty nice of you, Evangeline."

"You the nice one, keepin' an ole lady compny."

Out back, three acres of blue stem crowded a small pond. And there was a well: he primed the pump and water came up quickly. Good water. He pulled back a board and dropped a pebble: a pool maybe twenty feet down. A dull roar indicated an underground flow. Some dug wells west of Jericho Springs had already gone dry. This one wouldn't.

Euly ducked into the dim compartments of the barn, banging his cast against tools and piles of lumber until he found a broad implement door that he rolled open. No sign the roof leaked. Cavernous storage with plank floors, and stalls that would make bedrooms. He'd invest five dollars for a box stove.

He smelled potatoes frying. He'd never known his mother but hoped she'd be pleased he'd treated her namesake fairly. He turned his father's railroad watch toward a spike of daylight that leaked through the siding. Much work to do.

KIND WORDS, HARSH ONES, had no effect on his rented horse, a listless chestnut gelding with whip-welts along its rump. Euly took off his vest in the still air, and wished he'd worn a short-sleeved shirt. He jostled over the fairgrounds south of Caldwell, then along murky Bluff Creek, past a saloon in a tent and a barber working in the sunshine with three chairs, a barrel, and a mirror hanging from a blackjack oak.

Today was June 2, three months before the run. He estimated two thousand settlers had arrived and camped under the trees to escape the heat. They'd soon have all the game killed. Sides of bacon, he thought, and scribbled a note. Canned corn and peas.

He nodded to scrawny children, running with buckets of water, grasshoppers leaping ahead of them. He touched the brim of his straw hat to their haggard mothers. He wiped sweat from his face.

A trader and a farmer negotiated for a claybank mare. The trader took off his felt hat to wave at flies. Alkali streaked his long hair, and Euly could smell the man from atop the buckboard. "That's a good ole hoss. Crossed the desert with her and never did she falter. I reckon I could let her go fer fifty dollars."

The mare wouldn't see fifteen again and she was bowlegged. She'd been shod wrong. Not every blacksmith made a good farrier. You might correct her condition with bigger shoes, but the old girl should be turned out to pasture, where she could skip about barefooted.

The farmer looked toward a covered wagon tucked between cottonwoods. He wore a bulky cotton shirt and boots with worn-down heels. "Need somethin' make the run," he said, shaking his head, already regretting what he was bound to do. "Ain't she kinda skinny?"

"Crossed the Staked Plains, like I say. She'll fill out proper in all this bluestem."

"I could go forty."

Not worth ten, Euly thought, and flipped the reins to his sad little gelding. But what about Johnny's—and his grandfather's—horses? If that mare sold for forty, a good horse, a few days before September 16, might fetch two hundred.

And he had pasture for them.

A big man stood in his path, weaving a little from his trip to the saloon, holding a bottle of beer. Euly steeled himself as he pulled back the gelding. He was in no shape for a fistfight and reached for his rifle. Since fighting the lion, he carried it everywhere.

"What you take for that old Marlin?"

"It's new." It wasn't his father's. He'd oiled that one and stored it in a scabbard. "Fifteen."

"Ain't got no Winchesters?"

"Will have, sir. Watch for my wagon."

The big man grimaced, but reached into a vest pocket to produce three fives, clean except for tobacco crumbs. "Had a Marlin in the army, shooting them red niggers."

"Well," Euly said, handing down the rifle, trying not to wince at the man's language. A sale was a sale. "Man get a drink of whiskey in that tent?"

"They call it that. In my opinion, it's goat piss. Catridges?"

"It's loaded full. I'll throw in half a box, all I have today."

"Don't truly like a Marlin, 'ceptin' these little .25-.20s. Good brush guns." The big man cocked the rifle and fired with one hand. Something dinged down in the woods. "Jesus, Mary, and Joseph!" he said. "Bought a rifle off a Mennonite!"

Stores would soon open in the new country, trains would deliver goods, but settlers needed items for the first day, for the week or two when they made their claims. They needed pitchforks, shovels, axes, and picks. Sturdy gloves and shoes. Axle grease. Horseshoes, harness, saddles, and Spanish bits. Hammers, nails, staples. Rope.

Corn meal, flour, molasses, potatoes. Live chickens if he could find them, because chickens would keep you from starving through a long winter. Tobacco. Sulfur matches. Levi's. Bolts of muslin, maybe a sewing machine or two.

Most of all, men needed their guns. Shotguns for prairie chickens. Rifles, perhaps some handguns, for fighting off claim jumpers. By August rifles might go for twenty dollars. And often men were hazy on the cost of ammunition. He could mark it up 50 percent.

He tied the buckboard to a post and hobbled along Caldwell's main street toward Western Union. Among his other enterprises, Cabot ran the telegraph office.

SELLING MARLIN REPEATERS FIFTEEN STOP MONTY WARD PRICE ELEVEN STOP YOUR PRICE KANSAS CITY WINCHESTER STOP

Cabot replied immediately. WINCHESTER FORTY FOUR NINE FIFTY WHOLESALE STOP FIVE CASES STOP. Euly replied, TEN CASES STOP SEND CALDWELL SANTA FE STOP.

He had to return for Kate's wedding but he'd left things open with Jenny how long he'd be gone. He hadn't much to do in Jericho Springs other than to load his wagons and shut down the farm, and plans for setting up Evangeline's barn dropped into his head. He could use those piles of old lumber to partition some rooms. He could lay in feed for his stock and shore up the fences.

He sent another telegram to "the company," bragging of his progress and urging them all onto higher ground. He even suggested to Johnny that he might haul some whiskey from Carl Junction. Then he paid the operator, a nearsighted fellow who took a moment to decipher his scrawl. Euly lived by his Uncle Helmut's maxim, *Das Leben ist Arbeit*, and he'd turned in a productive day though handicapped by his cast.

He felt good about himself but when he turned toward the door his confidence melted into gloom. Sweat popped up on his forehead and trickled down inside his cast. Eddie Mole stared from the wall.

"Kilt our deputy," the operator called out. "U.S. marshals want him, too. Kilt maybe ten men."

Euly pointed. "The 'honest merchant.' That's my father."

"Your daddy! Aw, that's terrible." The operator came around his desk as if he were empowered to right wrongs. He stroked his bald head and squinted not quite in Euly's direction. "How'd it happen, you don't mind me asking?"

"He—" Euly mashed a thumb on the poster. "Didn't know my father. Shot him down for three hundred dollars! Shot him from horseback, like he was too lazy to dismount. Sir, it's going on a year now, and I can't bring my mind to an understanding. I don't comprehend how such a man could exist in this world God made."

"Nobody can. They've cleaned up this town some, but ain't a month goes by they don't carry some ignorant cowboy out of the Barn Dance, killed over nothin', killed over kissin' a painted whore. Mostly, the killer rides off free."

"Even if it had been a crime of passion—"

"You're thinkin' about a normal human bein', son. That poltroon cut down our deputy before he got a word out, no more thought to it than spittin'. I do not believe Eddie Mole is a-stayin' up nights burdened with regret. They hang him, I don't what the Good Lord is gonna do, because Hell won't take the man."

Das Leben ist Arbeit made a fine guiding light but it wasn't enough. No amount of work, planning, or diligence prepared you for that one violent moment. It was almost as though Eddie Mole wasn't a man but a malevolent force which came at you sideways, from crookedness, from laziness, from a dark alley or a gun on Main Street.

"The law will get him," Euly murmured, slumping on his crutches. "I got to believe that. Justice will prevail."

The operator nodded and let out a long sigh. "It's been known to, son," he said.

16

The Holy Estate

Pastor Peter McAfee announced Johnny and Kate's wedding date—the very next Sunday, June 11—along with missionary news and baptisms. Surprising everyone, Frieda Hausen rose to speak. There were times to speak, even for women, but unless a tornado bore down on the church, Sunday morning was not among them.

Perhaps because so many had attended her German classes, perhaps also because unmarried Frieda was so circumspect, the congregation grew still. Despite the heat, no one waved a fan. A hiss or two rose from the women, seated primly to the left, separate from the men seated on the right, also primly. Kate had forgotten about church.

"This marriage," Frieda said, in a timorous, courageous voice, "is an abomination before the Lord." Frieda's white face flushed with blood and she sat abruptly, as if to avoid fainting. She waved her cardboard fan.

Her marriage an abomination? Kate didn't understand. An abomination like Abner Pierpont? No, it was a union between a woman and man who loved each other, who happened to have brown skin. She glanced across the aisle at Johnny but couldn't read his face. At first, he didn't seem outraged and Kate didn't know if she was. The idea of marriage still seemed abstract. She'd never saved needlework, flatware, silver dollars in a hope chest.

She'd never had a beau except for Johnny and he wasn't a beau; he was body and soul.

She heard another woman's voice, steeped in that special piety people deployed when quoting scripture: "Thou shalt make no marriages with them."

Now she grew angry. She wanted to scream at Frieda Hausen. Again she glanced toward Johnny, hoping for guidance, but he stared forward. She had an insight into the supposed stoicism of Indians—and Nancy, and Jo. If you wanted to survive in a sea of hostility, if you wanted to avoid a beating, what else could you do?

She was among the gentle Mennonites, not the Ku Klux Klan!

Pastor McAfee nodded to Sister Nora Kreider, Kate's Uncle Ronald's wife, who tore into the brand-new pump organ with "Wonderful Words of Life." The congregation sang heartily, some in German, some in English. The song was a Methodist revival hymn and therefore controversial. The organ was also controversial, debated over several years, the younger generation at last winning out over the hidebound Ukrainians. Helmut himself had been dubious, though more about the expense than the sacrilege.

Everything among the Old Ones was like that, Kate thought, their safe, cloaked-in-black Ukrainian ways mounted against what they thought of as decadent modernism. The Young Ones went courting in buggies, and installed telephones, and some even voted for the Englische offices. Scandalous!

Did others agree with swooning Frieda? From the pew behind her Annelise's veined, pale hand descended on her shoulder, and Kate turned and summoned a smile. Annelise cried but everything made her cry these days.

Johnny's mother, Mira, offered a stare as unexpressive as Johnny's, but Kate knew her well enough by now to see the rage behind the stoicism. Mira was so excited that her son had found a wife that she'd ventured into the white, white world of the Mennonites, and the two old women had become confidantes. She put an arm around Annelise.

Kate didn't hear the sermon but it was short and with uncharacteristic quiet the congregation filed out. Taller than any of the other women, she scanned them for a sympathetic face but every black hat was downturned. Johnny took her hand, stared gravely, shook his head. He strode before his mother and Annelise as if he were a bodyguard, and in fact he blocked two women with friendly, then irritated, faces, who probably meant to express sympathy. "Don't worry. Everything will be fine," Kate called out. Annelise looked up in horror and Kate forced yet another smile.

She wanted to take her aunt and Mira somewhere quiet, to show her anger only to her family. But Pastor McAfee had positioned himself on the steps and spread wide his hands, beckoning to two loosely formed groups. The Old Ones. The Young Ones. His face grew stern, more like a judge than a minister, and even the children quieted, knowing that God's law was about to be adjudicated.

One group stood with Annelise, loyal to her and the memory of Helmut; the others stood fifty feet opposite, and seemed less cohesive. Several families hurried toward their buggies, as if fleeing a fire, and seemed reluctant to return. The division wasn't strictly Old versus Young, Ukrainian versus American-born. Several of the old-timers passed Johnny and Kate, shaking their heads ruefully. And Jenny Muenster stood with her father, the universally disliked Henry—the man who, fifteen miles distant, with two sheep, had killed Helmut Kreider. Kate glowered at Jenny and the girl's eyes flitted up and down, showing doubt and defiance at once. They disliked each other, but did the girl understand what she was doing? Poor Euly!

"Deuteronomy 7:3," Pastor McAfee said. Kate had never warmed to the man and she knew Euly despised him for lecturing on revenge in what should have been a eulogy for their father. Really, Pastor? Barney Kreider is dead. You can't find one good thing to say?

"Neither shalt thou make marriages with them; thy daughter thou shalt not give unto his son, nor his daughter shalt thou take unto thy son."

Frieda's eyes blazed with fervor, and Jenny made a step forward, intent on the pastor. These people didn't understand love. Abiding love. Overcoming love! She slipped an arm around Johnny. She felt the muscles in his chest tense, as if he might have to fight, but Mennonites warred only with words.

Annelise cried openly and beside her Mira shrank and seemed out of place. Johnny drew his mother near and that's how the four stood, together to challenge the world, three tall, brown-skinned people and a grieving old woman white as an egg.

"But may I remind you that this oft-quoted, *misinterpreted* passage refers to the Canaanites, an idolatrous people and a fierce enemy of the ancient Jews. We in Jericho Springs proudly give five hundred dollars a year for our missionaries at the Darlington Agency, to uplift our brothers and sisters among the Arapaho and Cheyenne. These poor people were once the enemy of all Kansans but now they are defeated and hungry, and they are not Canaanites. They love the Lord! The passage should not be used, my brethren, to support race prejudice. We of all people should rise above such sentiments."

What? The dour pastor had taken their side and murmurs of assent rose from both groups. Jenny Muenster slipped behind her oafish brothers. Frieda Hausen stood alone, no one to catch her should she faint again. The black heads of the old Ukrainians lifted as if to Heaven, their faces softening. Guidance. That's what a pastor was for.

McAfee hadn't finished. "Friends, let's dispense with that other popular verse, Paul's admonition: 'Be ye not unequally yoked together with unbelievers: for what fellowship hath righteousness with unrighteousness? And what communion hath light with darkness?'"

The pastor said "unequally yoked" did not refer to race, but to marrying outside the faith. "Kate grew up among us, and is a fine, Mennonite woman."

Thank you, Sir, Kate thought. Race was all but imaginary, wasn't it, real only if you were filled with hatred? When people thought she was white, she was white. If she married an Indian, she was brown. She'd be white again, visiting Newton or riding on the train.

"John Baxter is the son of a Baptist minister and has attended our services here faithfully."

An exaggeration on both points but Kate appreciated McAfee's words. Everyone—except Frieda, and the Muenster family—smiled in good fellowship. Then the pastor, pedant that he was, went too far:

"And if one *were* to object to consorting outside the race, the error has already been made by the late Barney Kreider. Would any of us seek to punish our blameless Sister Kate—"

She couldn't take anymore. She was a brown bastard, and her home was not her home. She threw her head into Johnny's chest, glanced up at him almost in apology, then walked toward the school house. She refused to run.

She sat at her desk of eons ago and tried to read the grammar lessons on the blackboard. Her thoughts swirled so violently that a moment passed before she realized the language was German, and the handwriting Frieda Hausen's. She filled with hatred but simultaneously lectured herself that hatred did not lead to understanding. This was the point of Pastor McAfee's cautions, no matter how coldly he delivered them. He had no heart, but his mind was in the right place.

Forgive Frieda, she told herself. She is a miserable person. No one such as Johnny has entered her life and no one ever would. Then, as if by the Lord's hand, or the Devil's, Frieda came through the school house door. She stood confused, blinking from the sunlight. Kate called out, "Here, Frieda."

Frieda rushed forward and dropped to her knees, though

she wore a corset and her upper body couldn't bend. "I am so sorry," she said, sobbing, sniffling. "I was wrong! We've always been friends, I don't know—"

"Get up, Sister," Kate said. "Don't crawl around on the floor like a dog."

"I *am* a dog. I'm nobody and I've ruined everything."

"I believe you have, Frieda." Kate sighed. "Did you mean to?"

A shadow crossed the doorway and Johnny stood silently.

"No. Yes! I never thought of you as an Indian, but you *were*. All along! You don't understand, Kate. My parents, they were from the Old Country, too, but they didn't get along here. They couldn't find good land. They had no money. All we ate, day after day, was salt pork and molasses. So we got in the wagon, we had Johnson the Horse and that old ox, we went to the Territory. It was 1878. I was nine years old! I went down to the creek for, for nature's call, and then I hid in the brush as they . . ."

"You mean Indians," Kate murmured. "The Osage?"

"They just knocked them in the head, these huge, *naked* men with their hideous topknots. They wanted the animals, that's all. I was so little! They went away and I crawled over there, beside my mother. Her face was all mashed and there was blood everywhere!"

"Oh, Frieda."

"I'm *so* sorry," Frieda said, through tight lips. She could no longer speak. She rose and ran blindly into Johnny, who caught her arms.

"Woman," he said, as if he had come upon a thief. Frieda shrieked, fell, and lay trembling like a freshly killed deer. Kate hurried after her, thinking to comfort this comfortless woman, but Frieda sprang up, ducked under Johnny's arm, and walked toward the church, body pitched sideways as though she were drunk.

SEVERAL CAME FORWARD TO express their outrage, including Pastor McAfee, who apologized for his remark about Barney Kreider. He seemed genuinely sad they'd decided to marry on the reservation. "Don't let a backward few rule your heart," he said, suggesting, after all, that he had one. "Jericho Springs, our church, is your home."

Perhaps it was Helmut's death as much as the insult from friends, but Annelise didn't want to stay, either, at least through the summer. With Euly gone, she turned over management of the farm to Helmut's brothers, and she and Mira boarded the train for Kansas City, where they'd take two days to shop before going on to Bartlesville. Kate kept her counsel on this adventure. She drew a map to Bernheimer's Department Store and suggested two hotels that might accept Mira. Kansas City seemed remote to her.

At Cabot's, they discovered Euly's day-old telegram:

FOUND STORAGE STOP AND ROOMS STOP CAN
SELL HORSES FANTASTIC PRICES STOP LIKEWISE
WHISKEY IF GAME STOP JOHNNY BARRELS BARN
MULES CONESTOGA WAGON STOP SEE FRIDAY
NINTH STOP SO HAPPY YOUR WEDDING STOP
JENNY LOVE STOP

"Do you wish to sell your horses?" Johnny asked.
"The money, Johnny. We need it."
"Hauling whiskey can be dangerous."
She nodded. Euly had a postscript:

KATE DONT LIKE WHISKEY THIS TIME ONLY
STOP MAYBE FIND MOTHERS GRAVE STOP BILLS
LADING FATHERS DESK STOP

"My brother isn't entirely honest," Kate said.
Johnny rolled his eyes. He would never criticize his Little Hero. "You should find the truth about your mother if you can. Ulysses tempts you, yes, but it is as you say about the horses. Ulysses wants us to make money."
"It's dangerous?"

"I believe where we must go is on the Spring River, three days, perhaps four, east of Emmet Baxter's farm. It is safe to go there. But hauling whiskey, we should travel by night."

"Why do you call your father, your stepfather, by his full name? Isn't he a good man?"

"He does not seem like my father." Johnny looked away. "He is good, yes. He does not know this for himself."

Kate handed Cabot their answer:

NO MARRIAGE CHURCH STOP PREPARATIONS
UNDERWAY PAWHUSKA STOP ANNELISE THERE
STOP PLEASE COME STOP WILL BRING HORSES
WHISKEY AFTERWARD STOP ARRIVE CALDWELL
JUNE 22 EARLIEST STOP

She had so much more to say—her disillusionment with the church, Annelise's frailty, her misgivings about Jenny—but subtleties and telegrams didn't mix. They returned to Annelise's farm for Kate's trunk and painting supplies. Johnny threw out oats to lure the horses—King Arthur, Soquili, and Kate's bride-price of the stallion and his four pretty mares. Then back through Jericho Springs again.

Euly's hardware stood closed with no sign of Jenny, but Kate didn't allow herself to speculate. She still hoped to get along with her future sister-in-law, at least through the summer. After that, Kate would live in Oklahoma on their homestead.

Kate Baxter, Pioneer Artist. She visualized the flourish with which she'd sign her paintings.

Feeling like a burglar, she opened her father's old office to retrieve an envelope with bills of lading, which would tell them where to go in Missouri. Meanwhile, Johnny loaded Euly's heavy wagon with eight empty whiskey barrels and hitched Prince and Pauper, the mules. They knew Johnny but were skittish. They had water, still, but hadn't been fed in several days. The horses, too, had been neglected, and Maude wouldn't get up at first.

"Where is that yellow-haired girl, Jennifer?" Johnny asked. Kate shrugged.

JOHNNY PICKED THEIR WAY along rough trails, avoiding towns, riding up crests and scanning with his binoculars. If there were dangers in Kansas City, there were more on the open prairie, and their fine horses made them prey. The Daltons were dead but plenty of outlaws rode free. Eddie Mole, Kate thought.

They'd make the run not randomly but for the killer's homestead. The wonder of it!

On the second night Kate urged Johnny to show her how to fire his Winchester. She enjoyed cocking it, ejecting the shells. She hit a rock two hundred yards distant, then hit it again, and she looked up for his approval. He nodded. Since the affair at the church he'd grown distant.

Unused to driving a wagon, she stood much of the time to relieve her soreness, and then doubled a blanket over the seat. She felt a new sympathy for Euly's long freight runs because the trail was jarring and slow. By the third day, every muscle aching, she begged to move onto the smooth main road. Johnny ignored her and she grew angry. Why wouldn't he talk to her?

And yet Kate knew, like the husband he soon would be, Johnny meant to protect her. If he erred it was on the side of caution, and maybe she wore on his nerves, too. They had never spent entire days and nights together. She laughed and called out, "You only care about your horses!"

He didn't answer, his eyes intent on the horizon, but she thought he smiled.

She brewed coffee, made biscuits, and fried bacon. She discovered that an open fire was much like a cookstove: you moved the bacon to a cooler place when it began to sizzle, and scooped up the grease for another day. Did the Osage, her people, eat bacon and biscuits? Sometimes she pulled her head back from the smoke, looked up at the cottonwoods shuddering in the wind, and felt homeless.

On the fourth day, no dangers in sight, they drifted through the waist-high bluestem, down gentle, sweeping slopes, and her wagon seemed like a boat on an ocean. To her surprise, because he spoke so little, Johnny began to chant, a peaceful, repetitive song offered in thanks to Wah-Kon-Da. Wah-Kon-Da, not much like Jehovah, inhabited everything. "Thanks for what, John Baxter?" she called.

"The tall grass," he said. "The horses. This beautiful day. My beautiful wife."

She couldn't answer.

A flock of passenger pigeons clouded the sky, surprising her. They flew fast and left a sound mournful as a receding train. When she was a little girl, they migrated down from Ontario and slept in the Zimmerman Woods, so many on a tree they broke the branches. She hadn't seen them in a long time. She'd read they were extinct.

There were plenty of prairie chickens, however. A rooster made his ridiculous mating call, as if a duck had been crossed with a lamb.

The dry air smelled of asters and sage, but she learned to guide the mules around stands of buffalo gourd because the big, orange flowers stank when you mashed them. The gourds were dazzling in their coarse way, thriving despite the drought, while green parsley cones and violet morning glories seemed almost to gasp for water as the day warmed. Whether the prairie was dry or verdant, she was eager to paint it.

Johnny knew where to find water. That evening they camped at a spring flowing out of a crack in a range of low hills. Johnny hobbled the stock in a robust stand of grass, while Kate prepared stew over a small fire, cutting up a hen Johnny had shot, adding potatoes, sage, and wild onions, a dash of flour and salt. She felt strong. Her legs didn't hurt anymore and she was ravenous.

Her face was chafed, her hair snarled, and she needed a bath. When was it she'd studied art and business in the big city? The splendid farm she'd grown up on, the church with its limitless rules, even her aunt had become blurred memories. The prairie toughened her. She could drive that damned jolting wagon to California and fire a rifle with one hand. She could eat raw meat and sleep on a board. She could give birth in the woods and cut the umbilical with her teeth!

Well, no. But she could do what her man did. What necessity called for.

Johnny feasted on stew and yesterday's biscuits and grunted his approval. "Fine, Kate," he said, in exactly Helmut Kreider's tone. He'd sat at their table, listening both to German and English, a stranger in the strange land of the Mennonites. Of course, Helmut was the true foreigner.

"You liked my uncle, didn't you?"

"He taught me how to farm. He was a man of peace."

"Stingy, though. Everyone said so."

"I had a warm place to sleep, with a light to read by. German food is good fuel for working." He looked at her gently. "I have never understood money. It is paper or metal, but seems to be pulled from the air. It is only recently I have had need for it."

He lit his red pipe with its foul tobacco and slouched against Soquili's saddle. Munching bluestem, the mare nuzzled his cheek, and he reached backward to stroke her face. He smiled as if he had everything he needed in life, though she knew better; sometimes, she caught his sidelong, doubtful glances. He was so much older than she, with a forced boarding school education. Sometimes, though she knew him as a girl and now as a woman, she didn't understand him at all.

He said, "I am of the Sky People, the *Tsi-Zhu*."

"I will paint them," she whispered.

"They marry the Earth People, or *Hon-ga*. I suspect your mother was *Hon-ga*."

"Does this matter?"

"It will please my grandfather, Buffalo Dancer, but no. You are half-white and I am partly French. We will marry in the middle way, *o-mí-hon*, without rituals. Many white men enter the clan this way, because the Osage are not the Comanches. We did not fight the white man; we negotiated with him. We paid for our land, *our* land; we have deeds the white man must recognize. Therefore, we are a little rich."

"I'm marrying you for your money?"

He tapped out his pipe and smiled again. "It is as if you were a widow, I a widower. My stepfather is white, as are your uncles, and could not understand how brides are bartered for. It is fortunate you have no sisters. I might need to marry them as well."

She thought she detected irony in his tone, then wasn't sure. "A fine custom for the man," she said at last.

"Not so fine. Think of all the horses this requires, and how sisters quarrel." He took her hand like a knight of old and kissed it. She leaned forward, expecting a kiss on her lips, but he didn't offer.

Soquili lifted her head as if the conversation puzzled her. Johnny leaned against the saddle again. Kate read in his eyes he was unsure of himself, in love with her, but doubtful how an almost full-blood Osage might consort with an almost—a half, a somewhat—white woman. Rather than distant, she understood he was shy. They had swum together many times, and lay on the banks of Zimmerman's Creek, but never dared to make love. Making love would seal their fate.

"This is such a peaceful place," she told him, her voice soft. "It is like your song. The air is clean, the water pure, and we are together as we should be. Do not worry so much, my love. The trail is hard, who knows what will happen to us, but have you ever been happier?"

He nodded. "I have not, Kate."

She meandered up the creek, glancing backward, beckoning him without being conscious of it. She floundered in dry grass, then stumbled onto a deer trace that led to the pool, deep as Johnny stood tall, below the spring. Thick cottonwoods rose high, shading the water, cloistering the pool. She unbuttoned her long dress, pulled it overhead, and dropped naked into the water, so cold her bones ached. In moments, she was accustomed to it, invigorated, and she swam to the little falls, where she gulped the water, balancing her torso with deft, small kicks like a frog's. She threw her hair under the falling water and kneaded it with her knuckles, then threw back her head with cascades of laughter. She turned, knowing he was there, her sense of her man, of love, of the universe, all wrong if he wasn't.

Johnny drew her a little downstream and onto a sand bar. Entwined, they rolled over and over, their laughter a song of freedom. No matter how hard she looked, she'd never found a book on the art of lovemaking, but as it turned out you didn't need instruction. Johnny was diffident, then jubilant, then overwhelming. She lay looking up at the moon above the cottonwoods and cried with joy.

CROPS WERE DYING AND the prairie was dry. Wind rasped through the brown grass. To the west, smoke rose.

No rain had fallen for weeks—but now it did, in cold, almost impenetrable sheets, and despite the late Helmut Kreider's mackintoshes they couldn't stay dry. Johnny fixed a canvas above the wagon seat, but still Kate sat with her wide hat dripping onto her lap. Sideward gusts cut her like sleet. She thought, my paintings, my clothes, but she'd wrapped everything in oilcloth and Johnny had lashed down a tarpaulin.

She slept, starting awake to the same dismal scene. The mules followed the horses, which followed Johnny, whom she couldn't see. She felt the land rising under the wagon, dropping off again with the wheels rolling faster, and she fell into shallow dreams. She tried to command them, to imagine sunny pastures and stately trees, but instead she saw Annelise weeping over Helmut in the coffin, and Frieda lecturing. Eddie Mole appeared with fiery eyes, and she held up her derringer, and pulled the trigger.

The reins slacked in her puckered hands. It didn't matter: the stolid mules, barely visible from ten feet away, found footing in the mud and plodded onward.

Johnny drew her under a shelter where he coaxed a small,

smoky fire. He pulled off her clothing and wrapped her in a rough wool blanket, and after a while drew her next to his own naked body. She dreamed she had been transported to Bible lands. She carried water down the the long stone street. A swarthy man stared from a doorway.

"You are fine, Kate," Johnny said, handing her a steaming tin of coffee, a biscuit, a strip of jerky. Hours had passed. The rain had turned to mist again. "You are strong."

"I am strong," she repeated.

"Wah-Kon-Da sends the rain to hide us. Arkansas City is a mile away."

They'd cross the river there. "Tomorrow—"

"Is the last day. You will sleep in a warm place. Next day, we will marry."

"I love you," she said, and next to him, the rain hissing and cocooning them in the tent, she felt warm.

THROUGH THE FOG, KATE heard the dull clanging of a church bell. The wagon wheels squished down the long street, the river gray like sky at the end of it.

Arkansas City had many Indian visitors but Johnny was wary. Stealing from an Indian was no crime if white men judged, and already, with the land run imminent, horses fetched premium prices. Still, few people were about.

This was Sunday morning, because half a dozen wet worshippers stood at the steps of Catholic and Methodist churches, and the bells kept ringing. The town seemed sodden enough to slide into the river. They met no riders except for one black buggy, a doctor shrouded behind isinglass curtains beaded with rain droplets.

Her mules plodded and slid toward the foggy water, then climbed up from mud, their hooves echoing off the wooden ramp and onto the ferry. The animals milled and shook off the mist. Mist beaded in Kate's wiry hair.

The bearded white man took his fare and said nothing. Johnny nodded to an old Osage couple who boarded after them, then stood apart. They rode one horse without a saddle.

A white man in a soiled blue suit, carrying a small brown suit-case, got on with his tired-looking mare. He remained mounted and Kate wanted to say, *give your poor horse a rest.*

The ferryman shoved a pole into the bank and the ferry lurched along the cable ever so slowly. You turned the pulleys and the body of the ferry, one way to cross over, the opposite way to return. The lapping water was the only sound. Johnny walked among the restive horses. Kate talked to Prince and Pauper and they stood peacefully.

"I love those mules," Johnny called out.

They left the fog and Kate squinted from the assault of sun-light. Downriver, deer on a sandbar turned away in unison. A dozen black turkey hens took flight out of cottonwood sap-lings like those she'd seen on the Missouri. Overhead, a quick shadow traveled down the water: those pigeons again.

The little craft bumped the eastern bank and the ferryman drew on a rope to steady them. He leaped ashore, Johnny fol-lowed, and they muscled another ramp into place. The white man trotted off east with his suitcase balanced on the pommel.

They brought the horses and the wagon onto shore—the horses skittish, the mules unimpressed. They turned south on the river road.

"Where is our farm to be?" Kate called out.

Johnny shrugged and pointed elaborately to the south—as if to Texas. "Two days ride."

"Where did you find the buffalo?"

That place was almost upon them. Johnny pointed downriver into a broad swamp where buzzards soared. The ground steamed with evaporation from little pools. "Quicksand," Johnny said, pointing to where the river road disappeared under six inches of water. He turned them eastward and they climbed.

Kate peered down on the swamp as if she could see buffalo. She couldn't believe Buffalo Dancer made them appear. Yes, they appeared, but everything had a rational explanation.

Or not. To believe that Jesus died for the sins of every man, white or Osage, Mennonite or Englische, that He died even for Eddie Mole, wasn't rational.

The mules knew where to go. She gave up the notion that she guided them and dropped into naps in the sunshine. Twelve hours before she froze; now she sweated. She dreamed of sausage and spinach and new peas, the meal she'd made for wounded Euly out of Annelise's garden and Helmut's smokehouse, her cooking instincts resurrected from girlish indifference. She reached back into the possibles bag for a biscuit but they all were gone.

She woke to a narrow road where dry, springy brush closed in. A great orange moon emerged in a sky streaked with long, narrow black clouds.

They reached a valley bounded all around by woods. She'd lost her sense of direction but knew the river ran near. Coyotes yipped, and ahead the horses nickered. By the low barn, where silhouettes of horses lined up along a fence, King Arthur and Kate's bride-price stallion strained to break free. Speaking sternly, Johnny led them away, while hands reached to help Kate down from the wagon seat. In the moonlight an ancient, gaunt man, Buffalo Dancer, said, "Welcome, Daughter. *Tha tse.*"

She told herself not to fear him. Only God could create buffalo. "*Ni zhu ka,*" she blurted, it's raining, even though the rain had stopped long before and the land had turned dry again. She knew only the few phrases Johnny taught her and now couldn't recall them. "Thank you for the horses, Grandfather," she stammered, and wondered if "Grandfather" was too familiar. The old man smiled, patted her shoulder, and receded into the starlight. She stared after him until she saw fireflies dancing.

Kate stepped inside the dark lodge and her eyes leapt to a bright candle. A woman handed her hot soup flavored with onions, and rough bread. The woman spoke soothingly but

Kate couldn't find her face in the darkness, and didn't know how to reply.

She sipped something warm and tingly and her body grew weightless. She twirled her arms like wings, dropped onto a mat, and pushed her long legs deep into cotton blankets. A buffalo robe descended, covering all but her eyes and nose. Down the long lodge, a fire danced red and blue. Kate thought she heard Johnny's voice and almost lifted herself from the mat, but she had no strength.

She heard one of the mules, Prince, cry out. Pauper answered with a bray like laughter. Someone, maybe Buffalo Dancer, chanted the evening prayer. The chant drifted away like an echo.

KATE WOKE TO THE sounds of women and children laughing, horses whinnying, pigs grunting the way they always did at their morning feast.

Sunlight streamed through the lodge's one window. She smelled tobacco, sage, tallow, cedar berries, dill. This was Buffalo Dancer's, an old bachelor's, den.

Her clothes had disappeared, but folded near the burned-out candle she found a deerskin dress with blue beading. She danced about on the wooden floor, tugging the dress past her thighs. Because it fit tightly all the way to her ankles, she'd need to take short steps, but she liked how the leather felt on her skin. The dress smelled musty and she surmised it dated from Mira's wedding or had belonged to Buffalo Dancer's long-dead wife. She found a comb but dragging it through her snarled hair was torture. She tied it back with a blue ribbon, thought of Jo, and checked her tears. She washed her face with water from a basin and nothing remained but to enter the daylight.

Fifteen curious women's faces turned toward her. Most wore military jackets, Union blue, or Southern gray, and several wore even gaudier coats, with red cording and gold lace, perhaps from a military band. Wedding party clothes.

"*Havay. Dah heh ninksha?*" she said.

Hello, how are you. The women came near, touching her arm, making half-curtsies. One delivered a long speech, pointing angrily toward the woods beyond the pasture, and Kate nodded helplessly. The others said, *Way da han*, I am good, and retreated shyly.

"*Wa-thú-ga*," she said, meaning, I husk corn, rather than I take a husband today, *wá-thu-xe*. Her new kin stared but the children laughed, and Kate stood tongue-tied. A little girl held up a bouquet of red and yellow coneflowers, then snatched it back. Without thinking Kate chased after her, tripped in the tight dress, and all the children screamed. Several women rushed to Kate's side.

On her feet again, she wanted to flee to the woods. I'm here, she thought. I must get through this. No matter her clumsiness, she meant well, and she felt the women would understand. As she grappled for words the little girl tugged at her skirt, handed up the bouquet, and threw her arms around Kate's legs. Kate picked her up and, looking over the barnyard, saw Buffalo Dancer's scarred face, a wraith peering through the smoke of his fire. Fear stabbed her heart but then the old man smiled.

And so did Annelise and Mira, seated at a table piled high with gifts.

"*Thó-da*," she said, the girl's arms around her neck. "Peace to you all. I come from a clan that believes in peace. I must speak English, but I will learn the language of the Wazhazhe. Forgive me my awkwardness. I am a poor sinner, I am an ignorant woman, please forgive me. *Thó-da.*"

Mira hurried to her side. "Is it not a good speech?" she asked theatrically, opening her arms to all the women. "Won't Kate make our son a good wife?"

The women laughed and called out their encouragements. Kate—and the little girl with flowers, who said she was called Brown Pony, or maybe that she wanted a brown pony—had won them over.

Nothing here but good will. No cries of abomination, and all she needed to do was relax.

Kate took a post at the table with Mira and Annelise and passed out yellow-and-gray cavalry blankets; blankets with stunning Navajo designs; and blue blankets from the trading post. Blankets were akin to currency. The women brought embroidered shawls for Kate, moccasins, blackberry jam, smoked meats. "*Wĕ-a-hno*ⁿ," she said. I am thankful, humbly she said so, and as the morning melted into afternoon, the women took seats to gossip and eat. They could be Mennonites, she thought, if they dressed in black.

She took her aunt's hand. "Are you all right?"

Annelise nodded. "Ashamed of my church, Kate. Overwhelmed by . . ." She swept her hand over the women. "All of this."

"Was your trip hard?"

Annelise looked healthier. Some color had returned to her cheeks. "You know how difficult it can be for women to travel, but men tipped their hats and carried our bags. The sole advantage I've seen, thus far, to growing old."

"They did not want me in their big hotel," Mira put in, then broke off with a giggle.

Kate couldn't quite fathom it: an Indian woman, her mother-in-law, giggling. "*What?*"

"Annelise said, 'Do you know who we are?'"

Kate understood. "That worked?"

Annelise laughed. "The first man said, 'Who are you?' and how could I say, an old Mennonite woman from Jericho Springs? So we gathered up our dignity and marched to the Lindell."

"The city was frightening!" Mira said.

Kate nodded. "I found it so."

"Well, the same thing," Annelise went on. "No Indians can spend the night. But this time the clerk was, I wouldn't know, maybe an Italian man. I said, 'Do you know who we are?' and plainly, he did not. He gave us quite a fine room overlooking the river."

Kate smiled. "You are a bold woman, Annelise."

"She is your white mother," Mira said, her eyes sparkling.

"Yes," Kate said. "My dear Mennonite mother."

Kate looked out over the brown faces, most browner than hers, some whiter. Beyond them stood the corral and fifty fine horses, the oaks, the broad walnuts, the cottonwoods behind them. On the table lay Annelise's Montgomery Ward fountain pen and butcher paper from the trading post.

Brown Pony crawled up to her lap and Kate put one arm around her chest. With her free hand, she began to draw.

Now the men came up from the woods, some wearing long tunics with their hair in waxed scalplocks, some in military coats like their wives, some dressed like white men. More than one seemed too jolly even for a wedding, and Kate realized they were drunk.

Johnny emerged, leading a sort of parade of the bride-price horses which soon they'd sell for the land run. He rode Soquili, and his white-skinned brother, Billy, rode the restless stallion they had no name for. The two had dressed almost identically in brown boots, deerskin shirts, and Stetsons.

Johnny dismounted and stepped toward their table. He tipped his hat to Annelise but his eyes were on Kate. "My mother's dress fits you well."

If I don't try to walk, she thought. She smiled but couldn't speak. Johnny seemed a stranger in his fine clothes.

"Have you eaten, Kate? I will bring food for you."

"Thank you," she said. "*I-ni-ka.*" Husband.

The crowd swirled like flowing water and Kate couldn't follow it all. Some locked arms and danced, or shuffled, around Buffalo Dancer's fire. Brown Pony crawled down, and twirled gaily, as men lifted their legs high and shouted to the heavens. Others fell to the ground in stupor. Young Billy joined the dancers, stomping his new boots, drunk as well.

Some Mennonites made elderberry wine but she couldn't recall seeing one drunk. Yes, she had: Euly, when their father was killed. And she thought he drank on his long hauls.

Euly hadn't come. She supposed he'd missed her telegram.

Sketching the dancers, she melded with them. It didn't matter she had only a fountain pen and inferior paper. She caught the essence of faces, of dancers leaping. She'd refine them later.

Waving a cup that sloshed with something Kate knew wasn't mint tea, a heavy-set man, with a cavalry coat stretched over his paunch, laid a reddish longbow across her sketches. "I give this bow to you because your husband is *u-thí-sha-ge*. A lazy man who will lie around all day, drinking Cherokee whiskey. You must do the hunting in your family."

Quite a speech, but something in the man's eyes kept his words from offending. A mixture of humor and challenge, she thought, and she recalled the stories Johnny told. "You couldn't be . . . *u-thí-sha-ge* yourself, Red Deer, to make such a beautiful bow."

"You have heard of me!"

"You are legendary among the Mennonite clan!"

Johnny returned with Billy and handed her a plate of venison, squash, and a dark, nut-filled cake. He inspected the bow and handed it to his brother, who made several attempts to string it. "Red Deer is legendary with himself," Johnny said.

"My cousin, John Baxter, is so ugly a man, I thought no woman would have him. However, he is an acceptable marksman. Is that why you want him?"

"I love him," Kate said.

"Yes," said Red Deer, slurping his drink, throwing out a boot to catch his balance. "I remember love."

"You could bring down a bear with this thing," Billy said. He had at last strung the bow and tried to pull it. He smiled at Kate and she thought, he will be friends with Euly. If he doesn't drink too much, maybe we'll hire him.

Buffalo Dancer began to chant. With no other cue, the clan circled the fire and joined the old man in singsong. They made a sort of responsive reading and, as if confronted with an unfamiliar hymn, Kate murmured recognizable words. Johnny stood at her side and he didn't know all the words either. Kate closed her eyes and thought of the church she'd left behind, all the good people. I live in Oklahoma now, she thought. A new country.

The chanting stopped and she opened her eyes. She stepped forward with Johnny and the old man gathered their hands, pressing them with his. The ground didn't tremble and lightning failed to strike. Buffalo Dancer was no conjurer. He was an old man like her Uncle Helmut, but with a fine face scarred by life. Soon she'd paint him.

Buffalo Dancer made a speech she couldn't understand but it was only several sentences. Sighs rose from the women. The men seemed to melt away; alarmingly, Johnny joined them. Buffalo Dancer stared, as if Kate should perform some ritual, and she panicked.

Speaking with low, calming voices, the women pulled her to the ground, then lifted her high on a blanket. Six of them carried her down a path toward the teepee that had gone up in the morning, and she laughed at the outrageousness of it. They laughed as well but taunted her with the fearsome things her man would do, this night and forever. They said he'd drink and go off by himself for days. They said he'd work her like a mule and run with younger women. He'd beat her if she didn't behave—and if she did.

The sky turned gray with pigeons, one undulating, suspended mass, though strays darted away like cinders from a fire. As she slid from the blanket and stood, the pigeons took over the woods, the fences, the barn, and clung to the poles of the teepee. They gave out a chorus so loud you had to shout to be heard. She glimpsed Buffalo Dancer in his rumpled Stetson, his arms folded. He nodded.

Had he summoned the pigeons?

Rattled, she entered the teepee. Incense burned and again

she smelled sage and dill. She lay on new blankets, every Mennonite certainty at risk.

Johnny came to her as the pigeons cooed.

"I want to paint him," she said.

"My grandfather?"

"To catch his eyes. His ancient, ancient—"

"Magic?"

"Did he call the pigeons?"

Johnny shrugged. "Buffalo Dancer is a priest of the old religion. One of the last, but to me he is like your Annelise. My grandfather, almost my father."

Kate sighed. She was exhausted but she'd made it through the day. "Did I do well?"

He laughed. "Every man, not only Red Deer, is envious of my fine new wife."

"It was so . . . easy. So happy and gentle. Except for the drink. Why do they drink, Johnny?"

"Because the old ways are gone." He frowned. "Because . . . they have not found meaning in the new ways."

Kate did not know the old ways. She did not know the new ways. After a while, she said, "Are we married now, my love?"

"We must be," Johnny said.

17

Love and Money

Both Gerty and Maude threw Euly betrayed looks with their big, trusting eyes. Their stall doors were open for access to pasture, and to the creek for water, but no one had grained them for several days, probably not since Johnny and Kate set off with the mules. This in itself puzzled Euly. It must mean that they hadn't married and had gone on to the reservation. They'd taken the empty barrels, so they'd received his telegram. Probably they'd replied, but he hadn't returned to Western Union.

He gave his horses extra portions of oats and hobbled about until he found three withered apples. He sat feeding them apples and talking of his exploits, and the horses snorted, calmed, and forgave him. Ulysses had come home.

The kitchen door to the dogtrot house stood ajar and a wasp buzzed past his ear as he entered. The furniture seemed displaced, though he'd been gone for two weeks and knew memories could gel around comforting lies. Three cups had been left to dry on the drain board. The bed was made, which Jenny didn't always bother with. But the barest lie sat on the window sill: the pipe that one of the Muenster boys smoked. Euly tried to think. Will, the tall one.

Of course, Will and Milton *were* Jenny's brothers, but still Euly felt disoriented. He threw aside his crutches and limped to his hardware, which was locked, but inside he again felt ill at ease. His inventory seemed thin.

He sat catching his breath and wiping away sweat with his bandanna. He inspected the wagon, which he and Jenny had rolled in with the notion she'd pack it while he was gone. Toward the front stood a keg of fence staples and a crateful of pliers. Jenny couldn't have lifted those.

There must have been a discussion. Jenny meant to pack the wagon and enlisted her brothers to help with heavy items. Then the brothers announced their true intentions and grabbed what would be easiest to sell. The tobacco was gone. The guns, and most of the ammunition. Some dresses, shirts, and trousers— not overalls, but Sunday outfits. They meant to travel?

Two pairs of men's boots had walked off, with the old boots tossed into the worn-out whiskey barrel Euly used for trash. Garden implements, harness, and fence wire hadn't been touched, nor stovepipe nor sheeting nor lumber. You couldn't carry those on horseback. They might have stolen his wagon, even his horses, but horses and wagons were easy to trace, easy to claim, and Euly could come after them with the Harvey County sheriff.

He found the cash register empty even of pennies. He was proud of the machine with its brass inlays and intricate scrolls, as professional as any in Newton. He still had *that*.

Several checks, one for forty-two dollars, remained. The checks would cover personal expenses and he needn't dip into the company account to feed himself. But because of the empty register, his eyes lifted to the fancy box on the highest shelf in his little millinery of straw hats and black bonnets. He held the thin hope Jenny hadn't been complicit.

He pulled over the stepladder and climbed it, dragging up the cast but then putting weight on it. The cast needed to come off. He had work to do.

The box contained a smaller one for chocolates. He'd bought them at Cabot's Miscellany, because he'd read in novels how women liked them. Jenny flooded his face with kisses and he stood tall, a sophisticated man who knew how to please a woman.

The envelope inside, containing his emergency fund of fifty dollars, was empty too. Unless Jenny had told them the brothers could not have known. Ulysses had come home, but his Penelope hadn't waited for twenty years. She didn't last two weeks.

He stood in his vegetable garden, judging what should be tended if he were gone until fall. He'd take along the ripe cabbages. The melons would ripen and rot. The sweet corn would grow hard but he could feed it to his horses. He could dig potatoes even in October. He hoed from his knees, herding black dirt around the potatoes, chopping out radishes and lettuce and spinach, striking as if to punish the Muenster brothers and even Eddie Mole. He relented when he visualized pretty Jenny, and sat on an apple crate for an hour, his thoughts swirling and dark.

He'd been robbed and betrayed. But when Eddie Mole killed his father Euly hadn't sought revenge, and he wouldn't do so now. Maybe he wanted revenge, but he didn't believe it could be had. If he killed Eddie Mole, the death wouldn't revive Barney Kreider. He doubted he could find the brothers, but if he did he wouldn't get his money back.

He despaired. He didn't understand how any man could kill another, or why two men, not friends but surely not enemies, had so low an opinion of him they'd violate all that was his. And Jenny had helped them! He remembered how long the winter had seemed after his father's death, and felt bleak loneliness descending.

The Muenster brothers were born, even bred, for trouble, but Jenny bewildered him. He remembered her handing him cookies at his father's funeral. Could so touching a gesture have been calculated?

All my plans, my dreams, were a fantasy. She had no faith in me.

Work, he told himself. That is all I can do. *Das leben ist arbeit.*

Many saleable goods remained in the hardware, and he set

about packing them for the trip to Caldwell. He put aside canned beef and potatoes to eat on the trail.

He supposed he was duty bound to go by way of the Muenster farm and have things out with Jenny—assuming she was there. One way or another, he had to end things, but mustering his courage was hard. Still, what kind of man would accept such an affront? Was he a man at all if he did?

Were all gentle people doomed to be victims? What matter how hard you worked, how honest you were, if thieves and murderers ruled the land?

They didn't. Their wildness caught up with them. They were killed by their own kind or brought to justice. He had to believe this. He had to believe the world held a little more good than evil.

Some horses ran away if you handled them clumsily, and he was clumsy as he moved about in the cast. But Gerty and Maude loved him and remained patient as he led them past the garden and backed them into the hardware. They seemed grateful to be in harness again. He talked to them, his voice high and emotional.

He scooted a box near to set his whole leg on, then lifted up the cast with his hands. At last he sat upright, rustled the reins and clucked to his friends, and they made the turn toward Jericho Springs. With the drought, the road was firm even through the Zimmerman Woods, and a breeze cooled him from his efforts.

He needed advice. Helmut might have summoned his brothers, any of whom could have cited a grievance, and they'd bring the judgment of God and man down on Henry Muenster. But Helmut was dead and Kate and Johnny had left for the Osage reservation. Then Euly thought, Giles Cabot, the man who'd driven such a hard bargain for Euly's apples, but now his partner.

CABOT STOOD SORTING MAIL into boxes, but nodded and motioned down the hall toward his office. "How's that leg?"

"I believe the cast could come off. I've been walking on it."

He read Kate's telegram from three days before, but Cabot, an

Englische, had no information what had gone on at the church. Euly described the warehouse he'd rented, the several sales he'd made and what they portended, and Cabot said the crates of rifles should be waiting when Euly returned to Caldwell.

Cabot poured hot tea and offered ginger snaps from a tin. He sat again. He tapped his fingers on his desk. "Trouble, Ulysses?"

Euly blurted it all out. Had he been talking to Annelise, he'd have fought back tears, but that wouldn't do here. Men kept their emotions under control.

"Remarkable," Cabot said.

"Sir?"

"Your powers of deduction. My guess is you have it right. Those boys went off on the train last Monday and they shipped six crates."

Euly sat forward. "Where were they bound?"

"Wichita, but I had the impression they were leaving the country. You grubstaked them, Ulysses."

"And Jenny—"

"Your young lady." Cabot reached for words. "No, she wasn't with them."

"What would you do, Mr. Cabot?"

"Nothing. You'll never find those fools. Call it a business loss." Cabot laughed. "You might bill the county for services rendered, since we're all better off without Will and Milton Muenster."

Euly stared. The man's cynicism was almost inspiring. "I meant about Jenny."

Cabot's nostrils flared and irritation swept over his angular face. "When it comes to affairs of the heart, Ulysses, I am not the man to consult."

Euly nodded.

"But since you are my partner, I will say it again: do nothing. She has shown her true self. You might say she has done you a favor and the cost can be borne. Be grateful to the gods you did not marry this girl."

"We—"

"She is waiting for you. She has a story to tell. Perhaps she will cry and beg forgiveness. Why bother with it? This is the opinion of a lifelong bachelor but you asked for it. Were it me, and I am not a drinking man, I'd buy a bottle of whiskey—which, by the way, has been difficult to find since your father's death—and take a long walk in the woods. I'd shout, I'd beat the ground, I'd fire that Marlin of yours at turkey buzzards. Maybe I'd pray, too, and then I'd be on my way to Caldwell."

"Yes, sir," Euly said, his head low.

"While we have been talking, I saw Doc Hostetler pass in the window. He has had his lunch. He will be reading his paper and smoking his pipe. Let's walk down there and get that damn cast removed."

CABOT'S LOGIC COULDN'T ACCOUNT for the human heart. Euly knew that's what Annelise would say. He could almost hear her: "I'm sure there's an explanation. Jenny's still a very young woman, Ulysses. Give her a chance!"

Logic couldn't explain why Jenny had stolen from him, only that she had. He feared Cabot was entirely right. But halfway to Newton, resolving all along to keep going, he found himself turning up the weedy lane onto Henry Muenster's farm. He drove past an overgrown hay field, then a plot of corn that had flooded and hadn't been replanted. Topping a hill, he pulled back the reins and steeled himself. From a quarter-mile's distance he made out Henry, sitting in the middle of his barnyard as always, contemplating his ever-dwindling farm from his rickety chair. The sun burned over the swamp and as Euly watched, the barn's shadow swallowed Henry Muenster.

I can't reach Newton before nightfall, he thought, as he urged his team down the eroded lane, allowing them to pick their way because of the heavy load. I'll take the quarry road that heads straight for Wichita and stop at that little lake.

Euly reached under the tarp for the bottle and took a long pull. It was bad whiskey, not the good stuff his father imported, but good whiskey was over-rated. They were all the same after the first drink.

He did not greet Henry Muenster. He aimed the wagon between the old man and the barn and made a wide turn toward the house, so that his horses pointed uphill again.

Henry stood shakily. "Euly Kreider! Jest in time for supper. Well, you know we ain't got much, but you're shore welcome."

Euly didn't reply. He lifted the Marlin from its scabbard and laid it across his thighs.

"Now, Euly. No need for that rifle. You jest climb on down from there, you know we're friends, we'll have a good long talk."

Gerty pawed at the barnyard mud and Euly pulled on the reins. He sensed movement in the house but kept his eyes on Henry. From behind the old man, a dozen geese marched forward, flapping their wings, bending back their long necks.

Henry sat again in his chair and tapped out his pipe. He looked up at Euly blearily. "It's them boys, ain't it? I'd tell you where they is, Euly, if I knowed myself. Cecilia and I, we been grievin', we been prayin' for their souls, because we know they taken the path of iniquity, the path that leadeth to destruction."

The geese waddled onto the long porch and lined up to study Euly. They pulled their necks back and hissed like snakes. He thought of the cobras he'd seen long ago at a traveling circus.

"They left us in terrible shape. We might have to move to town, my legs how they is, but I tell you, Euly, you had a pile of work to do after your daddy died. It all goes back to that, you want my persnal point a view. If you'd hired them boys, if they coulda brought home a mite of cash—"

"Where's Jenny?" Euly said, his voice without inflection.

As if awaiting her curtain call, Jenny emerged onto the porch, wearing a long red dress Euly recognized from the hardware, and no shoes. She is so pretty, he thought. In his mind, he organized rebukes, but they didn't reach his lips.

"I been worried about you, sweetheart," Jenny said. "Down

in the Territory with no one to watch over you. You got your leg back!"

He nodded.

"Mama has supper on, you wanna come in. Don't you want to come in?"

"I could have married you."

She pulled back her head like one of the geese. "When, Euly? Not before you took me down there, all those nights on the trail, and then have to live in some shack. With those savages."

His sister? Johnny? Was that what she meant? He swallowed. That Jenny hated those he loved only now occurred to him.

"Red niggers, that's what they is," Henry threw in. "We dealt with 'em we first settled in this country, they'd come around beggin'. Steal you blind."

"Your brothers," Euly said, his voice a thing apart. "They forced you."

"Church wouldn't have 'em," Henry went on. "Now, personly, I'd let 'em get married. Bible says we'se all God's children, niggers and Bohemies and Injuns, too. But I tell you, sir, I have no influence in worldly affairs. They wouldn't listen to me. Entire congregation rose up against 'em!"

Jenny's eyes met his without a flicker. "They're like me, Euly, no chance at all in this life."

"You stole."

She shrugged. "They went over to the cash register, and if they were going to take that—for a grubstake, Euly, for a chance in life!—they might as well take the guns. My *brothers*, Euly."

"The hat box," he said. "They couldn't know about it."

She blinked and pride fled her face. She stepped off the porch and put down her bare feet carefully across the barnyard. She looked up, reeling a little. "What difference does it make, Euly? You'd never marry me!"

He'd practiced how he'd say, "Thank you for the cookies, Jenny," and drive off. Such biting words would inflict a wound that never would heal, but then again, they wouldn't. If she could steal from him, his measured retort was silly. Even if he hurt her, what might he gain? *Do nothing*, Cabot said.

Do nothing. He threw a last glance toward the porch, where Henry stood now with his scowling wife. Euly had never exchanged a word with her.

Euly looked straight ahead, called out to Gerty and Maude, and eased forward. He didn't crack his reins or shout. He'd been a freighter too long, and knew his horses too well, for theatrics. He sensed movement behind him, the geese honking and scolding, but he didn't look back even when he topped the hill and met twilight. Two miles down the quarry road he maneuvered the Belgians into a sycamore grove by the shining lake. He set the brake, pulled out his bottle, and stepped down.

He built a fire—and was surprised to see it had gone to coals. He sat on a dry log and joined in the chorus of coyotes, howling at the pale moon.

"Did me a favor!" he screamed. "Did me a favor!"

18

Whiskey Runner

In thirty-two years Johnny had mastered the craft of loneliness, but he was only an apprentice to worry. He worried
about protecting his new wife and the way they had been
going at things, maybe soon he'd worry how to feed a family.
He worried how they'd claim their land in the Outlet and the
ways in which whites could cheat them.

As the sun climbed overhead and the road east grew busier,
he worried about securing Euly's whiskey. They were not five
miles east of the reservation when he hid the empty barrels in an
abandoned soddy, even though they were worth one dollar each.

"We hauled those barrels all the way from Jericho Springs,"
Kate said.

"You see how men look at them."

A traveler could tell the barrels were empty by the easy way
the wagon rode. But they were on Cherokee land now and the
visible barrels announced their intentions. True, some Cherokees were bootleggers. Others were policemen, looking for bootleggers. And the Cherokees and Osage had never been friends.

"We should not haul whiskey at all," Kate said at last. "You
saw the men—the women, too. Our brothers and sisters, Johnny,
enslaved to the bottle. And at the lodge of Buffalo Dancer!"

He nodded.

"Were you never tempted?"

"In boarding school, yes. One long winter. Two."

Kate looked doubtful. "You overcame it. You didn't like the taste."

"It is the taste of evil and I liked it very much. It filled the emptiness."

Kate sighed. "Seemed to."

"Seemed to. I studied older men who did not drink. Buffalo Dancer, and Emmet Baxter, and Helmut Kreider."

"How did they fill the emptiness?"

"With belief."

She smiled. "What do you believe in, Johnny? In Jesus?"

"I believe in you. That I can be a good farmer. That perhaps I grow wise as I grow old."

Kate shook her head. "What if I am no good at working dawn to dusk?"

"You will need to be, our first years."

"What if I become bored and want to travel to Philadelphia with my paintings?"

"Unless you are bored with me, I will accompany you. If you are, I will go hunting."

"What if I die in childbirth?"

"Then I will drink."

IN FIVE DAYS THEY reached Joplin, Missouri. They followed a nameless stream colored a bluish gray by runoff from lead mines, and twisted through mountains of spewed-up, discolored slabs of rock. Smoke rose on either side of them. They heard the shrill hiss of steam and machines pounding nearby: *clunk, plank, clunk, plank.* Dust-covered men rushed past them in wagons, their horses winded, gaunt, with sores on their bellies. This was another world and Johnny and Kate were frightened. It was as though, around the next bend, the violated earth would erupt in flames.

Nature resumed near the village of Carl Junction, with tall trees and a clear stream where Johnny longed to fish. He'd been traveling so long, and so much work stretched ahead of him, that he was weary from his aching neck down to his soul. This is my life, he thought, with this woman, with our family to be. This is the time when I need to work hard, as hard as Ulysses and Helmut Kreider and Emmet Baxter, harder than any of them because I am Osage.

They found the trader. His rambling store, a series of pole structures plastered over with—maybe held up by—signs for plug tobacco and farm machinery, stood tucked inside a grove of hickories. One tree grew out of the building itself, with the tin roof split around it. Winston O'Reilly, proprietor, the sign read, just like the bills of lading. Johnny pulled back, and his stalwart mules stopped short.

"We're here," Kate murmured, as if she wished she weren't. Rotten boards had fallen through on the store's long porch, and quick red wasps swarmed around a nest at the eaves. The interior was dark as a root cellar. They stood a moment, allowing their eyes to adjust, until O'Reilly called out to them from a rectangle of light shining down from a lone high window. Kate fled to the dark aisle of canned goods and threw Johnny fleeting glances, while he laid down the bills of lading and tried to appear confident.

O'Reilly was a craggy-faced old man with a crooked red nose and full white beard. Johnny's proposition irritated him. "I do not sell whiskey to Indians. And for you to ask breaks the law, my friend, so it does. Would yeez in turn sell to the Quapaws? Would I then be receiving a visit from a United States Marshal?"

"I am the agent of Mr. Barney Kreider's son," Johnny said, pointing to the bills. "Mr. Ulysses Kreider."

"Yes." O'Reilly nodded doubtfully. He bent far over his counter to catch a glimpse of the mules. "Prince and Pauper! Aye, aye, no one but Barney could come up with names like that."

"Ulysses Kreider will sell to white men in Caldwell, Kansas."

"The Outlet? Quite the profit, if you're not murdered along your way." O'Reilly seemed to reconsider but shook his head once more. "Yeez made a long trip for nothing, lad."

Johnny wasn't displeased. O'Reilly's refusal gave him an excuse he could carry to Euly but he was relieved for another reason. Sometimes the Little Hero allowed greed to overcome his good sense—and so did Johnny. Temptation, not to mention danger, had been removed.

"There is another matter, sir," Kate said, stepping forward as Johnny stepped back. The light from the high window framed her face amid drifting dust motes, and for an instant she became an angel rather than his wife.

"Yes," O'Reilly said, staring.

"A personal matter. I am looking for a woman, I don't even know her name, but an Indian woman who died in these parts. I am Katherine, daughter of the Barney Kreider on that bill—"

Something sparked in O'Reilly's eyes. He came around from his counter and dropped into a rocking chair by the cold stove. He yanked a hickory stick from the woodbox and sliced at the bark with a butcher's knife. "A very long time ago it was, lass."

"You knew her."

"I couldn't conjure it, ye entered this old place. Ye resemble Venus."

"Venus!"

"Morning Star was her name but she wanted to be called Venus because—" O'Reilly threw down the stick and folded his knife. "I don't know. Because it didn't matter. She kept our books, mathematics being a challenge for me. Barney Kreider will be well, I trust?"

"I fear—" Johnny reached for the words a white man might use. "He has passed on to his just reward."

"Ah," O'Reilly studied Kate. "I would not say a word against your father."

"Say what you like," Kate said. "He did not acknowledge me until his death."

"Oh, dear." O'Reilly frowned. He studied the hickory stick as if it might talk. "Long, long ago, when me wife still walked this earth. Barney and the morning star. It is a sad tale."

MORNING STAR CAME TO the O'Reillys early in the seventies, when she was sixteen. She'd lived at the Jesuit mission in Saint Paul, Kansas all her life, but when the Osage were forced into Oklahoma, the mission declined. All the children went south except for Morning Star.

"Why not go with the tribe?" Johnny asked.

No relative claimed her. Without such standing she would have been a slave. And with her Jesuit upbringing, she could hardly speak Osage.

The nuns had filled her head with Bible stories, and Morning Star believed them all to be true, though only for the Holy Land. Nothing so magical as David killing Goliath, or Eve tempting Adam, could occur in a place as dreary as Saint Paul, Kansas. Morning Star longed to visit exotic Israel and Greece, but they lay far to the east, in the vicinity of Philadelphia and London.

The Jesuit god lived in the East, too, though the nuns claimed he was everywhere, invisible like Wah-Kon-Da but not the same at all, because Wah-Kon-Da was pagan. This Jesuit god punished you to show how powerful he was, rather like Sister Johanna and particularly Sister Jane, the mixed-blood Choctaw. Claiming she did the will of God, Sister Jane sometimes whipped Morning Star's legs with a willow switch, though quite as often the girl ran away from the clumsy old woman.

Morning Star was a wicked child, the nuns claimed, the demon offspring of children banished from the tribe because they'd yielded to carnal temptations. Where were they now? Dead, of course! Morning Star's blood was poisoned and she must devote her life to penance. When she was little, Morning Star cowered in the mission garden expecting, almost hoping, to be turned into a pillar of salt.

As she grew older Morning Star rejected what the nuns said. What use was a god so whimsical as to create you, then scorn you for your imperfections? She was *not* wicked. In *The Student's Little Book of Philosophy*, she learned what she was: a *tabula rasa*.

A blank slate. An empty vessel. Not good but not wicked, and thus—she thought—she could *think* her way into existence.

Johnny liked books in which men did things, such as Little Hero's namesake, Ulysses, in *The Odyssey*. Otherwise, Johnny knew only McGuffey, the Bible, and enough arithmetic so the whites couldn't cheat him. He knew nothing of philosophy but understood Morning Star's plight. It was the plight of every Indian given a white man's education, but worse because the girl had no family.

"The girl devoured every book in the school," O'Reilly said. "This was how she understood the world."

"Or misunderstood it," Kate said.

Morning Star visited the great Father Jenkins, who said, "Perhaps our holy sisters worry too much about the Old Testament. Concentrate on the Gospels, Mary."

Mary was her white name. She couldn't be called Morning Star because the name was pagan. She didn't understand the word pagan but that's what her people were.

Morning Star thought, I have no people.

"The words of Jesus," Father Jenkins went on. "His great example."

Jesus told a beautiful story about a prodigal son whose father welcomed him home despite many sins. I am no one's son, Morning Star said. And I have no father unless he is you. Are you my father? Yes, child, Father Jenkins said, but try to understand. The story is a parable. The welcoming father is the great Jehovah of the East and the wayward son is everybody.

"That's right, Mary," Father Jenkins said. "*You* are the prodigal son. And so am I."

Jesus seemed like a man who should be in charge of everything, but how he could sweep up all the sins of the world, why he would want to, and why such a good man had to die, made no sense to Morning Star. The sense it made required an ingredient Father Jenkins called faith and she had only logic.

When Morning Star was fourteen, a carpenter forced her

into the tool shed by the garden. He kissed her roughly and thrust his hands under her shirt. He began fumbling with her skirt but then Sister Jane came out of the mission. When she called, "Mary! *You*, girl!" the man fled.

Morning Star had been reading the *Inferno*, and that night dreamed of the ferry across the River Styx, which looked much like the Neosho River except for being darker. The ferryman, Charon, became the carpenter. His face twisted with lust, he grabbed for her legs, and Morning Star woke screaming.

The nuns ran with their heavy feet and shook her until she lay quiet. They watched her after that. They liked to catch her talking to herself because it proved she was demon-possessed.

"Sister doesn't like us," Morning Star said, as she scrubbed the big pots. "What can I do?" Morning Star addressed herself as two people and answered as one, because she was her only companion. She knew the difference between *we* and *I*, but such subtleties were lost on the nuns. They hated her because she was Osage. They hated her because she was young. They hated her because she was pretty, and read books, and had beautiful handwriting.

The nuns locked her in the toolshed, letting her out only for work. They always had boxes of castoff clothing to sort, dishes to wash, rows of turnips to weed. Even stalls to muck out, though Morning Star hadn't the muscles for such chores. The nuns worked her so hard she grew sick and lay in bed all day, turning to the wall when the nuns threatened to send her to the madhouse in Topeka.

Maybe she should have hated it, because the carpenter had tried to rape her there, but the toolshed was almost like living outdoors, and sometimes the nuns forgot about her entirely. She stole candles from the church, canned peaches from the pantry. Father Jenkins's library was well-stocked, and she filled her *tabula rasa* with Don Quixote's noble quest and the strange animal stories of Aesop. She decided they were like the parables of Jesus—that is, about something else. Sometimes, she asked Father Jenkins what that something was, and he'd tell her, always cautioning her to listen to the nuns, to listen to his homilies, that all she really needed to do was muse over the Gospels.

She read and reread *The Life and Adventures of Robinson Crusoe*, because it seemed like her story, to be given up, to be lost, perhaps one day to find her way; and *Moll Flanders*, which she didn't understand at first, except that Moll Flanders was an outcast like she was, and men wanted to sleep with her. The carpenter came after Morning Star for the same reason: she was a woman. What did it mean to be a woman?

The *Odyssey*, being full of monsters, was more comforting. It swept her away for days. She dreamed she was Circe, the witch.

She learned to climb on the work bench and pry out the old window. Afterward the window sat loosely in its casement, but the half-blind nuns didn't notice. And it was a while before anyone discovered her raids on the communion wine Father Jenkins kept in the church basement. He ordered it by the wagonload and drank a bottle every evening.

Morning Star drank until she could no longer read and the world grew fuzzy. Then she crawled out her window, crept away from the mission, and stumbled along the banks of the Neosho. She longed to steal a boat and float south into Indian Territory, but she knew she was an Osage only to whites. She could not be Morning Star. She had never been Mary. She decided to call herself Venus.

One day when Sister Jane harangued her, Venus screamed. She backed the Choctaw nun up the stone walk, hurling vile curses that surprised Venus as much as Sister Jane. Perhaps demons really did inhabit her. "Wicked old woman," she said. "*Your* blood is poison!" Venus was delighted to read fear in that simple old face, but she knew her performance had doomed her.

The nuns accused her of stealing books and food, and Venus couldn't deny it. They said white students were coming to the school now and that unless Venus worked very hard, and didn't talk to herself, and never complained, Father Jenkins would send her to the place for crazy people in Topeka. So Venus packed a satchel with books, fruit, and two bottles of communion wine. She stepped out on the road that ran due west as far as she could see, and due east as far as she could see. In the East she might find the meaning of life her books hinted at but never quite revealed.

Kate laughed. "She was walking to Greece?"

Venus walked one hundred miles, swimming rivers, dodging coyotes and two lecherous white men, until hunger drove her to the O'Reilly door. She wore her drab mission school dress, torn in several places. Her eyes were wild with fear, yearning—and maybe a dash of lunacy. With little debate, the childless O'Reillys took her in.

"Like me," Kate said. "An orphan."

"She was too innocent, too much a child for this world we live in. But she kept our books and she swept the store room every night. And she had a deft hand with leather. Deer hides came to me on trade, and she worked them soft to make moccasins and boots and gloves. It gave us additional products to sell.

"She kept a garden plot and made a trifling little from her cucumbers and squash and blackberries. She had her own room, a stove to cook on, but often she slept under the stars. In the fall, even in winter, I would come upon her in the forest, eyes shut, talking as if to spirits in the air."

"Praying," Kate said.

"But to what god? We loved the morning star, I believe she loved us, but we were all of us marooned here in this lonely land like her Robinson Crusoe. The morning star read through me little library of Burroughs and Burns, Audubon and Edgar Allan Poe. She filled pages with her writings and sketches." The old man laughed. "She came to realize that this was not the East."

"She drew?" Kate asked.

"Deer, flowers along Center Creek, hummingbirds—all kinds of birds. Eagles. Buzzards. Me wife, Ellen, told me she drew strange creatures as well. Pookas and changelings in the shadows of the forest. Venus claimed she saw them."

Again, Kate's face took on that angelic look. "A little touched," she murmured. "The nuns were right."

"She was fanciful, aye. Talked to herself. Remember: Venus had only the likes of Ellen and me for company—and dogs, always. Three-legged orphans, wandering up from the mines. They lived in the woods, quiet as she. She was lonely. She made up things."

"Men?" Kate said.

"None that I knew. Me business was with a rough trade, too rough for the morning star; and from the mines, Irishmen like meself. A rude lot. Your father, in due course. A grieving man—"

Kate nodded as if she'd been a witness. "He'd lost his wife, Evangeline. In childbirth."

"So he said. Barney was a well-spoken man—a gentleman, an odd duck for such a dangerous trade. He could talk literature, and sometimes I'd hear a fiddle in the woods, Old Country tunes, German he said they were, and Russian. I never had me any music, and Ellen loved me despite me plain soul, but poor Venus was stricken as with disease. How could we object? What could we do for this wild girl? 'Venus has never had a moment of happiness,' me Ellen said. 'She never had a friend.'"

Kate almost snarled. "Because of this 'friend,' she died in childbirth."

"She did not." O'Reilly made a sudden gesture toward the dark rear of the store. "Me wife delivered *you* right there. The morning star lived another year—died of heartbreak, you could say, as in some old pub tune. Afterwards, poor Barney came to visit."

Kate's voice rose in bitterness. "Poor Barney?"

O'Reilly sighed. "Barney gave her money. He brought her dresses and shoes. He carried apples and hams from his country in the West—"

"*Hams?*"

"He built her a little house by Center Creek. It still stands."

Kate began to cry. Johnny stood in wonder, dumbfounded by the ways of women and men in love, until O'Reilly threw him a sharp glance. He put an arm around Kate's shoulder.

"Go on, sir," Kate said.

"'Marry this poor girl,' I told him. 'Could you do better for a wife?' I shamed him, you see. We knew by then that the morning star—that your father and she—"

"Yes," Kate said.

"Barney went home with me whiskey. I thought Venus would die, so sad she was, and he is but a vagabond, we thought. Like many a white man with the brown girls. But he did return! And soon! Why do I care what they think, he said to me, when I am already a renegade who runs whiskey? 'Precisely, sir,' I said. 'I will marry her!' he announced. And he said so to the morning star! But this time, he did not return for almost a year, and Venus was dead."

"By her own hand!" Kate said.

"By hers and mine. By your father's. By her passion, I fear, for John Barleycorn."

"Sir!" Kate said.

"For me whiskey. She couldn't hide it anymore. She couldn't mind the store or read her useless books. She couldn't care for the wee one."

"For me."

"Aye."

Johnny took Kate's hand again but she stared at him as if revulsed. "May I see the cabin?"

"That you may." O'Reilly said.

JOHNNY DROVE THE WAGON downhill to Center Creek to let Prince and Pauper drink and cool off. He threw water along their shoulders and flanks, and they snorted and twitched their ears. He unbridled them for their oats but kept them in harness. Five hours of daylight remained, and as soon as Kate finished her reverie they'd be on their way.

He made out Venus's clapboard cabin upstream, one room but with a broad chimney, two hardware windows, and a long front porch. The two chairs on the porch had nearly reverted to dust and the north wall was stained green with moss. But Barney Kreider had nailed on a galvanized steel roof that showed no rust after almost twenty years, meaning the cabin's interior probably remained intact.

Johnny made a mental note to use galvanized steel on his own buildings. Then again, those new asphalt rolls were cheaper and quicker, and he'd need to put up buildings fast before winter. Some kind of barn, some kind of house. He wouldn't allow Kate to live in a hole in the ground.

The trader came down the hill, startling him. "Want to buy some whiskey, Lad?" O'Reilly pointed downstream toward a wooden shed. "I can sell you four barrels made from me own barley and corn, aged a year now in white oak barrels I charred meself."

"But you said—"

O'Reilly laughed. "Barney Kreider was me only client. With the poor fellow dead, I have no market. I will sell to his son and that ends me business. Ulysses, you called him?"

"Yes."

"Even his son's name from a book. Come along by the other shore, lad, and I'll help you load."

Johnny bridled the mules again and pulled up to the bank, but he was troubled. I cannot blame Ulysses for this, he thought. Money might be the root of all evil but I have a wife now and need it. My cattle and horses won't care where it came from.

And how could I disappoint this lonely old man?

You are full of lies, his Osage self said. Money from evil cannot be purified. It leads to dry wells and locust hordes. Dead cattle. Dead horses. So Buffalo Dancer would counsel. Do not walk down this dark path, Grandson. Wah-Kon-Da will not light your way.

Johnny pulled into the shed and maneuvered the mules until the tailgate could drop onto a split-log ramp. They rolled the four barrels near and Johnny braced his legs to turn them upright—a task for two men.

"No necessity," O'Reilly said. "I have some shucks of barley straw."

When they were done the wagon appeared to be loaded with straw, though a careful observer could see how the wheels cut into the soil, pressed low by a ton of whiskey. Still, they'd made a good camouflage.

"I estimate six nights," O'Reilly said. "Even then, yeez must avoid the Cherokees."

"I will travel across Kansas. At night, yes."

"Good." O'Reilly sighed, and sat on a mildewed parlor chair. "Good it is finished."

A mouse ran out of the chair and down the dock, stopped at Johnny's boots, and looked up with its whiskers twitching. Johnny stumbled to avoid stepping on it and O'Reilly handed him a cup. "To seal our bargain."

Johnny took the cup. One wouldn't hurt. "Ulysses authorized me to pay—"

The trader waved a hand. "The last of Winston O'Reilly's famous whiskey. Going out into the world to render joy, mischief, and misery. Tell the boy to pay me what he believes it to be worth."

Johnny threw back his drink. He remembered the strong taste. At the school, after drinking, George Snapping Turtle and he fought until one of them couldn't get to his feet. Whiskey lent you a sort of courage but it also turned you stupid.

And reflective. The trader looked up with blurred eyes. "Your wife despises her father."

Johnny nodded.

"Me Mary, she'd ne'er talk to him afterwards. Only God

can forgive him. But I swear to you, though he came too late, Barney meant to take her and your Kate to his own country."

Johnny gulped his second cup. O'Reilly's whiskey was mellow and fine. The old trader's life was finished and Johnny felt free to talk to him. "It is hard to understand men. I have encountered regret, and guilt as well, but not like what this white man must have felt. As you say, only his god could forgive him."

O'Reilly stared over the woods. On the far horizon, you could see smoke drifting from the mines. "'There be three things which are too wonderful for me.'"

"What?" Johnny asked. The words were familiar, from boarding school or perhaps his Baptist stepfather, but he couldn't pinpoint the memory. He stood.

"'Yea, four which I know not: The way of an eagle in the air; the way of a serpent upon a rock; the way of a ship in the midst of the sea; and—'"

"The way of a man with a maid," Johnny finished.

WITH THE SUN HALFWAY down the sky, they turned west. The steel tires clicked on fine gravel from the mines, and the wagon rode easily. A week's more work for Prince and Pauper, and he'd have to find water for them. Johnny liked how eventempered they were. They were far less emotional than horses. "I wonder if Ulysses would sell these mules," he said. "I believe they would take the plow."

Kate didn't answer. She had retrieved her mother's notebooks, dating to the bewildered girl's mission days, and couldn't stop reading. She looked at Johnny with a sadness so intimate she embarrassed him and he smiled crookedly. She'd found pencil drawings, too, smudged and faded, only a few. A deer and a fawn, a misshapen man hulking in the trees behind. Leaves sailing above a waterfall. A bearded, half-naked man propped up in bed, laughing. Like an image from a dream, and then he realized: Barney Kreider.

Johnny tore his eyes away. "It is a violation."

"So true." Kate said, her eyes soulful, teary. "Art is a violation."
He knew she'd credited him with a lofty thought. "That your
mother was also an artist must strike you in the heart."

"You've been so patient with me." She leaned across to kiss
him but then she erupted. "You've been *drinking*."

"It was a matter of courtesy." He swallowed. "Between men."

"Drinking when you'd just heard—the same as I heard—about
Morning Star. My *mother*!" Kate turned on the seat. "What is
this? We're hauling straw?"

"We are hauling whiskey, Kate. As we proposed to do."

"Let me *off*!" She pushed a boot down to the running board.
Johnny caught her arm. "We're miles from anywhere, Kate.
You are my wife—"

She pulled away. "Take me to the train."

"You can't—" he began, but stopped, doomed to see all sides
of a question. Kate's wifely duty required her to stay with him.
She ought to insist. Some men would strike her or tie her down—
but on the other hand, the trip across Kansas would be hard,
even dangerous. It made sense for her to take the train. Why
hadn't he thought of it earlier?

The whiskey. He had given up on hauling whiskey.

"Baxter Springs," he said. "About four miles. I believe there's
a station."

Her lips trembled in what he read as disappointment he'd
capitulated. "I will *not* haul whiskey."

"I understand. I didn't believe it was destined, but this—"
Again Johnny stopped. Whiskey killed her mother. Whiskey
made by the same hand as the barrels they hauled. Whiskey
meant for Barney Kreider, the man who abandoned her mother.
"It's money, Kate, that's all. I'm not going to roll these barrels
into the weeds and take an axe to them."

"Pull up *here*."

He drew back the reins. If he'd told her the trip was too dangerous for her, would she have insisted on going?

She reached into the straw and found her bag, then hurried

into a grove of blackjacks along a dry creek. He waited in the sun, sweating. The mules brayed and Pauper turned back his head as if with a question. At last Kate returned in Mennonite garb, complete with black veil and gloves. Train travel could be dangerous for a woman, particularly an Indian woman, but Kate had turned white again. A white woman in mourning.

They didn't talk. In another mile, they reached the station, little more than a step-up stool in such a small village, and luck was with them. Perhaps the white god sided with Kate—or was it Wah-Kon-Da, knowing what whiskey did to Indians? A north-bound train stood dripping and wheezing as it took on water.

"You have your derringer," Johnny said.

Kate patted a pocket. He couldn't see her eyes but knew she wouldn't say goodbye with a kiss. He sighed as she turned toward the tracks. The way of a man with a maid. The way of a maid with a man.

"Will I see you in six days?" he called out.

She turned, lifted the veil, but gave no hint of a smile. "For better or for worse."

THAT NIGHT JOHNNY MET a traveler pushing his horse so hard it stumbled and half-fell. Not long after, four men followed at full gallop, their horses wheezing, the froth down their necks gleaming in the starlight. Then he heard ordinary prairie sounds: coyotes with their incessant complaints, owls querying every passerby, and the whizzing of flying insects. The hot wind rustled through grass like some invisible spirit. By four, even these sounds died away, and Johnny heard only his wagon wheels in the stillness and Prince and Pauper's monotonous clumping. He did not seem to be moving and slept for short intervals.

At dawn he turned up a drought-shrunken creek with a flat rock bottom. He guided the wagon onto a little island dense with sapling cottonwoods, fed his weary mules, and waded around the island to see if his wagon was visible from the road. He ate cold biscuits and jerky, rubbed coal oil on his arms and neck as a strategy against mosquitoes, then lay upon the wagon straw, a round chambered in the Winchester and his shotgun near.

He dreamed of Comes with the Snow, bathing in the creek. She made no effort to cover herself and he was aroused. She reeled toward him through the water, holding out her hands. "Drink," he thought she said. "Whiskey!" Her tone was guttural like a pig's. She fell at his feet, still holding up her hands, gulping water, drowning. He woke, dripping with sweat, terrified, and crawled down to the creek to sit in the tepid water. The trees were still in the heat and locusts shrilled.

Through the second night Johnny met no one and felt strength in his solitude. Here's how a man should lead his life: with a good rifle, a good horse, alone in the wilderness. Kate could never be corralled, and anyhow an Indian marriage meant nothing in the white world. When he'd delivered Euly's whiskey, he'd saddle Soquili and ride down into Texas, toward the great ocean, maybe Mexico. Here's your damn whiskey, he'd tell Euly, delivered by your Indian lackey. Give me the money.

Kate be damned!

Yes, he understood why she objected to hauling whiskey. It reduced proud Indian families to squalor and shame. Her mother died from it. He agreed whiskey was bottled evil but he merely pursued what they'd both agreed to. That would be the end of it! Would she spurn the money, when he placed it in her hand?

Johnny led a monastic life into his thirties. Sometimes women pursued him, even white women, and he never understood why. He was a farmhand and not frolicsome. They brought him meals, sewed him shirts, laughed at what they perceived to be his witticisms, but their behavior confused him. After a while, also confused, they let him go.

Then Kate turned his head, a woman he hadn't even thought of as female. She was a foundling, apparently part-Indian, a Mennonite good deed. She was a gawky, lonely kid from the church who liked to draw pictures on ledger paper. He posed for her half-naked, her noble savage—nothing but a joke. He didn't understand how she stopped being a kid and he couldn't do without her. When she left for Kansas City, it seemed an arm had been severed.

By the fourth night Johnny was overcome with loneliness. A solitary man defined misery, and he knew he'd been lucky to have found such a spirited wife. It was a mystical kind of luck, a luck inhabited by Wah-Kon-Da. Kate was his spirit guide, not Comes with the Snow, and he prayed he hadn't ruined things. They were one being. They should never be apart. He'd do all he could to encourage Kate's painting. He'd listen to her shrewd counsel—as he should have listened! He'd never again taste liquor.

On that night, under the bright moon, he met the horsemen.

He thought there were three, and listened. The horses traveled at an even, deliberate canter, and he counted the falling hooves. Two men, not three. A big horse, a smaller one. He recalled the horses tied at a dim roadhouse several miles behind him where he'd heard voices even at four in the morning. The canter worried him. It was the gait of pursuit, and who might there be, on this moonlit road, to pursue?

Johnny stepped down and stood between the wagon seat and the headboard, where a shot, at least an accurate shot, wouldn't hit Prince or Pauper. He could dodge the other way, and maybe the straw, or the barrels beneath it, would catch a round. A burst of light broke through the woods to the east. He raised his Winchester high so the sun would strike the barrel.

Johnny heard white men's voices, murmuring, and soon two riders emerged from shadow, silhouettes outlined by a faint red. They drew up and turned their horses ninety degrees to face him. One man was tall and rode a restive black stallion. The other was short, on a smaller, docile mare. The men had pulled their hats low. Johnny couldn't see their faces.

Prince brayed and the stallion pranced forward to the wagon, sniffed, and nibbled at the barley straw. Pauper neighed softly and the mare drew near with precise steps, like a show horse.

The tall man said, "Whatcha doing out here, Chief, middle a no place?"

The short man raised high his reins, so that the strengthening sunlight struck his hands. He let out a cackle. "What you say you're doing with your mule?"

Johnny looked from one dark face to the other but didn't reply.

"That wagon's sure riding low fer a load a straw," the tall man said.

"I have a two-bottomed plow under there."

"I figgered. You being an honest Injun, Chief, you mebbe don't realize what some jaspers do. They haul guns, or whiskey, and cover it with straw jest like you done. Not likely to fool your undesirables, and they're up and down these roads all night long. Some friendly advice, Chief. It was me, I'd pull that straw away, so's people kin see you jest hauling farm equipment. Del and me, we'd be glad to—"

"Move on," Johnny said.

"Cain't say as how I care for your tone," the tall man said. He pulled on the stallion and it backed off a step, twisting its head, fighting the bit. "Del and me, we'se kinda the lawdogs, this part of the road."

"That's awright, that's awright," the short man said. "Got no quarrel with you, Cochise. Wouldn't have a little sumpin to eat, would you?"

Holding the rifle with his index finger above the trigger guard, Johnny reached with his left hand for his possibles bag, then held up a cotton sack in the half-light. He tossed it at the tall man, who fumbled it, then shoved a biscuit toward his dark face. He threw the bag at the short man.

"He throwed it to *me*," the tall man said.

The men turned their horses. "Shore thankee, Cochise," the short man said.

"Be carebul, Chief," the tall man said, his mouth full of biscuit. They rode toward the darker side of dawn, laughing. Johnny climbed to the wagon seat and watched them until they were out of sight. The road curved into a woods at the foot of a hill, and though he couldn't see it in the weak light, he knew a river ran there—the Verdigris. The woods would open again at water's edge, where there had to be a bridge. The two men would take positions on the far side, meaning to catch him midstream.

Or they'd ride on, but his every Osage instinct told him they wouldn't. He urged Prince and Pauper south into the grass and pulled the wagon under two locust trees. He set the brake and gave the mules feed bags to keep them quiet.

The border lay two miles farther south. Maybe the men would follow, maybe not, but he didn't want to deal with the Cherokees. He could strike north across open country but it would be slow going, and he'd be easy prey.

He could stay where he was and wait for daylight. But another wagon might not pass for hours, and the two men still would come for him, night or day, in this forsaken place. They knew where to sell the whiskey—and the wagon, and the mules. They were border trash. They were white and had no qualms over killing an Indian, in particular an Indian with the effrontery to haul firewater.

He slipped another box of ammunition into his pocket and ran until the trees grew sparse, perhaps one hundred yards, then turned west toward the river, running on stones and hard ground, almost soundless in his moccasins. The river was low because of the drought but still four feet deep at its center. He crossed with agonizing slowness. He looked north but the stream curved into utter blackness.

The trees thinned out again where the hill rose. He paused to pull off his wet socks, then ran north until he reached the road, shivering in his sopping clothes. He moved east barely inside the woods, once disentangling a blackberry briar that caught his shirt and dug a trench in his neck. In one hundred feet he dropped and crawled to the road. He made out a steel bridge not fifty feet away, and the orange scallop of sun directly down the road. Every leaf glowed red, with the trees casting long shadows to the west, black on less black. He looked for something to climb and finally spied an outcropping of limestone, wafer on wafer reaching upward, dropping off, he surmised, in rubble at water's edge. He glided forward thirty long steps. On his belly again, he elbowed his way up the limestone, reaching ahead to secure loose rocks. Sweat stung his eyes. An hour seemed to pass before he reached the top, trying not to gasp.

The bridge trusses had turned a fiery red, but the river below remained black. He heard the bubbling water and birds in their tentative morning song. A coyote wailed.

"Where is he?" This was the tall man, speaking in a rasping whisper. The voice came from a pocket of darkness north of the bridge but Johnny couldn't see the man himself. There seemed to be a rectangle of darker black, leaning over the water. Johnny followed it up until it spread into branches in the gray-and-red sky. The tall man stood behind a tree.

"Shut up!" This time the whisper came from directly below him. Johnny inched forward another foot and made out the short man, squatting on the bank, invisible except for the crown of his white hat. Johnny stood, with a scraggly cedar between the tall man's spot of darkness and himself. The cedar smelled like kerosene. He heard breathing and a little snort.

"He's waitin' for daylight," the tall man whispered.

"Don't matter. He cain't get that heavy load acrost nowheres else."

"He *knows*."

"Shut up!"

Johnny's fired straight down and the short man slumped forward with a grunt. Even as the man slid toward the river, Johnny leaped, keeping his toes pointed downward, holding his rifle high. The tall man fired two rounds that pinged off the bridge. Johnny twisted one foot on a submerged rock but got off a round. He fell deeper, slipped in mud, and the Winchester dipped under water. Johnny had grown up with Buffalo Dancer's muzzle loader and it wouldn't fire if it got wet. He'd never quite trusted the miracle of it, he never had attempted it, but he knew Winchesters fired as long as the barrel remained clear. The tall man was in the water now; Johnny could just make him out. He was wounded. He screamed and fired twice, the first round hitting the water to Johnny's right, the second going wild, ricocheting off something, whistling into darkness. Half-convinced the Winchester would explode, Johnny fired once more, and the tall man fell backward with a wide splash, droplets of water arching high and turning red with the rising sun.

Johnny crawled up the western shore and walked out onto the bridge. Sunlight burst through the trees and warmed his neck. He cleared his Winchester's breech, his heart pumping wildly, his ears deaf to nature's screams. He took off his moccasins, squeezed the water from them, and collapsed on the bridge, strength gone from his legs. He'd been in a kind of trance. A hundred crows called out raucously from the trees and he looked down at the dead men.

The short one lay on the bank, a leg twisted under him. The tall man was mostly submerged, his legs snagged by a rotting tree limb, but his head remained above water. The head bobbed and the dead man appeared to look up at him.

Sweat popped out on Johnny's forehead and cheeks and he felt empty inside. The world was as in the Bible, without form and void.

At last he stood. In a matter of hours—or minutes—people would cross this bridge. Even such lowborn men had friends, wives. They would not be widely mourned, but someone might identify them and try to find the killer. Johnny had talked to no one since leaving Baxter Springs, and if not this morning, he'd never be connected. It would be hell to pull them from the water but if the bodies were off the road even one hundred feet, then weeks might pass before they were discovered.

A horse whinnied, startling him. Why hadn't he thought of the horses as he sneaked through the darkness? If they had sensed him, the dead men would have been warned. He sniffed the wind: north to south. That was why. Pure luck.

The stallion reared high as Johnny approached, but the little mare co-operated, and she carried a coil of rope. Johnny crawled into the stream again and tied the rope under the short man's shoulders. His shirt had soaked in blood and he was slippery as a fish. The mare pulled him out with little difficulty but skittered sideways when Johnny tried to throw the body over the saddle. So he led the mare and they dragged the corpse down the road and a little up the hill, stashing the limp, bloody thing behind a boulder several hundred feet from the road. The mare nuzzled the dead man's hand and Johnny pulled her back. "You are a good horse," he said.

The tall man was heavier, and his wounds still seeped when Johnny touched him. He half-dragged, half-floated the body downstream until he found a landing, then pulled it behind a fallen elm, dropping it into a colony of toadstools.

He unsaddled both horses and chased them until they raced off to the north. He threw away his bloody shirt because he had another. Then he plunged into the stream again and scrubbed his Levi's until the blood disappeared. He'd bought the jeans for the wedding. He owned another pair but had left them in Kate's bag.

The sun shone brightly now. Birds sang and flew between trees. He looked at the mules as if they might accuse him of murder but they were calm as always. He sat wearily on the wagon, forty miles yet to travel.

At the crest of the hill he met a man and wife on a buckboard. A boy and girl rode in the bed.

"Mornin'," the man said, as the wagon drew near. The woman looked away as if she suspected something. White women could not be trusted. They might say, he had a knife, he tried to rape me.

"Morning," Johnny said. His face felt molten and he knew

he had to seem stoical. The kids waved as they passed. "Look at the mules," the girl said.

In a quarter-mile, at the crest of another hill, Johnny reached for his binoculars and studied the open road between the hill and the trees by the bridge. Seconds before he expected it, the buckboard emerged, then entered the woods again. He scanned the horizon and at last spied the stallion on a far ridge. The tall grass was filled with wild horses. The stallion might be one of them. He lowered the binoculars and spotted the buckboard again, coming out of the woods east of the bridge.

They were evil white men who meant to kill me. I should not be troubled by their deaths.

He shut his eyes and prayed to Wah-Kon-Da, then to the Mennonite god, but his prayers were hollow. Gods did not approve of hauling whiskey. They did not approve of murder.

I am not a murderer. I did what I had to do. Where are you, Comes with the Snow? Have you truly drowned? She stayed his hand when he drew a bead on Eddie Mole. You are not a killer, John Baxter, she said.

He was like the man holding the horses at a bank robbery. Inside, innocent people were murdered. Holding the horses, he became a murderer, too.

But they weren't innocent and I am not a murderer. I had no choice.

You chose to run whiskey.

In olden days, did a warrior lie awake at night, torn by regrets for the men he'd killed on the battlefield? Did Misai, his father, fight back tears, and overflow with fear, and feel revulsion? He did because he was my father. And yet Johnny knew that men existed who killed without regret, like the men he'd killed or Eddie Mole. Did they? Maybe even Eddie Mole had nightmares.

THOUGH IT ADDED TEN miles to his journey, Johnny turned north toward Oxford with its bridge over the Arkansas. He did not want to deal with that slow ferry at Arkansas City. Likely, the dead men hailed from there.

Gloom overtook him. The plan to seize Eddie Mole's homestead worried him. He couldn't make the run himself, because he had no birth certificate and couldn't prove American citizenship. He thought that his brother, Billy, could make it, but Billy was unreliable. He might ask his friend, Ulysses, though Ulysses was less of a horseman than Billy, and if trouble arose, Johnny wasn't sure Ulysses could handle it.

He pulled his hat low to shield his eyes from the westering sun. He realized a crowd had gathered in Oxford. Men stood on a platform to make speeches. Brightly dressed women hung on the arms of men in suits. Ripples of laughter passed through the crowd and a brass band struck up. Rowdy boys skirted the crowd, throwing firecrackers, until several men ran after them.

What white men called a holiday. It meant little to the Osage or even the Mennonites, but it had to do with how the United States began.

Thank you, Wah-Kon-Da, for rendering me obscure. His trip would be easy now. He turned up an alley, parallel to the celebration, then cut over to the bridge. He crossed the dried-up river, struck south again, and Prince, then Pauper, came to a halt.

"Go, mules," he said. "Go. Go."

Johnny stepped down, realizing that mules weren't horses. Horses would work until they dropped but not mules. They'd pulled hard for three days and had their rest. Now he'd pushed them through a long night, and nearly another day, without a break. Their heads hung low.

He talked to them. "I forgot about you, mules, but over there is water," he said, pointing down a sweep of bluestem to the shallow Arkansas. "I'll take you out of your traces."

Johnny would never beat an animal. All in all, they were superior to human beings.

"Good mules," he said, standing between them in sorrow,

reaching out to them both and rubbing between their ears. At last they lifted their heads and followed his lead.

A TENT CITY SPREAD out before him—wicked white women outside saloons, promising heaven on earth; impromptu preachers warning of hell below. Redemption. Damnation.

Liveries with blacksmiths and farriers, pouring out sweat in the heavy heat as they fanned coals and struck their anvils. A shoe store. A realtor with maps to the finest parcels of land. Farmers selling vegetables for astounding prices. A stinking, crowded lot of horses for sale. Pigs, cows, chickens, and skulking dogs. A wheelwright who also repaired wagons. Many cafés, one of which sold oysters. Blue soldiers walking in pairs. Clumps of Mennonites all in black, bargaining for horses and beans.

Johnny spied a woman in a frilly dress, singing a sad song. An old man behind her stroked a violin, and passersby threw pennies into a bucket. Johnny paused, staring at the woman's long red hair. Osage women didn't have red hair, nor did Mennonites. Johnny almost cried at the woman's song, not at the words but at the high sadness in her voice. The sensation, the pain in his cheeks, amazed him. He hadn't cried since boarding school.

The tents grew more sparse and he made out the road into Caldwell. He knew Ulysses's warehouse stood north of the town and he supposed he could find it. Then he saw a familiar Mennonite, selling goods from the tailgate of a wagon fitted with shelves and drawers. Ulysses!

Johnny's friend and partner sold cans of beets and corn and peas, and a cured pork shoulder. He sold a chicken, a lantern, and six boxes of ammunition. And he sold water. Women held up every sort of container and Euly turned a spigot on a keg.

Johnny stepped down. "You sell water!"

Euly looked up as if Johnny were a customer, then grinned. "You made it!"

"It is good to see you, Little Hero."

"And you, my friend. Yes, Fall Creek is dry and it hasn't rained for weeks. We can use that straw for bedding, Johnny. There's whiskey under it?"

Johnny nodded.

"No one would ever guess," Euly said. He motioned toward the town. "Kate's been worried sick about you."

"Kate's here," Johnny said. Despite himself, his voice veered into a higher range.

"Of course, she's here. She's your wife!" Euly threw him a curious look. "Any trouble on the trail, Johnny?"

He shook his head. "The mules are tired, as am I."

"You've done well. You can sleep through tomorrow."

Johnny followed Euly's directions down Main Street, bustling with people, though he hardly saw them. He had come out of lawless, foreign lands, and Ulysses did not know. Kate did not know. No one would ever know.

They saw him coming. Kate ran onto the rutted street, twisting her hands, and then an old white woman and she rolled open the heavy door. Kate glanced up once and a wave of gentleness soothed his skin like a breeze.

He pulled the wagon inside and stepped down. He was stricken with shyness and Kate looked at him almost in shame. Then they rushed into each other's arms.

"Are you all right, my love?" Kate whispered. "Was there trouble?"

He met her eyes. "No trouble. Not much sleep."

"I've hardly slept myself. Oh, Johnny! I should never have left you. I—"

"You were right. You are always right."

Kate laughed.

"The trail was difficult. It was hot. It could have been—"

He turned from her. "I must care for Prince and Pauper. They are good mules."

"You'll find a pump out back, if you want to wash up. We have soup and bread. Johnny—"

He nodded again.

"I love you."

Once more he felt the tugging at his cheeks but he couldn't cry. Misai, his warrior father, wouldn't cry. "I love you as well, my beautiful wife. I need you. I am . . . thankful."

19

Life Is Work

Through the dust-choking, boiled-dry days of late summer, Caldwell's tent-and-wagon suburb grew south from the edge of town to the territorial line, about three miles, and stretched at least three miles east to west. The *Caldwell News* reckoned the number of settlers, merchants, adventurers, speculators, gamblers, prostitutes, horse thieves, and sundry ne'er-do-wells exceeded ten thousand, and might reach fifteen thousand. There were saloons to accommodate them all, and Euly had helped raise the tent for one of them. Monte Truman came to him in late June with a proposal but no money.

"I'm busted," Monte said. "Them temprance women worryin' me to death and I cain't find good whiskey since Barney left us. Wanna build me up a nest egg here. It's all over, mebbe I'll light out fer California."

Euly loaned him five hundred dollars at 5 percent, to be repaid on September 17—the day after the land run. They brought in a carload of Anheuser-Busch beer from St. Louis and Monte sold it for a dime a quart bottle, then a quarter, then thirty cents. They brought in ice, too, which Euly delivered every morning not only to Monte but three other merchants, and then he carried away forty icy bottles to sell along sweltering Fall Creek for forty cents each. Soldiers guarding the line bought it, too, descending on Euly's wagon like big flies.

Early in July Johnny hauled in the last of Winston O'Reilly's fine whiskey, and Monte all but fell to his knees in gratitude.

"Two hundred gallons," Euly said. "That will provide over seven-thousand two-ounce shots."

"I dunno," Monte said. "Never figgered it that way."

"That's my conservative estimate. At seventy-five cents a shot—"

"I walked around some. Highest price I seen is thirty-five cents, and some places sell it for fifteen."

Euly nodded. He breathed through the bandanna he'd tied over his nose and mouth. It hadn't rained for a month—one gullywasher that brightened the prairie flowers, but wasn't enough to save anyone's corn. He'd never seen it so dry. Outside the tent the wind carried along leaves and dead cinders and so much dust you couldn't see. "You know well as I do, Monte, that's grain alcohol, which you can ship legal if you call it medicine. They water it down from 190 proof, throw in brown sugar or pepper or maybe black powder—"

Truman held up a hand. "I know what they do, Ulysses."

"Do it yourself, if you need such an offering. I'll order it in for you. Long and short of it, I must have three hundred dollars a barrel for my fine whiskey."

Monte chuckled. "That's stiff, Euly. Your father—"

"In these circumstances, who knows what my father would have done? This is the last batch of a fine whiskey, Monte, and I feel three hundred to be generous. I have to pay my supplier, and divide my little profit with shareholders, while you could sell your shots for a quarter each, and still make eight hundred dollars. Likely you'll bring in double that, and be on your way to the land of milk and honey."

What Euly said was true, more or less, and Monte grinned, more or less. "You know I ain't got no money, Euly. I already owe you five hunert."

"Payment will be due after the land run, no carrying charges.

Because you and my father were friends. Because I'm your friend. And also—I know you understand, Monte—it's just business."

ANNELISE AND KATE RAN the chicken business, taking the train back to Jericho Springs, crating up every bird in the Kreider coop, then buying out Helmut's brothers, Ronald and Ananias—and their neighbors too. Johnny and his brother, Billy, slapped together nests for the layers, while the fryers ranged in a pen outside the warehouse, their wings clipped so they wouldn't roost in the trees. Euly sold eggs for a nickel each, laying hens for two dollars, thrice what either brought even in Wichita, and Annelise scolded him.

"These people have no money," she said. "Farmers from Indiana, and immigrants like we were. Those chickens, and a wheelbarrow full of turnips, might get them through the winter."

He frowned. "The poor ye always have with ye."

"Euly!"

Euly's basic rule was to double the going price, then back off if his goods didn't move. But they moved. He never sold shoddy merchandise and plenty in this temporary town did. If you could find eggs—or axle grease—at a better price, delivered to your hands in the hellish heat, you were welcome to do so. It was just business. Euly was honest, more than could be said for most of his customers.

Euly knew better than to argue with Annelise, and he believed in charity, of course, but how could you tell which of the poor were like Henry Muenster, chiselers and cheats, and which were good people, but unlucky? How many of the unlucky ones had been defeated by their own foolishness? Quite a number, Euly learned, as he moved about the camp: men who'd thrown their last money into stocks, in this panic year of 1893; men who planted corn in the midst of drought, with a note due. Was it bad luck, or stupidity, when you opened a store in the wrong location and sat on an inventory no one would buy?

You made your own luck. Euly had been poor but was about

to be rich through his own industry. Anyone could do it, if you were willing to work. Yes, work! Night and day. He remembered Eliza Cook's little poem in the *McGuffey Eclectic Reader*:

Work, work, my boy, be not afraid;
Look labor boldly in the face;
Take up the hammer or the spade,
And blush not for your humble place.

He had a limited time in which to make money. Annelise didn't understand the burden of it, how he worked and worked not for himself but for all of them, guarding every moment against saboteurs coming at him sideways. One settler in three was a thief, whether hailing from Indiana or Ireland.

"How honest would you be?" Kate asked. "If you were down to your last dollar-fifty and had babies to feed?"

He wanted to say, why have the babies if you can't feed them? "I sell your eggs and chickens at the front of the wagon and their sweet little tykes rob my potatoes from the rear."

"Maybe they're hungry," she said.

"I been hungry, too. Doesn't give them the right to steal."

"Not the right, Euly. The necessity."

Euly sighed. "Kate, they play tricks." Time and again, the sturdy mothers stood at a distance, while their pretty daughters batted their eyes and begged for chickens. No money at all, they claimed, and maybe this was true, with their fathers sitting in saloons. After his experience with Jenny, Euly wanted nothing to do with pretty daughters.

"So *that's* it." Kate laughed. "Were it up to me, Jenny Muenster should be drawn and quartered, Euly, but women are half the human race. Yes, you had a bad experience—"

Euly glowered. "Bad enough to last a lifetime."

"You're silly. You don't need to marry every girl you meet. When all of this is over, you'll be quite the eligible bachelor, Euly. Look around!"

Euly nodded. Kate was almost two years younger than he.

How did she become old and wise? "I don't have time for girls, Kate. I don't have time to drive along Fall Creek, currying favors with, with . . . *poultry.*"

"I understand," Kate said, reaching out to stroke his arm. "I know how hard you're working, and that we'd be rudderless without you. You're doing a magnificent job, Brother of Mine."

A soft answer turneth away wrath, he thought. Euly grinned at his sister, embarrassed by his own speech. He wasn't wrathful, merely piqued. He recalled something his father said: "Compliment a man, Ulysses, if you can bear to do it. We all of us hope for a morsel of praise and seldom receive it."

"Thank you, Kate," he said. "I don't work any harder than you and Annelise."

"Why don't you put Billy on the charity wagon, while you sell your boots and rifles?"

On Kate's say-so, Euly had hired Johnny's half-brother, Billy, a good-looking cowboy, to drive the mules around a second route. Billy was twenty-four but looked sixteen. He wore a Colt revolver on his hip and carried himself with an air of carelessness. He showed slight profits, and Euly suspected Billy gave merchandise away if his customer was comely enough.

Billy was a marvel with horses, a champion in Indian rodeos, and with Johnny had scoured the reservation for every fine horse, mule, and nag. Horses were their most profitable commodity, and, driving them up into perilous Kansas, the two armed brothers had proved sufficiently fierce to hold off thieves.

Billy would make the run for his brother. He was of age, looked white, and had a birth certificate. He didn't put much more weight on a horse than Kate, and of course he could ride.

Yes, Billy was useful, even vital, though you'd find him in a saloon by midafternoon. One night, or morning, he'd returned to the warehouse at four, as Euly began his day. But if I stocked him with tobacco at fixed prices, and some clearly-marked bitters and beer, maybe that would offset losses with eggs and chickens. Maybe, he thought, the charity run would at least break even.

Euly laughed. "My sister—"

He knew she mocked him. She was his sister and loved the role. "Yes, my brother?"

"Is very smart."

EULY SOLD BOOTS AND shoes, belts, suspenders, shirts, and Levi's. He sold several hundred pairs of blue denim overalls at one dollar each, still a bargain, though he'd marked them up forty cents.

Selling shoes was a quiet sort of business and Euly could adjust the price according to the customer—proving, to himself at least, that he wasn't the heartless capitalist Annelise thought him to be. He memorized the Montgomery Ward catalog descriptions and had brought down his sizer from Jericho Springs. And in his black hat, brown shirt with suspenders, and black trousers, he seemed sober as his partner, Giles Cabot, in his undertaker role. "Madam," Euly intoned. "Think of your most prominent toe."

Most women, penniless, bestowed a withering glance and turned away. Euly wanted the ones who giggled. "My big toe?"

"You are correct, madam! The length of your foot is the distance between two parallel lines—"

If she'd giggled before, now she laughed. "What!"

Euly held out two hands a little apart, east to west. "Lines that go off infinitely and never touch. These lines are perpendicular to the foot—" Euly turned his hands north to south. "—in contact with your big toe and the most prominent part of your *heel*. For best results—if I may, madam—" Euly knelt to help the woman off with her old boot. This was an involved process with high boots, and almost always the woman shooed him away, laughing and flustered, to do the job herself. Some allowed him to proceed, meeting his eyes as he worked. Euly thought a lesson lay in this and almost knew what it was.

"For a good fit, we measure the subject—you, Madam— standing barefoot in the sizer, with the weight of your body distributed equally on both feet." The women knew Euly's sales speech was silly but they were weary and worn, and seemed to find him entertaining. And once that old boot was off, he had a sale. If the customer didn't like his price, he dropped it until she did, and threw in a cup of cold water as she left.

With men he stressed the quality of cowhide, the water-proofing, the indestructibility of lasts and soles. Some dandies with pistols strapped to their hips wandered among the tents, but he sold no fancy boots.

One day he sold twenty pairs of boots, men's, women's, and children's. He sold mid-ankle work boots for women or men at $4.50, cattlemen's high boots for $5. His inventory of children's shoes grew as well. Children were everywhere and he kept his prices at cost, disliking the thought of barefoot children with winter not so far away.

But when it came down to it, the three items with the highest markup, the things men couldn't do without, were horses, liquor, and rifles. Horses you could ask almost anything for, and if one buyer stalked off in anger the next wouldn't. Rifles and pistols were sold everywhere, but Euly offered new Winchesters at a fair price—still profiting by almost 50 percent—and included a box of ammunition. With liquor he was a wholesaler, but he kept on hand several cases of Dr. Bersuch's Medicinal Bitters, which was cheap at double the wholesale price and wouldn't kill anyone. He sold snuff and the makings at a mere 10 percent profit, because they turned over fast and drew other sales.

Every two days he drove along the hundred-foot no-man's-land soldiers had cleared at the territorial line. With so much traffic grass had disappeared here, and the soil had ground as fine as corn meal into ten inches of dust. Maude and Gerty raised a cloud as they pulled through it, no matter how slowly Euly worked them.

The soldiers came running when they saw his wagon, call-ing, "Preacher! Preacher!" He also sold them cabbages, toma-toes, green beans—and chickens, if he could liberate them from Annelise. He pitied the soldiers, who made only twenty a month.

Twenty was still enough, however, to buy beer. Euly dropped his price to thirty-five cents out of patriotism.

Euly made a friend, Jacob Kosciusko, a private from Warsaw, Indiana. His father and grandfather operated a tannery there, a lucrative though hard enterprise that Jacob had joined the army to escape. He said girls wouldn't go riding with him, even if he took a bath and a bath after that, because of how the tannery stank up Warsaw. Tanners were like buzzards. They were essential but everyone wished they'd land elsewhere.

Jacob had longish hair that fell over his eyes and he couldn't keep his campaign hat straight. He continually glanced over his shoulder for the lieutenant, who rode along the line twice a day, looking for men who'd retreated to their tents under the hot sun, or clumped together under the two lone blackjacks, where they drank and gambled.

Jacob wore a coating of black grime like all the soldiers. They'd burned off the grass for several miles to the south and had little water to wash with. Burning the grass was supposed to keep settlers from crossing the line before September 16, but many got through at night, then hid in gullies or caves near choice parcels. Officials claimed forty-two thousand quarter-sections were available, though much of it would prove untillable. The Cherokees had rented it for range land, its best use.

"They're crazy," Jacob said. "Crazy ole farmers, went bust in Ohio and Indiana and Io-way. Hunert thousand lined up in Ark City."

And fifteen thousand in Caldwell, five in Kiowa, and God knew how many gathered to make the run from the south, out of Stillwater and Goodwin. Thus, the Sooners.

"We catch 'em every night," Jacob said.

"They go to the land office, their claims won't hold up. Every plot's got a number."

"They can buy the true claim or drive the man off, then pay some jasper to be a witness."

"Still. It's poor land, most of it. Salty. Could you even dig a well?"

"I seen a patch to the west, sand dunes for miles and miles. They say it was nothin' but ocean, onct."

Euly smiled. When this was over, what was the next thing? "You ever seen the ocean, Jacob?"

"Never seen nothin'. Never done nothin'. You think the army would take you places but you end up pulling guard duty in the middle of the middle of nowheres. I'm not a man of the world like you, Euly."

"Sure." Euly laughed. "I'm a man of the world from Jericho Springs, Kansas."

"You got your own place, good ground, and you're making money hand over fist. You got a lady friend, I imagine, and I bet she's nice."

"Oh." With increasing success, Euly suppressed thoughts of Jenny. Jacob had come at him sideways, and Euly felt a momentary lust, imagining Jenny lying beside him. Just as quickly, he felt a spike of anger and sighed with resignation. Work was 80 percent of everything. The rest, the 20 percent governing outlaws such as Eddie Mole and sweethearts such as Jenny, puzzled him profoundly. "Of course, Jacob. She's sweet."

"You gettin' hitched?"

He looked Jacob in the eye. "Truth is, we are no longer a couple."

"Well, then. You and me, let's sow some wild oats."

Euly looked north, where workers raised the army's triangular registration tents. One of them motioned to Euly for water and he pulled back on the reins. "Jacob, when it comes to . . . *oats*, I'm not much of a horse."

Jacob waved a hand at the patchwork tents stretching toward town. "You move around everywhere, Euly. You know the good places. Can't you show me? Ain't we friends?"

"Maybe one of the other soldiers would be better."

"They're old men. Euly, I never been with a woman!"

Euly couldn't bring himself to say, "Neither have I." He tried to analyze what he felt. Upright disapproval for what went on in those tents. Puzzlement. And fear, because the tents belonged to that mysterious 20 percent.

"If you want to, Jacob. Saturday night?"

EULY QUIT AT FOUR on Saturday and changed into Levi's, cowboy boots, and another of the plain gray shirts he'd bought from Montgomery Ward at $4.86 a dozen. He'd never be Billy Baxter but felt energized drawing the strawberry roan from the corral. She was a fine, spirited cowhorse, and he was young and strong and tough.

Then he fitted her with an English racing saddle that weighed six pounds, and understood again he was a merchant, not a range rider. For fifty dollars he'd ordered two dozen of the silly things on the theory that racers had to keep their weight down. He'd sold nine for $6.50 each. He'd have to drop his price.

A voice issued from the shadows by the well. "Are you going to a rodeo, Little Hero?"

Man of the world Euly grinned crookedly. "I have been invited to sow wild oats."

Johnny didn't laugh much lately but now he did. "I believe I know what this means."

Euly turned over a steel bucket near his friend and sat. "I have a theory, Johnny Heart of Oak. Eighty percent of life is work. It's all I know how to do."

Johnny held up his pipe and drew on a match. "I have tried to imitate this Mennonite trait of yours."

"I should imitate *you*. I work harder and harder and come no closer to understanding that 20 percent. Love. God. Evil. You've mastered it, Johnny!"

"The part of life with wild oats in it?" Johnny laughed again. "I am no wilder than you, Little Hero. You might study my little brother."

"Yes, I envy Billy." Euly walked back and forth. "Even when he makes me angry. But I'm talking about women, Johnny. That's why I'm headed out tonight. Women are the 20 percent I can't understand."

"I would say, 'Be calm. Let them talk.' I don't always understand your sister but I know she is a good woman. We will prosper if it suits Wah-Kon-Da."

"*Why* did Jenny cheat me?" Euly burst out. He thought himself weak to burden Johnny with his love life but couldn't help himself. A great principle operated and its nature eluded him. "I . . . *listened*. I was fair! I was honest!"

Johnny nodded. "Admirable qualities which she did not admire."

"A hard-working man who makes money—I thought every woman—"

Johnny shrugged. "I know little except Kate and I were destined. The yellow-haired girl and you were not destined. She wanted more."

"More than me." Plain, boring me.

"More than there is. She wanted a place to hunt where no one has hunted. She had nothing but aspired to be queen."

Euly sighed. "You, Johnny? You and Kate?"

"I am fortunate."

"So is Kate."

"Also, I am Osage. If I fail to look behind me, someone will hit me with a shovel. So maybe I am not so—" Johnny went silent. He turned his face away.

Euly saw that his friend was distressed but he plunged ahead. "The things, the scary things, I can't control! Not Jenny anymore—I *almost* understand her—but Eddie Mole! All the crazy stuff, the violence! If I understood it, like an apple tree or a pig or even a rifle, then I wouldn't be afraid of it. Where does evil come from, Johnny? Eddie Mole killed as if pulling on his trousers or saddling his horse. How can I understand that?"

Johnny coughed. "This problem you speak of, this puzzle,

it is everyone's. I cannot explain Eddie Mole. All you can do with such a man is—"

"You had him in your sights!"

Johnny tapped out his pipe and stepped on the still glowing embers. He stood tall in the shadow, a full head above Euly. "He killed your father, Little Hero, not mine."

"Of course. We've talked about this before. I always come back to . . . what is the use in killing one evil man? I don't understand, Johnny! Won't there always be another?"

"Always." Johnny's voice dropped to a whisper. "Little Hero, you *do* understand."

THEY SAT POURING OFF sweat in a saloon with no name. Two coal oil lamps lit the place dimly and smelled it up like a furnace room. They drank from quart bottles of Anheuser-Busch while little gray moths circled their heads and their boots stirred the dust. "Kinda strange to see you all dressed up," Jacob said.

"I suppose we're both out of uniform."

Jacob wore civilian clothes, though they were old and unclean. He'd scrubbed the soot from his face. "We got the Aim-ish in Indiana," he said. "Up by Shipshewana. Is that what you are?"

Euly sighed. "I'm Mennonite."

"What's the difference?"

"The Amish have more rules."

"Rules," Jacob said. "That's all the damn army *is.*"

After two beers each, they staggered onto the twisting concourse, past lit-up gambling joints where men played poker and faro. At the Can-Can women lifted their skirts and threw out their legs on a narrow stage. Jacob and Euly stood watching, but they couldn't see well from outside and the barker wanted a dollar to let them in. "Not worth it," Euly said.

Jacob looked regretful. "Yeah."

They passed the Elephant, the Red Light, the Oasis, the Sazerac, and Monte Truman's quieter Santa Fe—where often Euly stopped at day's end, because Monte offered a square meal.

Women in purple or yellow dresses stood at bright entrances and called out, "Need some company, handsome?" or "Come here, come here, come *here*, sweetheart." Euly didn't approve. He'd never consort with a soiled dove.

Still, how much did they cost? He reached into his Levi's to check on his four five-dollar gold pieces, and shifted one of them to his shirt pocket.

"Let's go in there." Jacob pointed to a red barn set back five hundred feet from the concourse. They walked up a lane toward a sprawling tent, lit with scores of gas lanterns, between the barn and a boarded-up house—not a farm anymore. Drought had overcome the farmer.

But the piano music—Strauss, Euly thought, remembering Annelise in the school—seemed unthreatening. They didn't have to pass through the usual gauntlet of barkers and aggressive women, and on parts of the floor—formerly, the barnyard—the house had laid down plywood to suppress the dust. "Barn Dance," the place was called.

They found a small round table on the house side, where the flaps were rolled up and you could hope for a breeze. Behind them, nailed to a post on a high picket fence, a sign in crude red letters warned, "NO GUNS NO NIFES." Up front, sitting on a high stool in a dark corner by a side door to the barn, a big, bearded man, the bouncer, sat with a shotgun.

On the dance floor there was indeed a sort of waltz going on, but the cowboys didn't understand it or were too drunk to execute it. Like chickens trying to fly, they flailed with their arms and fell down, leaving the women to spin by themselves like dying tops. Or the cowboys yanked the women off stage right, toward the bouncer who collected money—but the women always pulled back. Cursing, the men paid the bouncer and went through the blanketed door alone, into the dimly lit milk barn.

Perhaps you made other arrangements with the dancing girls. Or dancing was all they were hired to do other than cadge drinks and talk to lonely men.

PART 5

Behind, to the barn, was where Jacob should go when he worked up his nerve. Euly had heard of the cribs but had difficulty envisioning them. Here in the light you drank and laughed and danced if you could stay on your feet. Back there . . . he almost shuddered. If that was what you had to do to become a man—but it wasn't! Not his Uncle Helmut! Not Johnny!

For an instant Euly contemplated leaping up on the table and delivering a sermon on consorting with prostitutes, but he knew he wasn't qualified. That sort of testimony had to come from a true sinner. Such as my father, he thought, and fell into reverie, thinking a vital element had been omitted from his creation. Some men belonged here. He didn't.

Two young women appeared as if from thin air. "Buy me a glass a wine?" one of them, a blonde with sausage curls and eyelids painted blue, asked Jacob.

Jacob blushed. "Sure."

The woman waved at a bargirl and sat beside Jacob. She reached to sweep his long hair from his forehead. "I'm Betty. What's your name, soldier?"

The woman who sat near Euly was Chinese. She wore a long red dress with the neckline pulled down on her shoulders and half-exposing her breasts, though her breasts were small and the dress hung like a sack. "Hello," Euly said. "My name is You-Lisssss-Eze."

"That's Clara," Betty said. "She can't talk."

"Can't, or don't?" Euly asked.

Betty shrugged. Up front an old man struck his fiddle, and a red-haired woman called out, "Promenade!" Euly paid no attention to the Chinese girl because he knew the red-haired woman from Monte Truman's place. She sang sad tunes at day's end while Euly ate his supper. The woman's pure voice, and a glass of whiskey, transported you to a peaceful place where your muscles didn't ache.

Four cowboys leaped onto the plywood, pulling along four bright women. The couples followed each other in a revolving

260

circle, their hands clutched and held high. The fiddle heated up and the red-haired woman called out:

My true love's a blue-eyed daisy
She won't work and I'm too lazy

The Englische held square dances in Jericho Springs and Euly enjoyed watching from the street, though dancing was a scary proposition for him. Jenny would have gone. She'd have been delighted. Wasn't he here to sow some wild oats? Square dancing, even in a saloon, wasn't *that* wicked.

The wine arrived with two beers which he hadn't ordered, but they were cold, and gave him something to do with his hands. He surrendered his five-dollar gold piece and the bargirl twirled away before he could demand change. He almost ran after her but then Betty said, "Wanna dance, soldier?"

"How you know I'm a soldier?" Jacob said.

"You look so sad," Betty said, tugging on Jacob, and she led him—unsteady on his feet after so much beer—toward the dancers. They joined with three other new couples, crowding the floor, while singing rose from all around. Every time the red-haired woman made a call:

I got a gal she's ten foot tall
Sleeps in the kitchen with her feet in the hall

the crowd clapped and sang:

Hey lolly lolly lolly
Hey lolly lolly lolly lo

The tent rang with joy but Euly felt hot and miserable, and as soon as he could excuse himself he'd ride back to the warehouse and prepare for another day's commerce. Reeling to his feet, he saw that his new brother-in-law, Billy Baxter, was up there dancing his life away. Billy was the most energetic of them all, though he inspired a humoring frown on the red-haired woman's face, because he kept breaking out of her routines, puffing up his chest and high-stepping toward the crowd. Men shouted and women screamed to encourage him, and the chant of "Hey lolly lolly lo" grew deafening. Billy's partner laughed, lifted her skirts, and mimicked him, and then another woman rose from her table. Billy grabbed the new woman and held her on one arm, his partner on the other, and the three danced around backwards. Euly smiled. He wished he were Billy, if only for one night.

"Ulysses," Clara said, pronouncing his name perfectly.

Euly stared at the Chinese girl in wonder. "You *can* talk."

She matched his stare with glistening black eyes, neither friendly nor hostile.

The bargirl returned, glared, and slapped two dollars on the table. Three dollars for drinks? Outrageous, but he'd asked for it and it was a lesson learned. I sampled what the Englische think of as fun, he thought. In the future, when I undertake dealings with them, I'll understand their decadent ways. As he reached for his coins, Clara threw her arms around Euly's knee and he almost fell. "Go behind," the girl said, pointing to the blanketed door that opened into the barn. "Good time."

Euly pitied her. He couldn't imagine her long journey, how she'd ended up a crib girl in dusty Kansas, but the visualization of sex with her horrified him. Controlling a grimace, he shoved his two dollars across the table. The girl slid one dollar into a dress pocket, pushed the dollar piece toward him, and rose.

One dollar. She's worth one dollar. "Take it all," he said, his eyes downcast. "I'm—I'm leaving."

The red-haired woman called out:

Pretty little gal won't you come out with me
There's a side of me I want you to see

Hey lolly lolly lo!

Threading his way among the tables, Euly stopped for an instant to admire the red-haired woman, thinking that a woman so pretty, so graceful and assured, would always pass over a clod-hopper such as himself. There was probably a federal law that she had to. She was sophisticated. She knew the world.

He enjoyed spying on her. Like attending the play he'd taken Jenny to in Newton. Voyeur that he was, he could sit in darkness and watch Ophelia declaim, studying her mannerisms, even lusting for her, while remaining a stranger. He stared too long. The red-haired woman turned her blue eyes on him, in an instant conveying amusement, even intimacy—and Euly was a simple fellow, wasn't he? He had no secrets; the smart lady sized him up instantly.

Embarrassed, he assumed a stern expression and spotted Jacob. He motioned that he meant to leave.

At the same time a bald-headed, square-jawed man with massive arms and chest yelled out, "Baxter!" and veered toward the dance floor, knocking down tables and chairs as he came. Raising high a table leg, he weaved toward Euly's brother-in-law.

The fiddler stopped playing and the red-haired caller retreated to his side. The dancers shrank toward the stage, falling on one another, and the chant of "Hey lolly" died in an excited murmur. Billy turned, his face amiable. He reached for his Colt revolver but he wasn't carrying it, and lifted his hands skyward instead. He looked toward the bouncer as the bald man swung his table leg. Billy held up an arm to deflect the blow, then fell, clutching at his ribs.

The barker fired his shotgun into the air and rushed forward. Euly leaped, throwing his body into the attacker's knees even as the man swung again. The bald man lost his grip on the table leg, and meanwhile Jacob jumped the distance and kicked it away. Euly tried to hold the man down but it was like grabbing a mountain lion. The man bit Euly's hand and began to squirm away but it didn't matter: the bouncer arrived, raised his shotgun by the barrel, and struck the fallen man's head with the stock.

Euly collapsed backward, propping himself on his right hand, bringing his injured left to his lips. The fallen man's head poured

blood. His upper lip had curled back where it struck the plywood, showing two yellowed teeth. His entire body quivered,
then lay motionless.

Billy's dance partners knelt over him, kissing him and combing his hair with their fingers.

"Aw," he said. "I ain't hurt." He tried to push up to a sitting
position but cringed and fell back. One of the girls pulled up on
his shoulders, while Euly grabbed his unhurt arm, and together
they brought Billy to his feet.

"Can you sit your horse?" Euly asked.

"Shore," Billy said, and wriggled free. He dropped a hand to
his ribcage, winced, and wobbled as if to fall. Euly and Jacob
hurried to catch him. "I could go for the wagon," Euly said.

"I'll make it." Billy motioned toward the blanketed door.
"Horse is behind the barn. Aw, Euly, he caught me unawares. I
didn't have no weapon—"

"Good thing you didn't," Jacob put in. He threw a glance
over his shoulder, perhaps looking for Betty. "You'd a killed
him and they'd haul you off—"

"Why was he so mad?" Euly asked.

"Come after his wife. Martha don't want on that damn farm
and he mebbe thought I was a-doodlin' her." Billy giggled, then
moaned in pain. "Aaah!"

The bouncer was no help. He stood with the barrel of his shotgun upraised, glowering at the crowd, barking out commands.
A bartender joined him, and they bent to hoist the bald man
by his feet and drag him across the dance floor, trailing blood.

Euly tried to reach for the blanket but a hand appeared before
him and pulled it back. Euly looked up and met the redheaded
woman's wide blue eyes. He murmured thanks, and without
thinking, lightly stroked the back of her hand. She bent her
head in what might have been rebuke. In moments he wished
he'd asked her name, but now Jacob and he, holding up Billy,
shuffled into the dusty barn.

There wasn't much to see among the cribs. Rather, the light

was so dim and dust-filled you couldn't see much. They followed a jagged aisle, covered with plywood, toward an orange
door at the rear. A gray shape in a stall to Euly's right, big as a
hog and grunting like one, thrust and pulled back. To his left
Euly made out what he thought was an old woman, or perhaps a gray ghost. She lifted a lantern above broken milking
stanchions and the light made her eyes gleam red. When they
reached the exit, he felt a peppering along his backbone and
turned in alarm. It was the Chinese girl, pelting him with her
little fists. She spat and cursed him with a mixture of English
and Chinese. "Clara," he murmured.

They plunged into the outdoors, where a big, reddish moon
shone through the dust. They eased Billy down onto an apple
crate and Euly looked about for where the horses were tied.
"Whoo," Billy said. "Oh, me."

Euly sucked on his hand, which had stopped bleeding. Could
you contract rabies from the bite of an angry dirt farmer?

"That was one helluva good time," Jacob said. "What in thun-
der did you do to that China girl?"

Euly watched as the barker and the bartender dragged out
the baldheaded man and dropped him in the dust. He heard a
distant fiddle and voices singing, "Hey lolly lolly lo."

"I don't know," he said.

BILLY HAD A BROKEN arm and two busted ribs. He'd ride
in many another rodeo, but he couldn't make the run with one
arm in a sling and his chest cinched up.

Johnny had already left. He'd cross the river from the reservation at Ralston, a few miles from the claim, to guard against
Sooners. He'd be a sort of Sooner himself, an Osage snatching
land from the whites who had snatched it from the Cherokees
who had snatched it from the Osage, but he couldn't make a
legal claim. Nor could underage Kate, which was why the task
had fallen to Billy. Someone the government recognized as a
legal claimant had to register in Caldwell, gather stakes at the

site, and then stand in line at the land office in Perry, ready to produce a witness if a challenger appeared.

Johnny wanted two claims—the bottom land that he'd farm and pasture, and the superficially worthless land up on the bluff. Johnny knew of a spring there and timber good enough for sheds and corrals and fence posts. Billy and Annelise would take the train to Perry, stand in line, and wait for Euly or Kate to show up with the stakes. Euly and Billy would make claims and Johnny might never appear. He didn't dare leave his land unguarded.

First they had to register for the run, and even in the merciless sun some gallantry survived. Annelise joined the line five hundred deep, wearing her long-sleeved black dress and wide sun bonnet, leaning on a cane. Man after man waved her forward.

For the second registration Kate and Euly took turns through the day, and Billy, promising not to drink anything but water, stood through the night. After fifty-seven hours, on September 11 Euly paid the fourteen-dollar fee, and a tired-looking lieutenant signed his name below "Ulysses Kreider."

"I'll make the run," Kate announced over supper, looking up at Euly as if expecting his challenge.

Not so. She was Johnny's wife. The trip would be difficult but not remarkably dangerous. At least, no more dangerous than watching an evil stranger gun down your father on the main street of Jericho Springs. This was because of the particular way Kate had to make the run.

Johnny had found a golden piece of land tucked away at the Outlet's far eastern corner, fifteen miles from Buffalo Dancer's ranch, but fully eighty from Caldwell. Even if they had joined all those Texans coming up from Stillwater, the distance still would have stretched fifty miles. They hoped the parcel would be overlooked, at least for the first several days, until every obvious claim had been made.

A good horse had it in him to gallop ten miles. A great horse, twelve miles. Kate's King Arthur was a great horse, but if you pushed him beyond his limit you'd kill him. You had to walk him, canter him—and lead him over rocky ground. Let the desperate settlers fall on themselves and ruin their horses through their headlong runs. If Kate didn't need to detour for water or get lost (Euly would make sure she carried a compass and a pair of his lightweight binoculars, and Johnny had drawn for Billy a detailed map), Kate could strike a moderate pace, coming up behind the carnival and the carnage. Her trip should take two long days and a shorter third.

Meanwhile Euly would follow with a wagonload of water and supplies. For the first day, as far south as the Salt Fork, they could ride straight down the old Chisum Trail and he'd guard Kate's rear. After that he'd fall a day, even two, behind her, and this worried him, but he knew his sister was no tenderfoot.

"You know, Kate," Euly said. "You could go down through the reservation. Johnny's already at the claim. You don't have to . . . *run*."

Kate nodded and held up Johnny's map. "He's expecting me in three days—"

"He's expecting Billy."

"He's my husband, Euly."

Euly nodded.

"If I went through the reservation, it would take two days longer. At least. And that would mean two days that Johnny is worrying. And two days longer before we reach Perry with the stakes."

"Sure." Euly smiled. "Take it easy, Kate. I won't be far behind. Follow Johnny's map and you shouldn't have a bit of trouble."

IF ONLY FOR TEN weeks, Monte Truman had realized his dream: a roadhouse where you could eat, drink, socialize, and not be pestered by swindlers or whores. Monte's experiment wasn't as profitable as the Barn Dance or the Sazerac, but he drew plenty of customers, the most loyal of whom might have been Euly. In these last days Monte's Santa Fe had become his refuge, an escape from endless work and even the women in his family, forever urging him onto higher ground.

Two days before the run, finished with selling bridles and ammunition, Euly sat eating a steak, fried potatoes, butter beans, and a great chunk of brown bread. In a notebook he figured profits and inventory, calculating what he still might be able to sell at reduced prices. He'd run out of men's boots and work gloves, he was stuck with fifteen English saddles, but he knew the remaining Winchesters would move at twelve dollars each. They'd sell at his hardware, too, but he didn't want to ship them home.

He propped up his boots, rubbed his sore neck, and sipped from his forty-cent glass of Winston O'Reilly's fine whiskey. Alarming, how much he enjoyed the stuff. How much solace he could find in a bottle. And how much lethargy crept up on him: several mornings, he'd slept all the way until six and fought a hangover through the forenoon.

Twas in the merry month of May
When green buds all were swelling
Sweet William on his death bed lay
For love of Barbara Allen

Sad song! He thought of the hymns Annelise sang to him when he was little, but she'd never had that sweet, nostalgic violin behind her. Her voice never rose so high, with such purity. The words tingled down Euly's spine with a long sip of whiskey and he sighed. Maybe he'd float away to Heaven, his tasks on earth rendered mundane, the truth of his life revealed. He lifted his eyes, though he already knew: the square dance caller. The red-headed woman. And though fifty weary men ate Monte Truman's food, Euly knew in his heart that the pretty lady sang for him.

So slowly, slowly she got up
And slowly she drew nigh him
And the only words to him did say
Young man I think you're dying

So cruel! How could a woman be so cruel?

> When he was dead and laid in grave
> She heard the death bells knelling
> And every stroke to her did say
> Hard hearted Barbara Allen

> Oh mother, oh mother go dig my grave
> Make it both long and narrow
> Sweet William died of love for me
> And I will die of sorrow

She'd announced herself, hadn't she? At the square dance when he hauled out Billy. She pulled back the blanket to the horrors beyond—and their hands touched. What was her name? How did she get here?

> Barbara Allen was buried in the old churchyard
> Sweet William was buried beside her
> Out of sweet William's heart, there grew a rose
> Out of Barbara Allen's a briar

Yes, Jenny. A briar.

> They grew and grew in the old churchyard
> Till they could grow no higher
> At the end they formed, a true lover's knot
> And the rose grew round the briar

The whiskey turned the evening fuzzy and Euly, sitting alone, let his tears flow. Maybe it was because of the whiskey that he felt no shyness when the redheaded woman approached his table. Maybe, because of the whiskey, he rose to pull back a chair for her. "Are you as sad as that song?" he asked.

"Not at all. I am a jolly person despite me misfortunes." She thrust a hand out of a white cuff—like a man, sealing a deal. Euly understood he was drunk. He dropped into the pages of *Ivanhoe* and kissed the redheaded woman's slender fingers, though at the same time he might have pinched himself, to check if he and the redheaded woman were real.

She blinked. She held her hand sideways by her mouth and leaned forward with wide eyes. "I am Rebecca Donnelly. There are those who claim I'm a bonnie, redhaired lass from County Galway." She laughed and paused, as if displeased with her speech. "I am from Galway, for sure. I have red hair. Bonnie, oh, bonnie—that is a vanity, Ulysses. You prefer the woman with a brain between her ears, Ulysses, do ye not?"

He couldn't take her in as fast as she arrived. He was a farm boy, in his own estimation little more sophisticated than his horses. It defied his experience that this lovely creature named Rebecca could be nervous.

"You know my name," he murmured.

"I know ye well. Perhaps better than you yourself—though that, I realize, is an extravagant claim." She frowned, again as if her words had gone crooked. A reddish curl fell before her eyes. She pursed her lips and tried again. "Dear Monte, you see, he praises you endlessly. You are a knight in those somber clothes!"

Euly glanced toward the bar, where Monte sported a wide grin, and saluted him with a mug of beer. Monte had paid his debt the week before. He'd made enough, he said, to take his roadhouse to California.

"Hardly," Euly said. "Monte presented me with a sound proposition—"

"You stood him on his feet. So young a man . . ." Rebecca looked away. "You saved his life, Ulysses, as he saved mine and me poor old dad's." Rebecca pointed to the fiddler and a tremor passed through her shoulders. "Giving us honest work. Oh, boyo, we lived in Boston, *horrid* Boston."

Euly probed her blue eyes. They were not pure so much as wise. There was a subtle plea in them. Something leaped high inside him and he thought he divined her purpose. He saw her sweet soul and, if he was drunk, Rebecca was the vintage. "Marry me."

Those blue eyes leapt in alarm but he had to look away from the tenderness that followed. Why—for an instant—did she remind him of Annelise? Oh, he was clumsy and foolish—damn the whiskey; he'd never drink another drop! And now Rebecca laughed at him, merrily, like hard-hearted Barbara Allen. "You will build me a fine house, love?"

He hung his head. "The finest in all of Kansas."

"Not so fine, then. Will you take me to Kansas City, where I'll buy trifles with the money you work so hard for?"

He laughed despite himself. "Who cares about money?"

"No, no, you must be prudent. Always prudent!"

"I am. Dear Lord, Rebecca, I have always been prudent. I—"

"What would a foolish girl like me do with prudence? I want to be free as a bird."

"So do I. I want to be free as a bird and build you a fine, prudent house." Bonnie Rebecca, the girl with a brain between her ears, would explain it all. "I have a theory. Eighty percent of life is work—"

"Further proof! How could a free spirit like me marry such a drudge?"

"The other 20 percent is what you can't predict. Like, like . . ."

She stood. A part of him was like a part of her and he didn't want her to leave. They should talk through the night.

"Like true love," she said. "Like love that plays false—and jealousy! Like Sweet William and that poor, reckless boyo you saved at the dance." She paused and looked down on him with ambivalence and gentle reproof. "Like love at first blush, Ulysses."

"Yes." Euly grew sad. "I apologize. I spend all day bargaining with people, counting pennies and nickels, and for a moment I dropped my guard. Because you are so . . . *right*. I don't know how I know—your song—"

"You were struck with lightning." Rebecca laughed again. "But don't apologize, love. We are on the frontier, after all, and women are in short supply. If you had known in advance, you might have ordered out a dozen."

He couldn't reply.

"I have been privileged to entertain four proposals this summer and yours is . . ." She looked toward the fiddler and Monte, both of whom beckoned. "Abrupt. Flattering, yes, it is! I think you are a long way from home, boyo. You're lonely. Some young lady—of ye faith, surely—will be . . . fortunate."

He wasn't drunk. She represented a great aspiration and little time remained. He stood on a mountain. He looked out upon a horizon fraught with hazards and unpredictability but he was unafraid. If she'd studied him, for what purpose? She said she knew him better than he knew himself, but did she know her own heart? "Marry me," he said.

"Stop!" Her mouth twisted into an agonized frown. "You're drunk! All I wanted to say—the sole reason I came to your table—oh, ye are out of your sensible head. Ye don't know me. A girl in a saloon! I am twenty-eight, Ulysses, an old woman! I cannot—and dear Monte, of course, so good a friend—" Rebecca glanced toward the bar. "Ulysses, we—Monte has asked me and me old daddy to join him in San Jose. He has asked me to become his wife."

"Ahh!" wrenched out of him and Rebecca fell back as if struck. But Euly didn't voice the first words that entered his mind, "He's too old for you." He could be proud that he said, "Forgive me, if you can. He's a friend, Rebecca, and a good man."

Her blue eyes filled with kindness but not the kindness of a lover. A mother's, almost, and again he thought of Annelise. "Yes, Ulysses, he is surely that." She looked toward the little platform where she performed. Her father beckoned with his fiddle. "Pardon," Rebecca said, her manner suddenly formal. "Do let's talk again—tomorrow, love?—but now I must turn a lick of work for me supper."

Euly forced a smile.

"I'll sing you an Irish tune, a pub-rouser it is. Cheer up, love! Sing this as you ride through the Territory!"

The hours sad, I left a maid
A lingering farewell taking
Whose sighs and tears my steps delayed
I thought her heart was breaking
In hurried words her name I blest
I breathed the vows that bind me
And to my heart in anguish pressed
The Girl I Left Behind Me

There were several verses. All the lonely men clapped and sang along. Some had learned the words in the Civil War or marching off to kill Indians. It was not a song to be accompanied with tears and Euly stared at Rebecca with a stony face. Her blue eyes fled round the tent, urging the men onward, pausing for a long instant when they met Euly's. In fright, almost. And regret—but that's what the song was about.

AT 10:55, MOVING SLOWLY in the heat, Euly pulled onto a little rise, perhaps five hundred feet from the line. He stepped down and gave Gerty and Maude their feed bags. Maude concentrated on her oats, nodding contentedly, nuzzling his hand. The old girl knew what was important in life, but Gerty eyed the melee of animals and men ahead, shook herself, and stood trembling. Euly stroked her mane and talked to her soothingly. "Easy, girl," he said. "We're not going first."

With his binoculars Euly made out Jacob, a poor infantryman given a mount today so he wouldn't be trampled. Cavalry trotted east and west, pushing back excited horses, coming between settlers now screaming at each other in the whirling red dust. Euly saw one man drop—from heat stroke?—and never reappear.

The milling horses looked splendid, but here and there pairs of sleek mules pulled stripped-down buckboards. A better idea. The mules would run almost as fast as a man on horseback and with half again the endurance. They could reach the Salt Fork and the fertile land beyond it.

Some men would run with their own legs, carrying nothing but a rifle and canteen. Half a dozen even rode bicycles. Idiocy—you'd puncture your tires within twenty feet—but the cyclists looked like easterners, and perhaps the run was sport for them. They'd write books about the experience.

Then there were those wagons weighted down with kids and every poor thing the family owned, including a milk cow tied behind. They'd eat everyone's dust, blind luck their only ally. Sadder still, some men pushed wheelbarrows with all their worldly goods. They wouldn't get far but maybe the mad rush of riders and wagons would overlook the nearest claims. Maybe one or two of the wheelbarrow men could drive stakes within a quarter-mile.

Lowering the binoculars, Euly spied Kate on King Arthur, one hundred feet north of the line. He climbed to the wagon seat and waved but she had all she could do to calm her stallion.

He checked his father's railroad watch: 11:13.

Spectators milled all around him. To his left, a brass band fired up a Sousa march—Euly had never been able to tell one from the other—but then a heavy gust of wind strafed them with Oklahoma grit. The trombone and tuba dropped off with a gurgle and the musicians climbed down to chase after their hats. Two officials in black suits climbed up, looked at their watches, and spoke earnestly, but Euly couldn't hear them above the din of the crowd.

Eleven twenty-two. A man sold fried chicken, potato salad, and a cold bottle of sarsaparilla for a dollar. Cups of water brought ten cents. Euly carried two twenty-gallon kegs, but between the horses and himself he'd need it.

He lifted the binoculars again. Jacob, his faced screwed down to the unavoidable panic, had stopped to face the settlers. To his east a lieutenant climbed a tower, while behind him, on a second platform, a man in a blue suit pushed his head under a black cowl. The photographer.

Eleven thirty-seven. Euly brought down the binoculars and a hand grasped his forearm. He turned, startled, pleased—and confused. Rebecca sat beside him, bonnetless, her red hair blowing. The spectators, the agitated horsemen, fell away in a swirling blob of color like a crowd in a French painting.

She had been crying, but Euly did not think enough of himself to understand he was the cause. At last she looked up with clear eyes. "You failed to say goodbye, boyo."

She'd introduced herself, he'd blurted things best forgotten, and she'd bid him goodbye with a song. They didn't know each other. "After what I said, I didn't want to intrude."

"Oh, no, no, no, Ulysses." She tried out a smile. "We need to talk. About your theory."

Euly was worn out. So much work stretched before him, such a long journey. He thought of the pint of whiskey stashed in his bedroll. It would put a man to sleep as surely as a sledge hammer. "Oh."

"I believe ye've reversed things. The work we do, Ulysses, the work we all need to do to eat—*that's* the 20 percent."

Eleven fifty-one. Even without binoculars, Euly saw Jacob raise his bugle. "You can count on work. If you fail, it's no one's fault but your own. And I *don't* fail, Rebecca. It's . . . all I am."

"Plainly, love, that's untrue. You are kind. You'll risk your life for a friend. And ye like me music." She picked up his hand and played with his callused fingers as if he were an infant. "The 80 percent you don't understand, Ulysses, the mystery no one comprehends, is—"

"Life," he said. He understood but it didn't help. The mystery only grew deeper and there was more of it. He met her eyes. "You and me, Rebecca? I thought—we're so different, aren't we? I thought you made things clear. You're betrothed!"

Her eyes registered mischief. "Speak for yourself, John Alden."

Surprise followed surprise but he knew the Longfellow poem. "Won't we hurt old Monte?"

"We will." Rebecca looked up at him sadly. "And it's your fault, my love. You caused the lightning to strike."

Sweat, not tears, poured down her cheeks, and she brought out a handkerchief. He worried her fair skin would burn in the harsh wind. He reached into the wagon and drew a cup of water, then wet her handkerchief and stroked her face. He kissed her and put his arm around her shoulders. "You have freckles," he said, touching a fingertip to her nose.

Rebecca sighed and dabbed at her eyes with the handkerchief. "Do you want me?"

"How could I not? Yes, yes, what fortune! But—dear lady—I can't take it in! It's so strange."

"'She swore, in faith 'twas strange, 'twas passing strange . . .'"

What sort of woman quoted Shakespeare as the unlettered heaved into battle? Was she mad? "Rebecca. Rebecca. We have no time!"

She shrugged. "You may call me Becky."

"People are depending on me. I must—I have to—"

"Hush." Rebecca pointed toward the border. "It's history, love of my life."

"Love of my life," he murmured, and then Jacob blew his bugle. Another bugle sounded—down the long line, over a rise. The lieutenant leaned far out from his platform and fired his rifle. A roar went up as if the heavens had split, as if the walls of Jericho had fallen. In one dusty, seething, desperate mass, they were off.

20

The Run

 ate wore men's clothes with her hair pinned up under a wide slouch hat. But neither man nor woman could have held back King Arthur, who thought he needed to run faster than the chestnut mare. He did for more than a mile, jumping a writhing fallen man, veering around wrecks.

King Arthur dodged a wagon that bumped over a boulder, losing a wheel that rolled onward, hitting no one. The wagon itself careened sideways, pitching the man and woman into the dust, breaking their mule's leg. The mule screamed as she tried to rise from inside the tangled harness. Kate kept looking over her shoulder and the woman never stirred. The man limped over and shot the mule, then stood there in the sun.

The stronger, the faster, the luckier moved on, dispersing southeast toward the most desirable land, but Kate kneed King Arthur due south and found the Chisum Trail. She was alone now, half a dozen wagons far behind her. At last she brought the stallion under control and dismounted. "Bad boy," she said, tapping his nose, and King Arthur bobbed his head proudly. He hadn't lathered. He didn't even breathe hard.

She herself was covered in sweat and a black grime from the burnt grass. She kept thinking about the man who had lost everything. She reminded herself that all rules were suspended today, including a normal reaction to violence and pain. She tried to suppress thoughts of the fallen woman, the hysterical mule.

She'd hoped to find grass a few miles into the Outlet, but the army had been at work here, too, burning the tall bluestem to keep settled Kansas farmers from putting up hay. Winds rose, as they always did on the prairie, and the fires went wild. The result meant that forage for livestock would be hard to find and that the poorest settlers wouldn't make it through the winter.

She felt dizzy. She'd sweated too much without drinking. When the trail branched southeast, at the first significant marker on Johnny's map, she climbed a little hill where cedars grew out of a plain of rocks. She dismounted, drank a pint of water from one of her four canteens, and poured the rest into her hat for King Arthur. She put the hat on again and a little water dribbled through her hair and down her neck. It felt divine.

She judged she'd ridden six miles.

With the binoculars she could make out the man who'd shot his mule. His wife hadn't died, after all. She scolded the man and he argued back. She sat while he stalked around the ruined wagon, shaking his fists at the cruel blue sky, at God. Once again Kate scanned northward for Euly, but on the border a high wall of dust churned. She felt abandoned and fearful, but she'd done fine so far. She told herself to be calm.

A strip of jerky, a biscuit, and a swallow of water from her second canteen settled her stomach and seemed to cure her dizziness. She rode southeast into the black country, onto a hunting trail Johnny had marked. All the creeks were dry, but some of the blackjacks and cedars stood tall enough to provide shade. Here the grass hadn't burned, and she allowed King Arthur to graze for a few minutes, then put him into a canter over soft ground. They topped a rise covered with prickly pear and she reined him in. He had begun to lather.

She dismounted, talked to him, and together they finished the third canteen. She scanned the horizon to the north and spied a family who'd found their stakes. The wife and children raised a tent, while, beneath the merciless sun, the husband chopped the black sod. Such hard work ought to be done in early morning but she supposed the man was eager. With no rain, at least their dirt roof wouldn't leak. Where would they find water?

Kate despised sod houses. Knowing Johnny—with Billy and Euly's help, and with the reservation's resources not far away—he'd have a frame house raised by winter. He'd promised a wooden floor and a stone fireplace, maybe an indoor sink in the second year. Money made all the difference and they had some. That poor family on the ridge could claim nothing but their burned-off land. Well, some chickens and two scrawny milk cows. Maybe the man could shoot an antelope but those chickens were doomed, and probably the cows. If the family could make it until spring, and rains fell—

AS THE SUN DROPPED low, she rode downhill toward a winding line of cottonwoods and willows. King Arthur smelled water and broke into a canter again, and, sure enough, they'd reached the Salt Fork. She dismounted and plodded through a wide patch of sand. The river flowed a little but there were pools in it, some of them covered over with green scum, some almost clear. She dropped prone, drank, and spat. The water tasted like salt and mud. She drank again and swallowed. Her mouth puckered as if she'd bitten into a green persimmon. King Arthur, too, snorted at the water, but continued to drink.

She left him saddled because she'd need a better hiding place than this. He found a patch of brittle grass and pulled at it.

Catfish thrashed in the pools, trapped by the low water. Kate pulled one up with her hands like Euly and she used to along Zimmerman's Creek. The slippery thing flopped into the air but she batted it toward the sand. Driftwood abounded and she'd brought matches. Inside a ring of flat limestone she built a fire on the sand. She dug a small frying pan from her saddlebags, then one of those Barlow knives Euly sold. She'd never cleaned a catfish. She remembered her Uncle Helmut sticking their broad heads into a shop vise, then pulling off their skins with pliers. She stared at the fish with dread. Maybe she could slice away several long filets and boil them.

"Are you an Injun?"

Kate reached for her derringer. But the speaker was a boy, holding a pail of water, calling from across the little river. He wore jeans and a black hat but no shirt and stood with his shoulders squared—vain about his muscles, she thought. He was no more than twelve.

"You bet," Kate said, and held high the Barlow knife. "Come over here and I'll scalp you."

"You ain't no Injun. Papa said, look out, they're evrywheres, but you ain't one. Are you an outlaw?"

"I'm not even an inlaw. What's your name, young man?"

Before he could answer, a woman called out, "Ralphie, I need that water!"

Ralphie shrugged, grabbed up his pail, and ran into a thicket of willows with broad limbs that grew along the ground, pushing up sprouts. Kate crossed the river, stepping on stones and logs where she could, submerging her boots once, nearly falling. "Hello! Hello?" she called, as she followed the boy into the thicket, stepping over the low limbs. A leafy branch slapped her face and when she bent it aside she stood looking into a rifle barrel.

"Friend!" she said. "I'm alone, a friend!"

The woman grunted and lowered her rifle halfway. She was stocky, middle-aged, with thick, snarled hair. "What you doing out here by yourself, gal?"

"She's a girl?" Ralphie piped up. "I thought he—*she* was an Injun!"

Kate smiled. "Well, making the run, but not like other folks. I have two days' ride ahead of me, southeast."

"You'll get yourself shot." The woman looked her up and down. "Or mebbe worse."

The woman poured some of Ralphie's water into a cast iron pot hanging from a tripod. She didn't bring such gear in on horseback, Kate thought, but the woman, Blanche, said she wasn't a Sooner. She and her several menfolk hailed from Tennessee. The army had brought them in to dig wells back in July. They looked the other way when the clan found a piece of land to squat on: sandy in some places, rocky in others, but by the river.

Her uncle had taken the stakes and registration to Alva, while her husband and brother had returned to Caldwell with two wagons to retrieve a new drill and more piping.

"So here I am all alone," the woman said. "So young and purty."

"I'll defend you!" Ralphie said.

"I know you will, son." Blanche hugged the boy then looked up at Kate. "You do look like an Indian . . . what you call yourself, gal?"

"Kate." She frowned. "I'm mixed blood."

"Don't mean no offense. My husband's a half-breed."

"I'm one-quarter Cherokee!" said Ralphie.

Kate was tired. She'd sat in the saddle nearly eight hours, traveling thirty miles. She was hungry, too. Might be anything in that cast iron pot but she imagined it was tastier than her catfish. "Good to meet you," she said, turning away. "If ever a country needed wells. You folks will make some money."

"Make room, Mr. Rockefeller!" Blanche ladled stew from the pot and held out the steaming bowl. "Your company's welcome, gal. Come evenin', we'll put out the fire and crawl inside that tent. We're well hid here."

Kate found two pieces of chicken and half a potato in the bowl. Not even in Kansas City could you find such delicious fare. "I thank you, Blanche."

"We got nothin' to fear but coyotes and we'll hope none a them has two legs. Ain't you got no gun, gal?"

Kate produced her derringer.

"What's that little thing good fer?"

"You can kill somebody up close. I never have, but—"

"All righty. I'll take the far varmints and you take the close-uns. Don't shoot 'till you see the whites a their eyes."

SOUTH OF PONCA CITY, wagons jammed up twenty deep by the railroad bridge. Men threw down timbers, even disassembled their sideboards, to build up a road along the rails—which had to be taken apart whenever a train passed. Kate was thankful she'd remained on the southern shore. There was enough water in the Salt Fork here that she would have had to swim King Arthur across. She watched riders—with no patience to wait their turn on the improvised bridge—try to cross. One in ten made it but the banks were steep and slippery, and horses floundered, throwing their mounts into the water.

Kate turned southeast again and followed the tracks for several miles. The trains had brought in barrels of good water to a so-far-nameless tent city and Kate bought a dozen early apples out of an impromptu store. She fed one to King Arthur and they turned southeast again, needing to wring another fifteen miles from the day. In late afternoon she reached the Arkansas, wide and shallow, dividing plains of mud, sand, and salty pools where turtles and minnows swam. The river's edges looked firm and ensured quick progress but Kate retreated to higher ground. Another river flowed beneath the Arkansas, Johnny had told her, causing pockets of quicksand that could fool even the Osage. Kate turned due south again, her canteens sloshing with railroad water, and looked for a safe place to sleep.

A desiccating wind rose and she could feel her skin drying out and scaling. She'd reached the point of exhaustion where she hardly understood who she was. She looked down on herself, a poor creature, a grasshopper, crawling through the flat country.

Using her binoculars she spied a low west-to-east escarpment that broadened toward the river and dropped to nothing. She held up Johnny's now-tattered map and looked upon high, timbered ground, the northern side of his bluffs. She needed to skirt that rough land and go down to the river again. Their claim lay on the southern side of the escarpment, three or four miles west of the river. She was too weary to feel elation but she'd nearly reached home.

She had to sleep. Anywhere. That stand of oaks.

You couldn't kill an oak, her Uncle Helmut said, but these looked to be dying. Their brown leaves rattled in the wind. She slid off King Arthur and threw down his saddle for a pillow. The poor fellow flopped besides her and she fed him the last packet of oats out of her hand, fell asleep, woke to his rough tongue on her fingers. She thought she had one last cube of sugar but fell asleep reaching for it. She ran a hand over her face, alarmed by the caked alkali.

As the light failed, Kate understood she was not alone. On the plain to her south, two families had camped three hundred feet apart, one with a covered Conestoga, "Oklahomy or Bust" painted on the canvas, the other with an open, homemade wagon. Both families felt they had a right to the claim. The men shouted out insults, seemingly close to warfare.

"I got two hunert dollars for ye if you head on back to Ioway. Where you belong!"

"I was here fust, you spud-eater."

"Damn Sooner, that's what you is. Listen, I tried to be civil about this, but I'm reachin' the end of my tether. Evrybody is this family kin use a gun, and we're loaded fer bear."

"I'm a-shakin' in my boots. I got a twelve-pound Napoleon cannon over here and I'm loadin' it jest about right now."

"We'll come back atcha with my Gatlin gun, only I don't wanna waste my ammunition. I might go three hunert, jest to be done with a skunk like you."

"That's an insultin' amount fer land purty as this. You're gonna deal with me in court, you connivin' poltroon! I lined up a raft a lawyers 'fore we started."

They argued long after dark, just another night sound like the rattling leaves, the owls, and the protesting coyotes. Any wandering bad man would steer clear of such noisy rhetoric and Kate slept assured.

She left at first light, dividing the remainder of her apples with King Arthur, chewing on the last of her jerky. The ground lay flat with sweeps of long grass, sunflowers poking through it, and as the sun climbed halfway to noon, she came to a stream that flowed through the great meadow. She flushed six prairie hens and a scolding rooster. This must be *their* creek and she had only four or five miles to go.

Kate thought of Johnny, all she had to tell him, how she hadn't seen him in a long two weeks. She slipped from the saddle, scanned the undulating grass even though the notion of anyone within eyesight was ridiculous, and stripped off her clothes. Revolting, those socks, and in Jericho Springs she'd have thrown them away, but she wouldn't have any sort of wardrobe until Euly arrived with his wagon. She washed them out and lay them on a rock to dry.

She had no other trousers but had rolled up a new Montgomery Ward shirt. She'd brought a comb and a bar of Euly's Castile soap. She stood scrubbing herself from face to toes and then sat in the watery sand, sighing. King Arthur snorted and pranced off downstream twenty feet.

The water felt warm where the sun hit but down near the bottom it chilled her legs. "I dream of Jeannie with the light brown hair," Kate sang, and plunged her head under the water. She came up gasping, but soaped and kneaded her hair, plunged it under again, and then tried to comb out some of the snarls, the seeds and grass and beggar's lice. She'd take a lot of baths in this creek. Maybe they could build a pond one day. Johnny and she could go swimming like when they were courting. She smiled. They were so innocent then they didn't even know they were courting.

As she buttoned the new shirt, Kate heard hoofbeats. She might pass for a man with her hair tucked up and wearing Levi's, but she stood almost naked. For an instant she panicked, thinking what a man might do to her in this lonely place, but she forced herself calm and listened. The hoofbeats were distinct but not quite upon her and she believed they were receding. She yanked on her jeans, stuck her bare feet into her boots, and hurried toward King Arthur. He backed away, skittish, and she scolded him. He held still as she fumbled in the saddle bags for her derringer and then she swung into the saddle.

She saw the man now—the back of him, stopping at the creek to allow his horse to drink, almost a half mile upstream. Again she felt a stab of panic, because something about the man seemed familiar. Did she recognize that piebald horse? The man turned due west in the direction of the claim.

She began to gain on him and considered catching up and accosting him—with a hand clutching the derringer inside her shirt. The thought terrified her and she veered uphill, where the ground was rockier but she could camouflage herself amid red cedars and blackjacks. The horseman dropped from sight and when she saw him again he pushed his horse harder. Kate understood why. Not quite a mile onward a half-built cedar structure rose from the grass. A man swung an axe—a stick figure from this distance, but it had to be Johnny.

Kate dug her knees into King Arthur and he bolted forward. She thought how Euly had urged her to carry a rifle rather than a popgun, but she couldn't have hit a target at a thousand feet if she stood flat on the earth, let alone from horseback.

He must have made the run from Arkansas City. He thought this was his land. How could a wanted man, more than once a murderer, make a legal claim? Under another name?

Even he might not approach a stranger with a pointed rifle. Even he might first try words, but if it came to a fight with guns—

Eddie Mole. She'd never forgotten that one searing look across the street at her, at once furtive and aggressive, as he bent to swoop up Barney Kreider's money. Like a blow, she took in the mechanistic cunning of his eyes, forever calculating and then recalculating his odds for dominance. Kate was afraid but fear was irrelevant. With no plan but to warn Johnny, she bent close to King Arthur and urged him into the open again. Eddie Mole's mare was no match for King Arthur and Kate closed on the outlaw quickly. Her derringer was as good as a Sharps rifle for missing. She angled the pistol high and fired.

Eddie Mole turned in the saddle at the report and yanked up a rifle.

Johnny lifted his head, threw down his axe, and stared. No, no, Kate thought, as her husband climbed his cedar ladder and peered through his binoculars. She screamed. Get down, Johnny! Run! She pulled up her binoculars as well and focused on his beautiful face. She mouthed the words, "Ed-die Mo-ul," and pointed dramatically. Please, *please*. Can't you see?

Johnny leaped from the ladder and disappeared behind his structure. Eddie Mole got off two rounds but she couldn't see if they hit anything. Where did Johnny go? The grass lay flat all around his structure so he couldn't hide there. He must have dropped over the bank into the creek. He must be moving down it with his rifle.

Eddie Mole veered north toward a stand of cedars under the bluffs, no more than five hundred feet from Johnny's half-building. He pushed his horse so hard it stumbled but he sprang off the saddle and kept his feet. Crouching, he scanned the horizon and aimed his rifle toward Kate. She was in range now. She might as well have thrown the derringer but she leveled her arm and fired the last round at Eddie Mole. He jumped inside the cedars.

Now he had cover and could steady his aim. She imagined herself tumbling from King Arthur, bleeding out on the lone prairie as bullets whistled overhead. She turned King Arthur toward the creek. If she could cross it, she could hide under the high, northern bank, cutting off Eddie Mole's aim. Not far! Two rounds popped out of the cedars, one smacking the ground ahead of her, the other carrying higher. If she hadn't turned, that second round would have caught King Arthur. Or me, she thought.

King Arthur leaped. Kate shut her eyes and called out, "Jesus, sweet Jesus!" As they rose from the high bank, she heard four shots ring out from up the creek. That was Johnny. He was all right, and trying to divert Eddie Mole's fire. Oh, I left my socks on that rock, she thought, as her feet slipped out of her unlaced boots. She seemed to fly.

21

Home Place

An ancient path, followed by deer and once the Osage, led up the canyon beneath oaks and tall pines. Brown willow branches lay like great sleeping snakes, and then you reached flat ground and rich, green grass. Deep in the drought the spring flowed cold and clear. It would never go dry. The water flowed like a miracle, and if you came to this perfect place maybe you neared your time to die.

You will not die for a long time, John Baxter.

"Comes with the Snow," he murmured. He didn't need peyote to conjure the maiden seated on a broad willow branch, dipping her feet into the cool water. She turned her head and smiled. He remembered her glorious, long hair but it was shorter now. She looked like his new wife, Kate. Yes, Johnny thought, I have much to live for.

The army might oust him for a Sooner but only if they found him. For two weeks Johnny kept to the high ground, exploring paths through the big rocks, surveying the stands of scrub timber. He flushed deer but the sound of a rifle carried far in such dry air. He cut tall, straight cedars with a bucksaw, trimmed them with a hatchet, and looped a rope over Soquili's pommel to drag the poles down to the low cliff where, seven months before, he'd seen Eddie Mole.

No soldiers came, and on the great day of the run, he dropped his poles over the cliff and carried them near the creek, where

he wanted a corral and feed room. He stood for a moment and
stared at the ruins of Eddie Mole's cabin: nothing to use there.
Perhaps those flat stones from the collapsed chimney.

"And that was the first day," he announced to the sweeping
plains. "I see that it is good."

Do not blaspheme, John Baxter.

I am John Baxter, John Baxter,
I have horses,
I own land.

I am John Baxter, John Baxter.
I have a beautiful wife.

Wah-Kon-Da, Wah-Kon-da,
I am John Baxter,
My spirit soars,
One with all things.

On the second day of his creation he dug holes three feet
deep, two feet apart, in a rectangle fifteen by twenty. There
were no roots to cut through, but two feet down he had to pry
out rocks with his hickory pike. He made a slurry of gravel and
clay, dropped the poles into the goop, and packed in the rocks.
He had no level but walked around the frame, eyeballing it to
make sure it was plumb.

Then Johnny sat by his fire, frying bluegill from the creek in
a handful of cornmeal.

Next year he'd raise a barn here. A cavernous barn with a hay-
mow like the Mennonites built, and strong crosspieces for hoist-
ing up a cow or a deer carcass. The Mennonites had taught him
about sawmills too. One big oak would build a barn. But his
cedar poles, laid crosswise, chinked with clay or mortar, would
make a fine two-story house.

You'd lay down plank floors. You'd have to nail those green
boards tightly or they'd bow. Maybe he'd use the oak for sheeting, with tin over that. Buy his flooring from a mill, at least

for the downstairs. Tongue-and-groove as in Helmut Kreider's sturdy house. Kate would like that.

On the third day he lashed poles together for a scaffold, and began cutting notches in his uprights eight feet from the ground. He wished he had a chisel, but the cedar was soft and he could work it with the saw and his pocketknife. By noon he had plates tied up on all four sides. They held his weight but when Euly came, they'd nail them with twenty pennies.

Where is your rifle, John Baxter?

True enough. He'd seen no one but by now white men crawled all over the Outlet, some of them, the landless ones, desperate to the point of murder. He dropped down from the scaffold and found his Winchester leaning against his saddle. He pushed in four rounds and brought it up to his feed room frame. On the scaffold again, he scanned eastward with his binoculars. He expected Billy to appear by nightfall.

He began work on his ridgepole and first set of rafters. He had to angle the high ends of the rafters and cut notches where they dropped on the plate. The ridgepole needed to be flat where the rafters leaned in. The trick was keeping the assemblage from falling over as he tried to tie it together. If he raised the end rafters, with the ridge pole between, then—

He paused his chopping. He'd heard a rifle. Not a rifle . . . a pistol because of the staccato sound, heavy caliber. He stood tall on his scaffold and raised his binoculars to the east. A man on a black stallion chased another on a piebald mare. What was this all about? The man on the stallion—he didn't look like Billy—motioned in Johnny's direction, and Johnny leveled the binoculars. He knew the horse, that big . . . Kate? Kate! She tried to say something. Around, around—*get down*. Ready, be ready—*Eddie*. Eddie Mole?

A round slammed into wood as he leaped. The two half-rafters fell to the ground with the ridge pole as Johnny rolled toward the creek, gathering up the Winchester and getting off one shot in the general direction of the piebald mare. This was *his* claim. That's what Eddie Mole thought!

Mole turned on Kate now and Johnny fired again with better aim. His round must have hit near because Mole scooted back toward a clump of cedars. But Kate—well, that silly derringer held only two bullets. Johnny reached the creek bed and fired standing up, twice. Kate raced toward the creek. She'd kill her poor horse—

She was airborne!

King Arthur twisted sideways, bucking in midair like a rodeo bronc.

Kate threw out her hands as if to gather in something. She rose high in the blue, turned white as an angel in the sunlight, and fell from sight.

Johnny rushed down the creek, jumping from gravel bar to grass, climbing the bank every fifty feet to fire into the cedars. He rounded a bend and there sat his wife, her bare feet in a little pool. One boot had caught on a shard of limestone, protruding from the bank. The other stood upright in a quarter inch of water.

Johnny tried not to laugh. "You are well, my wife?"

She stared up at him as if he were a stranger. "Is he dead now?"

"No."

"I wanted to kill him."

"You have the right." He reached down to pull her to her feet, then held her close. Two weeks had passed and she was not the same Kate. She felt leaner. Her muscles had tension to them and wiry strength. "If you had not fired the little pistol—"

"If you had not given it to me in the first place—"

Johnny kissed her and she sat again, dazed. He climbed halfway up the bank, securing his boots in pockets of gravel. He fired two rounds and no fire returned.

"Is he dead now?"

Johnny shook his head. "Conserving ammunition. He hopes to draw us out."

"Husband, I *missed* you."

He nodded but couldn't match her passion. Yes, she had changed. "I missed you as well. I didn't expect you until tomorrow. I expected—"

She told him about Billy's injury. "I made the run to *be* with you. Because I am your wife!"

He nodded again. He understood she needed reassurance and he dropped from the bank, pulled her up from the creek, and kissed her again. She felt good next to him, softer now, and he wished there were no Eddie Mole to dispense with. "Were you in peril?"

"Not really. Not until now. But it was hard, Johnny—the land so dry, so hot."

"I'm sorry," he said. Of course, it was hard, but she could have come down through the reservation. Another day would have passed and they needed to make their claim in Perry, but he already occupied the land. Yes, she was his wife, and brave, and strong as an Osage woman should be, but a woman alone in that vast territory invited trouble.

"If you had done the sensible thing, Kate, and come down through the reservation—"

"I *had* to see you."

"I would be dead."

HE BUILT A SMALL fire and soon they'd have beans, biscuits, and bluegill. They lay side by side near his half-built corral, with a clear line of sight to the cedar grove. Kate turned on her back from time to time and he kissed her. He loved this brand-new woman but fondling her seemed risky, almost sinful.

"We're lucky," she said.

"Yes," Johnny said. "We have each other. We have land and good horses."

"Which we worked hard for! What do you see here in five years, on this beautiful land?"

He studied Eddie Mole's piebald mare. The mare had returned

to the cedars and stood cropping grass. Johnny turned to his wife, and for an instant, he thought she was Comes with the Snow. She stretched her long arms above her head and he was aroused.

He cast his eyes toward the mare again. "I see a prosperous farm. Corn, oats, sorghum to the south, pasture along by the bluff—with white horses from Buffalo Dancer's stock, running in the sun."

"Is there a house in this vision, John Baxter?"

The only one ever to address him as "John Baxter" was Comes with the Snow. Also known as Suzy Niabi, slain six miles from here by her drunken white lover, Eddie Mole. He stared at Kate. Her eyes glowed with love and living and he was a fortunate man. "A snug house made of wood and stone. With a long porch where you have set up your easel."

"Are there children?"

He rolled on top of her. He undid the top buttons of her Montgomery Ward shirt and kissed her breasts. "They are playing by the creek," he said, and rolled away again, and sat up to aim his Winchester. Her touch, her soapy smell, lingered. "Two daughters."

"Two daughters? What! Coming down, I had the same thought. How did you—?"

"I had a vision of our life here."

"A vision! What—what are you *doing*, Johnny?"

"I don't want him to get back to his horse."

She nodded. "Kill her. That's the easiest."

Johnny understood the tactic but hated the thought. It seemed uncharacteristic of Kate, the peaceful Mennonite, and he threw her a puzzled glance. He had killed because he had to. If he had to, he'd kill Eddie Mole, but never a blameless horse.

"King Arthur will make a powerful sire. With Soquili and the piebald mare, we'll breed strong foals that we can sell."

He fired behind the mare and she lifted her head in his direction. She stared like a deer would, waiting for motion before she sprang, so he obliged by waving his hat, exposing a hand and forearm. He didn't provoke a shot.

And the piebald mare didn't move. Johnny fired to graze her rump—an inch off, he'd cripple her, but he wouldn't miss. Once, he'd brought down a charging buffalo with a snap shot from a Sharps needle gun. The mare jumped and ran toward Johnny's corral. Eddie Mole's voice rose in a curse.

Johnny stood. The beans had begun to boil and he moved them back from the flame. He turned over the biscuits.

"Where are you going, love?"

"To tie up that mare. Make friends with her."

"Then what?"

Johnny looked to the west. "We should eat. And sleep. When Grandfather Sun falls from the sky—"

"We need to keep watch."

"Yes. But we have food and plenty of firewood."

"You will not . . . go after him? In the night?"

He looked down on his beautiful Osage bride, shaking his head. The bad man was doomed and hardly mattered except for the cash he'd bring them. Soon, after eating a little, they would make one of their daughters. "There is no need, my love."

Kate stood, too, and put her arms around him. Her eyes shone with dreams but also anxiety. "He has the high ground," she whispered.

"We have the water."

22

Call It Justice

The broken settlers, with no claim on anything, filed north again like the sooty stragglers of a vanquished army. Some begged for water, which Euly gave freely though only for drinking. He sold four boxes of ammunition. Others—men with claims—wanted his flour and onions, hammers, saws, and galvanized roofing, but he carried these for his family, for Johnny and Kate.

Deep inside the roasting heat, he hardly noticed any of them, because Rebecca had claimed the territory of his mind. He revisited her every word and gesture and knew her by deduction, but she was not a character in a novel, and mysteries arose. How had she and her father come to Boston? Did she claim any sort of religion? Had she grown up entirely in cities? Could she even ride a horse, much less follow behind one in a furrow?

She wouldn't need to do *that*.

Would Annelise like her? Kate? What about his uncles and their wives? The old Ukrainian Mennonites?

He compared Rebecca to Jenny and rejoiced. Rebecca was smart and witty. Jenny was a thief. Jenny had done him a favor.

If she wanted to, Rebecca could teach school.

Her father could run the hardware. He was perfect for it.

As for a house, whatever she wanted, nothing to it but money and work. A house belonged to the 80 percent—or was it 20?—that Euly understood.

Such thoughts transported him through the first two days and into the afternoon of the third, when it occurred to him that his wagon moved more and more slowly. He saw why: Maude was laboring. "Whoa there," he said, and jumped down, and ran a hand over her thick neck. Too hot, even in this oven of a day, and it might help to give her a bath. In Johnny's creek, he thought, assuming it hadn't gone dry, but he had at least fifteen miles still to go.

"Sorry, old girl," he said. He hadn't seen a tree for more than an hour but the land had begun to tilt upward, and he led the team into an outcropping of rocks that gave some shade on their westward side. He unhitched Maude and she stood with her head low. He had ten gallons of water remaining in his second keg, and he wet his handkerchief again and again, bathing her neck and head and withers. In a while she shivered and shook off the water, a good sign, but still she held her head low, as if it was too heavy to lift.

Euly reached behind her left elbow and felt for her heart. He lost the precise count but guessed it to be over fifty—too high; and she breathed rapidly. "Get down, Maude," he said, pushing on her withers, reaching low to bend in her knees, and finally she dropped, giving out a low moan.

"We'll spend the night right here," Euly said. "I'll get you all fixed up."

Her respiration slowed. By ten her heart rate was at forty beats—still somewhat high, but Euly felt encouraged. He placed oats on a corner of his blanket and stumbled about under the moon, collecting what grass he could find. Euly wished he had an apple or carrot for her. After midnight, he slept for several hours, and when he woke Maude had grown so quiet he thought she might be dead. But no: she'd eaten the oats and forage, and her breathing seemed normal.

He should have brought the mules. He knew how much Johnny liked them and he'd meant to offer them as a wedding gift, but the Belgians were his favorites and he hitched them without thinking.

At four he built up a fire for light, and watered and fed both horses. Maude seemed fine, holding up her head like a colt, and by beginning early she wouldn't have to pull through such punishing heat. "Maybe Johnny can tell us where to find a depot and we'll ride the train home. I can afford that, Maude, so you just think about home. You know our little place. You can eat timothy hay and run along by the creek, and you won't have to do a thing."

OUT OF THE BROAD basin, up a grade so slight it was almost indiscernible, they climbed toward a crest. Theirs was the only boat on a vast ocean of grass, here and there with ripples that twisted and ran off like waves. Euly looked eastward toward a greenish glow that could only be the Arkansas; he paralleled the long escarpment to his north. He knew where he was. Almost.

He brought up his binoculars and sighted west to east, pausing at every cleft, following down the draws, looking for water. He missed it the first time. An outcropping of rock hid it, but on his next pass he dropped the binoculars lower and saw the creek, the only cleft with flowing water. And then he didn't need binoculars because Johnny and Kate were down the grade from him a quarter mile. Gesturing violently. He heard Kate's scream above the wind.

A shot rang out, not much echo to it across the plain, and he snapped the reins above Maude and Gerty. They tried to accommodate him but down the uneven ground they gained only a little speed. Both Johnny and Kate fired toward a stand of cedars under the bluff, but rounds still peppered the ground near the wagon. Euly understood, when he reached the creek, that he'd be safe under the high northern bank. Then a round splattered into Maude and she stumbled.

She pulled onward, her screaming outraged, shrill. Euly dropped from the wagon and raced to her side. "Maude," he said, but she was already silent, hanging in her traces, her massive weight yanking at Gerty and tipping the back wheels off the ground.

He grabbed Gerty's bridle and they pulled. A round pinged off the water kegs as Johnny joined them. Together, with Gerty pawing mightily as she dragged her dead partner, they rolled the wagon onto the low ground below the rifleman's angle of fire. Johnny stood tall, his chest heaving. "Your good horse," he said, his black eyes fastened on Euly.

"Maude!" Euly said. He couldn't hold back his tears. "I should have left her at home, Johnny. She's too *old* to work. Why did I—?"

"Yes, Little Hero. A horse, more than a man, maybe, so much feeling."

Euly knelt by Maude and straightened her legs. When he looked up again his voice had steadied. "We need to bury her."

Kate ran up, carrying a Winchester. "I shot at him, Euly. If he stood here, if he stood here now . . . I'd *execute* him."

"What? Who is he?"

"It's lucky *you* weren't killed." Kate knelt by Maude and scratched between her ears. She hadn't bled much and looked peaceful. "I was never afraid of her. Euly, you remember how I walked down to Uncle Barney's—*your* farm to play? I had to climb up on the stanchions to feed her a carrot. Poor old gal. We rode out into the orchard—"

"*Who?*" Euly stared at Kate with such violence she turned her face.

Johnny placed a hand on Euly's shoulder. "Eddie Mole."

Euly didn't appear to react. He stepped to the back of his wagon and caught up his father's Marlin, gleaming in the sun, and a new Winchester still oily from the packing crate. Why, he thought, as he loaded both rifles and filled his pockets with rounds. Why do you create such men, whose sole purpose is to bring suffering? God in Heaven, are you there?

"We should wait," Johnny said. "He's only a little alive up there."

"All night we waited." Kate clutched Euly's arm. "We thought he must be dead, but—"

"He has no water," Johnny said. "Little Hero, it is wiser to *wait.*"

"I don't want to wait." Euly tore from Kate and leaped up the bank—and yet rashness was his plan. He studied the cedars, deliberately presenting himself as a target. He made a rational guess how many seconds might pass before a man could take aim, and before that instant passed, he leaped and rolled in the grass. No muzzle flash, but a round zipped into the soil where he had been and he saw a cedar tremble. With his elbows in the dirt, spreadeagled, he fired and fired again until he'd emptied the Marlin, and then he brought up the Winchester. He aimed left and right of the movement, his first rounds kicking up the dirt until he found the correct elevation. Two rounds returned, then none. As he reloaded, a Winchester cracked to the right of him, and then one to the left—Johnny, Kate. Euly stood with the Marlin at his waist and levered it empty. He threw it down and picked up the Winchester.

"Stop!" came a choked voice. "Goddamn you—"

"Show yourself," Euly called.

"I cain't walk!"

"Then slither on out of there, Eddie Mole. I got a case a dynamite on that wagon, and I suppose I can waste a stick or two on you."

He *had* brought dynamite.

One cedar trembled and the three of them converged, their rifles held at their hips. Eddie Mole's face emerged, bleeding from little cuts. He crawled into the sun and Euly came up to him, pointing the rifle at his head. He thought, dead or alive. I could end it now.

Up close, Eddie Mole didn't look fearsome. He was fat and

almost bald. Blood oozed through a patch of denim he'd cut from his jeans and tied around his thigh.

"Pack a damn Sooners," the outlaw said. "I done it legal and it was my place all along! Them slave soldiers burned down my house, you hear me? I stood there three days in Ark City, like to pass out in that heat, I done it legal!"

Kate kicked him hard in the ribs. Eddie Mole groaned and shut his eyes. His big belly shook like something molten.

"Wife," Johnny said.

Euly sighed, trying to comprehend this embodiment of evil. He'd never understood evil, except that it wasn't sneering or black or in any way definite, like they taught you in Sunday School. Evil was disappointing. It cared only for itself. It was almost boring. "Grab his feet," he said, staring at the hatred on Kate's face.

They carried him down near the creek and laid him under a tall cottonwood. Kate fetched water in a tin cup but then stared at Eddie Mole with her face still convulsed. She handed the cup to Euly and retreated toward Johnny's half-built shed.

The preacher said, if he is thirsty, give him a drink.

Euly cradled the man's head under his arm, then held up the water. "I ain't gonna make no trouble," he said, gulping the water. "I'se just defendin' my home! Hail, man's home is his castle. What they doin' here, damn Injuns, that's what I thought. And that woman, she jest lit into me, I done nothin'!

"'Course, I'm part-Injun myself, my mama was half-breed Choctaw, them soldiers taken her down the mountain, she never come back. I was an orphant, never had no chanct in life among the high-steppin' folks. I ain't gonna make you no trouble. You gimme my hoss, I'll skedaddle on south, I'se jest defendin' my home. You got here firstist. Ain't fair but they don't make the law for a poor man."

"Quiet," Euly said.

"I'm a-lyin' here bleedin' to death. I need a doctor! What I done to you? Jest defendin' my land, any man gonna do that."

"Shut your mouth or I'll gag you."

Kate returned with two Montgomery Ward shirts and began tearing them apart. "We should bandage that wound."

Euly bound Maude's legs under her long belly, knowing they'd stiffen and cause them to dig a bigger hole. The dirt was soft along the creek, but even so they worked until almost ten under the moon, with Gerty and Soquili and King Arthur nearby, nickering as they grazed on little bluestem. Kate cooked ham and cabbage from the stores Euly had brought down from Caldwell, and Euly carried up a plate to Eddie Mole and placed it on the ground with another cup of water. The bad man had fallen asleep.

If your enemy is hungry, feed him.

"I BROUGHT DOWN YOUR art materials," Euly told Kate, an hour before midnight, under a moon so bright you could read by it. They sat on cedar logs, huddled by a vigorous fire. "You'll be working around the clock but take an hour to draw in the heat of the day. Promise!"

"Very thoughtful, Euly," Kate said.

"I'm no artist but I try to read something from Father's books every day. Kate, we *need* such things. What's the point, if it's all just getting and spending?"

"Your famous 20 percent." Kate laughed and held up a sketchpad.

He made out the outline of Eddie Mole. "That's it! Sketch him, paint him from a dozen angles. Put him on a horse—stick his neck through a noose."

"So we never forget," Kate said.

Euly knew he should mention Rebecca but he couldn't form words. He'd been adamant how every woman would betray you and here he was in love again. He was so bewildered by love that even capturing Eddie Mole didn't mean much except the cash the man's hide would fetch. It might pay for a honeymoon in Kansas City, or even to Galveston to swim in the ocean.

He slept until four, waking to the smell of coffee. He pulled on his boots, walked to the fire, and yanked a strip of bacon from the skillet with his fingertips. He threw the bacon from hand to hand until it cooled. Then he poured coffee and munched on a biscuit. "This will be a beautiful place, Johnny," he called out. "In the middle of this terrible drought, you have good water. I'd like to walk up to that spring."

"Soon, Little Hero. Before winter?"

"Inside a month, I'll come down with the mules." With Rebecca.

Kate drew near, a blanket wrapped around her shoulders. She held out a tin cup and Johnny poured coffee. "You're leaving?"

"I don't want to, Kate. I'd like to help with your rafters, but—"

"It is a small building," said Johnny. "Thank you for bringing the tin and the nails."

"We can do it," Kate said.

"I will carry your claim to Perry, then I must go to Caldwell and rid us forever of this evil man. I'll send you the money the minute I receive it—to Pawhuska, I suppose? Oh, Lordy, Lordy." Euly visualized Rebecca. "I need to go home."

"Stay on the high ground, Little Hero," Johnny said. "You'll meet Billy."

REACHING PERRY WOULD HAVE added two days to his journey, but he did indeed meet Billy, driving a much-used buckboard pulled by a game little bay. Euly laid the stakes in the buckboard bed. Billy climbed down, favoring his right arm, but he offered to shake hands. He wore his Colt.

"How is Annelise?" Euly asked.

"We don't have to stand in line. They gave us a number. We'll appear in, hard to say exactly, maybe two weeks." Billy laughed. "I don't believe Annelise approves of me, Euly. I have sworn to improve."

Euly laughed. "So has every good man, Billy."

"What's *that?*" Billy pointed to the ragged heap Eddie Mole had dwindled to. Euly had changed the bandage twice but blood still soaked the cloth. The outlaw lay on two blankets with another blanket folded into a pillow, one arm and one leg tied to the sideboard.

"That's Eddie Mole. He killed Maude."

Billy nodded. "He ain't going nowheres. I don't believe you need to truss him up like that."

"All right," Euly said, and sliced through Eddie Mole's ropes with his pocketknife.

The outlaw opened his eyes and took up from where he'd left off. "Shootin' that hoss was pure accidental. And she's jest a damn hoss, orniest critter they is next to an ole sow with her piggies. You know, boy—" Eddie Mole meant Billy. "They dug a big ole hole for her while I laid there, my wounds a-festerin' in the sun. I ast you, is that how decent folks behave? A damn hoss! She was daid and they dug that hole in the ground."

Billy patted Euly on his shoulder. "She was a sweet-tempered ole gal, Euly. She always perked up when you come around."

EULY STRUCK UP THE Chisum Trail. The yellow moon rose and stars filled the sky. He could see for miles over such flat land, so he fed Gerty and drove through the night. At dawn he looked for a place to camp, but noon had arrived before he pulled under dusty cottonwoods by a branch of the Salt Fork with brown pools in it. He unharnessed Gerty, wet her down with creek water, and fed her again. She plopped in the dust.

Everywhere, grasshoppers jumped. A slight, hot wind rattled the cottonwoods.

Rolling out his bedroll, he found the last quart of Winston O'Reilly's fine whiskey. It had no appeal in the heat. He might enjoy it if he sat in a comfortable chair and Rebecca sang to him.

The outlaw had shucked off his boots and socks and Euly stared at his mangled right foot. He remembered the language from the wanted poster: "which he throws sideways when in a hury."

"How'd you do *that*?"

"I disremember. I believe it was in Fort Smith, Arkansas, or mighta been Denton, Texas. Woke up in an alleyway, vomit all over my shirt, big ole anvil settin' on my foot."

"An anvil?"

"Now, that foot don't hurt; got no feeling in it atall. Winter come, it's like I'm draggin' around a block a ice."

Euly handed him the whiskey. "We'll get going again at sundown, and reach Caldwell in the morning. Have yourself one last toot."

"You could shoot me. It would be a mercy. What you care, the wanted poster says daid or alive. Rather be daid. They'll patch me up jest to hang me."

"My religion prevents shooting you." If he were honest with himself, Euly had considered it, but such an act elevated Eddie Mole from vermin to man. And he didn't want a murder to haunt his memories. This way, he merely lent justice a hand.

"You an Old Order Sumpin?"

"I'm a Sumpin."

"Baptist would jest knock me in the haid."

Euly nodded. "I wonder if that's true."

"I didn't know your pappy. I seen this man holdin' a big wad a money and he wadn't gonna hand it to me iffen I ast nice. I got known evrywheres when we taken the bank up there in Emporia and they put out paper on me. So's hittin' and runnin' was the onliest way I could work no more. It weren't a persnal matter."

Euly lay down in the shade and let the bad man ramble. He'd come to realize that his father was flawed like every man, yet he'd taught Euly the art of commerce, how to use a hammer and the marvel of growing things, and to love literature. If I am ever a father, he thought, I hope I do as well.

"You remember Suzy Niabi?" he asked.

"Never knowed her."

"She was an Osage woman. Says on the wanted poster you killed her."

"Oh," Eddie Mole moaned. "She was purty. I killed her?"

"I imagine you were drunk," Euly said. "Out of your mind."

"Hell, yes. Demon rum done me in and here's to you!" Quite a lot of the bottle remained. "Wasn't always a bad 'un, boy. What's your name?"

"Rutherford B. Hayes."

"I served honrably in the Seventh U.S. Cavalry. Now, that ain't the same as Calvary, some folks get 'em turned around in they haids. I was a Bible-thumper onct, too, baptized me in the Red River."

"You with Custer?" Euly called out.

"The very peacock! With him at the Battle a Washita, you wanna call that thing a battle. Killed all them horses, never heard such screamin', and how the blood run, some kinda plague it was, *we* was. I could ride better 'an a Comanche. This here's real mellow whiskey."

"Glad you appreciate it."

"I mustered out after that and herd cattle for a while. You won't make no money that way. Had my eye on that little spread, water like that is a rare thing, only I never got together no funds. So me and—well, they's a bunch of us—we got to hittin' them Wells Fargo runs, easy pickin's most a the time. You could shoot the driver and them teams 'ud go evry which way. You know, a horse is a sensitive critter. I tell ya how sorry I am I shot your team animal? Pure accidental."

"You meant to shoot *me*."

"I'se jest defending my land. It's easy to kill people but I don't remember 'em all. They say I kilt some ole boy in Caldwell, too, and I disremember."

TEN HOURS LATER, IN Caldwell, Euly found Sheriff Turnstall, and they carried the unconscious outlaw into the jail. The sheriff stared at Eddie Mole, as though trying to find where the man was in the bundle of bloody meat. "Don't he smell," the sheriff said at last.

"He's not far from rotten," Euly said. "But he's worth two thousand dollars."

"Shore. Was he difficult to subdue?"

"He struggled some."

"I bet." The sheriff nodded. "What's your connection in this? You a bounty hunter?"

"I'm Ulysses Kreider from Jericho Springs. Eddie Mole murdered my father." Euly sighed. "And killed my poor old workhorse."

"I'm sorry, Mr. Kreider. You're shore gonna be a hero in this town. Must be satisfying to you to bring the murderin' bastard to justice." The sheriff laughed and slapped him on the back. "The Jericho Kid! Don't even wear a gun!"

Euly grinned and tried for a moment to feature himself in a dime novel, but he hadn't doggedly trailed the killer. Eddie Mole had more or less fallen into his hands. Euly's satisfaction came not so much from revenge as from finishing a disagreeable chore, like killing the last rat in the corn crib. And, by collecting the reward, from making the best of a piece of bad luck.

"Do I need to notify the court in Wichita?"

"I can do that for you," the sheriff said. "And I'll have a bank draft for the city's part of things tomorrow mornin'."

"Did your deputy leave a widow?"

"He shorely did. And two daughters—one of 'em, Ellen, about your age. Pretty little thing. She'd like to meet a big hero like you!"

"Don't know about that," Euly said, though the thought of meeting a pretty, admiring young woman appealed to him. He needed to go home. No woman anywhere could compare to Rebecca, not Ellen, not Jenny, not even imaginary Nausicaa.

"You oughtta look around some. Caldwell's gonna be a big city someday. I might even be in the position to offer you employment."

"A Mennonite deputy?"

"You brought in a vicious killer."

"Thank you, Sheriff." Euly laughed. "I'm headed back to Jericho Springs and mean to live a peaceful life if I can. But why don't you give the town's money to the widow?"

"Decent of you, son. Mighty decent."

Euly stood in the doorway. "Sheriff, I puzzle over it. Maybe you can explain to me how a man can kill another man and give it no thought. Not be weighted down with guilt. I want to say, you need an example of evil, look at *him*. But he doesn't care what you call him. Good and evil don't apply to a thing like Eddie Mole."

"Nope." Sheriff Turnstall nodded. "I seen a lot of 'em, how they bawl, and shit their pants, and go on about how innocent they is. You're right, they don't think like normal people. They'll say anything, they'll talk sweet as pie, but they got nothing inside 'em atall. All they cares about is what they need right now. One thing you can bet money on, alcohol's gonna be involved. That's how I explain it—the other thing, they lack motherin'. They have no tender aspect."

"Yes," Euly said, his thoughts already elsewhere. "He talked about his mother."

With his share of the federal reward, added to his profits from selling merchandise, Euly had two farms in the clear and nine thousand dollars in the bank. That is, the First Bank of Newton, not Ammon Krughoff's bank of Jericho Springs. Revenge was sweet.

AT THE TELEGRAPH OFFICE Euly sent one message: FINISHED STOP HOME THURS STOP LOVE ULYSSES STOP. Gerty was tired and so was he but they drove around the site of the run. Every tent had been pulled down. Men threw lumber into wagons and Euly grabbed some choice boards, black walnut and red elm, for himself. There were dozens of trash fires. A black spot spread out where he thought Monte Truman's roadhouse had been.

Rebecca had had to break the news all on her own. He'd had

no time to speak to his friend. All was fair in love and war and Monte wasn't a friend anymore.

With her father, Rebecca faced the daunting task of finding the farmhouse, then explaining to a parade of strangers what she was doing there. Giles Cabot would help.

Such behavior seemed unlike him, but what if Monte trailed Rebecca back to Jericho Springs? When it came to women, there was no end to the crazy things men did. If you need an example, Euly thought, look at me.

What if Jenny showed up at the farm, claiming *she* was Euly's true love?

Well, Rebecca could handle herself with anyone. His faithful Penelope would quote Shakespeare until they quaked in their boots.

He stopped to buy carrots and apples for Gerty, eggs and bacon for himself. He hoped Evangeline would take the hint and cook supper. She saw him coming and opened the warehouse door. She went off with the food while Euly unharnessed Gerty, rubbed her down, and threw her hay. He walked around the warehouse to assay the inventory worth hauling. He'd leave the canned goods for Evangeline. He'd take along the three kegs of nails and the English saddles.

"Not much farther, girl," he told Gerty. "And it's not much of a load."

He cleaned up by the pump, then ate scrambled eggs and a bowl of bean soup.

"Them Adventists is comin' back," Evangeline said.

"Don't they owe you money?"

"They said they'd pay. They said they got a wagonload a potatas."

Euly slept for fourteen hours. Next morning he walked over to the telegraph office. A message awaited him as he knew it would. The message read, "I AM HERE STOP."

Sources

Daughters of the American Revolution, Ponca City Chapter. *The Last Run: Kay County, Oklahoma, 1893*. Ponca City OK: Courier, 1939.

Fulbright, Jim. *Trails to Old Pond Creek: The Early Days of Trade and Travel in Northwestern Oklahoma*. Goodlettsville TN: Mid-South, 2005.

Hancock, M. A. *The Thundering Prairie*. Philadelphia: McCrae Smith, 1969.

Iorio, Sharon Hartin. *Faith's Harvest: Mennonite Identity in Northwest Oklahoma*. Norman: University of Oklahoma Press, 1998.

Janzen, Cornelius Cicero. "Americanization of the Russian Mennonites in Central Kansas." Master's thesis, University of Kansas, 1914.

Jones, Charles Jesse, and Henry Inman. *Buffalo Jones' Forty Years of Adventure*. Topeka KS: Crane, 1899.

La Flesche, Francis. *A Dictionary of the Osage Language*. Washington DC: Government Printing Office, 1932.

———. *The Middle Five: Indian Schoolboys of the Omaha Tribe*. Madison: University of Wisconsin Press, 1963.

———. *Traditions of the Osage: Stories collected and translated by Francis La Flesche*. Edited and introduced by Garrick Bailey. Santa Fe: University of New Mexico Press, 2010.

Liebert, Robert. *Osage Life and Legends*. Happy Camp CA: Naturegraph, 1987.

Martin, Dwayne R. "The Hidden Community: The Black Community of Kansas City, Missouri, during the 1870s and 1880s." Master's thesis, University of Missouri–Kansas City, 1982.

Mathews, John Joseph. *The Osages: Children of the Middle Waters*. Norman: University of Oklahoma Press, 1961.

McGuffey's Fifth Eclectic Reader. New York: American, 1896.

Wilder, Laura Ingalls. *Little House on the Prairie*.

Wilson, Terry P. *The Osage*. New York: Chelsea, 1988.

Witmer, Esther Mae. *Prairie Courage: A Mennonite Pioneer Story of May City, Iowa*. Sugarcreek O H : Carlisle, 2010.

CPSIA information can be obtained
at www.ICGtesting.com
Printed in the USA
LVHW042212120522
718626LV00005B/834